Luna Law

A Rattlesnake Lawyer Novel

Jonathan Miller

Rte 66

Thanks for everthing!

Library of Congress Cataloging-in-Publication Data

20170525
Casa de Snapdragon LLC
12901 Bryce Ave NE
Albuquerque, NM 87112
Printed in the United States of America

Author's Note

The views expressed in this book are not those of the author.
—Arthur C. Clarke.

I still don't know exactly what Clarke meant in that quote at the start of his classic novel, *Childhood's End*, or why I remember the quote verbatim thirty years later. The quote is my way of saying that this is a work of fiction. I am often referred to as the Rattlesnake Lawyer, but I am not Dan Shepard, Luna Cruz is not my wife, and I don't have any children. Dan's views of New Mexico and its peoples might not necessarily be mine. I would like to think I am a better lawyer than Dan, but I do wish I had his flashes of insight that usually save the day.

Luna Law is set in the year 2018, about a year from when I typed these final words. New Mexico is literally changing before my eyes with new construction, and I wanted that new reality in the manuscript. I used my imagination to describe the Albuquerque Rapid Transit buses, Innovate ABQ, One Central, Hotel Chaco, the Blake, and that new Facebook data plant in Los Lunas. Hopefully, my imagination is accurate.

This book is part of the *Rattlesnake Lawyer* series, but should stand on its own for the uninitiated. However, a Rattlesnake family tree might be helpful. Luna Cruz's father, originally known as Dr. Cruz, had four daughters with three different women. He had Luna with Ruth, and Jen with Nurse Song, both while he lived in Crater, New Mexico. He then fled to Mexico, changed his name to Mondragon and conceived Selena and Mia (Anna) Mondragon with Rosa.

Mia disappeared for eighteen years, and came back into

our story in *Conflict Contract.*

As for the next generation, Jen Song had daughter, Denise, with a lawyer named Dellagio, who is now deceased. Luna had daughter Dew (given name Sacagawea, don't ask how it became Dew) with Sam Marlow, and son Marley with Dan Shepard. Sam Marlow and Dan Shepard are third cousins, so Dew is Dan's third cousin, once removed.

Dew and Denise are now seventeen, but Marley is still only two. As I've said before, time flows differently in the *Rattlesnake Lawyer* universe.

There is no Dragon Moon corporation, no drug known as Crotaladone and no "magic thimble" technology as far as I know. All the Federal facilities mentioned are real, except for the AZ-NM facility in Crater County. All the courthouses are accurately portrayed, as I have practiced in all of them at some point.

Readers interested in the future of the magic thimble, shoftim technology and Dew's fate might want to check out my science fiction book, *A Million Dead Lawyers.*

As this story begins, there is no mysterious A-frame off the El Funko trail in Taos Ski Valley. The Culebra Kai dojo is fictional and *not* based on my own martial arts experiences. Still, all the martial arts techniques are accurately portrayed. "Crash of the Eagles, set two, final option" could indeed be lethal if done incorrectly with a half fist to the trachea. In any event, do not try any of the techniques at home.

- Jonathan Miller

Prologue

To Be or No?
June 29, 2018

"Where's Luna? Where's my wife?"

I took my fist away from Karl Kirlian's jugular. He crumpled halfway to the floor before straightening himself, a sad effort to preserve his dignity, which was difficult at this moment. The badge on his lanyard no longer displayed that he was acting CEO of Dragon Moon Corporation. The badge had no picture at all, and indicated that he was only an "employee." To me, he was still the enemy.

Kirlian looked behind me, looked down at the trail of bodies strewn along my path through the Albuquerque Convention Center and out to the plaza beyond. It was air conditioned here on the second floor of the convention center on this hot summer day, but he was sweating profusely. Kirlian was afraid of me. My martial arts training had finally paid off.

Fresh blood stained my "Team Turquoise" t-shirt. I wasn't sure whether it was my blood, or from one of the bodies behind me.

"She's in there, Mr. Shepard," he said, pointing to the entrance of the Kiva Auditorium. There was a turquoise-colored velvet rope in front of the double door. The electronic sign over the door announced: DRAGON MOON CORPORATION PRESENTS INTERNATIONAL MOCK TRIAL INVITATIONAL. The new CEO of Dragon Moon Corporation, Kirlian's replacement, would soon give a trophy to my step-daughter, Dew, assuming she'd won the mock-trial tournament.

I didn't care. Those bastards had kidnapped my wife. I could practically hear her heartbeat on the other side of that rope. My family was there in the Kiva. Dragon Moon might take them, too. In my padfolio, which was emblazoned with the logo of my wife's firm, Luna Law, I had paperwork that would take these guys down, but that padfolio was under a chair on the other side of the rope.

Dew, had once been in a high school production of *Hamlet.* re-written in contemporary New Mexico vernacular called *To Be or No?* It was forgettable except for Dew's *To Be or No* soliloquy. Now I faced a similar question. To cross or no?

"Will your new CEO take me to Luna?" I lifted my fist one more time.

He winced. "I have no idea. I'm not in control of Dragon Moon any more. They screwed me like they screwed you. They made a deal with a murderer. They're evil now."

Having a career corporate lackey like Kirlian call Dragon Moon evil was not only like the pot calling the kettle black, but more like the pot calling the kettle a black hole where no light escapes its gravity.

"What does that mean?"

"I don't know. Your answers, whatever they may be, lie on the other side of that rope." He straightened himself and looked me in the eye. "But you might not like what you find."

Had they killed Luna? What would I have to do next? I stared at the rope. My battle had just begun, but I wished I knew who I'd be facing on the other side . . .

PART I
Kimono Grab

1. El Funko

April 1, 2018, Two months earlier

Do I cross under the rope?

I was at the area boundary of Taos Ski Valley, a short distance uphill from the Kachina lift, off the El Funko ski trail. It was Easter Sunday, April Fool's Day, and the last day of the ski season. At three-forty-five in the afternoon, the season itself had only fifteen more minutes of funk left. Storm clouds hovered over the valley, but the outlook was for rain, not snow. Perhaps that was a sign that ski season was over and "mud season" was about to begin.

Should I cross under the rope?

I glanced at the sign again, hoping that it had changed colors and changed warnings. No, it still was yellow and quite clear: AREA BOUNDARY. *DO NOT CROSS*! There was even a hand-drawn skull and some crossbones, but this skull was wearing sunglasses.

The text on my phone was quite clear: MEET AT THE A-FRAME ON THE EDGE OF THE EL FUNKO TRAIL. This was the only A-frame here, funky or no, and it clearly sat well over the ski area boundary line. Why would anyone set up a meeting with a lawyer where the lawyer had to break the law to get to the meeting?

The answer was obvious. This was clearly a test. If I wasn't willing to cross under the rope this potential client would not hire me, Dan Shepard the Rattlesnake Lawyer, to be their lawyer.

Someone had already failed the test earlier this morning—my wife, Luna Cruz Shepard. Luna hadn't even gotten on the Kachina quad chairlift to check out the meeting. She had decided to stay at the Blake Hotel to "rest."

She texted me an hour ago, while I was skiing the outer limits of Taos to reclaim my lost winter as a twenty-two-year-old ski bum. DAN. POTENTIAL CLIENT. I CAN'T TAKE CASE. CHECK IT OUT. UP IN THE MOUNTAINS OFF THE EL FUNKO TRAIL."

EL FUNKO? I texted back. Hell, my life was in a funko right now.

all the way to ski area boundary off kachina lift, she replied. cabin on side of trail. you have to hike. client wants to see you at four.

why can't you take the case?

conflict. but this case might be a big one and we need the money.

In her forties, Luna was a former judge and a semi-retired lawyer, raising her seventeen-year-old daughter, Dew, and our two-year-old, Marley. Marley had a mysterious auto-immune disease and was confined to the hospital waiting for surgery. Hopefully, he would soon receive life-saving experimental treatment in Bangalore, India. Waiting for the surgery with Marley had become Luna's full-time job.

Luna and I were here in Taos Ski Valley on a rare weekend away, as Good Friday was an unofficial court holiday. Luna's late step-mother had willed her a weekend at a Taos Ski Valley timeshare right on the mountain. This was the last weekend we could use it before time, well, our share of the time, vanished into eternity. This weekend was supposed to be therapy for Luna, who suffered from caregiver fatigue while she stayed at Marley's side every day.

I saw my son almost daily, and lived for his smile. I usually saw him before my martial arts "senior classes," at the local Culebra Kai Martial Arts Academy. I practiced my *katas* for his entertainment—a choreographed series of blocks, kicks, and punches in various directions. He'd smile, and respond with a karate chop with his stubby little hands.

We had to pay for everything that wasn't covered by insurance, which was almost every test and test tube these days. The Indian adventure would cost a fraction of the equivalent American operation, but would still set us back. Luna was right, we needed the money. For Marley.

In another text, she'd sent me a pic of the meeting site, a pic of an A-frame off the El Funko trail the potential client had texted to her. El Funko was a hidden trail where you hiked uphill for a few yards before skiing down some choice powder through steep double diamond expert slopes. Double diamonds were a boy's best friend, and I wanted to prove that I still had some moguls left in my aging knees.

I didn't have any trouble finding the spot; this was the only dwelling this far up. The dark stained A-frame looked as if it had just been airlifted from Zermatt, Switzerland. No footprints heading in or out, and the black lace curtains were drawn, hiding the interior.

I tried to text Luna back, but didn't get any bars up here on my obsolete Samsung. I was alone. Suddenly, someone drew a window shade from the inside of the house. A young bearded man in sunglasses looked out from one of the windows and nodded. Then he lifted his hands as if to say "What the hell are you waiting for?"

I nodded, but didn't move. Even if the ski patrol pulled my ticket for crossing over, I would miss out on ten minutes of moguls at the most. Still, I wasn't sure if there was another way down to the ski area's base village.

"You realize if you go under that rope, you're on your

own."

Where had that come from? There was something odd about the unknown voice, as if it had been electronically altered.

"Do you hear me or no?" the voice said again. I turned around. A ski patroller stood a few feet uphill, the small form casting a big shadow in the rays of the setting sun. This patroller wore a silver racing helmet over a yellow ski patrol jacket, as if a robot had decided to take up skiing for the day and didn't know how to dress. With all the bundling and scarves, it was impossible to tell whether the person was male or female. The parka was way too big for such a small person, someone barely five feet and change tall.

Time to play lawyer. Hopefully I didn't have to play Rattlesnake Lawyer, and use my twenty plus years of trial experience just yet. "It's not against the law for me to go under the rope, isn't it?" I said. "I mean, it's national forest over there, public land, and I'm part of the public, right?"

"You know the rules. No skiing out of bounds." A voice this deep should not be coming from a body so small. When did Darth Vader start skiing at Taos?

"It's the end of the season. Is it such a big deal?" That was my closing argument, the "not such a big deal" defense. Some rattlesnake. I smiled. I'd been a lawyer for twenty-five years; I should do better. "I need to see that person over there," I pointed to the A-frame. "I have an appointment."

"An appointment? With who?" The voice grew even deeper.

"I don't know," I replied in my "preserving the issue for appeal" voice. "I got a text from my wife that the person needed to see me. I presume they've got permission to have that building there. I'm sure it's cool."

"What is your name? We need that for our records."

"Dan Shepard," I said. "Esquire."

The silver helmet nodded. "Like I said, Dan Shepard, esquire, you go under the rope and you're on your own. It's going to rain soon. You might want to find another way down, because in ten minutes this ski area is officially closed for the season and if you come back over the rope, it will be considered trespassing."

I could beat a trespassing rap in nearby Taos County Magistrate Court with my eyes closed, but that wasn't the issue. Was there another way down on the other side of the house? There was no going back on this side.

"I understand and accept full responsibility," I said. I could be one of my clients deciding to testify despite my fifth amendment right to remain silent. I took a final deep breath of high altitude air.

Before I moved, though, I thought about my son and his karate chops. And, I thought about Luna. I couldn't let them down.

I crossed under the rope.

2. The Z Word

Safely under the rope, I took off my skis and left them next to my poles. The skis were on a slight incline; I hoped the rain wouldn't wash them down the slope. My heavy ski boots waddled through the slushy snow. Thunder clouds rumbled in the distance and rain began to fall over the far ridge. Taos Ski Valley was closing at just the right time.

The ski patroller waited until I made it to the door, then glanced at a watch. Would he or she wait to see if I crossed back? As I opened the outer door the patroller headed downhill, down into El Funko.

A small man dressed in a black turtleneck sweater opened the inside door. It was cold inside, and I didn't see any source of heat. He indicated with a nod that I should take off my gloves, despite the chill. He did not shake my hand.

"My name is Karl Kirlian," he said. "I'm general counsel for Dragon Moon Corporation." He had a vague accent, a cross between Middle Eastern and Eastern European. He was in his late twenties, and had a jet-black goatee that matched his jet-black hair and jet black eyes.

There was something supernatural about Karl Kirlian, even though he was all business—as if he'd gone to Hogwarts for the joint MBA/JD/Defense Against the Dark Arts program. His black sweater seemed darker than any sweater I'd ever seen. Perhaps it was from an outlet store in Transylvania. Right next to his Taos Ski Valley season pass was another lanyard with a badge. This badge was a Dragon Moon ID and had his picture long with the words KARL KIRLIAN, ACTING CEO AND CHIEF COUNSEL. The ID had a hologram the size of a postage stamp. It showed a two-second loop of Kirlian in mountaineering gear, ascending to the summit of a mountain with a pickaxe.

I wasn't quite sure what swinging a pickaxe had to do with a Dragon Moon, whatever that was. Underneath the words, DRAGON MOON, smaller print had the corporation's division—LOGISTICS, CORRECTIONS, MEDICAL SUPPLIES, AND LEGAL TECHNOLOGY. Next to each title was a tiny symbol of a moon rising over a truck, a barbed wire fence, a medical RX symbol, and the scales of justice respectively. They were a one-stop shop. Their legal technology would convict you, a truck would transport you to their prison, and then to their hospitals after their guards beat you. I hated them already.

Inside, the A-frame was bare other than some high-tech equipment and a white card table. What a strange place for a meeting with a major corporation.

"I'm Dan Shepard, my wife Luna Cruz was the one who told me about this meeting. She said you were expecting me."

"Good to meet you, Mr. Shepard. Thanks for coming on such short notice."

"Call me Dan," I said.

"I hope you don't mind if my associate checks you for weapons and recording devices."

I hadn't noticed the "associate" who blended in with the wood. A very large, sunburnt man in a red ski sweater approached me. His badge read DICK SOBCHAK, and displayed a moving hologram of him doing a karate chop over and over. Dick looked like an uglier, low-rent version of Daniel Craig's smooth James Bond. Dick searched me roughly, found my almost obsolete phone, smirked, and put it on the table.

"He's clean," Dick said.

"Will you excuse us then, Dick?" Kirlian said. Dick

apparently didn't need a parka, and waded outside. "I'm sorry about that. You can't get good help these days."

"I guess not." I didn't know what else to say, never having a bodyguard before. "Why are we meeting all the way up here?"

"We cannot be too careful in these troubled times. My office is in Los Alamos and we're building a new facility in Albuquerque near the old Intel plant, but the corporation has what you might call a 'retreat' up here in the ski valley. We have cabins for our more *private* meetings. I grew up in an Armenian ski resort town, Tsaghkadzor, and my late father was an avid ski trekker. I look for any excuse to go skiing or trekking in the back country."

The words "back country" echoed in the small A-frame. "This is the back country all right," I said. "The way back country. How did you know that we would be here in Taos?"

"It's my business to know. The corporation has this place up here, and I was up here anyway. I never miss the last day of the season."

I couldn't tell if he meant that he was glad the winter was finally over, or that he just enjoyed change. "So why do you need to talk to me, Mr. Kirlian, away from prying eyes, prying ears, and cell phone reception?"

He remained standing. "Before we begin, what did that ski patrol say to you?"

"Only that if I crossed underneath the rope that I was on my own. Is there another way down? It looks like it's going to rain out there."

"I won't keep you too long. You can just ski down the snow-packed road behind us. It will take you right to the Kachina base area and then it's an easy slide down to the main village."

"I didn't know there was a road behind here."

More thunder sounded off in the distance, indicating more rain. I wanted to get this meeting over with before the rain caused an avalanche.

"You tried to hire my wife but she referred you to me due to a potential conflict of interest?" I asked.

"Regrettably so. Your wife assured us that you were a good second choice. Will you have time for these cases?"

I had a public defender "breakdown docket" caseload, where I took over lawyers' cases after they had their inevitable breakdowns. Now someone had taken over my caseload after I too broke down from constant travel and incessant client phone calls. Now my docket was free, all too free.

"Your late father-in-law was one of our earliest investors in Dragon Moon, along with my late father. Dragon Moon began as a pharmaceutical and medical supply company out of Juarez, Mexico. We expanded into the American Southwest to supply hospitals and military bases, and now we're poised to go world-wide as an all-purpose governmental, legal, and military contractor."

"I'm not a corporate, family, or probate attorney. All I do is crime. I mean, all I do is criminal law."

"We require your assistance on a criminal matter, not a corporate one. This matter concerns our truck drivers, and if we can't represent them in-house, we need to get someone out-house."

I thought he was joking about the outhouse, but it was clear that English was probably his third language, after Armenian and Spanish. "We had an attorney for one of the drivers, but that attorney can no longer assist us."

"What happened to him?"

"He died in an auto accident last week on the way to the Los Alamos courthouse."

"I'm sorry." I didn't know what else to say. Speeding to the courthouse on a winding road, practicing an opening statement from index cards while trying to pass the car ahead could be deadly.

Kirlian smiled, but it was not a warm smile. "Mr. Dorfman had already prepped the cases, so these matters should be no major concern for you. They are a possession of dangerous drugs --prescription pills without a prescription case in Clovis, and also in Portales; a receiving stolen case property in Carrizozo; and a conspiracy to receive stolen property in Los Alamos. Our driver, Albert Jackson Cage, was charged in all four cases in the span of a week. He also has a handful of misdemeanor traffic warrants that must be dealt with along the way. I'm personally representing another driver, Axtell Pile, and we thought it best to farm Mr. Cage's case to an outside attorney."

Albert Jackson Cage. I sure liked that name better than Axtell Pile. Albert Jackson Cage sounded like a president, or a presidential assassin. The name sounded vaguely familiar, though.

"He was a war hero, right?" I asked. "He rescued a girl in Afghanistan or Iraq, something like that?"

"That's correct. He was a driver who went back for his female passenger when she was captured in the Triangle of Death, or one of those triangles. He received a medal of valor for his loyalty. However, his return to civilian life has been a bit rocky, to say the least."

"When is court?"

"His hearings are tomorrow morning at ten up in the First Judicial courthouse in Santa Fe. They'll arraign him on all four charges in front of Judge Chairez. Can you be there?"

After a year of constant travel, my calendar was blank this week. Way too blank, as I had recently been taken off the public defender rotation, which might be for the best. I once took seventy-three phone calls from incarcerated clients in one day, and temporarily lost my hearing in one ear from pressing the phone so hard to my head. I ended up having to go to a doctor to clear my ear passage. Having only one client sounded much better.

My original plan for tomorrow was to go to the office early and pretend to work on a screenplay. I often wondered if they'd stolen my idea for a sleazy New Mexico lawyer and used it in the show *Better Call Saul.*

"That's odd," I said. "All four charges in multiple counties to be arraigned in one court before one judge?"

"It's the New Mexico Attorney General's office, it's their idea. The Special Prosecutions Divisions are handling all our cases. The New Mexico Supreme Court had already signed off on an order of some sort, and Mr. Dorfman, your predecessor, agreed. So, can you be there tomorrow at ten?"

"I can be there. Santa Fe is only a short drive from my home in Albuquerque. But, I would have to be formally retained first, if you catch my drift."

This whole situation didn't smell quite right, so I wasn't that eager. But times were tough in the Shepard household. Given our precarious financial state, we probably shouldn't have come to Taos in the first place, but Luna had insisted that this weekend was "use it or lose it." Her late step-mother would have wanted us to use it.

"We are prepared to pay you one hundred thousand dollars, plus any expenses for your time on these three cases."

I gasped, blinded by the zeroes flashing in my eyes. With my public defender contract, I received six hundred bucks for each case, plus a night at the Day's Inn and forty cents a mile. Even with a big corporate client, I didn't expect to get that kind of money. This case suddenly smelled a lot better.

"I can pay you now if you like, as a show of good faith, if you sign a retainer agreement forthwith."

Forthwith didn't sound like an English word, but it meant immediately. I'd seen something shiny on his index finger when I entered the A-frame. Upon closer glance, it was a silver thimble-like gadget on his left index finger. The "thimble" was a little thicker than those used for sewing and had a hole in the tip.

"Mr. Shepard, can you hold out your left hand?"

I held out my left hand. "This will feel strange for a moment, a slight electronic shock," he said. "But you will get used to it."

He didn't ask my permission as he put a silver thimble on my left index finger. Moments after it settled on my finger I did feel a shock. It quickly went down in intensity, but did not go away. The little device must be scanning my entire body. A small current even went between my ears.

"What is it?"

"It's a prototype of our e-thimble technology. It can do everything your smart phone can, but faster. Once the thimble is properly initiated, it can also be used to find out information that other entities have on file about you."

"Properly initiated?"

"It just scanned your body. See, it didn't hurt, did it? It is now interfacing with our network—and other ones as well."

"But you said there was no reception up here."

"That's correct. There's no reception for cell phones. There is perfect reception for thimbles however, using our dedicated satellite technology." I now saw a small satellite dish near a rear window.

He pointed his thimble to my thimble. "Transfer funds to Shepard trust account," he said. I don't know if there was an actual beam, but there was some crackling in the air, like a ham radio. I felt another small charge. He then said the money was coming from what sounded like the First Swiss Bank of Davos, which sounded impressive.

"Now check the balance in your trust account," he said. "With the thimble, just say 'Thimble, display trust account, recent transactions.'"

I was amazed by what happened next. The thimble emitted a beam of light that projected my balance against the wall. Sure enough, my bank statement was there, in a three foot by three-foot square, plain as day. Even better, it showed a recent hundred-thousand-dollar deposit that was labeled as "pending."

"Now the retainer agreement. You can sign with your finger right here."

He pointed down and a projection of a standard, albeit lengthy, retainer agreement appeared on the blank white card table. All nine pages were arranged like a tic-tac-toe board.

"Use your thimble," Kirlian said, as if reminding me how to use the "force."

I quickly reviewed the document. Despite the thrill of seeing a retainer agreement magically projected on a tabletop, the boilerplate language was standard.

"Thimble, sign document," I said and used the thimble to sign the final square with a few quick motions. On the table, my signature appeared. It wasn't quite signed in blood, but the tip of my finger felt lighter rather than heavier, as if I'd lost a pint or two of O negative.

"Thimble, store signed contract," Kirlian said. The nine pages disappeared. "I sent a copy to your email. Someday we hope to use holograms, and even brain waves, to operate the thimbles, so you won't have to articulate the words out loud."

"This is pretty amazing. How did it know my bank account number?"

"That would be public record of course, registered with the New Mexico Bar Association. With the body scan, your body, fingerprints, and DNA would be your password. Once the thimble is attuned to your body, you have access to considerable information about yourself."

I wasn't sure how Kirlian accessed all my information and passwords. They would be able to get my fingerprints through an attorney database of course, but how much else did they have on me?

"Don't be alarmed, Mr. Shepard, everything is completely confidential and can be synched with your other internet accounts. You can also use the thimble much like your smart phone. For example, just say 'Thimble. Display Albert Jackson Cage pending cases from 2012-2018.'"

"Thimble, display Albert Jackson Cage pending cases."

Within seconds, the NMcourts.com data was displayed on the table top, each page like the square of a chess board this time. The resolution was incredible, and automatically adjusted to my nearsighted eyes. With just a point of my finger and some body English I could manipulate images onto the wall. It wasn't quite Tom Cruise's moving holograms in the science fiction film, *Minority Report*, as the projection was confined to a blank surface, but this certainly was the future on my index finger.

"We are currently developing a system to replace the Odyssey and NMCourts.com system that utilizes the thimbles. It's called the 'shoftim,' but it's stuck in beta."

He pronounced the word as "shof-team." I vaguely remembered that shoftim meant "judge" in either Hebrew or Arabic. I think Luna had shown me a paper that her daughter had done on the role of the shoftim, the judges in biblical times. The paper had been published online, but I didn't remember where.

Kirlian looked at me. I couldn't read him very well, but thought he expected me to say something. "I hate when things are still in beta," I finally said. Then again, my entire life was stuck in beta.

Still, Beta was better than nothing. Per the thimble's display, Cage was charged with low level felonies. The Attorney General's office, Special Prosecutions Division was the plaintiff in each case. I would only have to communicate with one attorney, rather than a different one in each jurisdiction.

"The shoftim system can also give you an idea of likely outcomes," Kirlian said. "Ask it to compute outcomes."

"Thimble compute likely outcome of all pending Albert Jackson Cage cases."

The thimble vibrated for a second. "Ninety percent consolidated plea to all charges before trials," it said in a mechanical female voice. "Ninety percent probability outcome defendant will be placed on probation."

I smiled at those likely outcomes. It didn't mean that much work, or much risk, right?

"So, I must ask again, are these matters something you can handle, Mr. Shepard?"

I could still throw the thimble back in his face, tell him to take the money back, and ski down the back road. I felt a moment of discomfort. I still had a conscience after all. Ninety percent chance of a plea still meant a ten percent chance of a trial, maybe several trials.

"I just want to make sure that even though you are paying me, you understand that I still have to zealously represent my client, even if his interests don't necessarily coincide with yours."

He frowned. What the hell else did he expect me to say? I was famous for saying the "z word," zealously, usually when it meant that I was doing something I didn't want to do, but had to.

"Of course," he said. He handed me back my phone after looking at it as if checking it to make absolutely, positively sure it was not recording. "We expect nothing less than your usual, *zealous,* representation."

Did he just wink at me? I couldn't tell. I doubted that a truck driver would turn on his boss, so I'm sure the situation was moot. And, they had just paid me one hundred thousand dollars, so I would make the situation moot if I had to.

"I can zealously handle cases like this with my hands tied behind my back," I said, throwing down the z word again.

It must have satisfied him. We shook our thimbled hands, and I felt more electric current pass between us. These thimbles were awesome. He gave me a carrying case the size of a small jewelry box. "You can recharge it at night in here."

"I'll do that when I get home. Do you guys have a patent on these things?"

"It's pending. Your wife's stock options might become

quite valuable soon. I would advise her to hold onto them."

"I'll keep that in mind."

Kirlian rose from the card table, walked to the door, and opened it. "Good evening, Mr. Shepard." When he pronounced evening, he sounded like Bela Lugosi.

"Good evening back at you."

It wasn't quite evening yet, however. It was maybe half past four and the ski area was officially closed. Kirlian's bodyguard was gone. Maybe he had melted into the fresh puddle near the door. I put my thimble hand inside my glove and put on my skis.

"I would advise taking the road back there," Kirlian called from the doorway. "It will take you right to the base in a few minutes."

The snow-packed road wound down through the trees and along a brook. Although it was getting dark, I should make it to the base before the rain melted the rest of the snow.

Kirlian went back inside and I adjusted my bindings. Good to go. Last run for the season. The white summit pyramid of Kachina Peak now glowed pink with the setting sun. The thunderclouds had drawn closer, but a faint rainbow now shown over the high ridge to the west.

I wiggled my fingers in my glove. The thimble literally might be made of gold. It was already worth $100,000 dollars to me. After gliding downhill a few turns, I stopped to take a breath. I was winded here at ten thousand feet elevation. When I looked up, the rainbow had vanished.

As I skied further downhill, the road grew icier and then rockier. A spark lit up under my left ski when I crossed over a bare patch of pavement. I wondered if my ski pants were flammable, but they didn't catch fire.

I took another turn and my knees positively creaked. Over fifty, I didn't have the reflexes that I had when I skied every weekend. And, my metabolism didn't burn calories the way it did when I ran cross-country in high school. For the first time in my life I had a small gut no matter how many sit-ups and crunches I did each morning. I would never be under two hundred pounds again. I was going downhill in so many ways.

All that kept me away from obesity was my bi-weekly martial arts class at the Culebra Kai Academy in Albuquerque with its slogan *"Culebra Kai, there is no try!"* I had started going because Luna had suggested that I learn how to protect her after she had been shot at our wedding reception. I had rejected buying a gun because amid my depression after the shooting, I worried that I might use the gun on myself. Learning to fight with my fists sounded like a better idea.

Perhaps I loved the fact that the company's motto "there is no try" was taken from Yoda's advice to Luke Skywalker in *Empire Strikes Back*. "Do or do not. There is no try."

Culebra Kai was famed for its stable of world champion mixed martial artists, but they also offered senior classes for old farts who wanted a solid work-out a few evenings a week. I had hoped to become a flexible Karate Kid, but with every twisted stance I was turning into an un-limber Karate Middle-Aged Man. Still, after two years I was finally testing for my purple belt, the first intermediate belt.

Even gold belt, the first belt, had been hard to master with the simple defense to a Kimono Grab. Presumably back in the day, an ancient master was wearing a kimono. Someone tried to grab it, and the ancient master responded with a punch, a chop, and a rear kick to the opponent's groin.

After a few more zigs and zags on the snowy road, I slowed, reluctant to face Luna Cruz Shepard, esquire. It grew darker and colder by the minute, but now I saw pavement below me that wasn't snow packed. Civilization at last, ready or not. I could probably glide the rest of the way to the base village on the snow drifts to the side of the road. I might have to push a bit with my ski poles to get there, though. While I pondered my options, suddenly, out of nowhere, the ski patroller with the black helmet emerged from behind a tree. The patroller now wore hiking boots, rather than skis. Before I could react, the patroller grabbed my parka with both hands. This two-handed grab to the chest was the same attack that I should defend with the Kimono Grab technique.

But, I didn't respond. Instead, I lost my balance and fell forward. My head bounced against some ice and I rolled into the fetal position with my skis still on. I felt woozy. Perhaps it was the high altitude, but my heart was pounding like I was having a heart attack. Maybe the stress of the last few months was coming home to roost. Worse, my left glove and my thimble were gone.

"You shouldn't have gone under the rope," the ski patroller said, running away with the thimble. The figure jumped on a motorcycle and sped away.

As I lost consciousness, I didn't know if I wanted to wake up. Luna was going to kill me.

3. Ex Kachina

How long had I been out? As my eyes began to focus on shapes, I realized that I was in a clinic somewhere, maybe the small one I'd always walked by at the base of Taos Ski Valley. Through the window, I could see the vague outline of the Taos mountain against the dark gray sky, illuminated from the lights of the village.

"Dan, are you all right or no?" The voice had a slight New Mexican accent.

My wife, the illustrious Luna Cruz Shepard, stood in front of me. She wore a black ski parka that was opened to reveal an athletic turquoise ski sweater. The black hair of her youth was now colored, but gray was attacking the roots. Now in her forties, Luna had once been a judge and she still looked the part. She always dressed immaculately in dark colors, as if still wearing the robe and about to hear a murder case. Her big brown eyes were always darting around the room, assessing the evidence and credibility of all the witnesses, especially me.

With her impeccable make-up and grooming she could be a glamorous telenovela actress playing the role of a barracuda lawyer. Her beauty did not make her happy, though. She had been shot on our wedding day and always quipped that our marriage had been downhill from there. I couldn't tell if she was joking.

She looked at me, big brown eyes filled with concern, a tear running down her cheek. Luna often told me that she loved me more than life itself. I loved her that much as well. She held a piping hot to-go cup of hot chocolate from the nearby Blake Hotel. She handed me the hotel cup and I gulped it down.

"I stole it from the café when I heard you were here," she

said with a smile. I didn't know whether she was kidding. I didn't care.

"They found you passed out up the road," she said, holding my hand. "What happened?"

For a moment, I thought about telling her the truth, but that sounded ridiculous. Luna hated the complications in life that I caused her. She had often said that if she was OCD, I was "No CD," with no compulsion or obsession whatsoever. I certainly didn't want to tell her that I was mugged by a ski patroller. She wouldn't believe me, and then she'd blame me for causing it.

"I took a wrong turn near the Kachina base and ended up on the back road. I think I fainted from altitude and dehydration," I said.

"A wrong turn?"

"I took the back way down from El Funko."

A medical-type person came in. I wasn't sure it was a doctor, nurse, or just someone in white scrubs who liked hanging out in the clinic. I quickly nicknamed him Dr. Dreadlocks. He looked like he'd been skiing all day. His face was sunburnt, and his gray, dreadlocked hair looked like it had been stuck in a hat.

"You didn't suffer any frost bite," Dr. Dreadlocks said, "and you don't show signs of concussion."

They both stared at me. I contemplated filing a police report about the mysterious ski patroller. I checked my finger. The thimble was still missing. Then I did an inventory of my limbs. Other than the stiffness, I was fine. The ski patroller was probably just a figment of my imagination.

"You're saying you just fell or no?" Dr. Dreadlocks asked. He was only mildly suspicious. I was probably his last patient for the year.

"It was a silly accident." I said. "I'll live."

Dr. Dreadlocks looked at me dubiously, but didn't want to press. "Again, I don't see any signs of a concussion, but please watch him closely ma'am."

"Oh, I'll watch him all right."

Another patient entered the small clinic. He had a ski patrol sweater but no parka. "Somebody hit me in the head and took my parka," he said.

Well, the mystery of the oversized ski patrol parka was at least partially solved. But why would someone pretend to be a ski patroller just to mug me?

Dr. Dreadlocks headed for the door. "I'll be right back," he said. "You have insurance, right? There will be a co-pay."

Luna handed him a joint credit card that we reserved for emergencies. "So how was the meeting?" she asked when we had a moment of privacy.

It was a struggle to remember that far back, and I paused to take another breath of high altitude air. At eight thousand elevation of elevation, I still had problems breathing.

"It's not a big deal, just representing a truck driver on some low-level felonies."

"So, it had nothing to do with the shareholder dispute?"

"Not really. That barely came up. They paid me a hundred thousand dollars and already wired the money into the trust account. The arraignment is tomorrow in Santa Fe."

"I don't know. Dragon Moon is totally evil; they want to take over the world. Remember Halliburton, the company that made a fortune as a contractor during all the Gulf wars? Dragon Moon is like the Halliburton of New Mexico, except they're trying to take over the law as well. They're trying to set up software systems that will lock people up quicker, so they can make money with the for-profit prisons. I can't believe my father helped start them."

"You were the one who told me to take the meeting."

"I was just hoping that you could build your practice with real clients. If you had ten ten-thousand-dollar felony clients, that would be the same as one Dragon Moon for one hundred thousand."

"I don't know anyone with that many good private clients in this economy."

"Well. hopefully this will finally kick start your practice. You have such incredible potential."

I loved it when she said that I had potential. I lifted the hot chocolate as a toast to her. She had told me that working together, we could conquer the world. When I looked at the intent expression on her face, I believed her. "Hopefully."

After Dr. Dreadlocks sent in a nurse with mounds of paperwork for me to sign I stretched, and then limped out of the little clinic and into a cold rain. I could easily walk without help as I lugged my skis and boots back to the car. Unfortunately, I had to stop for breath halfway to the parking lot. The air might be pure up here, I just wished I could get more of it into my lungs.

Shadows were already growing behind the massive, luxury Blake Hotel that had gone in last season. The Blake looked like it had been designed for homesick Swiss bankers. The once funky Taos Ski Valley was welcoming more of the Alpine urban sprawl of Vail every day.

"I'll drive," Luna said.

My car was a gray Ford Focus, a non-descript car for a non-descript life. We didn't have snow tires. I would never be the Lincoln Lawyer, the sleazy but wealthy lawyer character in the film with Matthew McConaughey. Luna reminded me that the Lincoln Lawyer was successful and was passionate about zealously representing his clients. The Lincoln Lawyer never lost. Luna had hoped that I would become a Lexus Lawyer at least. Unfortunately, mid-sized Ford Focus with 100,000 miles and four dented doors was the best I could get with my credit rating.

The canyon road was dark in the rain. Luna drove us through the winding descent and then the valley opened onto a vast plain that stretched to the west, all the way to Arizona perhaps. Traffic began as we hit the turn-off for Taos Pueblo, a thousand-year-old settlement and one of the oldest continuously occupied structures in the world. In New Mexico, a "pueblo" was a Native American community that had received special designation from the King of Spain in the days of Columbus. Pueblos weren't just reservations; they were practically their own principalities.

Luna and I had visited the Taos Pueblo on the drive up here on Friday. I had hoped to see the ancient kiva, the spiritual center of the pueblo. On one of our first dates, Luna, Dew and I had descended into the underground kiva of the nearby Jemez Pueblo's thousand-year old ruins. I had felt a spiritual connection, not only to the kiva, but to Luna and her daughter. I hoped Taos Pueblo's kiva would bring our connection back.

"Could we see the kiva?" I asked a tribal cop at the entrance.

"Kivas are off limits to outsiders," the cop here said as if I had violated a serious taboo just by asking.

"I'm sorry."

I took a glance at the cemetery which the cop explained

was also off limits to outsiders. He pointed to the remains of an adobe bell tower, maybe twenty feet high. Apropos of nothing, he told me old me that the bell tower, which was straight on one side and gently tapered on the other, was all that remained of the original San Geronimo church. That church had been burned during a pueblo revolt with several families inside. The bell jostled a bit in the wind, as if issuing a slight warning.

I expected Luna to reprimand me for my stupid question, but she had been drawn to a jewelry table. A Native woman was selling earrings from several card tables set in front of the massive adobe structure that had been around for a thousand years. I didn't know that turquoise could have such a powerful magnetic field.

The woman's red shirt had Old English script spelling out HARD CORE REZ GIRL, and the table was filled with bulky silver and turquoise earrings.

"Those earrings are *you*," Hard Core Rez Girl said to Luna in a surprisingly soft voice. She didn't have to do the hard sell to a turquoise addict like Luna, and she knew it.

The earrings were indeed Luna—silver and turquoise in perfect harmony like yin and yang. Luna could wear them for a Supreme Court oral argument and then keep them on for the celebratory night out.

"They're five today," the woman said. "But we don't take credit cards."

I frowned when I saw Luna's sad eyes. "I'm sorry, Luna," I said. "I don't have five hundred dollars."

"No. Five *dollars!*" Hard Core Rez Girl said. "Cash. You're rich. You're white. You have five dollars or no?"

My pocket was cash free, but I ran back to the Focus to pick up five dollars in change in the car's nooks and crannies and handed it all to the woman.

Luna looked at me, the earrings already in her ears. "I love you, Dan."

"I love you, Luna."

As we had walked out, we passed a couple of Native youths in Taos Tigers sweatshirts who had a casual drum circle. We felt the beat and kept time with every step.

• • •

The earrings lost their luster as we sat in traffic in the rain, heading back from the ski area two days later. The rain finally thinned out after we passed the San Francisco de Asis Church in the little hamlet of Ranchos de Taos. The adobe backside of the eighteenth-century church faced the road. The back of the church was more famous than the front, as it was popularized in a famous painting by Georgia O'Keeffe. The signed painting, hanging in a museum, was probably worth more than the tiny church and all its parishioners.

While the Taos Pueblo might be an older structure, to me the Ranchos Church *was* New Mexico—the perfect marriage between architecture and nature, form and function. The tan walls weren't perfectly aligned, so every time shadows came they struck the church differently. Georgia O'Keeffe could paint it every day and find something new in the light and the angles. I wasn't Catholic, but I reflexively mumbled a quick prayer whenever I drove past. It was sacred.

Luna and I had our picture taken at the back of the church on the drive up that Friday. The woman taking the picture could have passed for Georgia O'Keeffe herself.

"That's my favorite place in New Mexico," Luna said, pointing to the church. "I feel like we're part of the painting."

"I agree."

"Can you hear that sound?"

"Could it be the Taos hum?" I was referring to the famed sound that emanated from the ground here that only certain people could hear.

"No, it's like a heartbeat." She made heartbeat sounds. "It's like the beating heart of New Mexico."

I listened and heard the beat. A clear thumping did vibrate up from the earth. With my shoe, I made a little heart shape in the ground and put DAN PLUS LUNA.

She smiled. With her heel, she added the word FOREVER.

• • •

I didn't hear any heartbeat as we passed the church heading southbound on Sunday. Luna cranked up K-Taos solar radio, which played some forgotten, depressing Bruce Springsteen guitar dirge about bad love in a bad economy. I loved it. Music just sounded better on solar radio, whatever that was. She drove the Focus quickly through the Rio Grande canyon, and that took up the next half hour or so. I woke up when we entered the Santa Fe city limits.

"I'm going to go through Santa Fe on St. Francis Drive through town," she said. Rain was now pouring down. On the left, off in the distance, I saw the big veteran's cemetery fully illuminated by floodlights. Luna shuddered.

"What's wrong?" I asked.

"Whenever I pass a cemetery, I think of funerals. First, my mom, then my dad, and then Rosa Mondragon last week."

"I'm sorry about your step-mom."

"Rosa Mondragon wasn't really my step-mom. She was my Dad's second wife, and the mother to two of my half-sisters. They all lived in Mexico so I didn't see them growing up."

"You have a really messed up family."

"Tell me about it. Rosa's funeral dredged up a lot of dark memories. My dad loved her more than my mother. He loved those two daughters—Selena and Mia—more than he loved me." Luna wiped away tears as she drove.

We both grew uneasy when she mentioned the named of her half-sister Mia. Mia had attacked us, and shot us on our wedding day. She was still at large.

We didn't say anything, even as the rain stopped when we left Santa Fe and merged onto I-25 toward Albuquerque. An hour later, we passed the Lomas Boulevard exit and saw the New Mexico Children's Hospital to the east. Our son was there.

I felt a pinging in my head, as if someone was tapping on my skull with a small hammer. Luna must have felt it too. "Marley's in trouble," she said. Somehow, I knew she was right.

We took the next exit and within moments, we were at the hospital entrance. Luna left the engine running, I followed her. I still felt the pinging, now it was worse. A security guard stopped us inside the lobby. For some unknown reason, instrumental versions of the Beatles songs always played on the Muzak. Today's feature was "The Long and Winding Road."

"I need to check on my son," she said. "I know it's after hours, but I feel it's an emergency." She faced him like she was making a motion for summary judgement.

Motion granted, somewhat. "Only one of you can go up," the guard said, after checking her ID and nodding at her name.

Luna nodded at me, there was no doubt that she would be the one to go up the room. The guard moved for her to enter the elevator.

A few moments later, the pinging stopped.

Luna returned, moments later. "I took care of it," she said.

I don't know whether she put back a loose tube, plugged a monitor, or just told the nurse to give him some water, but I continued to be amazed by Luna. She would do anything for our son. Anything.

. . .

After parking at home, we took the elevator to the fourth floor of the Bank Lofts on Central Avenue, an old office building that had been awkwardly converted into "Brooklyn" style apartments, complete with exposed bricks and protruding duct work. I couldn't help but compare myself to my late father. When he was my age, he lived in a mansion in the hills.

I had originally nicknamed the place Greystone, because it had grey stones, and figured it was a cool reference to Tarzan's ancestral mansion in England. I wasn't quite the comic book nerd I pretended to be. When she moved in Luna reminded me that the actual name of Tarzan's place was *Greystoke*.

"Don't you ever double-check things?" she had said. "That's what good lawyers are supposed to do."

"You're right," I said. "From now on, it's Greystoke."

"I'm always right," she said. "But Greystoke is a silly name for Albuquerque."

It was, but I didn't care. I had once joked that if Santa Fe was the City Different, Albuquerque was the City Same, because the suburban sprawl could be Anywhere, America. But my Greystoke was downtown Albuquerque, in the quirky self-proclaimed Innovation District. This part of town was trying to be a discount San Francisco, Seattle, or Austin.

And, it had almost worked . . . but Albuquerque would always be Albuquerque, the land of manana.

Our rooms had been home to an insurance agency in the nineteen-seventies, and they still smelled of moldy, lapsed term life policies. The building was mostly filled with young hipsters who worked in Albuquerque's high tech start-up scene. The hipsters ignored us.

"We need to move," Luna said in the cramped elevator that barely contained the two of us and our luggage. "To a real house so Marley can have his own room." Luna's house had burned down in a suspicious fire. Some time back she had convinced me to buy the unit next to mine, and to put a door in between the two units. Her seventeen-year old daughter, Dew, lived in the next unit.

The elevator door to the fourth floor opened. Dew must have heard us, because she stuck her head out of her door. She looked like a younger version of her mom, but dyed her dark hair a discrete lavender.

Dew's cousin Denise, the daughter of Luna's half-sister Jen Song, was staying the night. She stepped out as well. Denise didn't say much, even though she had lived with us ever since her mother took a mysterious assignment in Asia last fall. Denise was a few months older than Dew. With her pink hair, they looked like twins, except Denise's vaguely Asian eyes were brown, while Dew's more Caucasian eyes were green.

They were an odd duo—a yin and a yang on acid. Dew dressed in a style called sloppy prep. She wore an argyle sweater and khaki shorts as, if she was pledging a bad sorority. Tonight, Denise wore a shocking pink jacket over a black t-shirt with Korean lettering.

Dew and Denise—Dew was always first. Dew was the big

talker, Denise the silent one. If one was alone, the other was soon to join her. They were a sorority of two. Neither had any other friends at school. But with my mom retired to San Diego and my son in the hospital, along with Luna they were the closest thing that I had to family.

"We're practicing for mock trial team, for reals," Dew said, as if she was covering up for something else. I was too tired to care, a situation that happened a lot.

"Both of you?" Luna asked suspiciously.

"Denise is the witness." Dew replied. "The silent witness."

Denise smiled a guilty smile, which I couldn't read. Dew looked at me, hoping to avoid further cross-examination from her mother. "Dan, Luna said you passed out on the slopes, what happened?"

I was always Dan to her. She also called her mom Luna, unless Dew deemed Luna worthy of being called Mom for the moment.

"I'm not sure," I said. Dew had already turned her attention elsewhere, inevitably to her smart phone and the latest cool app. She was Luna's daughter, not mine. Suddenly, Dew's two cats, Sahar and Suri, snuck out from behind the girls' legs and emerged into the hallway.

Dew's given name was Sacagawea. She had given the cats exotic names starting with S, because "that's what I'll name my own kids someday, although by the time I have kids they'll come out of test tubes."

I grabbed Sahar, a white cat, and Luna grabbed Suri who was half white and half black. Sahar purred and licked my face. Were the cats the only ones in the household who truly loved me?

Luna and I entered our loft. The living room slash

kitchen felt barely bigger than the elevator, now that it was crammed with Luna's furniture. The last vestiges of my bachelor pad had been taken over by Luna nouvelle Santa Fe style. Our dining room table was big enough for a dinner party for eight.

Luna had obsessively reminded me of my slovenly ways before she moved into Greystoke. No CD, indeed. Now she said, "Just think of all the improvements we can make to this place now that we have a little money. New furniture for a start."

"I'll get you a dining room table and four chairs."

"Six chairs, in case we have guests."

"You got it."

For a moment, she looked at me romantically. Talk of new furniture was an aphrodisiac. I looked back at her. I did love her deeply, and it was undeniable that I was better off with her than without her.

"But not tonight," I said. "I am still a little sore from the accident and I have to go to Santa Fe tomorrow morning for the arraignment."

I went to the bathroom to get ready for bed and popped one and a half generic Benadryl allergy pills for sleep—the closest thing I had to a drug addiction. The pink generic Benadryl pill would make me nervous for about thirty minutes, and then I'd abruptly sleep for around four hours. Then I'd take another pill to make it through the night. I don't know if I ever took the pink pill for allergies. I had read that the oval pills caused early dementia and wondered if they were to blame for my grogginess in the morning.

Luna and I were about to go to sleep when Dew and Denise started playing loud music Sahar and Suri, the cats, must have been screeching along with the DJ. It sounded like gunfire with wailing.

I couldn't sleep, but it wasn't just the headache. I thought again about Luna's half-sister Anna, whom I knew as Mia. I thought back to that horrible night on top of the Parq Central Hotel when Mia had killed Dew's father, then wounded and tried to kill Luna, Selena, and myself. I still had a scar where the bullet passed right through me. Luna didn't have any scars, not on the surface anyway.

After the shooting Mia, had jumped off the fourth story roof of the hotel and landed face-first on the ground. She had been in a coma for months, but when she recovered, she vanished. For the last few years she had been presumed dead.

• • •

It was three o'clock in the morning, when I woke up screaming. Luna grabbed me. "You're having a nightmare."

She held me tight, and I felt safe in her arms. She kissed my forehead. "Don't worry," she said holding me even tighter. "I'll do whatever it takes to protect this family."

"I thought that was my job."

"It is, but together, we're invincible."

"I'm the Luna Lawyer then. Everything I do, I do for you."

As I struggled to get back to sleep for the last few hours of the night, I knew in my heart that everything—Luna, Mia, Marley, Dew, Denise, and even Dragon Moon—would come together at exactly the same time.

I wondered if I would be ready.

PART II
MONKEY ELBOW

4. Don't Cry for Me, Little Mia

April 2, 2018

I woke up early to prepare for the drive to Santa Fe, even though I had a generic Benadryl hangover. Did the little pink pill take a few more points off my IQ last night? I was often unable to follow complicated directions from Luna. With a generic Benadryl hangover, I was unable to follow *simple* directions from Luna. I never remembered which drawer to put the ice cream scoop for example.

I took a quick shower, chugged a Killer Cappuccino energy drink and slapped on my nicest blue suit. I still had an old purple Jerry Garcia tie that I wore for some of my biggest trials. The purple in the tie had faded quite a bit, but Garcia and the Grateful Dead were the patron saints of traveling defense attorneys who did a lot of "truckin,'" like their famed song of that name. I was never a hippie, but I did enjoy a good Garcia guitar lick. Perhaps the tie reminded me that I wore a "touch of grey" in my hair because it "kinda suits me anyway."

I left my famed rattlesnake boots in the closet. When I wore those boots, I hoped to transform into the legendary Rattlesnake Lawyer and slither through the badlands of New Mexico. What was a Rattlesnake Lawyer? A lawyer who could slide into any courtroom and tell the judges, juries, and opposing counsel, "Don't tread on me or my client, dude!"

Instead I went with some narrow, pointed black Ekko shoes made of ersatz snakeskin. That made me the garden snake lawyer at least.

Unfortunately, in my haste, I forgot to put the Killer Cappuccino can in the trash. Instead, I just left it on the counter and it must have sprung a leak. I also hadn't noticed that the can had dripped little brown drops onto the floor. Luna walked into the kitchen and looked at the brown drops of guarana taurine mixed with one percent real coffee dripping onto the already dirty floor as if I had dragged in a corpse and hadn't bothered to clean up the blood.

"Can't you ever pay attention to your life?" she asked. "Isn't that what they teach you in martial arts, to go slow and get out of your head?"

She came over to me and gave me a hug. "You can do this," she said. "I have faith in you."

I hugged her back. I could do this. When I was with her, I did have faith.

. . .

I shared an elevator down with a guy I called "Facebook," as his lanyard held a badge for the new Facebook data facility in Los Lunas. The guy couldn't be more than twenty-five, but he had a full beard and tattoos for the cool bands of my day. The Clash had recorded "Should I stay or should I go?" before he was born, but he had it tattooed on his arm in Olde English script.

"I'm interviewing with Google next week," he said as we went to the garage. He drove a new, black BMW convertible.

If like Tarzan, my Greystoke was symbolic of civilization, I was about to commute to the jungle, and it was a hard commute. I had trouble backing out and dinged the side of my Focus yet again. Yeah, I needed to focus all right. Just before I got to the turn for the northbound interstate, I noticed I'd forgotten my padfolio, a black folder that contained important legal documents and other lawyer necessities. I did a U-turn and headed to the office.

Yes, generic Benadryl made me stupid.

Albuquerque grew more urban every day. Today I was nearly side-swiped by one of the new Albuquerque Rapid Transit (ART) buses that ran up the middle two lanes of Central Avenue. The construction of the bus lanes had taken a long, congested year, and the town was still recovering. The jury was still out on ART.

After passing the four stories of the new "entertainment complex" One Central, I crossed under the railroad tracks and looked for parking on Broadway Boulevard. Albuquerque's Broadway was dramatic in its own way—a chorus line of addicts heading to a rehab center performed a perpetual song and dance number with the young hipsters who walked toward the Innovate ABQ complex.

As I parked near my office, I saw that a mysterious figure was pacing on the sidewalk in front of our door. The figure had seemingly removed a wooden staff from her jacket and placed it on the ground. I approached our firm's front door with a tinge of apprehension. No one ever waited for me in front.

"Can I help you?" I asked. It was a woman with buzz cut.

"You don't recognize me?"

She did remind me of Luna. A distant relative perhaps?

"I'm your sister-in-law, Selena."

No, I didn't immediately recognize Luna's half-sister with her lack of hair and the addition of her masculine wardrobe. The staff was really her cane, a cane that she now leaned against for support, a result of her injuries from Mia on our wedding day.

"I'm supposed to meet with Luna about Dragon Moon. We have to strategize," she said. "Can I wait inside? The cold is getting to me a bit."

The Law Office of Dan Shepard, esquire, was a renovated

adobe house that held both our offices. My firm was technically a sole proprietorship, but I felt as if I was the employee and Luna the boss. She called her firm LUNA LAW, because it sounded better than Cruz Law.

I had agreed. "People don't want to get cruz-ified by their lawyer."

She hadn't found that funny.

The entrance was made up of double glass doors. On the right door, white lettering spelled out THE RATTLESNAKE LAWYER, DAN SHEPARD, CRIMINAL LAW.

On the left door, turquoise lettering announced LUNA LAW, LUNA CRUZ SHEPARD, CRIMINAL LAW, CORPORATE LAW, FAMILY LAW, SECURITIES LAW, WILLS AND ESTATE, DIVORCE.

A tiny crack in the glass punctured the "o" in DIVORCE.

Was that crack a bad omen? Sometimes our business felt like a marriage and our marriage felt like a business. The small suite contained my office, a lobby, and her bigger office that had the better view of the brand new Innovate ABQ complex that had just opened. My office had a view of the rear of the Albuquerque Convention Center. From the front, the convention center was a direct architectural descendant of the block-like adobe stylings of the Taos Pueblo and the Ranchos style of church, albeit it was the Ranchos church on steroids. On the third street side, one bell tower—with its tapering on one side and straightness on the other-- even looked exactly like the rebuilt tower of the San Geronimo church at the pueblo.

Unfortunately, my window looked out at six stories of ugly industrial gray convention center parking garage that was more Newark than New Mexico.

Selena and I walked inside the lobby of the small, three

room suite. Selena sat in one of the plush chairs in the lobby, and grimaced with pain. Her injury had never healed properly.

"I only have a few minutes before I have to go to court up in Santa Fe," I said.

"For Dragon Moon? Luna told me about you meeting with Kirlian. What are you doing for them?"

"Just some minor felonies for one of their truck drivers."

"It's probably more important than you think. Their business relies on access to government, on security clearances. If they lose access, they could lose everything."

"What's your connection to them? Your father was an original investor in Dragon Moon, right?"

"He changed his name to Mondragon and Dragon Moon was a play on that. He liked it better than Moon Dragon."

"What's a dragon moon?"

"Maybe some kind of bad moon on the rise, like the old blues song. Dragon Moon started as a trucking company in El Paso, and my father ran a chain of pharmacies that provided discount drugs for Americans just over the border in Juarez, Mexico. Do the math."

"I've already done it. They were shipping pills *sans* prescription up from Mexico."

"It was some kind of money laundering thing. He had profits from his chain of pharmacies and didn't want to pay taxes on them. Old Man Kirlian, the man who started Dragon Moon with my father, didn't want to pay taxes either, so there was some kind of quid pro quo at the beginning. My father had considerable stock and property that went to his daughters after my mother, Rosa, died last month, as you know."

Considerable stock and property? Luna hadn't told me

much, except that it was all tied up in litigation. I couldn't think of anything except "I'm sorry for your loss."

"Thanks. We had grown apart after my father died, but I did love her. But here's where things get tricky. He left his fifty-one percent of the company stock to the four daughters, but not in equal shares. Luna got some, and Jen, Denise's mom, got some. The lion's share went to Mia and myself."

"The Mia who tried to kill us? She inherited stock?"

Selena pantomimed using her cane as a sword, stabbing a phantom Mia. "That's her, the fugitive murderer *puta*. And for some reason she received the plurality of all our shares when her mother, *my* mother, Rosa, died. Remember that our father died before we knew Anna's new identity as Mia the Murderer. When he made the will, she was still missing, and he hoped that the money would help her get a fresh start in life if she ever surfaced. If not, it would revert to us. Unfortunately, after Mia shot us and then went to the hospital, it was confirmed by DNA that she was indeed Anna, the true heir to my father's fortune."

"Can a fugitive murderer *puta* inherit stock?"

"That's the issue. Kirlian said that since she's a fugitive, her shares would revert to the company, to him. Kirlian became the acting head of the company after his father and our father passed. We're saying that they revert to us—to Luna and myself. I have a feeling that if Mia is ever arrested she would still be entitled to the shares, because that's what the will clearly stated. There was nothing in there about a morals clause, even if she's in prison."

"Does Jen Song, your other half-sister, get a share?"

"Jen won millions in that lawsuit with Susie Song, so she doesn't need any money. When Jen went away on her little Asian excursion a few months ago, she left her shares in trust for Denise until Denise turns eighteen. That will be in a few weeks."

Jen had simply vanished from our lives along with Susie. They had billed themselves as "The Laser Geishas" after the popular cult animated TV show, and Jen said something about "official Geisha business" over in Korea. Were they were going to fight the forces of evil in the anime world?

"Your family has issues," I said.

"We tend to go to extremes under pressure," she said. "It's in our genes."

That was certainly true. Mia had gone over the edge of course, Jen had as well. I knew Selena had once been involved in a gunfight up at Acoma Pueblo, but didn't know the details. As for Luna, who knew how she would react if our current situation continued?

Regarding the next generation, Dew and Denise had certainly inherited the crazy gene. I just hoped that Marley would survive long enough for us to find out.

"So, what's going to happen?" I asked.

We still aren't sure how much the shares are worth after all the stock splits and what not. The shareholder meeting is coming up in a few weeks, and they don't have a permanent CEO yet. Young Kirlian wants to take over his father's company, and supposedly someone from Cannon Air Force Base in Clovis, a Colonel Herring, is in the running too. There's another group that wants the former governor, Diana Crater. Or maybe some Chinese scientist from the Los Alamos labs who invented their new legal software."

"Does it really matter who takes over?" I asked.

"Several groups want to do a hostile takeover and keep the company private," Selena said. "Other groups want to do an IPO to cash in while the timing is right. They have this thing called a 'thimble' that could replace the cell phone."

"I had one," I said. "Kirlian gave me one, but someone mugged me yesterday and took it while I was skiing."

"That's unfortunate." Selena let out a soft moan of pain and touched a spot on her pant leg. "We can talk about that mugging some other time. I feel like I've been mugged every day. Could you get me some water, *por favor*?"

I got her some water and she gulped down a few pills. Of all the survivors, she had suffered the most. "Thanks. I just want to hold it together for this shareholder meeting."

"When and where is it?"

"Albuquerque on June 29 at the convention center over there." She pointed to the large complex on the other side of the railroad tracks. "Dragon Moon's biggest clients—Los Alamos, all three air force bases, Sandia Labs, and Spaceport USA—are all based here in New Mexico."

"Aren't they also trying to take over the courts or something?"

"The New Mexico legal system is currently on two computer programs—nmcourts.gov and Odyssey. Dragon Moon wants the contract to make sure it runs on only one, their shoftim system."

Someone put a key in the outside lock, we both looked at the door with dread. Was Mia coming back for us?

Thankfully, it was only Luna. Today she was dressed in a black pantsuit and blazer, business casual like she was off to argue before a mere Magistrate court. She hugged Selena, who remained seated.

"I like the haircut," Luna said.

"I'm finally me," Selena said.

She looked at me. "You okay?"

I nodded. She had a paper bag. She opened it to reveal

three piping hot muffins, which she placed on her desk before handing one to Selena and one to me.

"How did you know I'd be here?" I asked.

"I knew you'd forget your padfolio," she said with a smile.

I ate the muffin. She came over and gave me another hug. "For luck," she said. "Sounds like today you're going to need it."

"Thanks," I replied.

"I love you," she said.

"I love you too."

"Sorry Dan, this is a family matter," Selena said. The two of them went into Luna's office and closed the door.

I hurried out the front door of the office, and then remembered the reason I had come back into the office in the first place—my padfolio.

When I re-opened the door, Luna had returned to the lobby with the padfolio. She tapped it against her chest. "I knew you'd forget this." She had stocked it with a fresh pad and some pens. There was even a bulge from all the business cards she had stuck in the inside pocket.

"What would you do without me?" she asked.

"I'd be lost." I grabbed the padfolio and hurried back out the door. On the yellow pad, Luna had written the words HAVE FAITH!

5. Yada Yada La Bajada

My padfolio in hand, I headed north like any of the everyday La Bajada lawyers—lawyers who lived in the same old Albuquerque but worked in Santa Fe, the City Different. La Bajada hill, a steep ascent forty miles north of the Santa Fe county line, marked the divide between the Albuquerque and Santa Fe metropolitan areas.

Along the way, I passed the exit for Rio Rancho, New Mexico. Rio Rancho had become the go-to suburb for lawyers who practiced in both cities. If I had played my cards right, I'd probably be living there right now with a three-bedroom home, a yard, and a mortgage. It was probably too late for suburbia and me.

Even from this far out, I noticed the abandoned Intel plant that had once housed three thousand workers that would be the new home of Dragon Moon. Damn, they really were taking over New Mexico.

Within moments, the exit was far behind me and I was in the high desert. Some of the north facing hills still had snow on them. Dotted with the dark junipers these hills resembled sleeping Dalmatians.

After the long climb, I stopped at the La Bajada rest station on the top of the hill for a rest break. As I unzipped and did my business, I was struck by the fact that Luna and I had not had sex since the shooting. Sure, there had been medical issues as she and I recovered, but was our passion gone forever?

La Bajada meant "the descent" in Spanish, and after I got back into the car it was downhill toward Santa Fe.

I often thought of odd things when I drove. Today I wondered which moment was the high point of my life? Probably at twenty-two when I graduated from an Ivy league college and held the class banner at graduation. Life had been La Bajada since then.

A quick glance at my watch told me I still had time to meet with my client and get ready for the case. I took the St. Francis Drive exit and drove through the main part of Santa Fe. Everyone here drove a Subaru or a Prius. My Focus felt completely out of style. Parking was scarcer than usual today. Was there an art gallery owners' convention in town? I couldn't find a space anywhere so I parked in the state lot. The massive three story adobe building didn't charge any fees and didn't check for tags, so it was a good place for Santa Fe insiders.

I hurried across the street. Santa Fe was, at seven thousand feet elevation, nearly as high as the Taos Ski Valley base village. I gasped for breath as I passed the adobe monstrosity that was the Paul Bardacke building, the main office for the New Mexico Attorney General. I hated those guys.

The three-story building looked like an adobe fortress— the Alamo with better internet connections. My old law school girlfriend, Mary Alice Forrest, was now the attorney general for all New Mexico. She only hired the best guns to work there. I didn't even get an interview when I had applied.

When I arrived at the First Judicial courthouse a few blocks over, I headed to the metal detectors and asked a guard for the location of Judge Chairez's courtroom. He gave me a dirty look. "Her court's in Los Alamos today. Didn't you check the court website?"

My heart sunk. Where was my head these days? Well, even if I didn't have my thimble, I could have checked this on my smart phone. Suddenly my notion that I had plenty of time to prepare had been thrown out the window. I was going to have to wing it. In martial arts, not all attacks came from the front. The defense to a punch from the left side, from three o'clock, was called Monkey Elbow. I had just received its equivalent attack, but had failed to respond.

6. Lost Almost

North of Santa Fe, I drove into the crossroads town of Pojoaque, which was another Indian pueblo. I drove under the speed limit because the town was famous for arresting non-tribal members. I once represented a Chinese scientist who was on contract with the national lab up at Los Alamos. He was issued a ticket in Pojoaque for going seventy miles per hour right where the limit abruptly became forty-five. Because he exceeded twenty-five miles over the speed limit, the cop threw the book at him and charged with reckless driving in addition to speeding. Reckless driving sported a mandatory four days of jail time if convicted.

The scientist explained to me that if he spent even the mandatory two days in jail for the speeding, he would lose his security clearance. If he lost his security clearance, he lost his job. If he lost his job, he lost his visa and "very bad things" would happen to him if he was deported back to China.

I won that case when the cop didn't show, and the Chinese scientist told me that I was the best lawyer in the world. Whatever the hell had happened to me since then?

I took the Los Alamos turn-off, and a few miles later crossed the Rio Grande where it ran deep through a narrow canyon. On the other side of the river, the road began a steep ascent up to town. My scientist client had deemed the town "Lost Almost," and perhaps he was correct. With every mile up hill, I was reminded of the opening scene in *The Shining* where Jack Nicholson drove his family on a scenic route to certain doom. I could hear the movie theme in my head as the ascent went on longer than I expected, but finally I ascended to a mesa, a great plateau high above the craggy red rock formations in the valley below.

Just before I made it to the top of the mesa, I saw a break in the shoulder guard, as if a car had burst through the metal then plummeted off the cliff. Alongside the shoulder of the road, there was a *descanso*—a roadside shrine consisting of a small cross along with some flowers to indicate that someone had died in an auto accident at this very spot. There was a New Mexico statute that allowed these shrines if they were far enough off the road so they didn't interfere with traffic. That usually meant the cross stood three feet off the shoulder.

This shrine with its simple cross and two dozen roses followed the statute, but I still shuddered. It was as if a cold hand had grabbed the back of my neck. Maybe I did have a bit of the shining after all. Thankfully, the first hotel I passed when I hit town was a Hilton Garden Inn, as opposed to *The Shining's* Overlook Hotel.

I could see the massive concrete structures of Los Alamos National Lab (LANL) off to the left. They developed technology for nuclear weapons, among other chemical innovations. Much of the lab's architecture was the "brutalist" style of the sixties—very boxy and hard. I took the right fork of the road toward downtown, which felt more like a small college town in the Midwest. I soon became stuck at a light next to a Starbucks in downtown and I wondered if they served a plutonium pumpkin spice latte here. Or, maybe a nitrogen iced tea?

Finally, I parked at the courthouse next to a small pond. This building also had the brutalist style of LANL. To add to the mood, the mountains off in the distance were scarred by fire, and the bare trees looked even darker over a patchy cover of the season's remaining snow.

After I hurried, beeping, through an unguarded metal

detector, Kirlian greeted me next to the stairs. He wore a black suit and blood red tie, as if he'd just picked a jury in Purgatory.

"Where were you?"

"I'm sorry," I said. "I didn't know court had been moved."

"Where's your thimble?" he asked. "You would have received an alert."

I had a moment of sheer panic. What should I say? He could still take the hundred thousand dollars back.

Time to think fast. "I'm having some kind of allergic reaction to it. Is there a way to turn the intensity down?"

"I'll have one of our techs look at it later in the week."

Before he could ask anything more, a bailiff came from inside the courtroom. "Court is in session." The ancient bailiff looked like Albert Einstein in a blue polyester blazer.

"Could I see my client?" I asked.

"Do you have clearance?"

"Clearance?"

He didn't answer and instead ushered us into the courtroom. Kirlian walked to the podium and greeted his client. Axtell Pile was a wiry Anglo man with a military haircut and a *semper fi* tattoo, but seemed to have too much nervous energy to be a marine. He couldn't stand still, much less stand at attention.

This overly nervous dude was not someone I would want around loaded firearms. He had WEAK LINK tattooed on the back of his neck. Had his marine buddies tattooed it on him as part of a Code Red hazing?

The attorney general herself, Mary Alice Forrest, was at the prosecutor's table on the right. She looked every inch the modern Lady Justice in a charcoal, pin-striped business suit. Mary Alice had been my law school girlfriend at American

University. I once joked that she had spent her entire life in the 88th percentile. She was a solid B plus student while I had As and Ds. Somehow that B plus lifestyle had carried her on to become the top prosecutor in New Mexico. Slow and steady wins the race.

Mary Alice stood with Jesus Raphael, a prosecutor of about my age, who had made the news after winning high-profile cases all over the state. Raphael had long hair, a stylish beard, and could pass for a noble out of the Renaissance, or perhaps the Spanish Inquisition. He had been a prosecutor his entire adult life and now he probably felt secure enough to let his hair down, literally.

Behind them a very short paralegal sat in a folding chair, as if they didn't want to put her at the table with the big guns. The woman looked Native American, or perhaps Mongolian, and had very wide cheekbones. There was also a puffiness around her eyes. Her hair was gray, so it was impossible to guess her age.

The paralegal carried an iPad tablet and stared at it intently. I wanted to say that the new thimble would make her obsolete, but with the power of her gaze, I wasn't so sure. I walked over to introduce myself to the group, then noticed the paralegal wore turquoise earrings identical to Luna's.

"Nice earrings," I said as I sat on one of the benches right behind her. "Are you a member of the Taos Pueblo?"

She didn't say a word. Before I could shake hands, the bailiff, the Einstein look-alike, asked us to rise. Then the judge came out onto the bench wearing a bright turquoise robe, as opposed to basic black.

It was like a homecoming; I knew the judge as well. There were only a few hundred people in the criminal field throughout the entire state, so after a while everyone got to know everyone else. The honorable Veronica Chairez was the former Veronica Arias, from the small town of Aguilar, New Mexico. She had started as the receptionist for the jail there, and I saw her every day when I did my time in the Fighting Fourteenth, the conservative judicial district in Southeastern New Mexico. We had even dated for a spell.

Some homecoming. She didn't even nod in my direction.

Veronica was related to the famous singer Anna Maria Arias. Today the judge wore dramatic make-up and tall dark hair that made her look like an opera diva. Veronica, excuse me, the Honorable Veronica Chairez, had moved to Los Angeles some time back. Before she left she'd emailed me that she was on a schedule and either I was on it or I wasn't. I didn't email her back quickly enough, so I apparently wasn't on her schedule. Last I heard she was living with a rich movie producer. The producer must have moved back here to work on some of the numerous projects filming in New Mexico these days. Veronica needed a day job, and being a judge was as good a day job as you could get.

The final necessary party for the hearing, a court reporter, scurried over to a space near the judge's bench, just like the parasite that nestled near Jabba the Hutt in the *Star Wars* films. While the paralegal looked Native American, this court reporter was short and looked Middle Eastern. Persian perhaps? She, too, wore turquoise, as if to copy her boss.

"Shaharazad, are we ready?" the judge asked.

Shaharazad, the court reporter, nodded.

The judge called the case to order. Kirlian used his thimble to project his notes onto his desk. I could see five separate pink beams emanating from the hole in the thimble. He also had a printer next to him. The printer did not make a sound, but paper magically emerged from a narrow slot.

"Your honor, here are the waivers we printed out so that you could hear all the arraignments in these cases as well as in his co-defendant's. We also had the necessary paperwork filed with the New Mexico Supreme Court so you could be appointed to all the cases."

Luna had once told me that this could happen in complicated cases in multiple jurisdictions. With the proper paperwork, the Supreme Court could order this unlikely scenario. Kirlian handed the papers to Einstein who handed them to the judge.

The judge scanned the papers dubiously, but then nodded. "Mr. Kirlian, there are cases in Los Alamos County, Curry County, Roosevelt County, Lincoln County, and Luna County."

Another beam came out of his thimble and pointed at the table, as if the tiny metal computer was feeding Kirlian his lines. "Your honor, we waive a formal reading and enter a plea of not guilty on all charges."

Axtell Pile nodded. The paralegal for the state was apparently in a race to keep up with the machine and she now handed Mary Alice all the needed documents. She was fast.

"Conditions of release?" the judge asked.

The small paralegal handed Mary Alice a few additional documents.

"Your honor," Mary Alice said. "Mr. Pile's a flight risk. Had he and his co-defendant not tried to enter Los Alamos National Labs, they might still be on the run."

Why would anyone with warrants on their head try to enter one of the most highly secure areas in the country?

There was a spirited argument for a few moments, and Kirlian used his thimble like a wand to project information onto the courtroom's big screen. Meanwhile, the paralegal kept pace, handing Mary Alice the appropriate paperwork. Kirlian then asked if the parties could approach. The paralegal walked up right there with them, holding the tablet. Mary Alice turned to her whenever the judge said something, and the judge turned on "white noise" so we couldn't hear a word. The white noise gave me a headache.

Finally, all the parties went back to their tables and the white noise machine grew silent. Unfortunately, all the whiteness kept echoing in my head.

"It's agreed then. Mr. Pile will be released on his own recognizance, but is confined to his residence unless he has court hearings."

What had happened up there? Both the Mary Alice and Kirlian looked happy, so an appropriate compromise must have been reached. The short paralegal pointed to something on her tablet and Mary Alice nodded.

"I'm getting out baby!" Pile shouted to someone in the gallery. "Free at last."

"Be quiet!" Kirlian yelled at him.

If Pile could get out, that should mean that Cage could get out as well. Before I had too much time to think about that, the judge called Albert Jackson Cage.

The bailiff shouted out the name as if announcing a prize fight. "Albert . . . Jackson . . . Cage! Now appearing in Courtroom Number One!"

"Your honor, may I have a minute to consult with my client?" I asked, trying to rise above the echo.

"No, you may not," the judge said. She echoed her earlier statement to me. "I have a schedule and either you're on it, or you're not."

Cage strutted into the courtroom wearing an orange jumpsuit that barely contained his bulk. He looked like a former middle linebacker who had gained weight after retirement. Some war hero. I wanted to call him Fat Albert, but his intense stare indicated that he didn't take kindly to nicknames.

Cage stood next to me at the podium. It was as if he was a world heavyweight champ and I was the ref who was supposed to hold up his hand in victory. This man had a presence. Maybe he was bulletproof. Once a war hero, always a war hero.

Before I could introduce myself, the judge banged the gavel. "Mr. Shepard, do you want to waive a reading of the charges?"

"I think we all want to know what my client is charged with, your honor," I said.

The judge frowned. Cage grumbled. This would be a waste of their time. Judge Chairez spoke quickly. "In Clovis, Curry County, there was a possession of drugs case. Another possession of drugs case in Portales, Roosevelt County. It was receiving stolen property in Carrizozo, Lincoln County and in Los Alamos County, Cage was accused of a conspiracy to receive stolen property.

"Your honor," said Mary Alice said. "We've amended the final count of conspiracy to be conspiracy at receiving stolen property. While he was apprehended in Los Alamos County, the actual conspiracy to receive stolen property took place in Luna County, so we will be asking for a change of venue to that jurisdiction."

Luna County? Where was Luna County? I thought Luna was from Crater County. Did my wife have a county named after her? Then I remembered that Luna County was somewhere down south, near either Mexico or Arizona.

"How do you plead?" the judge asked. "Are you with us in the here and now, Mr. Shepard?"

I returned to earth. "Your honor, we plead not guilty to all the charges."

The paralegal tapped on Mary Alice's hand and pointed again to a tablet. "Your honor, we might be amending these charges," Mary Alice said. "Some additional evidence is coming to light."

The judge frowned. "Normally, I would not be handling the arraignments on these cases in various jurisdictions, but I must compliment the parties on getting all the necessary papers filled out."

I hadn't filled out any paperwork. It had been filled out by Dorfman, the attorney before me, the one who died. The paralegal came over to me with the papers, but didn't make eye contact. A New Mexico judge in good standing could handle an arraignment for cases anywhere, right? I had never seen paperwork like this before, even though some statutory citations allowed it. I was very aware that I didn't have my thimble and that my smart phone wasn't particularly smart.

I didn't have time to research the statutes with my phone. If Kirlian had signed them and his client had gotten out, my client would probably get out as well, right?

"Just sign these," I said as I handed Cage a pen.

"You aren't on their side, are you? Who's paying you?"

"Dragon Moon is paying me, but I'm on your side," I said.

"Are you sure?"

Time to play lawyer. "I took an oath to zealously represent you, even if they are paying me." I had just used the z word, zealously. Did I mean that?

"You promise that?"

"I promise." I looked him in the eye. He might have had the scarier gaze, but I didn't blink. Perhaps martial arts had enabled me to control my facial muscles for the necessary second so I could pass for a Culebra Kai/ There is no try to a zealous lawyer.

He lowered his eyes and signed all the forms waiving arraignment in the other jurisdictions so Judge Chairez could arraign him here.

"Why is this in district court already?" I asked Cage.

"I waived prelims back when my lawyer was Kent Dorfman. Didn't you know that?"

"Of course," I lied. "I'm just getting up to speed."

"You better hurry up and get up to like the speed of light, man. This is my life here."

"Mr. Shepard?" the judge asked.

We signed the necessary paperwork, handed it to Einstein, and the judge looked it all over. "Let's get the scheduling over with, right now."

"Your honor, these cases are all relatively simple and time is of the essence," Mary Alice stated as if she was the judge rather than the prosecutor.

"And why is that, counsel?" the judge asked.

"Your honor, the shareholder meeting for Dragon Moon Corporation is on June twenty-ninth, the end of their fiscal year. We need to get Mr. Cage's issues resolved prior to that, so let's set the trials over the next few weeks."

"What do Mr. Cage's cases have to do with a shareholder's meeting of his employer?"

"Your honor, we are exploring charging the current board of Dragon Moon with numerous violations of the New Mexico

Securities Acts, as well as Federal regulations. Those charges will certainly be a factor in who they choose to be on their new board prior to the IPO this fall. We are coordinating with the Justice Department."

The paralegal handed Mary Alice a stack of papers, and then handed an identical stack of papers to me. She still avoided eye contact.

I looked at the attorney general's table. I now had some sense of what was going on. The attorney general wanted to pressure Cage to testify against Dragon Moon in time for the shareholders meeting. On the other hand, Dragon Moon probably wanted me to plead Cage out quickly to get the cases behind them. Both parties wanted to get this case resolved soon.

"Mr. Shepard?" the judge asked. I wasn't sure what she wanted me to say.

"Say something, damn it!" Cage whispered to me. "You're the lawyer, right?"

"Your honor, I am entering on four cases all over the state. It would be ineffective assistance of counsel *per se* for me to handle four cases in the next few months."

"Your honor, Mr. Shepard signed a contract with us." It took a moment for me to recognize Kirlian's voice. "He said he would handle all the cases, come what may."

"Mr. Kirlian, please do not interrupt me in my courtroom." Kirlian may be a powerful lawyer, but Judge Chairez ruled her courtroom with a turquoise first. She scanned all the documents as if she was a speed reader.

"Counsel, I agree that time is of the essence on these cases and they have been delayed enough because of the warrant situation."

Delayed enough? I didn't know about any warrant

situation. Why didn't I prepare?

She then printed out a scheduling order that she handed to Einstein, who handed it to the two parties. I would indeed have three jury trials before June 29. This was going to be one busy spring.

"Thank you, your honor," I said, and started to turn around.

"What about me getting out?" Cage said. "Axtell Pile got out."

"Your honor, conditions of release?" I asked.

The judge shut me off. "He had three warrants for his arrest. He still has pending misdemeanor warrants in Alamogordo. He will remain in custody, but you can file the appropriate motions. We are in recess." The judge left the courtroom like a blue streak. Things moved faster up here in Los Alamos.

"All rise!" Einstein said, but the judge had already disappeared. I was still shaking when the door slammed behind Cage as the guard took him away.

"Good to see you again, Dan," Attorney General Mary Alice Forrest said. "I didn't realize that you were still practicing law."

The words cut through me. "Malpractice makes perfect," I said trying to joke it away.

"We definitely want to cut a deal on this one; that's why the clock is ticking so quickly."

That sounded great. I remembered the prediction of the thimble that this case would easily resolve itself. "I figured. None of these cases are that major. Would you be willing to give him a consolidated plea to probation?" I was basically asking her to wrap everything up to a single plea document and let my client walk, just as the thimble had predicted.

The paralegal handed Mary Alice her tablet, and Mary Alice smiled an evil smile as if she had just drawn blackjack at the nearby Buffalo Thunder casino. "I don't know if you realized that Cage has a prior felony. Originally it had been a conditional discharge which meant it wouldn't be a felony if he had finished probation."

"So that won't count as a felony for a one-year habitual offender enhancement purpose, right?'

"Unfortunately, he lost his conditional discharge through a probation violation, so it does. Since he has ten pending felony charges in the four counties, we can give him a one-year habitual offender enhancement for *each* charge in each case. As of right now, the plea is ten years in the Department of Corrections."

She looked at the paralegal, who handed me one of Mary Alice's business cards. "Keep in touch," Mary Alice said.

Keep in touch? She did not touch my hand, did not even wave as she walked away. Raphael and the paralegal followed behind. Within seconds, I was the only person left in the courtroom, except for the bailiff.

"Could I finally have some private time with my client?"

He laughed. "Maybe. But I don't know if he wants to see you."

7. Cage in a Rage

Einstein reluctantly let me through the back door to see my client. "You have five minutes." Everything moved so fast here that five minutes probably meant four.

The prisoner waiting room looked like it doubled as a storage closet for a mad scientist—Dr. Clean, perhaps. There were boxes of old files stacked in the corner, as well as potentially toxic cleaning chemicals. Inside, Cage was still in cuffs, pacing next to the bench. The lone guard looked too intimidated to tell him to sit down.

"What the hell just happened in there?" he demanded.

"Sit down for a moment and I'll tell you, Mr. Cage," I said. "I just talked to the attorney general herself, we go way back."

He sat down. "You were a war hero," I said. "You saved that nurse with your bare hands when she was captured by the Taliban or whoever."

He still had the million-dollar smile that I remembered from his fifteen minutes of fame on CNN, and he was clearly flattered. "Call me AJ. Not exactly. She was a lab tech in a clinic, not a nurse. And we were sort of AWOL when it happened, if you catch my drift."

So, he and his girl were out with each other when he was not supposed to be. "But you did save her, right?"

"Yeah, I did. I had forgotten my gun, and when those guys grabbed her when we were stopped, something just came over me. You gotta understand this wasn't about patriotism. I just didn't want to get caught because we both could have been slammed for deserting."

"But you kept going, AJ. You took out four guys. That had to be patriotism, putting your life on the line for a fellow soldier."

"Nah, taking out the first guy was about saving our asses. But punching out the second guy and then the third, that was about love."

A man who saved someone for love, he was a man after my own heart. I hoped I could be as brave as he had been. "You fought them with your bare hands?"

"I have a fourth-degree black belt in Karate."

"I'm testing for my purple belt, maybe you can give me some pointers."

He pantomimed the Kimono Grab technique for me in the air. Even with the weight of the handcuffs, it was crisp and clean. I could almost visualize him wearing a kimono, the Taliban grabbing it and then Cage responding with some kicks and chops to neutralize the opponent.

"That's Kimono Grab," I said. "That's the first technique I learned for gold belt."

"I just wish there was a handcuff break technique."

"I'll try to get you out of your handcuffs with my flying daggers of justice."

He laughed. I was reaching him at least. "They're offering probation, right?"

"Unfortunately, right now they're offering ten years in the Department of Corrections."

The million-dollar smile became a fifty-cent frown. "Talk to Axtell Pile. He's got my thimble hidden somewhere. The thimble has information that might make ten years turn into a get-out-of-jail-free card. Because as of right now, him and me are on the same side, which is not necessarily Dragon Moon's side. Get my thimble and put it into your safe."

I didn't want to tell him that I didn't have a safe and that I had already lost my own thimble. "Did you hit it off with your last lawyer, Mr. Dorfman?"

"We did great until he got murdered."

"Murdered! I thought it was an auto accident."

"Things aren't always what they seem." Before Cage could expand further, he was taken away by the jail guard. By sheer force of will, he stopped the guard after the third step. "I need to finish up with my lawyer!"

"You got five seconds," the guard said. "We'll pretend not to listen."

"You got to prove yourself to me. You've got to get me out of here so I can tell you what's really going down."

The guard then yanked him away, and this time Cage didn't resist.

· · ·

As I walked outside, Axtell Pile sprinted out of the small jail facility that was attached to the courthouse. He wore a t-shirt for either a heavy metal band or a first-person shooter game called Full Metal Racket.

Initially I made eye contact with the red-eyed dragon on his shirt, but soon turned my attention to his equally red eyes.

"Meet me at the lab," he said. "I've got something to give to you so you can give it to AJ Cage."

I was unsure. "I don't know if I can talk to you, without your lawyer present."

"I'm not going to talk to you, just go to the lab. I'm in TA 99 and I've got Cage's thimble there. TA 99, that's Technical Area 99. They'll tell you how to find me, but you got to show your ID."

He was picked up by someone in a black van. I got in my Focus, and drove across a narrow suspension bridge that spanned a steep canyon. The misty canyon might as well be a moat that separated the gigantic lab complex from the rest of the world. I was crossing into another land, another dimension of sight and sound, a Federal twilight zone and I worried about radioactive monsters coming up from the depths.

The mist lifted once I arrived on the other side of the bridge. I found myself on another mesa rising above the gorge. LANL might be in New Mexico, but it was not *of* New Mexico.

There was still time to turn around before I got to the gate. I was worried because a co-defendant whom I knew was represented by counsel wanted to give me some information without informing said counsel. There would be a record of me going through that gate, and I was a little unsure about the ethics of this. Could someone represented by counsel give me information about the co-defendant?

But then again, didn't Kirlian have an obligation to disclose information to me as co-counsel if he had it?

I was confused. I was no rocket scientist and could barely understand the New Mexico Revised Statutes. I didn't even understand relativity or why "e" could possibly equal mc squared. Ultimately, I didn't go through the gate. My meager brain could only concentrate on one thing: Cage said his last lawyer was murdered and Kirlian had said it was an accident. One of them was lying.

8. Albuquerque Turkey

Before I headed home, I stopped at the *descanso* on the highway near Pojoaque. I pulled off by the break in the shoulder. After exiting the vehicle, I googled the name of the late Kent Dorfman, the last attorney for Albert Jackson Cage. Despite what Cage had alleged, per the local Los Alamos paper's website, Dorfman had died in a simple, single car accident at this very spot while trying to avoid a motorcycle.

Simple accident? Perhaps not.

As I stared off the cliff and into the red valley below, I played accident reconstructionist. The ski patroller who mugged me drove off on a motorcycle. Could that cyclist be connected to Dorfman's death? Dorfman presumably had a thimble. Did the motorcyclist steal that one too?

I recalled the Monkey Elbow technique—the defense to an attack from the side, a punch to the shoulder. I had no way of knowing whether the motorcyclist had tried to run the vehicle off the road, or if the cyclist had pulled alongside the car and then aimed a gun, forcing Dorfman to swerve off the road, across the shoulder and over the cliff. Dorfman had not defended himself.

I eased the Focus back onto the highway. This road had so many twists and turns that someone could drive off the road trying to avoid a collision. I passed a motorcycle or two heading down, but the drivers ignored me.

Despite some tourist traffic in Santa Fe, I finally arrived in Albuquerque around two in the afternoon. Speaking of accidents, I had some near misses while reviewing texts from Luna along the way. This afternoon, Luna was in the hospital room with Marley. Unfortunately, Marley had a little episode with his oxygen tube, but was now stable. After missing lunch, she wanted me to bring her food from Subway. She mentioned the Albuquerque Turkey sandwich.

I didn't have time to return to the office, so I drove directly to the Subway near the hospital. In line at Subway, I froze. What kind of dressing did she like? It was weird, but I had done a high-profile arraignment and stood eye to eye with an accused criminal, yet ordering a six-inch sandwich at Subway was the most stressful part of my day.

Did I have I limited storage capacity in my brain even without generic Benadryl? Even though I had memorized all twenty-three exceptions to the hearsay rules, I inevitably forgot where I parked.

Albuquerque Turkey sounded appropriate for me today: turkey with green chile. Luna wanted onions, no pickles, zucchini and no green peppers, right?

After a few failed attempts at direction, I just told the server to put in whatever she thought my wife would like. I didn't order a sandwich for myself. I must have lost my appetite up in Los Alamos.

A few minutes later, I arrived at the gigantic UNM Hospital on Lomas Boulevard, brown bag in hand. After its recent renovation, UNM Hospital was incredibly modern. In fact, the hospital looked more like a nuclear weapons lab than LANL did.

The Muzak featured an orchestra trying to get through "She loves you," with violins trying to do the "yeah, yeah, yeah" part.

Did she love me? Yeah, yeah, yeah?

Inside Marley's hospital room, Luna had turned the cramped single suite into a corporate law office. Luna Law indeed. She had stacks of law books scattered around the room on topics that ranged from corporations to securities law. She also had medical textbooks and computer print-outs from hospitals all over the world. Luna even had a primer on how to speak Hindi. With all the information she had amassed, Luna could probably assist the Indian doctors in surgery, if necessary.

She held Marley's hand, but kept glancing at her phone for the good word from Bangalore, or wherever the hospital was. Our son was connected to a machine that indicated with each beep that he was still alive. He raised his chin when he saw me, and made a feeble karate chop, as if to say I love you. I chopped back in the air—I love you back.

"How is he?" I asked, handing her the bag.

"He's going to be fine. Well, as fine as he can be. We should be getting notice any day about *the* surgery."

Not just surgery, *the* transplant surgery. This operation would give me my son back.

"Are you still sure about going all the way to India?"

"Yes. You know Dr. Gandi was Susie Song's doctor when she was here at UNM, and that he started his own hospital in India focusing on promising experimental treatments. Susie can walk again, so if anyone can perform a miracle, it's Dr. Gandi and his team of medical experts."

It was hard to argue with a miracle cure. Gandi was an American-trained doctor who had a personal connection to a family member, albeit a distant one, and that took away some of my reasonable doubts about this Indian excursion. Luna saw Dr. Gandi as Marley's only hope.

"And he will work with us on whatever the insurance won't cover?" I asked.

"Yes. There's no other way, Dan. Marley's on too many waitlists at American hospitals and the treatment protocols are not as good. You want your son to live, don't you?"

"Of course, I do. I just hate waiting." I knew a little bit about waitlists from my college and law school applications. I admired Luna for taking initiative. Saving Marley was indeed a full-time job. I gave her a kiss, then sat by the bedside and held Marley's other hand. It was very cold.

"We're going to save you, Marley," I said. "I promise. We'll do whatever it takes."

He didn't respond, didn't even move his eyes in my direction. He tired so easily. Did a two-year-old understand about life and death? As I watched, he fell asleep, his eyes moving under his eyelids. What did he dream of? How I wished his body could just start functioning normally.

Luna put her hand on my shoulder. "Whatever it takes."

I nodded. We had a quiet moment. God, I loved my family. I would be the Luna Lawyer, and the Marley Lawyer.

Luna got up from the bed, walked to a table and unwrapped her sandwich. When she bit into it, she immediately spit it out. It was as if I had just told her that I wanted Marley to die. "You know I'm allergic to onions!"

"I'm sorry. I'm sorry. I'm sorry."

"Why can't you just be better?"

This was a recurring theme between Luna and me. I always wondered when she asked me to be better, if she was asking me to become someone else.

"I'm trying to help my son live while planning a hostile takeover of a billion-dollar corporation. You're handling traffic tickets for their truck driver and can't remember about the onions. It shouldn't be that hard. Get your head in the game!"

"What else do you need?"

She gave me a long list via text, even though she was right in front of me. There were several errands that I needed to handle before the end of the day. Most important was to transfer money from my personal account to our joint account. After a computer hacking of my account a few years ago, I did such transfers in person with the tellers.

First, I went down the six lanes of Lomas Boulevard to the bank downtown, to check my balance and transfer the money. This bank was in a nice three-story, gray building. It was also in the same building as the Albuquerque office of the New Mexico Attorney General, which was on the third floor.

Yes, I could do a lot of banking online in this modern world, but I still liked human tellers with nice smiles. I especially liked Josephina (pronounced like Jose), who was hearing impaired. She had a discrete ear piece under her curly hair, but always stared intently at me to read lips.

"I can only transfer five-hundred dollars from your personal account."

"Fine," I said. "Could you also check my trust account?"

Josephina frowned when she pulled up the screen. "There's a hold on your account."

"A hold?"

She looked at me. "Could you speak slowly and distinctly?"

"There is a hold?"

"Yes. It should be available in seven business days."

"Do I have any other funds?"

"You have some money in savings. One thousand, two hundred."

I transferred a thousand bucks from my savings account to Luna's account. Luna was always overdrawn, but that was something I knew in advance that I was signing up for.

Next, I had to pick up prescriptions for Luna. I drove up

Lomas Boulevard and took a left on Medical Arts Drive to a place the locals called Pill Hill. I hadn't known that medicine could be artistic, but this complex resembled the Ranchos church up in Taos. Georgia O'Keeffe could have picked up her arthritis medication here in this adobe complex.

Nurse Song, Jen Song's mother and Denise's grandmother, was a nurse-practitioner who now owned one section of the complex. She was a small Asian woman in pink scrubs, and she gave me five small bottles for Luna's medications. I didn't recognize the new ones—some seemed to be for pain and others might be psych meds. Luna's doctor was a woman named Mary Ann Romero, who was practically a member of the family after all these years.

"Tell Luna to call me about the new prescriptions," Nurse Song said. "I actually need you to leave a fingerprint for the Crotaladone. That's the new heavy duty pain pill."

I had never heard of Crotaladone. Nurse Song explained that it came from rattlesnake venom, and was the next Oxycontin. She said that as if it was a good thing. "But be careful, if you don't have the right genetics it has nasty side effects."

I didn't ask about genetics, just gave my fingerprint and signed for the bottle, feeling like I was a defendant. I also reluctantly bought another bottle of generic Benadryl for my insomnia. If the choice was sleep or stupidity, I went with sleep.

After Pill Hill, I had to pick up dry-cleaning from the Hollywood Cleaners, which was just down Central Avenue from Greystoke. The cleaners catered to the film productions that came through Albuquerque, and I always enjoyed seeing the many autographed photos of celebrities on the wall. The man working there, "Hollywood Joe," often talked about leaving dry-cleaning for directing action thrillers.

"I've started a new script," he said, handing me a massive pile of men's and women's suits. "It's called *Heavy Starch*."

"What's it about?" I asked, despite myself.

"It's one of those heist films—like *Fast & the Furious* or *Mission Impossible*. Lots of disguises, double crosses and plot twists—all set at the dry cleaner for the CIA. Do you want to hear the quick pitch?"

I didn't have the time or patience for the quick pitch for *Heavy Starch*. I politely stepped away, but he kept talking about the act one inciting incident as I closed the door. It was now six o'clock, and time for my only pleasure of the night—martial arts. I often joked and called it *marital* arts, but no one else thought that was funny.

I had originally intended to go to the program at Downtown Sports and Wellness, which had a reputation for excellence and a caring attitude. The instructor at downtown was a grand-master. I didn't go with that one however. Instead, a jail guard at the Metropolitan Detention Center, a beefy African American man with the unlikely last name of Spartan, told me that I needed to go hardcore if I truly wanted to protect my family with my bare hands. "*Culebrai Kai*, there is no try."

After the shooting incident with Mia, I wanted to try something, anything, so I signed up for the Culebra Kai Senior Class. The class ran every night in a big complex off Martin Luther King Boulevard near the university. In this case, the brutalist architecture of concrete blocks with a black roof was totally appropriate. Like the Los Alamos labs, they dealt with deadly weapons here.

At fifty, I was in the middle of the age range for the senior class, but I certainly was on the lower level of ability.

The class was half black belts, and half "belts of color," as our sensei didn't like using the term "colored belts" for the lower levels of yellow, orange, purple, blue and brown. Some of the black belts were in their sixties, but could still do the crane stance, balancing on one leg—a basic move for any karate kid. With only an orange belt, my crane leaned to the left before it toppled over after twenty seconds.

Tonight, as I entered the building I saw the mural of various mixed martial arts champions that had trained at Culebra Kai. Maybe I could retain some paying clients here as well; fighters tended to require legal assistance. The late Heidi Hawk, the famed Native American Mixed Martial Arts fighter was featured prominently, her body in a fighting stance. In the mural, she had a tattoo of the sacred Navajo rock formation, Window Rock, tattooed on her abs, with the "window" surrounding her pierced belly button.

I had represented Heidi in a few matters, and she was the hardest core Rez girl of them all. Culebra Kai there is no try, indeed. When I saw her in the mural on the wall, I realized that I wanted to make her proud.

I changed into a white "ki" with an orange belt, and remembered to go to the bathroom before putting on my athletic cup under my black polyester training pants. Out in the main training room of the facility, I warmed up and practiced my katas with the other members of the senior class. A *kata* was a series of moves that was more like a dance, if you were blocking kicks and punches from the other dancers. I nearly hit one of the other senior members and he shot me a dirty look. I moved to a corner so I wouldn't come close to hitting anyone else.

Moments later, Spartan came into the gym wearing a crisp white ki that had a faded blood stain on the left shoulder. The crowd immediately bowed to him as if he was the ancient grandmaster from China's famed Shaolin temple. That was same temple that was featured in all those imported martial arts films. Before retiring and becoming a jail guard, Spartan had a successful martial arts career. He had received his nickname from playing football at Michigan State and growing up without luxury in Detroit. He liked the moniker so much that somewhere along the line he had legally changed his name.

I was so intimidated by his august presence that during the first class, I called him "your honor," by force of habit. It could have been worse. For some reason this African American jail guard reminded me of my father back when I was six, when my father yelled at me for not being able to tie my shoes. At least I had never called Spartan "Dad."

There were ten people in the senior class, a class that I called the Dojo of Dementia. The class had a few lawyers and doctors, and one attractive woman, Martiska. She was very short, but had the flexibility and strength of an Olympic gymnast.

After fifteen minutes of push-ups and stretching, we started a technique line and went through every technique in the black binder. I called the binder the "Hong Kong Book of Kung Fu," after a mythical book in *Hong Kong Phooey*, a cartoon of my youth. In a technique line, each person in line attacks the person in front of them and the defender demonstrates the technique. The defender then attacks the person next in line. The rule was "hit as hard as you want to get hit." I did not hit very hard.

The first technique in the Hong Kong Book of Kung Fu was of course the Kimono Grab, even though we wore the white kis instead of kimonos.

Martiska did a grab to my ki and I froze, forgetting which leg to move back. She kept pushing and I lost my balance. The whole class laughed.

"Get out of your head!" they kept saying when I ran through the orange techniques and onto the purple belt chart.

"Go slower!" "Pay attention to your body!" And then there was my favorite about my posture: "fornicate the air." I was supposed to have my pelvis thrust forward as opposed to keeping it back when I punched. Or was that when I kicked? Posture was not one of my strong points, then again, neither was fornicating.

Many of the martial arts techniques involved numbers on a clock—a punch to twelve or a rear kick to six. I envisioned a Mickey Mouse watch, and I was Mickey with the seven dwarves and five of their friends surrounding me.

I also continually confused Whirling Mantis, which is two outward blocks, with Circle of Glass, which is an outward block followed by an inward block. One was a defense to a left/right combo, the other a defense to a right/left combo. I always forgot which was which.

The last technique of the night was Crash of the Eagles, set two final option. This attack was a choke from six o'clock, (directly behind) and the technique was supposed to involve elbows and moving to two o'clock and then a half-fist to the opponent's throat. I wasn't sure how this involved either crashing or eagles, but I did get the idea of the meaning of "final" in "final option." Done too hard, a half-fist to the throat could be fatal.

Martiska performed Crash of the Eagles, set two, final option on me first. As the attacker, I was supposed to choke her, but I felt uncomfortable making the slightest contact with her thin ballerina neck.

"Choke harder," she said. "The technique only works if the attack is real."

As she took down my weak chokehold with her elbow and stepped to two o'clock so the half-fist came toward me, I ducked. The entire class laughed.

"Just think what would have happened if I'd made contact," Martiska said with a smirk.

The others went off to learn some cool techniques that involved levitation or walking through walls. I had never heard of them. Instead, Spartan made me perform a kata called Coordination Set off in a corner by myself. Coordination Set was a series of kicks and blocks in each direction, while turning counter-clockwise. As I was neither coordinated nor set; kicking and punching the air was not a fun way to spend the last fifteen minutes of class.

With each kick, punch, and turn, I prayed this skill set would transfer into the courtroom. I visualized myself as the Bruce Lee of law, or perhaps the Jackie Chan of jurisprudence. By the tenth set of coordination, I got into a groove. The kata might as well be Tai Chi, as I would often do a kick to one side and then a kick to the opposite one. I felt the *chi*, the life force, flow through my limbs.

At eight, class over, I took a quick shower. Being uncoordinated made me sweat more than usual. When I left the locker room, limping, I had to do a walk of shame past Spartan—right under the angry eyes of Heidi Hawk. I always worried that Spartan would tell me that I was too old, too uncoordinated, too clumsy, too whatever, and that perhaps I would be happier at another dojo.

Luckily, Spartan ignored me today. When I walked past, he was talking with Martiska about her black belt test. She had started at the same time as I had and was already testing for black. That made me feel even worse.

Just as I was ready to come home after this day from hell, I received one more text from Luna. STILL AT HOSPITAL. PICK UP GIRLS FROM MOCK TRIAL PRACTICE. I groaned inwardly at having to drive the girls. How could Dew have a perfect SAT score, and fail the New Mexico driving test three times?

But, I drove to Albuquerque Academy, a fifteen-minute drive to the far northeast heights, the more suburban part of town. When I arrived at the lush campus, Dew and Denise were waiting in front, like pink haired twins. Dew was talking, and Denise was listening—as usual.

"How did practice go?" I asked as they got in the car.

Dew was hyperventilating with excitement. "Okay. But there's big, big news. After we go to state, the internationals are going to be here in Albuquerque for reals."

"Internationals?"

"It's on June twenty-ninth. It's like an invitational for the best of the best in the whole world. They're sponsored by that big corporation, Dragon Moon, who I guess is having their big meeting here. Their new president or whatever is going to hand out the trophy. Even better . . . they're going to give free scholarships to the winning team. Like the team who wins gets their college *and* law school paid for, for reals."

Talk about a perfect PR move. I could just envision the ad campaign. The new Dragon Moon CEO comes down from above to give the free scholarships—probably worth millions of dollars altogether—on live TV to Dew. Perhaps Dragon Moon wasn't so evil after all.

"What's a free ride to Stanford college and law school worth?" she asked.

"Hundreds of thousands, maybe millions after inflation kicks in. I hope you guys win. How many teams?"

"It's all-stars. They pick the best four from the state—two kids will be lawyers and two kids will be witnesses, so Denise can be on the team too. We'll be going against teams from Russia and China."

I was about to tell her that it would be tough for both to be in the top four in the great state of New Mexico, but then again, Dew could achieve greatness if she put her mind to it. She was already a gifted advocate with her mother when it came to avoiding cleaning her room.

"We have to get through state first, though." Dew frowned for a moment. "And I have to stay academically eligible."

"You're still on academic probation?"

"More like parole, or what was it called in that film? Double secret probation? I'm on zero tolerance. Even a C minus will get me kicked off. But that's cool. My dad failed high school physics five times and he was like the best lawyer ever."

I never knew what to tell Dew about her dad, Sam Marlow. Luna and I had named Marley after him. He was a great lawyer and my third cousin, which made Dew my third cousin once removed, so we were technically blood. As the Rattlesnake Lawyer, my greatest case was when I had represented Marlow when he was charged with kidnapping Mia, who eventually killed him on our wedding day. Someone else had stolen the idea of a rattlesnake wedding and turned it into a book. I didn't get a dime.

"Your dad really was a great lawyer. I have a feeling he's arguing cases up in the great courtroom in the sky."

"I highly doubt that, but I do hope I see him again."

"Maybe someday you will. Who knows? He was cryogenically frozen, right? Maybe they can wake him up in a hundred years."

"I hope I'm still alive in a hundred years. I might not survive summer school."

I hoped that these two girls won the competition, not for the scholarship, but for themselves. They needed a boost like that to reach their potential. Hell, we all needed to reach our potential.

I swerved suddenly on Academy Boulevard and nearly cut off a massive Ford F-150 pickup. The driver honked angrily.

"Sorry," I muttered.

"Are you all right, Dan?" Dew asked. "I failed my driver's test and I'm a better driver than you."

"Just tired."

Denise said nothing, she had a tear in her eye.

"What's wrong?" I asked.

She didn't reply. For one second, I felt that pinging in my head again. Then nothing.

Denise wiped away her tear and shook her head.

• • •

We finally arrived home around nine PM to find that Luna had prepared a delicious green chile pasta dish. The dish smelled so good that the girls decided to join us even though they'd had pizza at their practice.

Luna was still in lawyer attire—her usual black and turquoise ensemble and looked absolutely fabulous for a woman of a certain age. After dinner, she got her computer running and looked up various SEC regulations. I knew that Luna would always be smarter than I was. Despite that, and despite all my bitching and moaning, I did love her so very much.

Right before I went to sleep, Luna jumped up, waking me.

"What's the matter?" I asked. "Is it Marley?"

"No, it's Mia."

"Your sister?"

"*Half*-sister. Selena just texted me that Mia is back in New Mexico. Police are investigating her for stealing a motorcycle in Santa Fe. They found a bloodstain on the ground near there and the DNA sample matched her records."

"Do they know where she is?"

"She could be anywhere."

I didn't sleep that night. The person who stole my thimble drove away on a motorcycle. Dorfman, the lawyer, was killed in an auto accident when he swerved to avoid a motorcycle, and presumably his thimble was stolen as well. Mia had stolen a motorcycle and had a billion-dollar motive to mess with anyone connected to Dragon Moon including Luna and myself.

I was no Los Alamos scientist, or even a Los Alamos lawyer, but even I could figure this one out. Forget rattlesnakes, I would have to be the Luna Lawyer for real.

PART III
CIRCLES OF GLASS

9. Clovis, Baby, Clovis

The rest of the week went slowly. In the elevator, my neighbor the Facebook intern told me that his interview with Google went well, but he would also meet with Apple next week, just to be sure. He had kept his Google visitor's pass lanyard to impress his friends back at Facebook. I could barely google my own name, much less master the iPhone. I couldn't imagine interviewing with those companies for full-time jobs with stock options.

That afternoon, I went to the bank and talked with Josephina, the hearing-impaired teller. The check, she informed me, hadn't cleared yet. "It's just such a large amount and it's come from an international account. It's bank protocol."

"Is it from a Swiss bank?"

"The money transfer was drawn from an entity called the First Swiss Bank of Lagos, in Nigeria."

Lagos was not Davos. The First Swiss Bank of Lagos sounded like the most crooked bank in the world. I had fallen for the oldest scam in the book, the fake money transfer from Nigeria. Now that I had entered my appearance in all of Cage's cases, I could not withdraw.

"Is there anything else I can help you with?" Josephina asked.

"My life," I said.

• • •

When I picked up the dry cleaning from Hollywood Joe, I asked, "How's your script for *More Starch Please* coming along?"

"It's *Heavy Starch*. Trying to make the female lead more sympathetic. It's hard."

"Tell me about it."

After handing me my suits, he handed me some of Luna's business suits. "Is your wife working again? She's a sharp dresser. I love her black power suits and turquoise tops combo."

"I'll tell her you said that."

"I'm trying to write a part for a lawyer who gets the gang out of trouble when the heist goes bad."

"I didn't know there were lawyers for big time heists. It would be great if Tom Cruise kept me on retainer for the next *Mission Impossible*."

"I was hoping to ask your wife for a 'friend read.'"

"She's really busy with Luna Law right now."

"Is that a script?"

"It could be."

After nearly dropping the suits in a puddle and then lugging them up the stairs, I needed to release some aggression, so I hit Culebra Kai again. Was it my imagination or had Heidi smiled at me when I came in?

Unlike Heidi, Spartan was not glad to see me tonight. During class I still had problems getting my knees bent low enough into the twisted stance without leaning over too far. My body didn't twist very well, and I couldn't kick with my left leg.

After I confused the Circle of Glass defense with the Whirling Mantis defense, Spartan made me go into the corner to keep practicing the Coordination Set kata so I could work on simultaneous kicks and punches. I worried that if I had to kick, punch, and chew gum at the same time, my head would explode.

As I repeated the kick-punch-turn pattern for the tenth time, I saw Spartan talking with the black belts.

"He's just not getting it, is he?" I heard Spartan say to

Martiska.

Maybe I would be better off if I couldn't hear what I didn't want to her like the bank teller.

• • •

Every day during the next three days, Cage called me at my office precisely at four in the afternoon. That's when the Los Alamos inmates were let out of their cells after the afternoon lockdown count. On Wednesday, we somehow ended up talking about *Star Wars,* and I found that Albert Jackson Cage considered himself the real life equivalent of Lando Calrisian—or at least the reincarnation of Billy Dee Williams, the actor who played Han Solo's rapscallion friend.

When we talked on Thursday, Cage told me about a fight between the mechanical engineers and the astrophysicists in the Segregation Pod at the Los Alamos County Jail. "When I first heard I was going to Segregation, I thought it was a racial thing, but in Los Alamos, it's just 'cause I work for Dragon Moon, I'm some kind of security risk. They're worried I might lure away one of the LANL employees into private industry. Being in Seg sucks."

"Well, AJ, I'll get you out as soon as possible and get you back on the road again."

"Man, I live for the open road. Being locked up in a cell is bad for my health," he said. He started a fair imitation of Willie Nelson singing "On the Road Again."

"Did you like driving in a war zone?"

"You know what they say about driving: long hours of boredom and a few exciting moments of terror."

"I thought they said that about flying."

"Driving is flying, just lower to the ground. You got to get me out of here. Isn't there a motion you can file?"

After hanging up, I checked my computer's data base and found a boilerplate conditions of release motion. I immediately filed a Motion to Reconsider his Conditions of Release for the Clovis and Portales cases, and asked for a setting as soon as possible.

Moments later, I received a response from the Ninth Judicial District Court, as both cases were in different counties, but within the same judicial district. The first conditions of release hearing was set for Monday morning, April 9, in Clovis, and the second later that afternoon a short drive away down in Portales.

Friday, when I told Cage about the motion hearing for Monday, he kept insisting that I meet with Pile to get his lost thimble to find out "what's really going down." I still didn't know if I could ask Pile directly, or if I had to subpoena the thimble through the court.

On Saturday, I finally could visit Marley at the hospital and give Luna a brief respite. I practiced my entire eleven-minute martial arts repertoire in front of him, from Kimono Grab through Whirling Mantis to Crash of the Eagles. I was a little disappointed that I only had eleven minutes of material, and that was counting all my katas, including blocking sets one, two and three.

Marley gave me two karate chops in response—one with each hand. I then started going through the katas, but nearly kicked over his IV with my Coordination Set.

Sunday night Luna stayed with Marleyl. "Remember, he's depending on you," she said over the phone. "You have to man up and do whatever it takes. Hopefully once he has this surgery, everything will change."

"Whatever it takes," I said. "Culebra Kai, there is no try."

"What does that even mean?"

"I'm not sure."

. . .

Monday morning, April 9, 2018, I woke up well before dawn and started the Focus on the drive to Clovis, 219 miles east from Albuquerque. I kept my eye out for Mia on a motorcycle, but I had more to worry about from the speeding trucks and commuters on the first stretch of I-40 through Albuquerque.

The next part of Interstate 40, through steep Tijeras Canyon, was where Albuquerque ended and the wilderness began. I had driven this way in my last lifetime when I began my public defender career.

Near Moriarty, New Mexico I crossed the county line for Torrance County, which I called *Jack* Torrance County, after Nicholson's character in *The Shining*. I heard voices when I passed by the spooky abandoned buildings on the barren plains that lined this part of New Mexico. There was a lot more than just Indian burial grounds out here, a few cowboy corpses littered this neck of the plains.

Eastward ho! Within a few miles, I had to go to the bathroom, but the next rest stop was closed. I passed Exit 203 which boasted a topless truck stop in the heart of Jack Torrance County. I thought of the film *From Dusk till Dawn* and its vampire strippers preying on truckers, but I doubted I'd find Salma Hayek dancing with a snake out here re-creating her famous scene from the film. I sure didn't want to use the facilities there.

Luckily, I saw the exit for San Ignacio, New Mexico, exit 263, just as the sun was rising. I put on my sunglasses.

At the bottom of the exit, there was a shallow pond, probably the size of a baseball infield but only a few inches deep. Cattle stared at me from the other side of a wire fence, but there were no other signs of life, especially not at dawn. I hid behind an empty dumpster near the fence, the only sign of civilization, and did my business.

When I emerged, the spot was perfectly aligned to the rays of the rising sun, and the light shimmered across the perfectly still water. I was in the high desert, yet felt like a sailor greeting the sunrise over the Pacific. Was it red sky at morning, sailor take warning? The sky was blood red this early in the day.

My glutes were a little tight from driving, so I performed some of my martial arts katas as the sun rose over the tiny lake. For some reason, alone with a sunrise over a pond, my martial did feel artistic. Each kick, each punch, was aimed at some ancient warrior from a forgotten Chinese period film.

"Your *wu shu* kung fu is no match for my rattlesnake law," I said out loud, paraphrasing a line from an old martial arts film, as if overdubbing the hero's response to the villain's challenge.

When I returned to the interstate it was only a few more miles until the turn off to the small town of Santa Rosa. With its rolling, spotted Dalmatian hills, and townsfolk with lilting Spanish accents, Santa Rosa reminded me of Taos.

During the next thirty-eight-mile stretch, I left the hills of northern New Mexico behind and then entered the plains when I hit the small town of Fort Sumner. Fort Sumner boasted of the "real grave" of Billy the Kid, the famous outlaw gunslinger. A cop car was parked on the far side of the street, and the officer pointed something at me. I couldn't tell if it was a radar detector or a six-gun.

As I drove thirty-four miles an hour down Main Street, I saw constant pictures of young Billy in that classic pose where he looked more like a stoned teenager than the fastest gun in the west. Billy the Kid was lucky he died young. There would have been no famous gravesite of Billy had he lived and become Billy the Middle-Aged Man.

On the other side of Fort Sumner, I passed a body of mud called Red Lake, which was neither red, nor a lake, just a mile-long patch of mud. Today the mud glistened with a few recent drops of rain. Behind, on a ridge, gigantic wind turbines slowly spun their three-pronged propellers.

On the other side of Red Lake, I thought I entered "Taliban," but upon closer inspection the sign indicated I was in Taiban, without the "l." Taiban felt like hostile territory that had been recaptured for the moment. War is "l." Many of the buildings were hollowed out, and graffiti on one building reminded me to STAY HAPPY! I looked around this deserted outpost as I sped past and wondered how anyone could be happy here.

The next stretch of Route 60 East was like a bad zombie movie. It wasn't quite plains, not quite desert, just open space and abandoned buildings. There was even more shine to these buildings in this part of the plains than in "Jack" Torrance County. Twenty miles later, I entered the village limits of Melrose, New Mexico which was the polar opposite of the youthful fantasy soap opera, *Melrose Place*, a television show set in glitzy Southern California. In this Melrose, there was an off-white grain elevator, no swimming pool in sight, and no one at the only gas station in town even remotely resembled the blond actress Heather Locklear.

On the other side of Melrose, the land's transformation became complete. I might legally be in the land of enchantment, but I passed grassy plains instead of desert, farms instead of ranches. It was also one notch more humid and I could taste the wetness in the back of my throat. Route 60 finally became four lanes as I approached Cannon Air Force Base. The base's airplane hangars were on my left, and suburban housing flanked my right.

Cannon was famous for something called "skunk works." Per Google, skunk work or works was a World War II term that now consisted of heavy duty military intelligence work, often with drones. Occasionally, mysterious air craft flew overhead here. Perhaps flying saucers lurked in those gigantic hangars. After all, Roswell was only a hop, skip, and jump away.

Moments later, I crossed under the interchange with the turn off for the base. A few hundred yards later I saw a billboard sponsored by a local church that listed the Ten Commandments.

I pulled off the road and changed my clothes near the Ten Commandments signs. I hoped there was no biblical injunction against pulling my pants off in public, even if I was in my car. Tucking in my shirt was always difficult on the side of the road, and I had to open the car door to put my shoes on.

After tying my purple tie in the rearview mirror, I was finally ready for court. Remembering how I had screwed up last time, I used my phone to double check the Ninth Judicial District Court website. Glad I checked. Court had been delayed by an hour.

Just then my phone buzzed. It was a message from Kirlian. COURT DELAYED UNTIL TEN. MEET US AT THE HOLIDAY INN.

on my way, I messaged back. we need to talk about the first swiss bank of Lagos.

He did not reply. I drove into town and a sign under an

old fighter jet read CLOVIS, A COMMUNITY FOR FAMILY. The jet looked as if it would take off at any minute, if anyone came between this community and its family.

Down Seventh Street, the next sign described Clovis High School's various state championships. The sign proclaimed that Clovis High was THE BEAST FROM THE EAST. The beast must eat a lot of grain, because there was a gigantic grain elevator in the heart of downtown. It was just a few blocks from the eight-story Hotel Clovis, which must have been a very grand hotel back in the thirties.

Clovis felt more like Kansas, certainly not like New Mexico. I turned left onto Prince Street, the main drag, and then drove a few miles until I came to a Holiday Inn on the far northern edge of town.

Another tall grain elevator guarded the north side. How much grain could there be in this little county? As I got out of my car, I spotted storm clouds off in the distance over the flat plains. No, I wasn't in my New Mexico anymore.

It was only nine in the morning, but several wait staff were picking up the scraps from the breakfast bar. I could smell the skunk works as military men and contractors did deals. Some wore air force camouflage uniforms. Other young men looked like computer hackers who hadn't slept in years. They drank their coffee black, like their turtlenecks, and went with donuts as opposed to fruit.

In one corner, there were a few families who obviously were on the great American road trip. One family looked exactly like a young Chevy Chase and the gang in one of the Vacation movies. They were nervous about all the skunk-workers that surrounded them.

Kirlian sat with Pile at a far table, next to the automated pancake maker machine. I had thought Kirlian was thin, but

Pile was practically anorexic. A third person, a woman in an air force camo uniform, excused herself after shaking some hands. I heard the words skunk works. The woman was accompanied by two large air men who looked like they had just left the front. One looked at me as if he was trying to decide whether I was a potential target that needed to be eliminated.

"Thank you, Colonel Herring," Kirlian said.

Colonel Herring. The name sounded familiar. Selena had mentioned a colonel with that name being linked with Dragon Moon. The colonel, a tall woman in her late forties, sat with her group at another table. Two computer geeks went to her table and one showed her his computer screen, as if sharing some top-secret data. Another, a mercenary wearing a bulletproof vest, joined them. He looked like a tall Tom Cruise. What were they doing? Planning the next *Mission Impossible*?

I stopped looking at their table and sat down. Kirlian frowned. "Where's your thimble?"

"Still at home charging," I said. "Getting used to using it."

Kirlian frowned. "Please be honest."

"I lost it," I lied.

"It will take a few days, but we will get you another one and deduct it from your pay."

"How much are thimbles?"

"That's to be determined."

"Well, hopefully we can come to some kind of a resolution. The money from the First Swiss Bank of Lagos hasn't cleared yet."

"It will," he said.

"I hope so."

"We have court in Clovis and Portales today. Are you prepared this time?"

"I am," I said. "I won't let you down. I would be a lot more gung ho if I knew the First Swiss Bank of Lagos was a real bank."

He pointed his thimble at the table, and the thimble produced various documents and news clippings relating to the bank. "It's very real," he said. "We can send you money from another account if you prefer, although that might delay you receiving the money even further. It is not too late for us to find another attorney and give him or her the hundred-thousand-dollar retainer."

"I'll give it another week," I said.

"I don't know why you are so zealous about getting your client out. Trial is only in a few weeks."

"He tells me there is a lot he can help me with if he's on the outside."

Kirlian frowned. Suddenly Colonel Herring shouted in our direction. She had a thick Texas accent. "Mr. Kirlian, here's some of my old boys I want you to meet."

"If you'll excuse me," Kirlian said. He stood, and walked to the colonel's table, leaving me alone with Pile. Pile glanced around nervously, but Kirlian's back was turned to us as he greeted Colonel Herring.

"I can talk to you after my court in Portales today," I said to Pile.

"I can give you Cage's thimble," he replied.

Before Pile could say anything more, Kirlian called Pile over to the colonel's table. "You'd better get on to court," Kirlian called to me.

• • •

I drove south down Clovis's Prince Street. Many of the

street and business signs were purple, but in honor of the Clovis Wildcats purple football uniforms rather than Prince, the singer of "Purple Rain."

Stuck at a light on 21st Street, I googled Colonel Herring. She was high up at Cannon Air Force Base, but I couldn't check her military records online. I was a limited hacker at best, and didn't know how to access military websites. What was interesting about her was that her name was mentioned as a possible CEO for Dragon Moon. That made sense. To be a big time military contractor you needed big time military connections.

I arrived at the big, gray brick courthouse with time to spare. Clovis's Curry County District Courthouse was right in the middle of town, across from a big church. The Ten Commandments were posted on a stone tablet next to the courthouse, right next to a statue of a purple cow.

As I climbed up the steep staircase, I encountered three bailiffs in crisp blue uniforms. At first glance I thought they were cops. They took security seriously down here.

After I passed through an ancient metal detector on the second floor, the uniformed bailiff directed me to a small room to talk to my client and shut the door behind me. I wasn't sure whether it was locked or not.

Cage had gained weight eating the jail cooking in Los Alamos. His orange jump suit had another missing button, and his stomach was escaping through the gap.

"Did you get the thimble yet?" he asked.

"Not yet."

"Your life might depend on it."

I wasn't sure what he meant. Just then the bailiff returned and told us that the judge needed us.

Inside, the courtroom felt like it was right out of the

fifties courtroom drama. There were even black and white photographs of Matlock lookalikes on the wall that dated back to the early days of New Mexico statehood.

Judge Chairez would ultimately do the trial, but she wouldn't be here for a simple pre-trial hearing. Judge Fredrick Blaine was an African American man with a purple bow tie, and was already on the bench. He had been a local football hero who had married a Playboy model and brought her back home to this small town. Supposedly, the Playboy model was up for election as a magistrate judge in November. I loved small towns and football heroes.

Raphael was here for the attorney general's office, as the attorney general herself didn't need to be here for a short pre-trial hearing. He wore a black suit with a purple tie. I soon noticed that everyone in court was wearing the same shade of purple tie. This was the kind of town where everyone wore school colors on Clovis High game days, or like today, on the Monday after a Clovis victory. Purple Reign indeed.

I recognized Shaharazad, the court reporter from Los Alamos, who was sitting up front. The state was in the process of shifting from court "monitors" who merely recorded the proceedings, to court reporters who took down the proceedings word for word. Perhaps there was a shortage of reporters, and she had to travel from district to district.

Shaharazad wore dark blue, matching the look of the bailiffs. If she was trying to fit in, she was doing a good job of it. I felt a tinge of suspicion as I looked at her. With plastic surgery, could Mia have become Shaharazad? A court reporter sitting the courtroom would know everything about the case, both on and off the record. I only turned my gaze away from her when Shaharazad gave me a dirty look.

"Mr. Shepard, you may begin," the judge said. He pointed with his chin that I should go up to the podium. My client stood next to me. If this was being videotaped, it should be in black and white, like a mash up of *Perry Mason* and the *Twilight Zone*.

"Your honor," I said, "my client has no felony record. He grew up in Las Cruces, played football at NMSU, and then joined the air force where he served his country overseas. He has a commercial driver's license and this charge will affect his ability to continue as a professional driver."

Raphael smiled. "Your honor, we are not opposed to releasing him on his own recognizance. No bond would be required."

Released on his own recognizance? Excellent! Was this too good to be true?

The judge smiled. "I agree. The defendant will be released on his own recognizance in this matter."

There at the podium, I felt a sharp punch to my gut. Why had my client punched me? What was the defense to left punch to the gut? Don't let it happen, of course. No one saw the punch as it occurred below the sight lines. "Ask about the other cases," he whispered.

"What about his other matters, your honor?" I asked.

"Those will be decided by Judge Chairez. I'm not going to step on her toes."

We then argued about the pre-trial and trial settings. Upon Raphael's insistence, the trial would be set before the shareholders meeting. "We can provide Mr. Shepard with discovery today, and there would only be one witness who has already been interviewed by prior counsel."

One witness? And that witness has already been interviewed? This was almost too easy for one hundred thousand dollars.

"We will be ready, your honor."

"Then I'll put you on the trailing docket for a few weeks from now," the judge said.

I wasn't quite sure what a trailing docket meant out here. Sometimes a case could be on a trailing docket for all of eternity. This case was sounding better and better every day.

Once we signed a pre-trial order, court was in recess. I had driven 219 miles for a two-minute hearing.

I followed Cage and the bailiff on the way out.

"One down, a few more to go," I said, in front of a cramped prisoner-transport elevator. The bailiff frowned. "You can't follow us anymore," he said. He held the elevator door, but indicated that he couldn't hold it forever.

"Do I get out now?" Cage asked.

The bailiff laughed. "Don't you get it? You've got five cases holding you."

"Don't worry, AJ, I just have to get you out on the other cases," I said.

"But I still get credit on this case, right?" Cage asked. "So, if I get sentenced to ninety days, these seven days in jail count to the total, no?"

That's when the horrible realization hit. On this case, in the eyes of the records people in the Department of Corrections, he might as well be a free man sitting at the beach in Baja. If he had to wait another year to resolve this case, he would get absolutely no credit on his cases at all. With the trailing docket, if this case didn't go right away, he could be locked up for months until it was.

I remembered a case where a guy had been sentenced on a few fourth-degree felonies, and was sentenced consecutively with no pre-sentence confinement, and ended up doing eighteen years instead of eighteen months.

"You better get your shit together in Portales," he said as the door closed, "or I will fire your ass and go with the public defender."

I returned to the courtroom in time to see Kirlian and Pile go before Judge Blaine. Despite his technical prowess, Kirlian was no great trial lawyer, or even a particularly good motion hearing lawyer. Via his thimble, he had the information literally at his fingertips, but there wasn't a high-speed connection between his thimble and his brain. He mumbled a few vague talking points, but the judge corrected him each time.

Kirlian might be running a billion-dollar corporation, but he was a fifty-cent lawyer. Until the arraignment, he had probably never appeared in person a real courtroom. I couldn't be cocky, though. Pile got to walk away unaided, while my client was escorted to the podium by a burly deputy.

Pile smiled at me. "See you in Portales."

10. Enema You

I had an early lunch at Jalisco's, a Mexican restaurant across from the courthouse. This was Curry County, but I didn't know if there was any place to eat something with authentic curry. I didn't see any East Indian food here, but Mexican should be safe. This place seemed to be popular with the camouflaged folk from Cannon. Colonel Herring was there with her driver and half the 101st airborne, plowing through multiple bowls of chips and salsa.

I went with the Mexican buffet. The food was delicious, but it wasn't true New Mexican fare. It was Tex-Mex, but more Tex than Mex. They spelled chile with an "i" on the menu and certainly didn't have blue corn or green chile. In between bites, I checked the official state court website, nmcourts.com, on my phone. Thankfully, the hearing in Portales was still set at one o'clock sharp, and one meant one for an out-of-town lawyer like me. Over the last of the chips and salsa, I did some legal research the old fashion way—through old law books that I kept in my car.

I spilled chunky red salsa on one of the books and it seemed fortuitous, because the salsa landed on the index entry for double jeopardy. God was telling me something.

"Have you ever briefed double jeopardy?" I asked Luna when she finally picked up her phone. "I got a guy who picked up two charges in two different counties for the same stolen computer."

"Dan, I'm busy. Can't you do your own work?"

"I really need help right now."

She hung up. I worried that something had happened to Marley.

Despite her seeming hostility, within seconds Luna emailed me an old brief on a double jeopardy issue similar to this one: someone arrested in two different counties on the same incident. I felt relieved, almost like I had been fed the answers for Final Jeopardy. With some squinting, I could read the tiny image of the document on my phone. Luna was a far better lawyer than I would ever be. She once said she hated law, and yet she was so damn good at it. I didn't know if this document was adapted from an old brief, or something she whipped up just for me. In any event, it was right on point, and I scribbled the case law down on my notepad.

After cleaning the chunky red chipotle salsa off my tie and the books, I drove the nineteen short miles to Portales, down the four lanes of US 70.

• • •

As I entered the town, a sign welcomed me: portales, nm, home to 17,000 friendly people and a few old grouches.

While, the Clovis to Portales highway was a straight north-south shot, once the road hit downtown, it made a few sharp turns and suddenly headed diagonally southwest toward Roswell, ninety miles away. At least I thought it did, but then the road turned again, and again. The streets here were named by letters and numbers, but I couldn't remember which were north/south and which were east/west. Well, technically the numbered streets would be northeast/southwest and the lettered streets would be northwest/southeast. Or was it vice versa? A few blocks later I came to a gray concrete courthouse in the center of a square at the corner of A and First. I did a lap or two around the courthouse and parked in a small lot on the edge of the building.

If Clovis was stuck in the fifties, Portales was still fighting the Second World War. There were more flags per capita in Roosevelt County than anyplace I had ever been.

Patriotic signs and slogans hung on nearly every building.

I checked my watch as I hurried toward the courthouse door. Unfortunately, that door was locked, so I walked around the building to find an open door on the other side.

Inside, there was no metal detector. I just walked right into the cramped courtroom on the second floor. The judge was an elderly white man who was clearly one of the old grouches. I was surprised to see Shaharazad was, once again, the court reporter. Shaharazad had changed clothes, and was now in a charcoal outfit. This afternoon she looked like she was trying to blend in with her machinery. The New Mexico court system must be running out of warm bodies, if this one reporter had to be everywhere.

Then I wondered if it wasn't coincidence.

The old grouch called Pile's case first, and Kirlian and Pile went to the podium. The hostility between Pile and Kirlian seemed to increase every moment that the two were side-by-side. They kept jostling each other during the hearing, and barely made it through without coming to actual blows. Kirlian recited some words about being ready for trial and receiving discovery from opposing counsel. He sounded like he had memorized the phrases before court. The judge gave him his scheduling order. Court would be in a few weeks.

When the judge recessed the case, Kirlian walked toward the doorway and then smiled at me, a cocky smile. He hadn't realized that there was a double jeopardy issue. Pile walked to the defense table, to me, as if to see if the grass was greener with another attorney. A bailiff had to escort him back to the gallery.

Time for the Rattlesnake Lawyer to do some rattling, thanks to the Rattlesnake Wife.

Cage was brought in by two guards, who were even burlier than the guards from this morning. If Fat Albert had eaten during the lunch hour, he didn't show it. I heard his stomach growl. After a few preliminaries, I brought out my double jeopardy argument and read from Luna's brief, but added some rattlesnake charm.

"Your honor, you can't do extra time for the very same crime," I said.

The old grouch smiled. "I like it when lawyers actually do legal research. It's very old school. Mr. Raphael, your response?"

Raphael the renaissance man didn't have his little paralegal with him. He asked for time to brief the issue, but the judge denied it. The judge reviewed the file and ruled from the bench. Case dismissed!

Luna and I were an incredible team when we wanted to be. I felt like a real lawyer—until they started to drag Cage away. He still had way too many other cases holding him for him to get out just yet. I was in the process of gathering my things when I realized Cage was already out the door, and had to run to the elevator to go down with him and the deputy.

"Get my damn thimble," he demanded when we were scrunched together in the tiny elevator, "or I will bar bitch the shit out of you."

A bar bitch was a disciplinary complaint. While most bar bitches could be handled with a one-paragraph response letter, an ill-timed bar bitch could jack up an attorney's malpractice insurance premium.

After he exited the elevator, I tried to return to the courtroom to retrieve my briefcase. Had I gotten off on the wrong floor? I seemed to be back where I started. When the elevator stalled, I just took the stairs. Inside the courtroom, Kirlian had left, but Pile sat in the front row, trying to figure out what to do next. We were the only ones there—both the old grouch judge and Shaharazad must have gone into chambers.

"I'll meet you outside," Pile said. "Give me two minutes. It's in my car."

That would give me time to think. I hurried into the bathroom. I now had a minute and a half to decide about whether I could ethically take evidence from someone represented by another attorney. Time to reach out to my favorite lifeline, Luna.

one more question, I e-mailed. can someone represented by a lawyer give a piece of evidence to a co-defendant's lawyer?

I had a reply within seconds. yes, but only if they waive counsel and you disclose the evidence to all parties if used at trial. She even cited some case law. professional courtesy is usually that you tell, but recent case law says you don't have to.

It all made sense now. Pile was clearly waiving the right to counsel by communicating to me. Pile was giving me a personal item that supposedly belonged to *my* client. He could do that, as well. If I used it at trial, I would have to disclose it to all parties, but I would cross that bridge when I came to it.

So, while I morally felt a little queasy taking something from Pile, ethically I was cool. As for courtesy, I wasn't a Boy Scout, so I didn't have to be courteous or kind in all situations. Clearly, if I didn't get the thimble, Cage would file a disciplinary complaint against me.

Even though I'd had classes on it in law school, I still

wasn't sure about the difference between morals and ethics. Luna sent another email. DOES THAT HELP? LOVE YOU.

it does, I emailed back. love you too.

I blushed. Then I flushed.

• • •

I must have exited the wrong door of the courthouse, because I completely lost my sense of direction. All the one-story terra cotta buildings and their flags looked the same. There were no mountains for me to get a sense of direction, and the sun was even hidden behind the clouds.

Which way was north? Didn't the roads go on a diagonal? I had totally lost my bearings and couldn't remember if I had come into downtown on 1st street or Avenue A.

Then I saw Pile get into his gray car near a corner of the courthouse. He waived, then pointed toward a one-way street near a corner of the square, indicating that he wanted to meet a block away from the courthouse. That sounded simple.

But first, I had to find my car. I circled back, clockwise, around the entire courthouse. Where had I parked? Everyone seemed to own a Ford Focus or the Toyota or Chevrolet equivalent. I thought I saw my car and started to open the door, but then realized that someone had a car exactly like mine. The car started to beep with a loud, annoying burglar alarm. I did another lap around, counterclockwise this time, and finally found my car. I had a suspicion that it might have been moved as it seemed to face another direction. Or perhaps I had just remembered it wrong.

I still could not remember whether I had come in on a street or an avenue. My phone didn't have enough power to reach Mapquest or Google. Even worse, my car wouldn't start. I had flooded it by nearly pushing the pedal all the way to the pavement. Finally, on the third attempt, it started. I then followed in the direction I thought Pile had taken.

Unfortunately, I soon passed the campus for Eastern New Mexico University. Eastern New Mexico University had the unfortunate nickname of Enema You. There was construction by the campus and a large no U-turn sign that I didn't remember seeing when I came in.

The road soon became a four-lane highway and I passed a sign announcing Roswell as the next stop. I was heading in the wrong direction like a lost UFO. Finally, I found a place where I could turn around and headed toward a sign that pointed toward Clovis instead of Roswell. That was a good thing, right?

I encountered more construction, and detoured until I arrived at Enema You again.

After nearly fifteen minutes, and three more U-turns, I drove north and finally spotted the car Pile was driving. Unfortunately, at the same moment a nice sports car pulled up next to it and rolled down the window to reveal Kirlian. He gestured Pile to get back on the road, and Pile started his car and followed.

This road was a straight shot back toward Clovis, so they would know I was following them. I would have to give up on getting the thimble for now. Cage wouldn't bitch me for trying, could he?

Instead, I drove the back way on Route 467, which took me northwest through the high plains toward Melrose. I felt like a high plains drifter, just like Clint Eastwood. After a few more drifts, I passed another entrance to the southeast of Cannon Air Force Base.

An MP indicated that I should stop before I got to the

base entrance, then signaled me to move to the right side of the road. Once I was off the road, a long military convoy emerged. Colonel Herring was in the third vehicle, a jeep driven by a particularly large associate. Behind her, several military flatbed trucks followed, their payloads covered by large green tarps. They could be carrying refrigerators or neutron bombs.

After the last of the flatbed trucks were well off in the distance, the MP signaled me to proceed westward. It was dark when I finally turned north in Fort Sumner. Once I was deeper into the desert, a giant red mist emerged from the horizon to my right. Had there been an explosion at Cannon that had mutated some lizard? Or worse, had the skunk workers created a nuclear skunk?

Curious, I pulled over and watched this crimson monstrosity emerge from the bowels of the earth. After the red cloud rose for a few more minutes, it abruptly lost color. I sighed with relief. It was only the very full moon. As I drove, I came up with a scientific hypothesis. This full moon rising over the waters of Red Lake had somehow interacted with the red lights of the wind turbines to create this giant malevolent cloud.

This must be a real dragon moon, the inspiration for the company name. The Beast from the East indeed.

· · ·

I finally made it back to Albuquerque late in the evening. Thankfully, I took the right exit for Central Avenue and home.

Luna kissed me as I opened the door. She gave me a glass of champagne and we toasted. "To Marley!"

"What happened?"

"Great news!" she said, hugging me tight. "We will be

able to get the transplant operation in India in a few days. I closed the deal myself. I told them I'd give my own heart if I had to."

"You're amazing," I said, sipping the champagne.

"What did you do today?"

I had to think about it. "Not much."

11. Zozo the Clown

I was stuck in Albuquerque for the next few days. I thought of a Talking Heads lyric, from the song "This Must Be the Place." *Home, it's where I want to be, but I guess I'm already there.*

Recently, I felt even less at home when I was at home. Albuquerque felt too big, too crowded, and I kept thinking that the ten-thousand-foot granite overthrust of the Sandia Mountains was about to fall over and crush me. I grew restless when I couldn't drive more than a block without hitting a traffic light. My open road had closed.

The next morning, after another generic Benadryl hangover, I picked up some paperwork at the district courthouse in Albuquerque and no one recognized me. The guards made me show an ID to prove I was a lawyer, and then I had to show my driver's license photo up close to prove that the lawyer was me. Luna and I had been married here a few years back in this very courthouse, but that might as well have been a lifetime ago. I had become even more invisible, if that was possible.

• • •

Over the next few days I did errands in Albuquerque just to see familiar faces who could acknowledge my existence. At the bank, I tried to talk to Josephina about the funds, but she had to keep asking me to stop talking so fast. She was having trouble reading my lips. I had to remind myself that I was lucky. Mia's shooting a few years back had caused me no permanent damage.

I wanted to wear my cowboy boots. After a cursory inspection of them in my closet, I could see that they weren't ready for action. The scales were coming off and the heels weren't even. So, I dropped them with Hollywood Joe, who also specialized in shoe repair. He recognized me at least. "Maybe they should do a TV show called *Rattlesnake Lawyer*," he said.

"Another sleazy Albuquerque lawyer show? I'm afraid it's too much like *Better Call Saul*."

I saw my neighbor with the Facebook lanyard while he waited outside to catch an ART bus. His new lanyard had an image of Mars on it, stamped VISITOR. He was either interviewing with NASA down at Spaceport America about a Mars Lander design team job, or interviewing on Mars itself. I sure didn't tell him about getting lost in the outer reaches of Portales.

Later, I undertook the most dangerous mission possible for the harried urban dad—the Costco run. Luna emailed me a long list and right from the start I felt that I was being set up to fail. First, there was the challenge of the parking lot. Invariably, I'd get hit by a wayward shopping cart. Cheyenne, the pretty Costco card checker, always stopped me at the front entrance, because I never had my black Costco executive member card on the top of my wallet. I once showed her my bar card by mistake.

Costco also invariably moved items around the aisles, and I always bought the wrong thing. "Hopefully you'll get it right this time," Cheyenne always said as she checked my receipts and matched them with my items on the way out.

This windy spring night, I was extra careful. I even took photos of certain items to have plausible deniability, just like one of the skunk workers. That's why I felt quite confident as I came to our front doorway. Feeling especially muscular from my martial arts classes, I carried the Diet Pepsi up with the Gatorade.

Unfortunately, I dropped the thirty-six pack of Diet Pepsi

and the eighteen pack of Gatorade just as I entered the loft. Each bottle exploded. Even the various mops, cleaning supplies and a gigantic jug of Windex were not enough to clean out the stickiness before Luna got back late that night. When her feet stuck to the floor, she just shook her head. There was even a tear in her eye.

Martial arts class at Culebra Kai did not take my mind off things the next night. Even the image of Heidi Hawk frowned as I entered the dragon. *Enter the Dragon* was a Bruce Lee film, by the way, but I must have entered through the dragon's exit door. Once again, my katas were too much martial and not enough art, and I was again stuck in the corner doing Coordination Set while the others learned how to do flying guillotine leaps. In the evening technique line, I screwed up Kimono Grab yet again, by committing the mortal sin of stepping forward with my left leg instead of back with my right.

At the end of class, Spartan announced to the group that I would test for my purple belt in a few weeks—ready or not.

"I'm not ready," I said.

"Martial artists are like sharks," he said at the end of class. "You constantly have to keep moving to survive. There is no try."

"What does that mean?"

He didn't even try to answer.

Martiska came up to me afterward. "Are you sure you want to keep doing this? You can barely handle Whirling Mantis and that's an easy technique"

"A mantis has to constantly keep whirling to survive," I said. "Right now, I feel like a crushed mantis."

• • •

After martial arts finished at eight, I visited Marley in

the hospital and sat with Luna. She offered me a chocolate chip cookie that tasted too good to have come from the hospital cafeteria. Had she snuck in and baked it herself in one of the staff break rooms?

The Muzak played "I want to hold your hand," but slowed down, romantic.

Right there, by our sleeping son, we held hands. She did love me after all, despite the toxic waste spill.

"You understand how important it is to keep working hard," she said with a gentle squeeze of her hand. "Insurance is not going to cover all the costs of the operation, much less my personal expenses when I travel with him."

"Why can't they all just come here for the surgery? Save Marley the travel?"

"You know why, Dan," Luna said, "This is an experimental operation they can only do in India and only at this clinic. As I have said, even if the operation was available here in the states, Marley might not survive on the waitlist long enough to have it done here."

The mysterious operation in India. I sometimes wondered if we were better off with a faith healer, except I no longer had faith. Luna had faith for both of us, though.

"I understand. I'm doing my best," I said.

"I don't know if that's enough anymore."

Marley snored, hooked up to a new machine. I heard the constant beep of his heartbeat, one second behind his breath. He looked a lot like me when I was his age. I'm sure that I had that same expression when I was having a nightmare. The only difference was that I woke up. I feared that Marley might stay asleep forever.

"I really hope that the operation does change everything," I said.

"I am sure it will," she said. "But that's just the start. For the rest of his life he might need constant medical attention that will come out of our pockets. Now do you understand how important it is that you keep working hard?"

"I understand," I said. I turned toward Marley and did an inward block and then an outward block—whirling mantis. His eyes were closed; he did not respond.

· · ·

Before dawn on Friday the 13th, I headed to court in Carrizozo in Lincoln County for another motion for conditions of release hearing. I wasn't superstitious, and this would be a routine hearing. The facts were relatively straightforward. Cage had made a delivery to Holloman Air Force base near Alamogordo. He had been stopped coming back from Holloman on Highway 54, just over the Lincoln County line, for speeding and the cop found a stolen computer.

I left Greystoke at six in the morning and enjoyed leaving civilization behind. In the darkness, among the thousand stars above me and the headlights coming straight at me I might as well be Han Solo flying the Millennium Falcon on the Kessel Run. I would make it in ten parsecs, whatever the hell that meant.

The sun rose over the wetlands of a bird sanctuary around mile 175. I understood why Albert Jackson Cage had loved being a driver so much. The moments of boredom he described could also be moments of beauty.

At mile 138, I turned east and traversed the hundred yards' width of the hamlet of San Antonio, New Mexico, which was not to be confused with the city in Texas. There certainly wasn't a Riverwalk, as the Rio Grande was bone dry at this crossing. Will Rogers once said that the Rio

Grande was the only river that needed irrigating. Not just irrigating, the Rio Grande needed love.

A few miles east on Route 380, I passed the Trinity Site, the site of the first atomic bomb test. The wooden historic sign displayed Oppenheimer's famous quote: I AM BECOME DEATH, THE DESTROYER OF WORLDS. He was alluding to Shiva, a god from the Hindu holy book. I had visited the Trinity Site with Luna and Dew a few years ago, and was disappointed. For a nuclear bombsite, the rocky desert there didn't look much worse than the rocky desert around it, except for a few green "trinitite" pebbles. Trinitite was the substance formed from the sand by the immense heat of the atomic bomb explosion. Considering the barrenness of stretch of desert, the green trinitite pebbles might be an improvement.

Other than a single dwelling/rock shop in a place called Bingham, there were no signs of life out here. Even the occasional cow looked lonely as she stared from behind a barbed wire fence. This area made the high plains surrounding Clovis and Portales seem as crowded as the teeming streets of Calcutta.

I crossed into Lincoln County, which was presumably named after the president. Talk about someone who died in the prime of life. It doubted that Lincoln himself ever made it out here; the county's most famous former resident was Smoky the Bear.

A few empty desert valleys east, I saw the turn-off for a "recreation area" known as the Valley of Fires. I do not know why anyone would want to recreate on these hills of black lava. This valley was created by natural causes, but the black lava made the site look more like the atom bomb test area than the real test site.

I stopped at the concrete outhouse in the parking lot of the recreation area, which was only a hundred yards off the freeway. I didn't bother to pay the three-dollar entry fee. This restroom smelled foul. Maybe the living dead were about to emerge from the bottomless hole in the ground.

I jumped up when I heard a knock. Was it a radioactive monster?

Thankfully, it was only a park ranger.

"You don't have a parking pass," he said.

"I'm not parking. I'm just using the facilities."

He started to write me a ticket. I pulled a five-dollar bill out of my pocket and handed it to him.

"Just get out of here and don't come back," he said.

• • •

If Clovis and Curry County felt like Texas, Lincoln County felt like Colorado. Carrizo Mountain to the north, the town's *almost* namesake, bore a striking resemblance in size and shape to Boulder's Flatirons, a mountain with rock formation that resembled giant sandstone irons. The mountain range to the south looked like the front range that ran from Pueblo to Fort Collins, with the white-capped twelve-thousand-foot pyramid of Sierra Blanca playing the understudy for 14,000-foot Longs Peak.

The town of Carrizozo scraped by with six hundred people and was the county seat. Someone once told me there was a law that required county seats to have railroad tracks, and Carrizozo had them in abundance. If Roosevelt County reflected the America of Roosevelt's Second World War, this stretch of Lincoln felt like it belonged in a Civil War re-enactment.

Most of the county's actual lawyers lived in the resort town of Ruidoso, a forty-five-minute hilly drive away.

Ruidoso, of course, had no railroad. It liked to think of itself as a discount Aspen for the day trippers from El Paso. Most of the jurors lived in Ruidoso as well, so during a jury trial Carrizozo's population swelled to about six hundred twenty, counting the lawyers, staff, twelve jurors, and two alternates.

There were only two open restaurants today: one for law enforcement and one for criminals and defense attorneys. Other than justice, the town's biggest export was a bottled beverage called Carrizozo Cherry Cider. I always wondered if it contained any cherry or cider. It was a totally artificial drink, but I loved the sticky reddish fluid so much that I stopped into the Valero gas station and bought a gallon jug. One enterprising lawyer had come up with something called a Carrizozo Cocktail, which was a mixture of cherry cider and Everclear. He had subsequently been disbarred.

The town boasted a handful of motels, none of which looked particularly inviting. Real lawyers stayed in Ruidoso, if they stayed overnight. I had once met with a homebound client in a room at one of the motels and feared that a drug deal was taking place in the next room over. Then I heard a chainsaw coming from the other side of the wall and was reminded of the chainsaw scene in the film *Scarface*.

After passing that motel I parked at the courthouse, a one-story, old-time ranching office that also combined the county treasurer's office and the sheriff's office. The town's only bank and a small grocery were right across the street.

There were two district courthouses in the twelfth district, one here in Lincoln County, and the other an hour south in Otero County in the small city of Alamogordo. Considering the shortage of legal resources in Lincoln County, sometimes a judge had to come up from Alamogordo to handle a case.

I parked in the lot and across the way Raphael and the paralegal exited a Subaru station wagon. It was a late model state vehicle, which must be nice. They wore matching outfits: blue suits with red and white bolo ties. With his wild long hair and a new, scraggly mustache, Raphael looked more like John Wilkes Booth than Abraham Lincoln.

The poor paralegal carried all of Raphael's files on a wheeled dolly, and had trouble navigating the dirt in the courthouse parking lot. She wore Navajo jewelry, which tended to be more traditional than the funkier Pueblo designs that Luna favored. Hmmm. I wondered if the paralegal was Navajo.

"*Ya ta hey*," I said in the Navajo language, Dine. I could only say hello and thank you. "Nice earrings."

"*Ahueh-heh*," she replied in a whisper. Most people in New Mexico knew how to say hello and thank you in Dine.

"You're welcome."

The courtroom also doubled as the county commission chambers and school board meeting room. There was an old poster that read TONIGHT'S AGENDA—KEEPING THE COACH?

An elderly Lincoln County sheriff's deputy in a dark green uniform brought Cage into the courtroom. He was in an orange jump suit and handcuffs. Had he gained even more weight?

"They moved me to the detention center here," he said. "There's green mold on the toilets. You got to get me out of here!"

"I'll do my best. AJ."

The deputy played the bailiff and called court to order. Today's judge was non-descript. I didn't even remember his name.

We first agreed on a scheduling order for the trial This would be the second trial before Judge Chairez and would be held on May 1. There were only two state's witnesses in the upcoming trial here in Carrizozo. Even with jury selection, we should finish the trial by the end of the afternoon.

"Anything else?" the judge asked.

When I made my motion to have Cage released, the judge frowned. "He is also being held in custody for violating his probation in Otero County, which is within this jurisdiction. We can address that matter in this hearing as well."

"I didn't know he had a probation hold in Otero County, sir," I mumbled. Why did I not know this?

Raphael sure knew about it, though. "Your honor, I call Officer Heydrich to the stand."

From behind the door a man entered and almost goose-stepped to the stage. Everything Probation Officer Heydrich wore was entirely khaki, even down to his short tie. He looked like an accountant for Rommel's Afrika Korps that had blitzed across the Sahara during the Second World War. On Raphael's direct, Heydrich revealed that he had been with the Luftwaffe, the German Air Force regiment that trained at Alamogordo's Holloman Air Force base, and then remained behind after he fell in love with a local girl.

I expected him to say a Spanish name, but he smiled and said, "I fell in love with a fraulein called Lady Justice." He was serious.

"So how do you know Mr. Cage?"

"He was assigned to misdemeanor compliance with me. I was on vacation back in Germany, but when I heard that Mr. Cage had a conditions of release hearing, I flew back from Berlin at my own expense."

How much did a plane ticket from Berlin to Carrizozo

cost? He flew all the way back just to make sure some guy didn't get out of jail for not going to defensive driving school? Probation sure worked differently out here in the badlands. Cage was being held on a ticket for speeding. He was supposed to have taken a traffic safety class online, but had failed to do so. This wasn't trivial. Heydrich had the power to keep Cage in jail for six more months.

Maybe I was getting better at this, but I knew how to respond. It was time for a legal blitzkrieg of my own. "Your honor, failure to take an online defensive driving class is terrible, but Mr. Cage has been in jail for ten days and counting. I'm sure he's used those ten days to ponder the traffic code and appropriate speed. I ask that you give him credit for time served and remove all holds."

The major stared at Cage. "What does a blinking yellow light mean?"

I was about to remind the court that my client had a fifth amendment right not to answer the question, but that could anger the judge.

Cage didn't hesitate. "Proceed with caution," he said.

"Proceed with caution indeed," the judge said. "I don't often release holds, but today I will release all holds on Mr. Cage in the twelfth judicial district."

I looked at Cage as the elderly deputy dragged him away. "One more conditions of release hearing to go, Monday in Deming," I said, "and you're out of here."

12. Deming Rock City

April 16, 2018

Another hot weekend in Albuquerque. I jogged around downtown and I was nearly hit by an ART bus when I crossed Central Avenue. During my run, I felt invisible. Even the homeless people ignored me, as if I didn't have enough pocket change to be worth their while.

Saturday night Luna needed a respite; she had spent forty-eight hours straight with Marley. I took Luna and Dew out to dinner at a gourmet pizza place, and Luna made us wait for an hour. "I think I lost those five dollar earrings," she said.

She ended up going with bare ears. It didn't matter. The place was deafening with conversations about Netflix shows I had never heard of. Everyone wore black. Black was the new black.

Our waitress was a girl who had piercings and tattoos that covered the left half of her face. She had left the right half untouched. The girl gave a dirty look to Dew. They must know each other.

"You have the same name as my cat. Suri," Dew said pointing to the waitress's name tag.

"It's a magical name."

"You did mock trial at Academy last year," Dew asked. "The team that won state."

"Yeah. You were the girl that had to drop out because of grades, right?" Suri said.

"I'm doing fine now," Dew said. "I'm back on the team and am lead counsel. So, you're just a waitress, now?"

"What can I get you, sir?" Suri asked me, ignoring the taunt.

Luna looked at me with an implicit challenge: you'd better order the right thing. The waitress suggested the special and I thought it sounded delicious. Both Luna and Dew rolled their eyes.

"We'll have the special," I said.

Wrong decision. The special pizza had artisanal sausage. When did sausage making become performance art? In the end, the food was a little too artisanal for our taste. Suri frowned when we left a small tip.

"Here's my tip for you, Suri," Dew said. "If you moved faster, you might make more money. You're going to need it because you obviously didn't get a scholarship."

Suri looked at Dew, as if Dew was personally responsible for her having to work her way through college. "The reason Academy took state last year in mock trial was because you failed out and weren't on the team. Hopefully you will fail out this year, too, so they can win again."

Dew's eyes narrowed. Suri could not have said anything worse to her. "Well, I hope you get murdered and the person who defends your killer is a good lawyer like my real dad, Sam Marlow, and that your killer is found not guilty at trial."

Luna pulled her daughter away before the two came to blows. I saw a sense of rage in Dew that I had never seen before. I also caught that she had referenced her "real" father as being a "real" lawyer, as opposed to myself.

Yet, that wasn't the weirdest part of it. I never claimed to have any "shine," the psychic powers Stephen King had described in *The Shining*. And yet somehow, even though it was utterly impossible, even if it took a hundred years, I knew that Dew's curse on Suri would come true.

• • •

When we got back to Greystoke that night, Dew went into her room and cranked bad music just loud enough to be irritating, but not loud enough to warrant a knock. What was this music called—electronic dance, techno, or just industrial? I wasn't sure if the screeching and/or rapping was in English or Korean. was becoming my dad with these darn kids today and their awful music.

Luna went to the kitchen and poured herself a shot of the whiskey, something she rarely did, then handed one to me. We toasted and then hugged.

"Now you see why I'm so intent on saving my son. I've already lost my daughter."

"She's just a kid. All kids act out."

"I don't think you get it, Dan. Dew's a monster. She's brilliant, but she's lazy and has no empathy for anyone, except maybe Denise. When she gets out in the real world, if she makes it past high school, she could do real damage."

"That's a pretty harsh thing to say about your own daughter."

She sighed. "One of the reasons I married you is that I saw you could be a father to her. Her real father, Marlow, was brilliant, but lacked self-control. I was hoping you would engage with her, discipline her, and be a father figure."

"Discipline? Dew threatens to call child protective services on me if I even take away her allowance."

"Who's the adult, you or Dew?"

"I'm not sure," I said. "Are you saying her acting out is my fault?"

"I just wish you had been better. A better lawyer, a better husband, a better father."

AI couldn't think of a response to that. I went to the bathroom, took two generic Benadryl, and lost consciousness.

. . .

Monday morning, April 16, at the bank. Josephina told me that she was calling corporate to get the hold lifted. I thanked her. "I will call you personally," she said.

That evening, martial arts didn't feel like *Fight Club*, it felt like Fight Calculus Class. I could never get my angles right and I misjudged acceleration and mass. Even my crane stance was crooked. Martiska tried to work techniques with me, but I sensed that it might be too little too late.

"Will you be ready for your purple belt test?" she asked.

"I have to be. There is no try."

I picked up Luna's Crotaladone prescription from Nurse Song and left another fingerprint. She warned me that Crotaladone was probably going off the market because of the bad side effects she had told me about before.

"I'll keep that in mind."

That night, the night before court in Luna County, I couldn't sleep. Luna County contained the small city of Deming and had nothing to do with my Luna, as far as I knew. She was from a place called Crater, New Mexico, which was no longer on any map.

This was my third Conditions of Release hearing for this client. If I won, Cage got out. If I lost, he stayed in jail for a few more weeks. It wasn't such a big deal, right?

I finally drifted off to sleep, but was awakened very early by a knock on our door. I shuffled to the door and when I opened it, I recognized Dr. Dreadlocks from the emergency room in Taos. His dreadlocks were even longer and grayer now.

"Is something wrong?" I asked.

"I'm a process server now that ski season's over," he said. "Does Luna Cruz Shepard live here?"

"Yes, she does."

"You got served." He handed me a piece of paper with Luna's contact information and a caption that listed a Federal case—the United States of America versus Dragon Moon for violation of several securities regulations. It was signed by a Federal judge.

It took a moment for me to decipher the language. This case had nothing to do with Cage or my case, this was the Feds against Dragon Moon. The Feds didn't want to talk to Luna, Dragon Moon did, and a Federal judge was putting her on notice that if she didn't testify at a deposition, she could be locked up.

As everyone had said, my cases were just fleas. This Federal action was the big dog. I now wanted to get off the flea very badly, as the big dog was starting to shake.

"Luna? There's a man here to serve you some papers."

"Nah, I don't need to talk to her." Dr. Dreadlocks turned to go. "They're officially served when I gave them to you. She's been served, dude. I'm out of here."

I handed Luna the subpoena in bed. She took one glance at it and then crumpled it up.

"This is serious!" I said. "You must appear for the deposition to answer all the questions posed by the lawyers. You are a material witness and it says that if you do not appear a warrant can be issued for your arrest. There's also a *subpoena duces tecum*, which means you have to bring all documents related to your father's investment in founding Dragon Moon, as well as all his will and trust documents."

"I don't care," she said. "What are they going to do, arrest me?"

"I don't know. It's signed by a Federal judge. You'll get arrested by the FBI."

"No, I'll be arrested by US Marshalls. I don't care. I'm going to be hearing about my son's operation any day now. I'll deal with it, don't worry."

I noticed she said "my" son instead of our son, but didn't want to upset her even more. "Is there anything I can do?"

"Be a better lawyer," she said. "Provide for your family. I can't help you with everything and still save my son's life."

That hurt.

"Don't you have to get on the road?" she asked.

I did. I put on a gray Brooks Brothers suit and an orange tie that would match Cage's jumpsuit. As I headed down to Deming, I passed Truth or Consequences, New Mexico. The former town of Hot Springs had received its strange name due to an old TV game show of the same name that offered a reward to any town willing to change its name. Truth or Consequences sure sounded better than Celebrity Apprentice, New Mexico.

Luna and I had stayed here on the Columbus Day holiday weekend a few months ago, at a place called Blackstone Springs. The hotel made it a point to have every room have a theme. Each room was different, and each had pumped in spring water.

We had stayed in the Twilight Zone room, which was in stark black and white with black and white photos from the old TV show. We were indeed in another dimension—one of sound and sight and hopefully of romance. After we undressed, we soaked in the mineral waters of the tub in the bathroom. I kissed her. She kissed me back. Damn, I loved her so much.

And yet, after twenty minutes in the steaming water, I

felt faint and light headed. The steam from the room felt like a malevolent force that was crushing my lungs. I wobbled, then fell and cut my hand.

"Drink water," Luna said, escorting me to a chair. She ran outside wearing only a towel and grabbed two bottled waters from the vending machine

"You saved my life," I said after gulping down the second bottle.

"I know," she said.

"How will I ever thank you?" I asked, trying to joke.

"Save me some day," she said.

I lifted my bloody finger and touched her hand. "I'm swearing a blood oath that I will save you if you ever are in danger."

"I'll hold you to it, you know," she said.

• • •

As I drove past the most southern of the two Truth or Consequences exits, I mused that Luna had saved more than my life. Without her, I'd probably be disbarred by now, or worse, stuck as a small-time lawyer in a town like T or C and drowning in a hot tub all by myself.

That was the truth, and I had accepted the consequences

After half an hour of driving south on the interstate, I cut back across the Rio Grande in the small village of Hatch, the green chile capital of the world. Real chile was spelled with an e. HOT DAMN CHILE, a sign warned the faint of heart as they entered town. Unfortunately, there still was no water in the river. Seemed like all the rivers in my life were drying up. I wondered if the lack of water would make this year's chile crop hotter or milder.

Cutting across the harsh desert on Route 46, I passed another gigantic wind turbine farm. I might as well be on

Mars now; the turbines spinning from an extraterrestrial wind. I tried to call Luna, but there was no reception this far out in the boonies.

The crime of the day was conspiracy to commit receiving stolen property. Per the police report, Cage had met someone while making a delivery at the Playas facility near Deming. The man, a janitor at the lab, was supposed to have given him an item stolen from a Los Alamos scientist's home. Had this incident taken place within the friendly confines of the Los Alamos National Laboratory, and involved something directly connected to the lab, it could be treason. Could you still get hanged for treason?

However, since Cage and the janitor had met in person near Deming in Luna County, and the item was the scientist's *personal* property, this was just a simple conspiracy to receive stolen property. Worst case scenario, Cage faced a fourth-degree felony with only eighteen months on the line. Usually with a non-violent crime such as this, the defendant was sentenced to probation, even if he or she had a prior felony.

Why was I so nervous about this simple little case that wasn't treason? Because I had no idea what was going on here. I didn't have a copy of the discovery, of the evidence, yet. I wondered what was stolen and why anyone would conspire to receive it.

Located in the southwest corner of New Mexico, Deming was close to both the Arizona and Mexican borders, and it absorbed the influence of both neighbors. It was also near the City of Rocks State Park, so I nicknamed the town Deming Rock City after the song, "Detroit Rock City" by Kiss. No one under the age of fifty ever got that reference.

There were native palm trees here, but every blade of

grass was planted. It was also surprisingly warm. A hot breeze must be blowing up from the high deserts of Chihuahua and combining with an even hotter wind from Phoenix.

On the main street headed south through downtown, I went to the old courthouse, a Victorian structure that had been there in pioneer days. Luna County was also famed for skirmishes between Pancho Villa and General Pershing during the early days of the twentieth century. That old, historic building was now the county building. Was the courthouse inside?

No. Someone directed me to the new courthouse across the street, which was still relatively new. While the old courthouse had old western charm, this new one mixed architectural styles with abandon. Then I caught a glimpse of something at the convenience store across the street. Was that a short figure in a silver helmet astride a motorcycle? It was too far to make sure.

Once inside the surprisingly modern courtroom, the judge was already on the bench chatting amiably with a few local lawyers. This judge looked a bit like an old west lawman with a long gray beard. I wondered if he had a six gun under his extra-bulky black robe. Raphael was there in a cheap blue blazer, clip-on tie, and jeans. Guess he thought he didn't have to dress for Deming.

Kirlian and Pile were off in a corner. Kirlian was in his usual black suit, black shirt, and black tie. Pile wore an old, white t-shirt for the band AC/DC. Appropriate, as he was a live wire who could go either direction. I watched as Pile pushed Kirlian, and then grabbed his lapels, pulling him in. In some jurisdictions that might be considered a battery. In martial arts, it would have been considered a Kimono Grab.

Pile let go before Kirlian could counter-strike. Kirlian didn't react, but did check his clothes to see if there were any rips. A sheriffs' deputy came over and stood with them, to make sure Pile didn't try another grab.

"I'm not going to do what you say!" Pile shouted at Kirlian. "You don't own me."

"As a matter of fact, I do," Kirlian said.

They kept arguing, but I made it a point to walk away. I didn't know whether the attorney-client privilege applied when two people were yelling as loud as they were.

I met up with Raphael in between the doors of the courtroom and the lobby "Luna got served on the Federal case," I said.

"I know," Raphael replied. "That has nothing to do with us. That's the Feds against Dragon Moon."

"I might have to withdraw," I said. "There might be a conflict."

"Let's wait and see," he said. "That's above my pay grade."

"This little case is above both of our pay grades," I said. I thought about Cage's thimble, the one Pile should be giving me very soon. "But maybe we can make a deal. Let's say I can get you some information that might help the Federal case against Dragon Moon."

"We'd have to talk to the Feds, but I'm sure they could make your client's case might go away."

Kirlian and Pile went first, and they made quite the contrast with Kirlian's black suit and Pile's white t-shirt. It was like matter and anti-matter. Even though they were just there for a scheduling order, I could feel the negative energy emanating from the podium. Kirlian was pushing the case forward, while Pile kept repeating, "We're not ready! We're not ready!"

"We *will* be ready," Kirlian said.

"I want a new lawyer!" Pile shouted. "I want Shepard!"

Who knows? Maybe I could get more private work through referral down here. This was a Rattlesnake Lawyer kind of town.

The judge banged the gavel. "We have a full docket today and don't have time to handle an issue like this right now."

Pile stormed out. He didn't say a word, but made eye contact with me. He pointed to his index finger and mouthed the word "thimble."

I nodded back. Kirlian chased after Pile, but I didn't see whether he caught up with him or not. We had our own hearing to do.

Before I went to the podium I received a text from an unknown number. It said very simply, PINK STORE.

I assumed that it was a text from Pile. He wanted to meet me at a pink store, presumably to give me the thimble. Everything was falling into place.

Our pre-trial/conditions of release hearing went very well. I began my spiel by bringing up the fact that this was the final case that was holding Mr. Cage in custody. "Your honor, he's not getting day for day credit toward any sentence for the time served on the other cases while this jurisdiction has a hold on him."

A woman came to my side. I recognized her as Yahima Finch, the woman Pile had saved in the Middle East. She was a redneck version of Luna with blond hair and a black pant suit of polyester instead of natural fabrics. "Your honor, my husband can stay with me," she said in a southern drawl. She carried a gym bag with her, filled with his clothes should he get out.

"Your honor," I said, seizing the momentum. "You might remember Ms. Finch from the Iraq or Afghanistan conflict. Mr. Cage saved her from enemy hands. Mr. Cage is a war hero."

The judge paused and checked something on a computer screen. "I remember you, Ms. Finch. I finally have made the connection to that news story."

Raphael mumbled something about Cage being a flight risk, but his heart was clearly not in it. I think he wanted the truck driver out at this point so the wheeling and dealing could begin.

"I will un-cage Mr. Cage," the judge said at last. "Now let's set the trial in this matter for Judge Chairez. What are the settings for the other matters?"

I scrambled to look it up on my phone, but before I even was online, the tiny paralegal handed the bailiff the scheduling orders in all the other cases, and the bailiff brought them to the judge. The judge looked down at the orders. "We are set for trial in this matter, but this is a pretty tight schedule. Will you all be ready?"

"The great state of New Mexico will be ready," Raphael said.

I looked at Cage. He nodded. "Defense will be ready!" I said.

"One more thing after that unfortunate outburst in the last case," the judge paused. We all stiffened. "Mr. Cage," the judge looked right at him, as if I wasn't there. "Do you wish to continue with Mr. Shepard as your attorney?"

Cage waited a moment, and then waited another. "Assuming he takes care of a certain thing, I'd be happy to have Dan as my lawyer."

I felt good, especially as he called me Dan, just like we

were old friends. But, I sensed that our friendship would end very quickly if there wasn't a happy ending to the case. We walked to the back room, the deputy used a fob to open the door, and I walked in behind Cage.

Inside, the big deputies took off Cage's handcuffs. I noticed that Yahima Finch's gym bag was already inside the room. She had faith in me.

"Free at last. Free at last! Great God almighty, I'm free at last," Cage sang in a baritone. He hugged me, and opened the gym bag to reveal jeans and a t-shirt. Without waiting, he started undressing right in front of me.

"Sorry AJ, but I'm not that kind of a guy," I said as he stepped out of his jumpsuit. He was naked. Looked like he had gone "commando" and spurned the jail underwear.

"Now close the deal with Pile," he said. "You do that, and I'll do everything for you."

I smiled and walked away. Get up, everybody's going to leave their seat. Get down, everybody's going move their feet! I had rocked Deming Rock City. Now where was this Pink Store?

13. Hotel Erotica Juarez

The courthouse parking lot was empty and Pile was nowhere to be seen. The Pic Quik convenience store across from the courthouse was vaguely pink. That must be where he wanted to meet. I walked over, but it was deserted except for the clerk. The motorcycle I had seen before was nowhere to be found.

"Is this the Pink Store?"

"That's in Palomas, across the border," he said, as if I was the world's stupidest tourist. "Everybody knows that, *ese*."

I checked my wallet. Might as well get some cash from the ATM. After a few attempts, I finally got online. Unfortunately, the small print of the ATM indicated I was overdrawn. I also checked the trust account and nearly fainted. The hundred thousand dollars was gone. No hold. No pending. Just gone. The balance was zero point zero, zero. WTF?

After announcing that I was ready in open court today, I was now stuck handling the three remaining jury trials. There was no way to delay after announcing three times on the record that I was ready for trial.

Trapped, I called Luna in a panic. "Dragon Moon stopped payment on the retainer! The hundred thousand dollars is gone!"

Bad move in a Pic Quik convenience store where the value of my retainer was easily greater than the value of the entire store. I didn't want to panic in a store so close to the courthouse. I also knew I had to change out of my suit to cross the border. Wearing a suit might as well be a sign that I was an easy target. I could handle a Kick Me sign, but my gray Brooks Brother pinstripes might as well say Kidnap Me!

I changed in the Pic Quik restroom, into shorts and a blue polo pocket T. I exited quickly, carrying my suit and pants in a heap. I felt surprisingly light, but couldn't figure out why.

It was a little over thirty miles south to the border town of Palomas. Outside of New Mexico, I was just the Rattlesnake Civilian rather than the Rattlesnake Lawyer. In Mexico, I feared I would be the Rattlesnake Victim.

I had gone to Juarez more than twenty years ago, back when it was relatively safe, but then it became the most dangerous city in the world. The small town of Palomas was far worse, as per one native-born Mexican lawyer friend.

"There are less tourist places to hide," he'd said, "and more desert to bury the bodies."

My friend and I had been talking about safe places to travel in Mexico. I once joked that there had been a TV series called *Hotel Erotica Cabo,* but I knew there would never be a series called *Hotel Erotica Juarez.* There certainly would never be anything called *Hotel Erotica Palomas.*

I headed south on a two-lane road past several abandoned ranches. I looked at my fuel gauge. Almost empty. I could get gas on the way back, in Deming. Just not at the Pic Quik. In the meantime, in addition to the ranches, I passed a small village called Columbus, New Mexico. There was a turnoff for Pancho Villa State Park, too, the site of a historic battle between Mexican and American forces. I kept going.

I hummed "Welcome to Hotel Erotica Juarez," to the tune of *Hotel California,* interspersing it with singing "Hotel Erotica Palomas." I wasn't a very good singer.

Thirty minutes of scrub land from Deming, America abruptly ended. There was a covered border crossing that looked a bit like a high-tech tunnel, or perhaps a docking bay for a small starship. The line of cars to cross the border stretched back for a half mile, but I could see a large pink structure looming over the fence.

With the back-up on the auto line, it would take an hour to cross by car. I also noticed that I had forgotten to give Luna the bottle of Crotaladone, and the bag was still lying on the floor. Could I be arrested for my wife's prescription when crossing the border? I didn't want to risk it. I better walk across.

Unfortunately, the parking lot next to the border crossing was full. Maybe they were having a clearance sale at the Pink Store? A pink light special? What all did they sell there?

I parked at a small Family Dollar store on the American side and reached for my wallet in my shorts. And then my situation suddenly grew even worse. My wallet was gone! My wallet held my ID. I must have left it at the Pic Quik in Deming, in the bathroom. I now had the immediate worry of having enough gas to get back home. Could I make it back to Deming? There was no gas station along the way.

A motorcycle drove past me. The petite rider wore a silver helmet. Was that Mia crossing over? The driver crossed in front of the line of cars, said something to border patrol, and was immediately waved across. Mia was a Mexican citizen, from nearby Juarez. Did she have special badge?

My phone rang again. Unknown number. It was Pile. "Are you almost here?" he asked.

"Almost," I said. "I'm at the border."

I panicked. The rules for crossing over from Mexico for US citizens seemed to change daily. If I crossed over without my driver's license, I might not be able to get back to

America without going through the consulate. I began to think of various scenarios. I'm sure the Rattlesnake Lawyer could talk his way back, right?

"I really, really need to see you," he said. "Like right now."

"There's a big line," I said. "I'll be there in a minute.

I had no other option; I had to get the thimble to save my client. I walked toward the small border crossing and suddenly I was in the middle of an Asian tour group. More Asian tourists suddenly appeared behind me, pushing forward as if Mexico was the promised land. Were they going for crafts, or the discount pharmaceuticals at one of the border pharmacies?

Pile kept talking as I was carried forward. He sounded increasingly worried, and his rapid breathing sounded like Darth Vader on meth.

"Someone's coming," he said. I heard him walk away, perhaps into an alley. I could see the big outline of the Pink Store on the other side of the border

When I was third in line from crossing over, I heard a gunshot on the phone, and then seconds later I heard it with my own ears. The phone went dead after another gunshot and echo. Had someone shot the phone, too?

The motorcycle with the silver helmeted rider crossed back over the border, again waving at the border patrol. If she was law enforcement, she didn't need no stinkin' badge for identification.

I was still in line with two Asian tourists to go, so I tried to turn around, but the surge of the tourists behind me was hard to push back. No identification was needed to get into Palomas today. The large, no-nonsense Mexican border guard was waving everyone through, not necessarily a good thing.

I pondered using my martial arts on the people behind me to stop from being pushed over the border. What was the defense to a push to the back? Kimono Grab only worked against a push to the front, but what about a push to the back? Crash of the Eagles, final option? I could plant my feet and try to hold my position. No, I certainly didn't want to chop at someone's neck in front of border patrol.

It was too late. I was now visiting Mexico, like it or not. And without a passport, I might not be coming back.

My phone rang again. Hopefully it was Pile, telling me that the shooting had been a weird accident and everything was all right. I was now right in front of the Pink Store, but an ambulance and a few Mexican police officers standing near an alley blocked my view. With the throng of Asian tourists, I was reminded of the final scene of *Chinatown,* where everyone walked right past Jack Nicholson.

I finally answered the call. "Hello? Pile?"

It wasn't Pile. "Dan, we got the call." It was Luna. "The doctors here at UNM cleared Marley for the international flight, so I'm taking him for his surgery in India tonight. We'll be there for a few weeks."

"I can be there tonight, please wait for me!"

No hesitation. "No, I've got to do this alone."

I walked away from the Pink Store, deeper into Palomas. Hopefully, I wasn't attracting attention from the police who were examining the crime scene. "What about the subpoena?"

"I don't care about the subpoena. My son is more important than a subpoena."

She again referred to Marley as *her* son as opposed to *our* son. "That might not be a good thing. The case is really heating up."

I was panting now, and the cops stared at me. I just nodded, and walked south as if I belonged here.

"You heard about the money?" I asked.

"Yes, of course. I'm going to have to scramble to move some of my own money out of my other accounts to pay for my last minute international ticket."

"I didn't know you had your own accounts."

The ambulance now took a body away. His face was covered, but I recognized Pile's t-shirt from court. Pile was dead. There was a long bit of silence, as if everyone here was mourning the loss.

"One more thing, Dan," Luna said.

"What?"

"I'm not coming back."

"You're not coming back from India?"

"I'm not coming back to you."

The phone went dead. I just stood there, numb, in the middle of downtown Palomas, Chihuahua, Mexico. I felt like I had just checked into the Hotel Erotica Juarez, and like the Hotel California, you could check out anytime you wanted but you could never leave.

I had crossed over the line and had no idea how to get back.

PART IV
WHIRLING MANTIS

14. Turquoise Kryptonite

The ambulance gone, I found a bench on the shady side of the Pink Store. Luna leaving me was too much too handle. I almost threw up as I bent over and stared at the dark Mexican dirt. I looked toward the border crossing. Was I trapped here forever?

My phone rang, startling me. I didn't recognize the number, but took it anyway. It was Cage. "This is my number if you need to call me," he said.

I almost started to cry. "AJ, Pile is dead. You gotta help me," I said. "I'm trapped in Mexico. I think I left my wallet at Pic Quik back in Deming."

"Pile is dead?" A dead friend trumped a broke lawyer.

"Someone killed him."

"Who?"

"I don't know. I think it was someone on a motorcycle."

"You know my last lawyer, Dorfman, he got run off the road by someone on a motorcycle as he was heading to Los Alamos."

I didn't want to tell him that someone on a motorcycle had pushed me down in Taos and took my thimble.

"Are you safe?" he asked.

"I don't know. I'm stuck over the border and don't know if I can get back."

"I'm here getting gas right now at that Pic Quik," he said. "Let me call you back."

I hoped he would. I half thought he might abandon me? If he picked up my wallet would he take everything in it and go on a shopping spree at Family Dollar? I didn't know Cage that well.

I sat for fifteen minutes on a ragged wooden bench, trying to figure out how to return home. Did they even have a consulate in Palomas? Considering that Mexican police were now swarming the area looking for clues in Pile's murder, I certainly didn't want to volunteer that I knew Pile and thus make myself a material witness.

Finally, Cage called again. "I got your wallet, man. It was on the ground by the gas pumps. You're lucky no one saw it. I'll bring it to you down in Palomas."

"You'll do that, AJ?"

"You know my code: never leave a brother or sister behind."

• • •

Cage must have sped all the way. This time of day, more people were leaving Mexico than entering, so he had no problem getting across.

When he sat down on the bench next to me, he was in jeans and a battered green t-shirt that said JOIN THE ARMY, TRAVEL THE WORLD, MEET INTERESTING PEOPLE, AND KILL THEM. Did the t-shirt have a bullet hole in it? He had gained more weight, and his big gut made the t-shirt almost horizontal under the word "them."

Yahima sat down next to Cage as he gave me the wallet. All the money and credit cards were there. Why hadn't I trusted him? I liked it when my clients were honest.

"I told you, I never leave a brother behind," Cage said. "Now where did Axtell get shot?"

I pointed out the alley where Axtell Pile had been killed. Cage betrayed his feelings for a moment with a single tear before he caught himself. "Axtell, I'll miss you my brother," he said.

"Now what?" I asked.

"In the case or right now?"

"Right now. We should probably go back over the border

to America."

"Right now, we need a drink."

"You're on conditions of release. You're not allowed to drink," I said.

"That only applies in America, *ese*."

He wasn't allowed to leave the New Mexico, much less America, so it didn't really matter at this point. The three of us had a drink at the bar at the Pink Store where everyone was either an American or a Japanese tourist. There was also a plaza that wasn't just pink. Some store fronts had vibrant blue, green, and red hues. I thought of the Laser Geishas of course.

As we sat in the plaza, Cage and Yahima went with margaritas, but I wanted to avoid anything with Mexican ice that came from Mexican tap water, so I went with a Dos Equis. I remembered the old joke, you can drink the *cervezas*, the beer, in Mexico, but don't drink the water.

We toasted poor Axtell Pile. "He had a good heart, even if he was a total Gomer. Gomer Pile," Cage said, wiping away another tear.

I tried to talk about the cases but Cage lifted his hand to make a stop sign. "Without the thimble we're up shit creek," Cage said. "We can't prove anything."

"AJ, I learned to paddle in shit creek with my bare hands," I said. I didn't know what that meant, but they smiled.

Uncomfortable talking about the case, possibly because his wife was next to him, our conversation shifted to love.

"Are you married, Mr. Shepard?" Yahima asked.

"Not for long," I said. "And call me Dan. If this was Facebook, my marital status would be 'It's complicated.'"

"I'm sorry, Dan. Once we got married it was til death do

us part, in sickness and in health, and in thinness and in fat. Isn't that right, Fat Albert?"

She playfully punched his belly.

"I'm working on it," he said. "I'll be 'Thin and Muscular Albert' again soon enough. After I finish these chips I'll go on a liquid diet."

He chugged his margarita, then rushed through the entire bowl of chips and salsa. There were red salsa stains on his shirt now that were slowly sliding downward.

"It's cool that you guys are still together," I said. "So," I said, turning to Yahima, "tell me the real story of how AJ here rescued you."

"Well, we were driving back to base after seeing some local friends and spending the night, but it must have been a set up. Those guys who attacked us pulled me out of the truck. They had their hands all over me, trying to tear my clothes off. Then I started to pray and the next thing I know I saw Cage take out those guys with his bare hands. That's when I knew he was going to be with me forever."

Cage laughed. "Of course, that's what my ex-wife thought before I met Yahima."

"You guys are made for each other," I said.

"He's lost his hair and part of his hearing, especially when I need him to get stuff at the supermarket. He goes away for weeks on end and drinks too much. He doesn't clean the bathroom after he stinks it up . . . but I love him just as much as I did on that day when he saved my life."

"That's the most beautiful thing I've ever heard," I said. "What is your advice for me to get back with my wife?"

Yahima thought for a moment. "She should be like me and accept her man for who he is."

"That's not going to happen," I said.

"You can become the man she wants you to be," she said.

"Ditto," I said. "Not going to happen."

"Well, you can save her if she ever gets kidnapped," Cage added. "It worked for me." She kissed him when he said that.

"I'll keep that in mind, AJ," I said, then took a last swallow of my beer. "We'd better cross over before it gets dark."

I felt a moment of apprehension when we crossed, but Cage flashed a special Dragon Moon ID and we were over as if we had made it past a Walmart security guard. "He's with me," he told the guard.

With Dragon Moon at my side, I didn't need no stinkin' badge as well.

Cage turned to me just after we crossed. "I've got to go check on Pile's body," he said. "Never leave a brother behind, alive or dead."

Quickly, Cage returned to Mexico, and Yahima followed. "Good luck with your wife," she yelled, right before she crossed the border. "Love conquers all."

"I sure hope so," I said.

As I saw them drive south, I realized there was a decent chance that they were not coming back. Mexico was a big country and it was doubtful that they would be extradited for a few low-level felonies that had nothing to do with the cartels. It was in everyone's best interest, including mine, if they kept going. The further south the better.

"Bon voyage!" I yelled. I wasn't sure how to say that in Spanish.

I have no memory of the drive home, even though it took four hours. I must have stopped for gas somewhere, and surely, I ate something from a convenience store. The Greystoke lofts were empty when I arrived. In a text, Dew told me she was staying with Denise at Nurse Song's place for the duration. Dew only had a few weeks left of high school over the summer. Presumably she would get her own place after that. She reminded me to take care of the cats while she was gone.

I fed the cats, Suri and Sahar, who seemed glad to see me, even though one cat pooped on the floor next to my boot. Once I cleaned up the cat poop and disposed of it in the downstairs dumpster, the two cats went to sleep on the bed, on Luna's side. It struck me then that Luna wasn't coming back, ever.

I sat motionless on the bed for an hour, unsure what to do. I thought about Marlow, the father of Dew and namesake of Marley. Luna had rejected Marlow, and didn't tell him about Dew for many years. I knew about Marley, of course, but would she keep him from me? Marlow then went to the next sister, so to speak, but Selena rejected him for another woman. After being dumped by Selena, he found the third sister, Mia, who lured him in and killed him.

Superman's weakness was kryptonite. The daughters of Dr. Mondragon—Luna, Selena, Jen and Mia—were turquoise kryptonite for guys like Marlow and myself.

I petted Sahar's belly, who nuzzled against me, purring. I finally got in bed and Sahar sat on top of me over the sheets. "You're not going anywhere," he seemed to say.

Just as my eyes closed and I drifted into sleep, my phone beeped. My screen revealed it was Luna—her old avatar had been an image of her wearing a business suit, her new avatar showed her holding Marley in her arms. I was not in the image.

I picked up the phone, but it was only a text with a link to a video. The video was a surprisingly clear eight second video of Marley in an Indian hospital room. The room was immaculate, and more modern than the American equivalent. There was some Hindi writing on the wall behind him. Marley wore a tiny hospital gown, and performed the duel outward blocks of the whirling mantis, and then the left inward block, right outward block of Circles of Glass.

I must have repeated it a hundred times.

15. Home Alone

April 18, 2018

Luna often spoke about being in constant motion. The next morning, I decided to move constantly to prevent falling into despair. I drove in to my office. Luna had already cleared her stuff out of her side of the suite. Had she called professional movers? At least she hadn't changed the locks.

I went to my modern glass desk. Luna had picked it out to replace a crumbling oak antique that had once belonged to my late father. I sat down. Time to play lawyer.

First, I used my smart phone to check the Ninth District Court's website for the trial in Clovis. Without the thimble, it took several tries. We were still set for jury trial, but were sixth on the docket. That meant five felony cases would have to go away before we had to go. Chances were good that our trial would be pushed back to the next docket, or even the one after that. Cool.

I tried to call Cage, but his phone provided an automated message that he was unavailable. In some ways, this could be the perfect scenario. If Cage had gone to Mexico, perhaps none of these cases would ever go to trial. Assuming the First Swiss Bank of Lagos finally came through with the hundred thousand dollars, I could receive attorney's fees without performing any significant attorney work.

I googled Kirlian and found a business number. I rang him and surprisingly he picked up. I asked him how Pile's death affected my role.

"Well, obviously, we still need you to handle the rest of Cage's hearings."

"Could you please pay me for my time so far and send it from a local bank?"

"I'll send two thousand dollars from my personal account. It's in an American bank, from Los Alamos, if that makes a difference."

"Thank you."

"Are you going to stick with the case?"

I didn't bother to tell him that we were sixth on the trial docket, or that Cage was on the run. "Of course," I said. "I'm working on the case right now."

"Do you think AJ Cage will testify?"

"My gut instinct is that he won't. We will rely on a 'sufficiency of evidence' defense." Sufficiency of evidence meant that the state couldn't prove the case beyond a reasonable doubt. It also meant that you didn't have anything else to stand on. I figured Kirlian wouldn't know that.

"That sounds appropriate." I figured right.

After I hung up, I stared at the walls of my office. My only client was now in Mexico. I had nothing else to do. So much for constant motion.

. . .

After an hour of staring at my blank walls, I went to the bank and checked with Josephina. Sure enough, the two thousand was in my personal account. Even better, one hundred ten thousand was "pending" in trust from the mysterious First Swiss Bank of Lagos. Kirlian must have thrown in another ten thousand for my troubles.

"You're in good shape," she said. "They've made some adjustments to their profile so it will take less time. It should work this time."

Selena entered the bank as I was leaving. She now

sported a white pant suit and could be Tony Montana's Miami estate lawyer if they ever made a sequel to *Scarface*.

I was surprised when she hugged me. "I'm sorry," she said.

"I'm sorry, too. I loved Luna. I mean, I love Luna."

"She can be a bitch sometime, and this corporate thing is putting a lot of stress on all of us."

"What's happening?"

"I heard from Mia. She called. She said she was sorry for shooting at us and wants to make amends."

"That's nice of her."

"She said everyone is trying to reach her regarding the Dragon Moon stockholder battle. If she votes with Kirlian, he said he would pay her a million dollars."

"I'm sure that's a violation of securities law. What else?"

"If she votes with Herring, the Colonel will transport her someplace where they don't extradite. She's still on the run, but she's reaching out to me through texts. She wants to make sure that she gets her share of the stock, and she won't give it up without a fight. She seems to know the corporate bylaws backward and forward. Under the Dragon Moon corporate by-laws, she needs to be *convicted* of a felony to lose her stock. She may get arrested, but she won't be convicted before the shareholders meeting. She will still be able to vote her block of shares, even if she's in jail awaiting trial."

"You were right when you said that your family has a crazy gene. You're the only sane one in the family."

"Am I? I'm crazy enough to believe Mia and maybe even forgive her."

"Are you serious? I know that Luna will never forgive her."

. . .

Dew texted that she and Denise needed a ride after school at Academy, as Nurse Song, Denise's grandmother, had to stay at the clinic. She also texted me to bring the cats in their travel carriers.

I said nothing when they got in the car, but the cats purred.

"I'm sorry you and my mom broke up," Dew said.

"So am I," I said. There was an awkward silence as we drove down the six lanes of Academy Boulevard, a golf course on our left. Dew pretended to watch the golfers.

"I'm sorry that I could never replace your dad," I said, when we got to the light at the intersection between Academy Boulevard and San Mateo Boulevard. "You girls have pretty much lived on your own for the last year."

"I never let you be my dad," she said, "but it's too late now."

"Are you two excited about graduation?" I asked, changing the subject

"Don't you pay attention? We're not graduating. I have to go to summer school, and so does Denise, but they're still letting us do mock trial."

Denise nodded. I felt that pinging again in my head, but she didn't change her expression. The pinging soon stopped.

"I'll help you in any way I can," I said.

We didn't say anything more. Even the cats stayed silent. Once we arrived at the Medical Arts Clinic, Nurse Song came out to greet us and Dew turned to me, "Once you get those trials done, maybe you can help me run some cross-examination questions."

"I'd like that," I said.

"Luna says that you aren't a very good lawyer, that your heart's not in it."

"Well, my heart has to be in it now."

Both girls carried a travel carrier into the clinic, and I felt even more alone. But, I didn't have time to mope. It was time for Martial arts. Hopefully this would be my one good hour of the day.

At Culebra Kai, Martiska ran me through my purple belt techniques and katas. I whirled a step too far with my whirling mantis and she clocked me in the back of my head.

"Are you with us tonight, Mr. Shepard?" Spartan yelled from across the room. "She almost knocked your ass back to Carrizozo or wherever you're going these days."

"I need more time," I told Spartan. "I'm not ready to test."

"You don't have time," he said. "This is your last chance to stay in the program. Culebra Kai, advance or die! There is no try!"

He didn't mean that, did he? That if I didn't advance that I would die?

16. Buddy Holly of the Law

April 23, 2018

A week flew by and suddenly it was Monday morning, time for the first trial in Clovis. We were still sixth on the docket, but that was far enough down the list that I hadn't prepared anything. The judge's assistant told me that I should probably come anyway, and I would be excused the minute one of the other cases started picking a jury. The actual trial itself would start on Tuesday, if it went at all.

I could bill my mileage at 40 cents a mile, so the 438-mile round trip would yield an extra 176 dollars or so. That would buy a really nice bouquet of flowers for Luna to say I'm sorry.

At dawn, I put on a blue suit and that ancient purple Jerry Garcia tie, as I knew those were the Clovis school colors. I also wore my boots. Once I entered the Clovis city limits, I noticed the state historical marker of the famous Norman Petty studios, where the late Buddy Holly recorded "That'll Be the Day." It was a non-descript brick building. It was a sad day when Buddy Holly went down in the plane crash with the Big Bopper. That was the day the music died.

You say you're going to leave me, you know it's a lie, 'cause that'll be the day-y-y that I die. I sang. Like Billy the Kid who never became Billy the Middle-Aged Man, I wondered what would have happened to Buddy Holly if he found himself in his fifties and still in a place like Clovis.

Cage hadn't called, so I planned to arrive at court at eight-thirty A.M., mention to the judge that that my client was "on his way," and then leave the second I was excused. One other option was that if we did have to go to trial and Cage didn't show, a warrant would be issued and then I would still get excused. Should be an early day.

Raphael was already in the courtroom. He wore a nice suit with an orange tie, the colors of the Artesia Bulldogs, a football rival to Clovis. I wasn't going to fill him in. The short paralegal was with him, wearing a black skirt and white top, and funny earrings that displayed the *cuchara*, the Hopi clowns that wore black and white body paint. I wondered if she was Hopi.

Judge Chairez was in the room, too, talking with Shaharazad. The judge wore a regular black robe. After Shaharazad indicated that her machinery was working, the judge called all the lawyers into a back room, the cramped jury room. Twelve jurors could fit in here, but there wasn't room for an alternate. There were probably eight lawyers and sixteen cups of coffee.

"Who is number one?" the judge asked.

A poorly dressed ancient lawyer announced that he was first and ready to go. Unfortunately, his client hadn't been transported from prison where he was doing time on another crime.

"Warrant issued!" The judge said with flourish, even though it wasn't the defendant's fault he hadn't been transported. "Number two?"

This was a public defender case. The lawyer was there, the client was there, but unfortunately the client had strong odor of alcohol emerging from his Budweiser t-shirt. Bad choice when you're on trial for DWI number eleven. The judge had the man arrested on the spot and hauled away to jail.

"Two down," the judge said. "Who is number three on the docket?"

I was hopeful that one of the other cases would go to trial, so we had more time to figure out what to do. The defense wasn't ready on the third case, and the state wasn't ready on the fourth. Why didn't anyone want to go to trial today?

I tried to call Cage, but received no answer. Good. He was probably all the way to Panama by now. I'm sure he was smart enough to go somewhere where they wouldn't extradite him. Brazil was nice this time of year.

"Number five on the docket. Is Mr. Salazar here?"

The attorney named Salazar wasn't there. He probably figured that as number five on the docket he was safe. Unfortunately, once his number was called, Salazar and his client were on the hot seat. The judge gave him three minutes, but didn't bother to call the attorney to let him know he was on the clock.

At exactly three minutes, as the second hand hit twelve, the judge, then issued a warrant for the arrest of both the attorney and his client. They didn't mess around down here.

"Number six on the docket, State v. Cage. Mr. Shepard, is your client here?" the judge asked.

I started to announce that we were not ready, and that my client wasn't here in the courthouse. They'd issue the warrant, but it would never be served on Cage at the Copacabana, Cancun or wherever he was. It was the best thing for all concerned.

Then the worst possible thing happened. Cage arrived in the jury room with Yahima in tow. A guard stood behind them. "Mr. Shepard, your client is here."

"Sorry I'm late," he said. "Are we going to trial?"

Cage wasn't in a Budweiser shirt. He didn't reek of alcohol. Instead, he wore a blue blazer and khakis with a red tie, as if he was going to an officer's club reception at Annapolis. Yahima wore a matching blue blazer and had let her hair go to its natural red. She also looked, dare I say it—

appropriate. Both appeared to be stone cold sober. They were ready for court.

"State is ready," Raphael said.

"Defense?"

I looked at Cage, as he tightened his tie. "Let's get this over with," he said. He pulled his tie a little too tight.

"Defense is ready."

The court brought in the prospective jurors. We had to pick a jury from the fifty people in the gallery of the courtroom. I recognized one of the jurors, a man I called Gollum, from Albuquerque. He must have moved to Clovis. The other potential jurors were retired military, retired cops, and a handful of employees from the nearby dairy plant. Except for Gollum, no one looked like they'd be sympathetic to an out of town trucker found with drugs.

I did not have the jury list; all I had was my gut instinct. Raphael did a long boring *voir dire* going through every play of the prosecutor playbook—beyond a reasonable doubt is not beyond all doubt blah, blah blah. Judge Chairez asked him to stop mid-question after he methodically went through the jurors, one through twenty.

Raphael was doing my work for me, since he could get people to disqualify themselves whenever they said they couldn't be fair or impartial. One woman said that she was married to a cop and the mother of another cop, so police always told the truth. I wouldn't have known that, so I was happy she bowed out. I then went up and it was time to be the Buddy Holly of the law. "Any football fans out there?"

Everyone raised a hand. This was a Friday Night Lights Texas kind of town that just happened to be in New Mexico. I talked about reasonable doubt in the state football championship, and as it pertained to Buddy Holly—how you didn't want to get in a plane unless it was beyond a reasonable doubt that it wasn't going to crash. I flat out home-towned the out of town prosecutor. I didn't go with profiles; I went with smiles.

"They love you," Cage said.

"I can learn to love being a lawyer."

Once the jury was sworn in, the judge reminded me that in Clovis we pick a jury on a Monday, and then start the actual trial on a Tuesday. I had twenty-three hours to cool my jets.

I looked at Cage. "What's this case about again, AJ?"

He laughed. "Well, if you don't know, I can't tell you. I'm going to check in at the hotel and sleep with my wife. Call me when you know what's going on and we'll talk."

17. That'll Be the Day

I wanted to avoid the Holiday Inn, where Cage was staying, so I went with the old Days Inn by the Burlington Northern & Santa Fe (BNSF) railroad tracks. Did anyone ever take the train from Burlington to Santa Fe? Instead of a business center, the Inn had a room dedicated to the BNSF folks who were staying the night on the railroad's dime. Every few minutes a train passed, either heading north to Burlington or east to Santa Fe, and the building's bricks vibrated like a faithful poltergeist. The day of this Day's Inn had long passed, and yet it still had soul.

As I found my room in the middle of the open air first floor, several railroad workers were busy lassoing a saw horse in the courtyard and drinking beer. I pondered all my techniques, but couldn't remember any redneck defense.

They had given me a two-room suite here at the Days Inn, so I felt like a railroad baron. I couldn't help but hum the song about working on the railroad all the live long day. Still, I wondered why someone would be in the kitchen with Dinah and why they would be strumming on the old banjo. When the train passed by me the third time that hour, I decided to stop caring.

I turned up the TV inside my room so I could concentrate on the case, rather than on the trains and the ruckus in the hall. Then I reviewed the file for the Clovis case. Turned out that Cage had been speeding on US 60 on the way to Cannon Air Force Base. A state policeman stopped him and found a medicine bottle (later identified as Crotaladone) that Cage didn't have a prescription for. The bottle was in plain sight.

There *almost* was a defense. The pill bottle was not labeled so there was the potential that Cage had lack of knowledge of its contents. No one had bothered to take fingerprints.

The only way we could possibly win this case was for Cage to testify that he picked up a valid prescription for someone else, and could show the paperwork. Or perhaps he had a passenger with a valid prescription who left the bottle by mistake. I called him from the room.

"Well, I've finally got a clue," I said. "I've thought of a defense. You had a valid prescription."

"I didn't. Try again."

"You had a signed authorization from someone to pick up the prescription and the prescription was valid."

"I'll think about that one," he said.

"You had a passenger in the car with a valid prescription who accidentally left it there."

"Can't you get the traffic stop thrown out? Don't I have a right not to be searched and seized? They didn't read me my rights neither. Don't they got amendments for that too?"

By "traffic stop," he was referring to his contact with the police where he had certain protections under the fourth amendment of the constitution. Under the latest Supreme Court decisions, in laymen's terms, police could search a vehicle if they had probable cause. They didn't have to read the person their rights, especially if contraband was in plain sight.

"You were going ninety miles an hour in a sixty-five. It's like you wanted to get caught. And they don't have to read you your rights when there's a bottle of some pain killer made from rattlesnake venom in plain sight in the cup holder."

"Do they have the proper chain of custody?"

"When did you become the lawyer, AJ?" I asked. I went back through the file. "Yep. It was picked up in person from the police station by a chemist and sent back to the cops in a sealed bag. It was always in a locked safe. Next idea?"

"Figure something else out," he said. "I don't want to testify. You need to be a better lawyer."

"A better lawyer?" I asked. "You need to be a better criminal."

"What do you mean?"

I remembered Hollywood Joe's pitch for *Heavy Starch.* "Like in one of those heist films like *Mission Impossible,* where the gang has disguises, government moles, and cool gadgets. You, on the other hand, just drove fast with drugs in plain sight. It's like you wanted to get caught."

"I'm sorry, but this is real life," he said. "I didn't want to get caught. It just happened. This is serious. I don't want to end up dead like Axtell."

"Then give me something to work with! Is there anything I can do to change your mind about testifying as to what really happened?"

He hung up. This had indeed become Mission *Almost* Impossible.

I channeled my inner Tom Cruise Action Hero and practiced some martial arts in the cramped room. In the process, I stubbed my toe against the bed's floorboard. I finally remembered whether it was Whirling Mantis as opposed to Circles of Glass that was a defense to the left right combo, versus the right left combo. When I was done, I was pleasantly exhausted, but again found it strange to sleep in a bed alone. I missed Luna so much. The king size bed needed its queen.

• • •

The train woke me before dawn, the next morning. Still, Cage arrived at the courthouse before I did, in same outfit he had worn yesterday. Raphael wore a black suit and a purple tie. Maybe he was following my lead on how to dress for success in the land of the Beast from the East, the Clovis Wildcats. The paralegal was nowhere to be seen.

The judge called the court to order and Raphael did his opening statement. It took less than a minute, counting the five times he said "The evidence will show." I waived mine. I still didn't know whether Cage would testify, and didn't want to make a promise to the jury that I wouldn't be able to keep.

Raphael called Officer Ruby as his first witness. Ruby looked eighty if he was a day and I wondered if he would live long enough to make it through direct examination. He testified that he made a traffic stop when Cage barreled past a speed trap on US 60 between the base and Melrose. While asking Cage for his license, the officer saw a bottle of Crotaladone pills in plain sight. The Officer asked Cage what the bottle was for. Cage didn't reply, but did give consent for the pills to be tested.

Raphael's direct examination lasted five minutes. Then he took a deep breath and smiled. How do you cross when you have nothing to cross?

I questioned the officer and mentioned that it was unlikely that someone would smuggle Crotaladone in plain sight.

He agreed.

"So, he probably wasn't smuggling them, was he?"

"What else was he doing?"

"I'll ask the questions here, sir."

It went downhill faster than La Bajada from there. I

struggled for fifteen minutes with any question that came to mind. Raphael kept objecting with "asked and answered" until Judge Chairez finally banged her gavel.

"Do you have anything else, counsel?"

"I guess I don't," I said and sat down.

"Next witness?"

The paralegal made an entrance into the courtroom with another woman, and the paralegal acted like a tour guide for a VIP. She must have been sitting in one of the witness rooms along with the witness. The paralegal escorted the woman, who turned out to be the chemist, up to the stand. The chemist identified the pills as Crotaladone, and this time the whole presentation took less than ten minutes.

I tried a cross, but had absolutely nothing to work with, other than "You weren't there, were you?"

"No, I'm a chemist not a cop. I tested the illegal drugs. That's what I do."

"Anything else?" the judge asked twice. I repeated the same question and Raphael did an "asked and answered" objection, which was sustained by the judge.

I sat down and the state rested. I made a pro forma motion for a directed verdict as I was contractually obligated to do.

Judge Chairez stared at me. "Is your client going to testify?"

"Give us a minute."

I met with Cage in a small room down the hallway and informed him again that the only way to win this case was for him to name the name of the owner of the pills and how they came into his possession.

"I can't tell you," he said.

"How did you get them, AJ?"

"I can't tell you."

"Why were you delivering them?"

"I can't tell you."

"What is going on here, AJ?"

"I don't know, man," he said. "One of the things I learned in the army is that you don't sell out a brother or a sister."

On the one hand, I admired his sense of honor. On the other hand, I didn't like him taking the fall for someone. Was it Pile? Or, was it Kirlian?

"Do you want to call Yahima from prison for the rest of your life?"

He was about to change his mind when Kirlian knocked on the door and pushed his head in without waiting for an answer.

Cage froze. Kirlian then closed the door after mumbling an apology.

When we went up before the judge I looked at Cage. He shook his head.

I meant to say the defense rests, but instead I blurted out "We got nothing, your honor."

"That's for sure," the judge said. She then read the jury instructions and we did closing arguments. I muttered something about reasonable doubt, then the case went to the jury.

Before I could even go to the bathroom, the bailiff came back into the courtroom.

"Do they have a question?" I asked.

"They have a verdict."

I was the Buddy Holly of the Law without the talent. I had crashed and burned in less time than a song on the AM radio.

The jury was excused after the guilty verdict, and I did

my only real lawyering on that second day of trial—I had to keep my client out of jail. Cage had been a jerk these last few hours, but he was clearly terrified of something. I owed him the z word, zeal.

Raphael wanted Cage remanded, locked up right there in the courtroom.

My inner rattlesnake lawyer finally awoke. "Your honor, my client was a war hero."

The judge rolled her eyes, then stopped mid-roll. "A war hero?"

"Your honor, he was a driver for the military and was transporting a passenger. There was a diversion stop, and he rescued her with his bare hands, and prevented her from rape, torture or worse."

"I recall that incident," the judge said.

"And, your honor, our county has let him down. He has had trouble adjusting to home after serving his country. On a personal note, when I lost my wallet he came for me. He crossed into Mexico to help me, which might have been a violation of his conditions of release. He could have kept on going south, but he came back. He always comes back.

"And, while I may disagree with him about not testifying who the drugs really belonged to, this is a man of honor, your honor."

"I'll let him stay out if he keeps in contact with you."

"Thanks, your honor."

"See you next week counselor for round two."

I glanced at my watch. It was four o'clock. I could still make it back for my martial arts test.

18. Praying Mantis

I almost stopped at exit 263 off I-40 to practice my moves as the sun set. Unfortunately, I was running late and figured I'd better power straight though. The avatar of Luna holding Marley appeared on my phone. She had texted another video of Marley. Well actually, it was the same video. But this time she had added the words GOOD LUCK DADDY!

God, I loved my son.

When I arrived at the Culebra Kai parking lot five minutes before the test, my legs felt like lead from the drive. Inside the locker room, I almost forgot to put on my cup in my haste to get ready. I didn't have time to go to the bathroom, much less stretch.

As soon as opened the door to the gym Spartan called me to the center of the room. "Is the candidate ready?"

"Yes, your honor."

He laughed. "I'm not your honor," he said. "This has nothing to do with honor."

Martiska acted as my sparring partner, but even holding back, she still made contact. I moved the wrong foot for Kimono Grab. I did Circle of Glass instead of Whirling Mantis and was clocked in the head twice by the left right combo. My Coordination Set was uncoordinated. Spartan stopped the test after the second option of Crash of the Eagles when I hit Martiska in the shoulder instead of the neck.

"I think we've seen enough," Spartan said.

A few minutes later he called me aside into the lobby, and we stood under Heidi Hawk's left glove on the wall poster. "It's not working out," he said. "And to make it worse, your dues didn't go through. I'm asking you to leave Culebra Kai."

"Is there any way I can retest?" I asked. Then I said the

worst thing. "Could I try again?"

"There is no try here, you know that. You're never going to get any better. I don't want to waste my time or yours."

"This is all I've got now."

"Give me your belt and your book," he said. I was reminded of a clichéd sports movie where the stern coach cut a football player, and asked for his locker and his playbook.

Thankfully, I had left my book in the car. I wasn't going to give that book up for anyone. I could teach myself Karate after court.

"I'll bring it by tomorrow," I lied.

When I walked out of the dojo I swear that the image of Heidi Hawk had a tear.

"I won't let you down, Heidi," I said out loud. "I'll be back!"

19. Breaking Winds

April 30, 2018

I didn't sleep that night; I had to prepare for the next trial in Lincoln County in the Carrizozo courthouse. We were number one on the docket for Monday, April 30, and I felt like I was Lincoln going into Ford's Theater.

Luna texted me to say the preparations for the operation were going well and that Marley's Indian medical team was optimistic. I tried to call her, but she didn't pick up.

Dew and Denise went away for a week for a mock tournament. This tournament would determine whether they were selected for the Mock-Trial All-Stars invitational. Dew had dropped by her apartment to pick up some supplies, and gave me a hug before she left. "I wish you could help me on my cross-examinations," she said.

"I wish you could help me with mine," I said.

. . .

On Saturday, I took a few phone calls from Cage as I reviewed the file for the Lincoln County case. This charge was one count of receiving stolen property—a laptop computer. The circumstances were bizarre. There was an accident at the one traffic light in the town of Carrizozo. Cage was driving his truck and got into a fender bender. While inspecting the vehicles, the cop noticed the shiny new computer that had an officers' name engraved on the back.

Cage claimed he had bought the computer at a pawn shop in Alamogordo, but was unable to provide a receipt or any recollection of the location of said pawn shop. He wasn't being charged with stealing the computer, just for receiving a computer that he knew, or should have known, was stolen. Pile had been in the cab with him, attempting to log on to the computer when the accident occurred.

Without being asked, Pile had shouted, "We didn't know the computer was stolen!"

For a moment, I thought I could get Pile's statement suppressed as "hearsay," but I remembered that his statement would be admissible as an excited utterance under Rule 802, or perhaps a "statement against interest."

"Again, it was almost as if you wanted to get caught," I told Cage over the phone. "You claimed that you bought a type of laptop that they only use on base, and that an officer had pawned it. But, you don't remember where you bought it. And Pile said the computer was stolen before he was even asked. That's what we in the business call 'bad facts.'"

There was a long wait on the other end. "Well, Pile was nervous."

"You can blame Pile," I said. "In some old lawyer show, they called it 'Plan B.' Blame someone else."

"I can't pin the blame on someone who ain't here to defend himself."

"We need to talk, AJ," I said.

"We can't talk over the phone."

"Then where?"

"I will be at the Inn of the Mountain Gods up in Ruidoso Sunday night before trial," he said. Maybe we can meet there."

"I'll try to make it."

I had planned to drive up for the trial before dawn on Monday, but a relaxing night at a luxury hotel sounded better than spending a night in Greystoke alone and doing dawn patrol. As if on cue, I received a call from Kirlian.

"As a show of good faith, we can book you a night in Ruidoso the night before the trial starts on Monday," he said. We agreed on the Inn of the Mountain Gods.

That sounded suspicious. I wondered if Kirlian was listening to my calls, but then again, I didn't mind staying at a beautiful resort hotel on someone else's dime.

. . .

I left Sunday in the late morning. I arrived in Carrizozo 149 miles later and stopped at a Valero gas station near the Four Winds restaurant. I grabbed a Carrizozo Cherry Cider then went out to examine Cage's crime scene at the blinking red light in the middle of town. This was the receiving stolen property case involving a stolen laptop computer. Cage and Pile had an accident in the truck, ran off the road, and when the officers inspected the car, they found the stolen computer.

The Four Winds was across the street from the gas station, and I could feel all four winds blowing in my face as I stood on the corner. I turned to the south, and in my mind's eye I saw Cage and Pile coming from Alamogordo on Highway 54. I then saw them make a left turn to head east on Route 380.

Why did they swerve?

In my file, I saw that the truck swerved to avoid a motorcycle.

Suddenly everything came into place at this barren crossroads in the middle of the desert. Cage's first lawyer, Kent Dorfman, had driven off the road while swerving to avoid a motorcycle. I had been mugged by someone wearing a motorcycle helmet, who then drove off with my thimble on a motorcycle. Someone on a motorcycle was seen near Pile when he died.

My client was being set up by the motorcycle rider. Did this rider work for Dragon Moon? Maybe. Perhaps that was why he was so afraid to tell the truth. He was afraid that he would, figuratively, be thrown under the motorcycle by his employer.

Back in the present, someone honked at me. Startled, I dropped my cherry cider and the blood red liquid spilled all over the pavement.

20. Mountain Gods

I drove southeast toward Ruidoso and began a steep ascent up Highway 37. Unfortunately, much of this valley had been ravaged by forest fires some time back, and still looked like a war zone all these years later. This was the real home of Smokey the Bear.

"Smoky the Bear died for our sins," I said to myself as I passed a grove of burnt trees.

And yet, once I hit the Ruidoso city limits the ravages of the fires abruptly stopped, due to a valiant effort by local firefighters. I was now in a mountain resort town that felt more like Aspen, Colorado than Albuquerque, New Mexico.

After driving through Ruidoso's quaint, historic western tourist district, I saw the turn off for the Inn of the Mountain Gods. What did a mountain god look like anyway?

Turns out, the inn was gigantic; it was set against a small blue lake that bounded the twelve-thousand-foot Sierra Blanca. Sierra Blanca was especially blanca today. The summit must have taken a late spring snow dusting.

After parking in the gigantic underground parking lot, I emerged into a spacious resort hotel. Unlike the Overlook hotel in *The Shining*, this inn had real Native American artifacts on display. Sierra Blanca filled the beautiful glass window on the other side of the lobby. Talk about an overlook.

Ms. Mescalero Apache, a beautiful young woman in tribal costume, stood and greeted all who came by. "Welcome to our homeland," she said.

I wasn't in a hotel. I was in a homeland.

On the way to the front desk, I passed the gift shop, which featured Apache jewelry from the local Mescalero Apache tribe. The design of this jewelry was more aggressive than most other Native jewelry offerings. No surprise, though, as Apaches were great warriors, since before the days of Geronimo. There was a choker composed of some type of bone. Luna would have loved it. Could I buy her back with jewelry? Maybe I would get it for her in the morning.

The room comped, I checked into a spacious suite with another view out to Sierra Blanca. I had once spent a romantic evening with Luna in this very suite before we were married. I could practically see her in her black lingerie sprawled on the king size bed.

Damn I missed Luna. I even missed Luna Law.

. . .

I called Cage and we agreed to meet at the patio outside Wendell's, a gourmet restaurant that featured wild game. It was a warm spring night, and I was comfortable in shirt sleeves. Cage was in a Hawaiian shirt, and I don't know if it was possible, but the hula girl on the shirt looked exactly like Yahima Finch. Yahima sat next to him and wore a Hawaiian shirt of her own. The hunk on her shirt was an image of Cage's face superimposed on a sarong, so he looked like a Samoan warrior.

We had perfect timing for the sunset. As it slowly descended, the sun reflected off the snow at the summit of Sierra Blanca to make it Sierra *Rosa,* and then it cast a pink glow on the waves of the lake.

Despite the high altitude, my pulse was the lowest it had ever been. To compensate, I smoked cigars with Cage after Yahima excused herself. "Keep my husband out of jail," she said.

"I don't want to lose her again," Cage said. "I missed her

so much when I was in jail."

"I miss my wife too," I said. "And I'm not even in jail."

He watched her intently as she walked down the steep staircase to the lakeshore. Was she doing an intentional wiggle?

"I found out more about Axtell's death," he said when she made it to the bottom. "I made some contacts down in Mexico."

"What did you learn?"

"Axtell was executed by the bad guys."

"That's cold."

"If I testify as to who gave me the stolen computer, I won't have to do time?"

"Well, AJ, we still have the first case where you were convicted. And we have the other case, but I have a feeling that if you cooperate, I can make everything go away."

Down below, Yahima Finch took off her shoes and waded into the water, even though there was a no swimming sign. She turned around and waved at us. No one seemed to be stopping her, so she dived in. She waved again from the water.

"AJ, do you really want to give that up to go to jail for ten years?" I asked.

He waved back at Yahima. "I'll testify tomorrow. I don't want to say anything now because there are ears everywhere, but I'll testify. Someone gave us a computer and then wanted it back. That's what this was all about."

A waitress had been hovering behind us. "Can I get you anything else?"

"We're good," I said. She went away. Cage excused himself and hurried down to the lakeshore to join Yahima. The sun finally set all the way, but the lake was illuminated by the moonlight. I couldn't tell, but maybe they were skinny dipping.

I went back to my room, resigned to watching television. Unfortunately, my key card didn't work. I tried three times to no avail so I went down to the lobby and talked to the clerk. I was surprised that my suitcase was already sitting there.

"I'm sorry sir," said the clerk. "But something came up with the room and we had to cancel your reservation."

"Something came up?"

"The card that was used to charge the room was reported as stolen."

"I didn't use a card, I was comped."

"Well whoever comped you, un-comped you."

"I do have an alternate card. I can afford the room. Really."

"I'm sorry sir, but we're all full up. I'm sure you can get a room in Carrizozo."

21. Heaven in Room Seven

The half-moon shone on the ravaged forest as I drove back. Wolves and coyotes howled as I descended from the Alpine paradise of Ruidoso back to the desert of Carrizozo below. There wasn't any room at any inn. After a frantic search, only one motel in Carrizozo had a vacancy.

It was ten when I checked into the Black Sands Motel, south of town.

If the Inn of the Mountain Gods was heaven, the Black Sands was worse than purgatory. It wasn't quite hell, but it was hell adjacent. There had to be a reason why this was the only room left in Lincoln County.

A group of men and women were gathered in the parking lot drinking beer. As I carried my luggage a beautiful woman dressed in leather came over to me. "Hey man, you want to party?" She offered me a can of Bud. Another man offered me a joint. I had to think about it.

It was going to be a long night.

It was loud, so I needed to get my generic Benadryl. I went out to the car and opened a bottle and popped a pill, then another. I stumbled back to the motel.

• • •

By eleven o'clock, room seven of the Black Sands Motel was hopping. I was getting into it; the drug must be making the experience more intense. First it was the drummers. The late Keith Moon of the Who must be challenging the late John Bonham of Led Zeppelin to a beat-off, while the USC and Ohio State band's drumlines kept dueling beats. The bands then spelled out "Carrizozo" in the parking lot, with Satan himself coming down to dot the "i" in Carrizozo.

Then came the guitars. Prince was jamming with Jimi, and the guitar licks were so funky that they acted as an aphrodisiac.

The singing started next, screeching mezzo-sopranos singing faster and faster—the Mormon Tabernacle choir on meth. The thin walls shook harder and harder to the incredible pounding beat. The mirror in my room even cracked from the high notes from either a soprano or an alley cat.

I wouldn't sleep tonight.

As for the women, first Salma Hayek resurrected her erotic vampire Santanica Pandemonium in the film, *From Dusk till Dawn,* right there in room seven of the Black Sands Motel. She started dancing on the queen-sized bed with a giant slithering rattlesnake behind her. The rattlesnake kept the beat with its tail as she moaned in ecstasy.

Next Ziyi Zhang and Michelle Yeoh of *Crouching Tiger, Hidden Dragon* fame floated down to room seven as if descending from the snows of Sierra Blanca. They wore their Chinese medieval costumes and levitated above the bed, performing an intricate aerial ballet mixing combat and passion.

The finale in room seven must have been choreographed by Stanley Kubrick—people in Venetian masquerade costumes and monk's robes recreating the orgy scene from *Eyes Wide Shut.* My eyes wandered through the nooks and crannies of room seven like a Steadicam tracking shot.

How many people had there been in room seven? How many climaxes? How much ecstasy? It would have been impossible to measure.

I finally fell asleep at five in the morning, only to awake seconds later to the sound of police sirens. It was still long before dawn, but I bundled up and walked outside my room. It hadn't been a dream.

There was a broken drum kit, a dead rattlesnake, and a monk's costume sitting in front of the door to room seven. Cops were leading a few men and women away. When I got back in the car, I realized that I had accidentally taken two of Luna's Crotaladone, thinking they were generic Benadryl. That explained a little.

Drugs or no drugs, I had to admit that the best sex ever, perhaps the best sex in human history, had taken place right there in room seven of the Black Sands Motel in Carrizozo, New Mexico that night.

Unfortunately, I had spent the entire night in room eight.

22. Yo Yo in Zozo

I was still feeling the effects of my sleepless night and Crotaladone hangover when I arrived at the Lincoln County Courthouse a few minutes later. I didn't even bother to eat, because I didn't know whether I could keep anything down. The battle of the band drumlines was still echoing in my head.

The jurors were already in the courthouse, and the bailiff asked me for my juror number.

"No, I'm a lawyer," I said.

"You forgot your tie."

I retrieved my orange tie from under the gas pedal, hoping that the mud stain on the bottom looked like part of the tie's polka dot pattern, then met up in the lobby with Cage, who wore the same blazer and khakis he had worn the last time. He clearly hadn't washed them; his clothes were wrinkled and smelled as if he had taken them with him into the lake for his tryst with Yahima. Who knows? Maybe he had.

Inside the courtroom, Kirlian was chatting with Raphael and the paralegal. All wore the same dark hue. Had they all aligned against us? To top it off, the paralegal was wearing the aggressive bone and turquoise choker that I had admired last night up at the gift shop.

I scanned the potential jurors sitting in the courtroom. These jurors skewed older, and per their questionnaires were involved in tourism in Ruidoso. No one in this Carrizozo jury pool was from Carrizozo. I thought I recognized Gollum, the potential juror from Clovis, in the pool, but it was someone who looked exactly like him. Had he been cloned?

Judge Chairez and Shaharazad came out after a bit, and

we began. Raphael asked these jurors the exact same questions he had asked the ones in Clovis.

I wasn't as good as Marlow at picking juries, but I used my weakness to my advantage. I said "I'm going against the best young prosecutor in the state, and my friend AJ Cage has to rely on little old me. You're not going to hold that against him, are you?"

Since I had spent at least part of the night at Inn of the Mountain Gods, I did a "casino *voir dire*" and talked about beating the odds and beyond a reasonable doubt. The jurors responded. The judge called a recess so we could pick.

During the recess, Cage didn't seem to care which jurors I picked. "I've got a lot on my mind," he said as an excuse.

"Is there even a defense to this case?" I asked. "You were found with a computer that had someone else's name on it."

"I don't know yet."

"You don't know if there's a defense."

"I don't know if I want to tell you what really happened."

Carrizozo wasn't like Clovis. Once the lawyers picked your jury, the trial started immediately after. Raphael's first witness was an airman from the base—a fresh-faced kid from Tennessee. He talked about how much the military meant to him, but that on one night out he took his computer with him. He had his name and rank engraved on it, and had it locked in the trunk of his car when he went into a bar to watch a basketball game.

At the bar, the Buffalo Wild Wings on Alamogordo's main drag, White Sands Boulevard, he met two attractive young women. They invited him to party. The young man stated that he had no ulterior moves, he just wanted to have a good time.

In the Wild Wings parking lot, just outside the

surveillance camera's range, one woman hit him on the head when his attention was on the other. They must have grabbed his keys and took the computer from the trunk of the car. When he awoke, he saw the women riding away on a motorcycle.

The women were never seen again. They were an interesting footnote, but they were not on trial here today. They must have been the ones who transferred the computer to Pile and Cage, who were not being charged with the robbery, but merely receiving stolen property. This computer did have the airman's name engraved on the back of it.

Raphael picked up the computer and showed it to the man.

"Is this your computer?"

"That's my computer. It has my name on it."

"I just want to make sure that there's nothing classified on it."

"No of course not. We're not allowed to save anything classified on our computers."

"Have you ever seen the defendant before?"

"No."

"Did you sell your computer?"

"No, I did not."

"Is there any reason he should have your computer?'

"No, there is not."

"Pass the witness."

My cross-examination focused on the fact that it was so obvious that the computer belonged to the airman, Cage must have assumed that everything was cool when it was in his truck.

The jurors rolled their eyes with that one. Raphael didn't

even bother to re-direct, a sign that I hadn't touched the poor airman.

"How many more witnesses do you have?" the judge asked Raphael. Should we take a break?"

"No, your honor' Raphael replied. "We can finish the state's case before lunch."

He called Officer Barbrady of the local sheriff's office. Barbrady wasn't the brightest cop, but he had no trouble with his part. He testified that there was an accident involving a motorcycle. Raphael didn't dwell on the accident, just on the search. The cop looked inside the cab of the truck and noticed a computer with the airman's name engraved on it. He had heard about the robbery in Alamogordo, as it had gone out on the wire.

I stopped listening. I was putting the pieces together. Someone wanted the computer for espionage. The computer probably contained no sensitive information, but its IP address would allow someone to hack into some serious defense department websites, especially if that person had a thimble.

I waived cross examination of the cop. Raphael was disappointed that I hadn't put up any fight at all. This case would come down to Cage admitting that he had been set up, or whatever the hell was really going on.

"The state rests," he said. I made a pro forma motion for directed verdict, but didn't say anything else. What was there to say?

"Are you going to call any witnesses?" the judge asked me.

"Let me talk to my client over lunch."

. . .

Cage and I walked over to the Valero station and grabbed some frozen burritos. After heating them in the microwave, we washed them down with Carrizozo Cherry Cider as we stood at the windy corner of US 54 and US 380 across from the Four Winds, the site of the incident. Hopefully, no one could hear us over the din of the winds and the truck traffic.

"I've got it figured out, I said. "This has nothing to do with the stolen computer."

"What do you mean?"

A military vehicle drove past us and turned east onto 380.

"You knew that one of you could use the computer to hack into department of defense sites, along with the use of a thimble."

He nodded.

"Will you testify that someone asked you to steal that computer?"

"Can you guarantee that I won't end up dead like Pile?"

Another army truck turned from Route 380 south onto Route 54 toward Alamogordo.

"I'll do my best."

"Then I'll testify."

"Will you tell me what's going on?"

"On the stand."

For one moment, I had hope that I would be a real lawyer and this would be a real case. I was wrong, of course.

"We call Albert Jackson Cage to the stand," I said after court had resumed.

Albert Jackson Cage went up to the stand and took the oath. I had a brief feeling of triumph. This man had stared down terrorists, he shouldn't fear testifying of twelve jurors in some rural American courtroom.

"Please state your name."

"Albert Jackson Cage, but you can call me AJ."

"AJ, why did you have the computer in your truck?"

He looked at me. He looked at Raphael and the paralegal. He looked at Kirlian. He avoided my gaze the next time, and stared at Yahima. She was saying something to him. "I love you," perhaps.

He looked like he was about to say something, almost like Marley. But then he shook his head.

"I'm sorry, Mr. Shepard,' He said at last, still avoiding eye contact. "You can't guarantee my safety and I would rather have my girl and my son visit me at the jail for the next three years then visit me at the cemetery."

I wasn't quite sure what he meant. I asked the question anyway. "So why did you have the computer in your truck?"

"I take the fifth."

He didn't think I could protect him after all. I tried two more times and then walked back to my seat. "Pass the witness," I said.

Cage started crying up there on the stand. One of the sheriff's deputies had to go up to the stand and escort him back to our table.

"Do you have anything?" the judge asked. Not asking if I had any witnesses or evidence, just whether I had anything, anything at all.

"I got nothing, your honor."

I don't really remember what happened next. We must have done jury instructions. We had to do closings. I am sure I said something about reasonable doubt in my thirty seconds or so while I addressed the jury. The jury must have been excused by the judge to deliberate. The jury may not have left the jury box before rendering a verdict.

All I know is an instant passed and then I heard the judge say "guilty" and ask me if I wanted to poll the jury.

"What for, your honor?"

The judge excused the jurors for good and ordered Cage remanded into custody. I couldn't think of anything to say to keep him out.

This big man started crying. "I wish I could tell you what was happening. I'm being set up," he said between sobs.

"I don't care," I said. "I don't care."

Four deputies carried the big man away. Could this day get any worse?

Of course, it could.

. . .

On the way to the parking lot, some jurors stood outside the men's room.

"I had to close my restaurant for this shit?" one said.

"Why did the defense lawyer defend someone who was so seriously guilty?" asked another.

"Won't he lose his license for being doing such a bad job?" asked a third.

I didn't want to go to the bathroom to give them the satisfaction of laughing at me.

I didn't want to stay in Carrizozo. Badly, I wanted to get out of this jurisdiction and out of New Mexico. I wanted, I realized, to get out of life.

It was starting to drizzle in the parking lot, so I walked directly to my car and got in, I wanted to avoid any interaction with a living soul. But a few miles out of town, my suit felt like lead. My shoes were killing me, and I had to go to the bathroom.

I pulled off to the Valley of Fires exit and hurried to the outhouse on top of the black lava hill. Before I could go inside, my phone indicated a text. It was from Luna. COMPLICATIONS FROM SURGERY. MARLEY MIGHT NOT MAKE IT.

My heart might as well be back at the high elevation of Taos, it was beating so dangerously fast. Marley might not make it? My son was going to die?

I didn't bother to text Luna back. An overwhelming urge came over me, and I knew that my entire body wanted to purge the pain from my heart, my guts, and my soul. I went to the hole in the outhouse and bent over.

I vomited up everything. I had failed as a lawyer. I had failed as a husband. My wife didn't want to share my name or my life. I had one thing that I had given the world—a son.

And now I had failed at being a father.

Luna had a healthy child with Marlow. She had a dying child with me. I had never made enough money to buy Marley all the care that he deserved. I was too busy wallowing in my own shit to be a real father, much less a real lawyer. I'm sure if I had tried harder we could have been able to get specialists in sooner and Marley would not be dying today in Bangalore.

My glasses fell into the muck below. Good. I wanted to be blind.

I kept heaving, over and over. It felt as if everything inside of me was coming out. Every ounce of failure. Every ounce of pain. Oppenheimer said he had become Shiva, the destroyer of worlds. I had become Shiva, the destroyer of my life.

The smell emanating from below the earth was

unbearable and it grew worse with every heave. I kept retching for five minutes. It seemed that only intestines and vital organs were left to come up at the end.

Finally, I wiped my face with a wad of toilet paper and walked back to the car. I had an old pair of glasses somewhere in the car and had to find them before I could check my phone again.

There was nothing more from Luna. Should I text her again? No, she would tell me Marley's news either way. As for me, I was at rock bottom in a sea of black volcanic rocks.

Just then the phone rang. Luna. I picked up quickly. "Luna? *Luna?*"

The phone connection went dead. I still had a few pills left in Luna's bottle of Crotaladone. I wonder what would happen if I took them.

PART V

COORDINATION SET

23. Fear and Loathing in Los Lunas

I was somewhere near Belen, the Hub of Enchantment, when the drugs finally took hold. I had purchased a Five Hour Energy, two bottles of Extra Strength Tylenol and three packages of generic Pepto-Bismol tablets.

"I'm feeling a little lightheaded," I said to myself.

And then it was quiet again in the car. It was almost six PM and I still had more than forty miles to go. They would be very tough miles. But there was no going back and no time to rest. Earlier, I had been listening to an audio book CD, *Fear and Loathing in Las Vegas*, to take my mind off everything on the drive home. I had turned off the CD player as the seriousness of my situation kicked in. The various pharmaceuticals had mixed with stress and caffeine to give me a mental state where I could process what was happening.

What would I do without Luna? Then I saw her name on a sign up ahead. I had to wipe my eyes to make sure. Why would her name be on a road sign? I finally realized that the sign with some faded letters was for the exit for the village of *Los Lunas*, New Mexico.

I drove past the exit and passed the Facebook data facility. The building was a hundred-yard long warehouse filled with computers. There were probably more computers inside the building than people. My mind tried to coordinate all the data within my own life, but my brain was on the edge of overheating. I didn't know whether my son was alive, or whether my wife was coming back. As for Cage's final, remaining trial, that would take care of itself, right? I would lose. Cage would go to prison for a few years. Dragon Moon would take over the world.

I wasn't sure how I felt about anything anymore, other

than I knew deep in my heart that I wanted Luna back. I wanted my son to live. I wanted my family to survive.

When I drove over the muddy Rio Grande just south of Albuquerque, my phone finally rang. I looked at the caller ID and heaved a sigh of relief when I saw it was Luna. Then I weaved through traffic like a drunken crazy person as I fumbled to answer the call. Despite my best tries, it was if her signal was stuck in the muddy banks of the Rio Grande *bosque,* the woods next to the Rio.

On the third attempt, she got through. "He's going to live," she said. "He's going to live!"

"Thank God!"

We talked for the next ten miles as the desert of small ranches on the Isleta Indian reservation transformed into urban Albuquerque. In a breathless voice, Luna reported that in the end, the operation had been a resounding success. But, Marley needed time to recuperate from the stress of the complications during the surgery.

"Once he rehabs, he'll have a normal life. His body is normal. His brain is normal. He should even start talking soon," she said.

"How long for him to recover?

"Best case scenario, he will be airlifted back to UNM hospital in a few weeks, and after a few days of rest would be able to move home."

"Where's home?" I asked. "For you? For Marley?"

I was passing the Albuquerque Sunport, the modern adobe international airport where Luna would fly in. Part of me wanted to jump on the next plane to meet them in India and fly back with them. I weaved into the exit lane and calculated the cost of an emergency flight.

"We'll see," she said. "We need to get home first and get

him out of the hospital. We'll see what happens after that."

"What will we see?" I asked.

Before she could answer the phone went dead. Luna wasn't taking me back—yet.

After driving through the desert, I was now surrounded by the million people of Albuquerque, yet I felt incredibly alone. I pulled off the interstate on the Central Avenue exit and parked the Focus on the fourth floor of Greystoke's garage. This garage was probably bigger than the town of Carrizozo, and with the lights out, I had trouble navigating my way to the elevator. I was lost in my own garage.

Inside, my apartment was unworthy of being called a pigsty, because animal control advocates could close a pig sty down. It was amazing how quickly the space had deteriorated since Luna had left. I had left milk out, my underwear was on the floor, and before Dew had taken then away, one of the cats had pooped in my shoe.

I looked at the clock. Nine-thirty, time for a late dinner. I had one frozen meal in the freezer, a Marie Callender's shrimp pasta. I followed the directions to open the package. Unfortunately, I couldn't get the microwave to work. I didn't know if Luna had re-programmed it, or if it had died. It would take forty minutes to cook the meal in an oven, eight minutes for each of the five shrimp.

I walked down the stairs and through the tunnel over to Luna Law to use that microwave, and was surprised to find a night maid cleaning inside. She looked at me with suspicion. It took me a moment to recognize the woman who was cleaning my office this late at night. It was Anna Maria Villalobos, the cousin of Judge Chairez. She had been on the show *American Idol,* but had fallen on hard times since she had sung at our wedding. She had a young girl with her, who was sleeping in a corner.

"What are you doing here?" I asked.

"What are you doing here?" she asked.

"Just working on a case," I said. I certainly didn't want to tell her that I couldn't figure out how to get my microwave to start.

"Who's the little girl sleeping over there?"

"That's my daughter, Jaylah. I take her with her on my late jobs. I don't like leaving her alone in our neighborhood at night."

Jaylah was the name of a warrior woman on *Star Trek*, and this petite warrior seemed healthy and well dressed in Hello Kitty pajamas. Nothing seemed out of the ordinary, so I let it go.

"How's Luna?" she asked. "Singing at your wedding was one of the high points of my career, just like being on *American Idol*."

"She's great," I said. "Just great."

After microwaving the pasta and wolfing it down I pretended to read a file while she pretended to clean. Her daughter lifted an eyelid, then pretended to sleep.

24. Inmost Cave

May 1, 2018

The next morning, I called Kirlian at exactly eight A.M. After some small talk, he agreed to meet me after lunch in Albuquerque at his office in the US Eagle Building, the tallest building in New Mexico. I wasn't sure whether US Eagle was a bank, a credit union, an insurance company, or an advocacy group on behalf of American raptors.

"I've got a present for you," he said, in a voice that sounded like a bird of prey.

On my way to the office, I dropped off some suits with Hollywood Joe, and picked up the one clean one I had left him last week. Luna had selected every single one of my suits, and decided that I looked better in black than in my preference for dark blue.

"I wear black, you wear black, and we look like a team," she had said. She had also thrown away most of my old blue suits. Plus, I had gone from a 44 long athletic fit to a 46 long and less athletic fit since I met her. That meant I was eating right, and I kidded myself that it was all muscle from martial arts, right?

"Your wife asked me to ship some of her suits to India," Hollywood Joe said as I dropped the pile on his counter. "You guys breaking up?"

"I guess so."

"Are you going to try to get her back?"

"I don't know yet."

"Boy gets girl, boy loses girl, boy wins girl back," he said. "That's the plot of *Heavy Starch*."

"This is real life," I said. "I don't know if I get the girl back."

"A lot of screenwriter's give up in the second act funk—they don't know where to take the plot next."

I thought about El Funko. My life was in a second act funk. "So, what happens in the second act funk?"

"Right now, you're in the inmost cave. This is where the hero is at his lowest, but then he gets his groove back."

"I don't know if I ever had a groove, and I don't know if there's going to be a happy ending."

"In my screenwriting critique group, someone said that the difference between good stories and bad stories is a happy ending."

As I walked out the door with my clean suit in hand, I realized that I hadn't asked him which one—the good story or bad story—had the happy ending.

After changing into my clean black suit at home, I picked up some files from the office. Then I decided to walk to the US Eagle Building. It was hard to tell which people were the sloppily young hipsters going to the Innovate ABQ building and which were the homeless headed to Evolutions, the drug treatment center. Homeless or hipster, I asked myself as I passed the bearded tattooed folk on the sidewalk. Did it matter? I didn't belong to either group.

I ambled west on Central Avenue and crossed under the railroad tracks via the pedestrian tunnel that was adjacent to the noisy passage for automobiles and the Albuquerque Rapid Transit busses. Other than the natural light coming in from the sides, the tunnel was dark but loud, like a New York subway tunnel. The electric lighting in the tunnel wasn't working and I nearly stepped on a gigantic man who was sleeping just inside the entrance. I apologized. He mumbled something about kicking my yuppie ass.

I hadn't heard the words "yuppie ass" in years. Maybe

the man had been asleep since the nineties. He was dead wrong as well. I was neither young, urban, nor particularly professional, all requirements of being a yuppie. Years ago, when I was a suburban Ivy league educated wimp, I would have been afraid of this challenge by this sleeping giant. He could have a knife, though, I reminded myself. Gingerly, I stepped over him and went through my martial arts repertoire. I was ready to unleash a downward block, if necessary, and then follow it with a round kick. The man didn't move, but nearly hit me with phlegm before I moved away.

My claustrophobia kicked in right in the middle of the tunnel. A second later the limited light at the end revealed two people stumbling slowly toward me. They grunted like zombies, and smelled of urine, vodka, and death. I could use either Circle of Glass or Whirling Mantis, depending on whether the first punch to me was a left or a right.

This felt like the inmost cave that Hollywood Joe put into his *Heavy Starch* script, and I was coming into the light.

When I finally emerged on the other side of the tunnel, construction on Central Avenue had closed the sidewalks. That put pedestrians very close to the train tracks and it was deafening when an Amtrak train pulled into the adjacent Alvarado station.

The Southwest Chief, the famed train, was heading on its daily journey from Chicago to California. I sang a few bars of the famous Journey song, "Don't Stop Believin'" with its line about the midnight train heading anywhere. Had I stopped believing in myself? I pondered taking a noonday BNSF train headed north to Burlington or at least Santa Fe to escape.

But no. I still believed in something. Even Cage deserved

a zealous defense. I sighed, and walked two blocks north to the Albuquerque Civic Plaza. If the Ranchos church was the heart of old New Mexico, this brutalist concrete urban plaza was the heart of the new.

I glanced at a small, faux adobe tower on the west side of the plaza. It rose from the façade of the convention center and I noted the clear architectural debt that this convention center complex owed to Taos Pueblo adobe cubes, and to the curves of the Ranchos church. Perhaps it was the light in that perfect blue sky. I imagined Georgia O'Keeffe painting the convention center in her inimitable style. She could have made the center's brown color scheme look exotic, romantic.

There were groups of college athletes jogging around. The convention center was hosting yet another indoor track meet. Luna had almost made the Olympics in the triathlon. I wonder how she'd do against these kids. I knew I'd be left in the dust by her, even now.

An electronic message board near the main entrance flashed advertisements about upcoming events. In addition to several high-tech conferences, the bright red letters boasted of the INTERNATIONAL HIGH SCHOOL MOCK TRIAL COMPETITION—JUNE 29 KIVA AUDITORIUM, WEST HALL, and the DRAGON MOON SHAREHOLDERS MEETING, EAST HALL, both on the same date. The two halls were separated by a skyway that ran above the railroad tracks. If Dew made the finals, I could find a way to crash the board meeting, right?

I turned to my right and headed toward the two, twenty-plus story towers on the south side of Civic Plaza. Both were capped with pyramids and radio towers. One tower contained the Hyatt Hotel, the other the aforementioned US Eagle Building. The two buildings shared a common lobby and a Starbucks. I passed through the Hyatt side of the lobby, which was teeming with young, high-tech folks with name tags, slurping *vente*-sized non-fat lattes. A banner announced WELCOME NORTH AMERICAN PATENT LAWYERS, YOUNG LAWYERS DIVISION. I thought I recognized one young lawyer from the Los Alamos Starbucks. Or maybe not. All those high-tech folks looked the same to me, and they all while they spouted the same high-tech gibberish. I didn't want to ask any of them what was new in patent law, as I didn't know what was old in patent law.

Wading through the reception area took a full five minutes, during which I caught the gist of many conversations. One young techie mentioned a new brew pub, then the other launched into the hoppy flavor of an IPA and a 10 percent ABV level at a brew put at the nearby One Central Entertainment Center. I wasn't sure what ABV was, or whether ten percent was good, bad, or dangerous. I googled it as I pushed myself through the crowd. ABV stood for alcohol by volume. A ten percent ABV beer would probably send me back to the outhouse to heave.

Through the scrum of young patent lawyers at the other side of the lobby, I showed my ID to a guard at the front entrance of the office tower elevator. Several muscular men in blue suits with red, white, and blue ties rode up with me and got off at the eighth floor, the home of the United States Attorney's Office.

I rode the elevator alone to the twenty-second floor. When the door opened, I faced an unarmed guard standing at the front entrance. His shirt featured a logo for Dragon Moon security. With his hands, he indicated that I would be frisked before I could enter Kirlian's inner sanctum.

The guard had a name-badge that said his name was Dick. I had met him before, at the A-frame. Dick's gun holster was conspicuously empty. "You lose your gun, Dick?" I asked when he got a little too rough tweaking my private parts.

"You didn't hear?" he asked, squeezing my leg. "After the last shooting one of our guards got sued, and now none of us can carry guns until we get this certification thing straightened out."

I remembered hearing about a court ordering staff at a security company to not carry guns until some paperwork and training had been dealt with. One of the guards had accidentally shot an unarmed teenager, the son of a judge, who was trying to get into an event where his dad was speaking. There had been racial overtones, of course. I hadn't connected the shooting to Dragon Moon Security. The company apparently did a little bit of everything including freelance security. They really were trying to take over New Mexico.

"That might be a good thing, Dick, so you don't shoot any more unarmed kids," I said.

After Dick released his GI Joe grip on my leg, he pushed my left shoulder. A push to the left shoulder? I should have responded with a defensive move called Brush of Danger, which involved an arm rake simultaneous with a twisted stance. Instead, I held my ground and shifted instinctively into a fighting stance, keeping my arms at my side, but ready to go up at a moment's provocation.

"I you think you can take me buddy, I'm ready," Dick said. He lifted his hands and moved his feet into a classic fighting stance.

I bowed and gave him the Culebra Kai salutation of a closed fist into an open hand. "I'll think about it. Maybe next time."

"I'm counting on it," he said.

Inside, Kirlian's office looked temporary, as if he had taken his few possessions from the A-frame and moved them here. The renovation of the former Intel plant in Rio Rancho would take years. As for Kirlian himself, he was attempting the evil business casual look—khakis and a black polo shirt. Upon closer inspection, the logo on the shirt was a dragon rather than a polo pony, a dragon spitting fire.

We sat down at the same card table in those same, uncomfortable folding chairs. Dragon Moon must have a bit of a cash flow problem right now. They were renting the most expensive office space in town, but couldn't afford to furnish it.

After some small talk about New Mexico weather, Kirlian handed me a new thimble, which he took from a small case. "We had this made personally for you," he said.

"You aren't disappointed in me?" I asked.

"No, actually we are quite pleased. The final trial should be over in a few days, and the matter will be behind us."

"Do you want me to lose?"

"We want the matter *resolved*," he said. "Resolved quickly with a minimum of distractions. All my attention right now is focused on the shareholder's meeting. You might want to tell your wife to get in line behind my group of shareholders."

"I can tell her," I said, "but she's not listening to me."

I put the thimble on. He gave me a complicated series of passwords to say to activate it, and to access the various judicial data bases. It worked fine in the office. Other than being able to project images on a flat surface, it was essentially a small smartphone.

• • •

After our meeting, I took the south exit out of the US Eagle building to avoid another gaggle of North American patent lawyers, and headed toward my office on the other side of the railroad tracks. This wide street was a far less claustrophobic crossing than the one under Central. Walking on Tijeras Avenue, I passed the entrance to a downtown health club, where there was a posting for a senior's martial arts class. There was also a small advertisement for free martial arts classes with a membership. I still had a membership there, didn't I?

Why had I chosen Culebra Kai rather than here?

That night, faced with the prospect of another night alone without a microwave or a wife, I went to the martial arts class at the downtown sports club. When I went to the entrance, there was a beautiful Latina woman at the door, whose nametag read JESUSITA.

"You're the *Culebra Abogado*," Jesusita said in the mellifluous lilt of a Northern New Mexico accent.

"The what?"

"The Rattlesnake Lawyer," she said. "I read an article about you once in the Spanish edition of the *Albuquerque Journal*."

"*Culebra Abogado*," I said. "I'll use that if I ever advertise. It's my brand."

• • •

I learned in the locker room that the founder of the group had been taught by the same sensei who had taught Elvis. I wore blue Nikes instead of blue suede shoes and wondered if there would be a move could Crouch Tiger, Hidden Hound dog. He wasn't there tonight, but the black belts would take up the slack.

Inside in the "group fitness room," which served as a

basketball court/yoga studio and dojo, one of the black belts there was a former lawyer who had quit his practice when he developed cancer. He now talked with a voice box. He'd also had a tracheostomy, and breathed through a short tube in his neck.

His condition certainly put my problems into perspective. This was the man who was assigned to take me to a corner to assess where I was in martial arts.

"I just failed my test for purple belt," I said.

"It's not about belts," he said through the voice box. "Tell your story."

"My story?"

He demonstrated one of the katas—a short form one. His voice box told the story. "Someone punches you from this side. You block him. His buddy comes at you with a kick from this side and you parry."

"Do I need character motivations for why they are attacking me?" I thought about Hollywood Joe and his script.

"That's up to you."

He watched me do my eleven minutes of material, and then demonstrated how to turn my katas into a lethal ballet. I could visualize his invisible dance partners. I even heard thumps on the ground when these imaginary foes hit the ground. He said I could do better if I articulated better, didn't rush and forgot about character motivations.

Articulate better. Sounded like good advice for law.

When I finished the class an hour later, I was grinning from ear-to-ear, even though I had taken an accidental punch to the chin. The guys here picked you up after they knocked you down. This was how martial arts was supposed to be—more arts than martial.

No more Culebra Kai, there is no try. It was time to try

something else.

I chatted with Jesusita on the way out. She was reading a Spanish poetry book by Pablo Neruda, and listening to some spoken word poetry.

"Culebra Abogado, she said. "I'll write a poem about you."

"Go for it," I said.

"Let's see," she said. "It could start like this: 'You're the *Culebra Abogado,* don't you mess with the crazy *vato.*'"

The crazy dude. "I love it," I said.

25. Geisha Hospital

May 2, 2016

Luna called me the next day to tell me she was returning from India with Marley in three weeks. Marley was going to spend a few days at our local hospital, UNM Children's Hospital, as a precaution, and then move with her to the new Hotel Chaco, which was near Old Town, until everything settled down.

"Why Hotel Chaco?" I asked. "That's the new one next to the Hotel Albuquerque, right? That's like the most expensive place in town."

"They're giving me a good rate on the Honeymoon Suite," she said.

"Honeymoon Suite? Is there something you're not telling me?"

"There's a lot I'm not telling you."

• • •

That afternoon, I checked my financial situation with Josephina on the bank. Some money had been cleared from the trust account, so I had access to two thousand real American dollars. Assuming I didn't pay my mortgage, and made only a partial payment on my Ford Focus, I could survive the next thirty days by living off the land.

"Your wife called yesterday and checked on the account," Josephina said, adjusting her hearing aid with her left hand. "Is everything all right with you guys?"

"I don't know. Did she try to withdraw money?"

"No, she just wanted to check the balance, but she is not an authorized signer on your trust account."

"When will the rest of the funds be available?"

"The remaining $98,000 should be available next week."

"You said that last week."

"This week I mean it."

. . .

The next three weeks were a blur. I managed to survive, but I realized how much I missed Luna. We were a team and I wasn't good at being solo this late in the game. She texted me pictures of Marley, but never called, and told me via test that after a few scares he was doing all right. I missed my son.

One weekday night, I was driving on Central Avenue near my loft and nearly hit a sixty-something man in a suit who was drunkenly crossing the street between The Library and Knockouts. The Library was hardly a place of higher learning; it was one of those "breastaurants" where waitresses wore short schoolgirl outfits that opened to their tattooed and pierced belly buttons. Knockouts was known as the bar where the old strippers went to die. I vaguely recognized the man as a lawyer, Woodford, who had handled a co-defendant back when I was a baby lawyer. Was he still practicing? It was like watching the ghost of Lawyer Future. Would that be me in fifteen years without Luna?

. . .

I had given up all hope of ever seeing my family again when Luna texted me to let me know that she and Marley had just arrived in Albuquerque. She said she wasn't ready to see me just yet, but I could visit Marley Monday evening after he had settled in. So on Monday, May 28, Memorial Day, I was finally able to see my son. My first family outing with Luna and Dew had been on a Memorial Day so many years ago. I could never have imagined that on this Memorial Day, I would have a son, but not have a wife.

Marley might as well have been in the honeymoon suite

at the UNM Children's Hospital. He had a room to himself, and none of the other three rooms in the suite were occupied.

Was our insurance paying for this?

"Hey Jude" played on the Muzak. Time to take a sad song and make it better.

Someone sat with Marley, right at his bedside. At first I thought it was Luna, as the shape wore a deep black blazer, but it was Denise who turned around. She must have inherited one of Luna's hand-me down blazers that had already been handed down to Dew. Denise had un-dyed her pink hair and I didn't recognize her looking normal—well, normal for Denise.

Underneath the blazer, she wore a t-shirt with LASER GEISHAS FOREVER on it. The animated TV show about the Laser Geishas had somehow become popular online with the cool kids.

Denise did have one pink bang in her jet-black hair, presumably as homage to Laser Geisha Pink. Luna billed herself as Laser Geisha Blue, the leader. Selena was Laser Geisha Green and Jen, Denise's mother, was Laser Geisha Pink. The Geishas were a girl thing that I didn't pretend to understand.

"Good afternoon, Denise," I said, not expecting an answer.

"Good afternoon, Uncle Dan," she said. "Aunt Luna went to get food. She's not ready to see you yet. She did leave these cookies for you, though."

I didn't know which shocked me more, Denise talking, or that Luna didn't want to see me.

"It's nice to see you, but when is Luna coming back?" I asked.

"After you leave the hospital. But don't call me Denise.

My name is a joke. Call me Pink."

"Okay, Pink. What's wrong with the name Denise?"

"Denise is my slave name. Do you know where my name comes from? My crazy mom was pregnant with me and a twin brother. She asked Aunt Luna, her half-sister, what she should name us. Aunt Luna said Denise for a girl."

"I like your name. I don't see what the problem is."

"But then Aunt Luna said it should be 'De-nephew' for the boy. Get it? My aunt Luna named us De-niece and De-nephew. De-nephew died at birth, so we were left with me––Denise, the living joke."

"No, don't think of yourself as a joke," I said, a little alarmed.

"I don't. And just because I don't talk that much doesn't mean I don't have anything to say," she said.

"I'm sure that's true, Pink. Do you ever hear from your mom, from Jen? You know she was the original Laser Geisha Pink."

"I heard from her last week. She's in Asia with her cousin Susie and either they're battling the forces of evil in another dimension or she's had a breakdown and is stuck in a mental hospital near the North Korean border. Then again, my mom could be fighting the powers of evil *from* a mental hospital near the North Korean border."

"I can see her doing just that. Your mom is an incredible woman." There would always be a special place in my heart for Jen Song.

"I've inherited some of her powers," Denise said matter-of-factly.

"Powers?"

"I can communicate with Marley," she said. "Without words. I'm a little psychic. He is too. Psychic that is."

She was serious. I stared at her, speechless, and then I sensed a strange electric current pass between us. "That thimble makes you a little psychic too," she said. "I heard about those."

I felt a little spark on my fingertip, but it quickly passed. "So, what is he thinking right now?"

"He's dreaming about the whole family being together. You and Luna."

I looked see his rapid eye movement behind his closed eyes. "Can you tell him I'm trying?"

"He knows."

"Is he mad at me for being a failure like your aunt Luna says?"

"He knows you're doing your best."

"Tell him I will save the day, somehow."

She shut her eyes. As if on cue, Marley woke up. He looked at me, smiled, and did an elaborate version of the kicks and punches of coordination set, all while staying in his crib.

"My other aunt, Mia, is trying to contact me."

"Through her mind?"

"By text," Denise said with a smile. "She used to be our babysitter, and we were kind of close until she went crazy and shot everybody."

"Do you like her now?"

"I can't forgive her for what she's done. Ever. She killed Dew's father and that warped Dew probably for the rest of her life. She shot my Auntie Selena, but I think she was possessed in her own way. Not all geisha spirits are good."

"Possessed or not, it will take a lot for me, and it will take even more for Luna to ever forgive her."

"Mia understands that, and she knows she has to make

amends."

"What are the amends?"

"She doesn't know yet. But maybe it has something to do with the stock shares."

The Muzak now played the next song – "A day in the life." How many holes did it take to fill the Albert Hall?

"I hate this old classical shit," Dew said.

"It's the Beatles," I said. "John, Paul, George and Ringo."

She stared at me blankly.

"I'm really John, but Luna wants me to be more commercial like Paul."

She shut her eyes as if receiving a psychic message from a Liverpool cemetery. "You're really George, but right now Luna thinks you're Ringo."

I didn't want to get in a conversation on music with a troubled teen who listened to K-pop, not with my son staring at me intently. "Can I spend some time alone with Marley?"

Denise excused herself, and I sat with Marley for an hour. We didn't say a word. We didn't have to. As I walked into the parking garage, I saw a Subaru with its lights off and a figure inside. It must be Luna. She was waiting for me to leave before she hurried back up to sit with Marley.

Luna wasn't ready to see me yet? Suddenly I knew I wasn't ready to see her yet either.

26. Beep Beep

May 29, 2018

The next morning, just as I got into the Focus to drive to work, I received a phone call from a New Mexico state government office. I was surprised that it came from Mary Alice Forrest herself, the attorney general.

"We have a new offer for you," she said in a very serious voice.

"What's that?"

"Your client gets probation on the charges he's already got, and we drop the third charge. He also has to testify against Dragon Moon when we go after them."

"I will convey the offer to him. What happens if he doesn't take it?"

"He had two prior felony charges that were converted into to a single charge for the purposes of a plea. Using the habitual offender enhancement statutes, we can give him up to twenty years. Plus, we are thinking of going after him Federally."

I grimaced. I wasn't a Federal lawyer, but they could stack a few more years on top of the twenty years he was doing in state court. A plea to probation sure sounded nice.

"Dan, I urge you to take this deal," she said. "You've been on a bad streak for the last few years. You never got your mojo back after Sam Marlow's trial."

"I have been through a lot," I agreed, thinking of my stint on the breakdown docket.

"As attorney general, I get to read all your docketing statements." She was referring to short summaries of trials that I lost that I filed with the court of appeals. "You're a great lawyer and a great writer, but you're a terrible legal writer. We email your docketing statements around the offices as training. Our beginning lawyers have to find every one of your mistakes as an exercise in issue spotting."

That hurt. "I just want to get the summary of the facts and issues out and let the appellate lawyers do the heavy lifting," I said.

"How's Luna?" she asked, changing subjects. "You should have her proof-read your work. She's the real lawyer in the family."

"I'm driving right now," I said. "I can't really hear you." Then I hung up. I had planned to drive to the Los Alamos county lock-up to visit Cage, but when I called the jail to check on him, the jail receptionist told me that he had been moved to a facility in Otero County. I didn't know whether that was a good thing.

• • •

A few hours later I was on Route 380 eastbound, deep into the desert, passing the turn-off to the Trinity site. It was 209 miles from Albuquerque to Alamogordo. When I hit the Alamogordo city limits I exited for the relief route, the two lane "beltway" around downtown. As someone who grew up in DC, I laughed that these two lanes within a few hundred yards of this small town would be anyone's definition of a belt, much less a way. Still, it was a relief not to pass through White Sands Boulevard, the congested main drag.

At the south end of town, Google Maps directed me to take the exit on US 70 toward White Sands National Monument. Unfortunately, as the town gave way to desert, I missed the turn-off for the Otero County Detention Center. When I saw Holloman Air Force Base on the edge of the White Sands dunes, I knew I had gone too far. Holloman looked like it was in Afghanistan Adjacent. Several war movies had been filmed here, including one of the Transformer films.

I Mapquested the Otero County Detention Center again, and made a U-turn at the edge of the base. Thankfully, the guard didn't have to use his AK-47. I headed east and found the place. Damn, I needed to learn how to make my thimble work while I was driving.

Unfortunately, when I arrived at the detention center the small woman at the front desk informed me that Cage had just been moved to the Otero County *Correctional* Facility, which was fifty miles south on Highway 54, in a place called Chapparal near the state line. Correctional as opposed to detention. Was it better to be detained or corrected?

"You're the Rattlesnake Lawyer, right?" the small woman asked.

"I was. The Culebra Abogado."

"My name is Haydn, you represented my pops here a few years back. You saved his life by getting him into treatment."

I vaguely remembered her father from my conflict contract days. Haydn had been a gorgeous convenience store clerk in Carrizozo then, and today she looked quite professional.

"You look good in uniform," I said.

She smiled. "I'll call ahead," she said.

"How's your father doing?" I asked.

"It's been a long time. He's dead now, but he was out of custody when he died. He got a real funeral, not thrown in some hole in the desert. That's a victory at least."

Some victory.

• • •

I headed south on the four lanes of US 54 through some

of the most inhospitable country I had ever seen. Per Wikipedia, this was the northernmost reach of the Chihuahuan desert. Other parts of the state looked either like Mars or the moon. Considering the incredible heat emanating from the gigantic sun, this stretch might as well be Mercury, the hottest planet in the solar system. Some military vehicles passed me on the road, while a few turned off onto vaguely marked military sites that were part of nearby Fort Bliss. I did not see a single tree nor a blade of grass.

Chapparal meant roadrunner in Spanish and further googling revealed that this Chapparal wasn't a town. Instead, it was a "census designated place." More roadrunners than people lived here, spread out over the vast desert.

I couldn't miss the gray boxes that suddenly popped out of the horizon. This hulking facility with several layers of barbed wire could be the prison for evil mutant foes of the X-men. This facility apparently was supposed to correct all kinds of people, from Federal terrorist suspects to the overflow of drunks from the county jail to the north.

Haydn, the receptionist at the Otero County Detention Center, had told staff here that the *Culebra Abogado* was coming. She must have raved about me, as I wasn't frisked by the wiry correctional officer. He was about to let me pass until he saw the thimble.

"What's that silver thing on your finger?" he asked.

"My fingertip was damaged when an automatic jail door slammed shut," I said, somewhat seriously. "After I sued, this was the bionic replacement."

"Okay, you can keep it," he said. "We'll try not to slam a door on you."

I waited in a small windowless room until the guard brought Cage out. He wore an orange jumpsuit from Los Alamos County Detention Center and based on the smell, it should have been treated by a radioactive hazmat team. The CO held his nose when he shut the door behind us.

Cage smiled when he saw the thimble.

"Finally," he said. "We can use that to work on the case right now."

"Before we start, I have to convey a plea offer from the attorney general. You get probation on the two charges you've already been convicted of, and the third one is dropped. Plus, you testify against Dragon Moon. If not, they can use your convictions to give you twenty years, and maybe more, if they turn it over to the Feds."

"Twenty years? I can't do that. Plus, call it honor, call it my code, call it whatever, but I don't testify against anyone else."

"You humiliated me up there," I said. "That was the worst moment of my legal career. You say you don't leave a brother behind, but you left me there to die in front of twelve people and two alternates. Throw me a bone. You don't have to testify again, but give me a hand."

"I'll show you how to work the thimble."

"That's a start."

Cage gave me a quick crash course. He demonstrated a few arm movements and body English that were apparently needed as well. Then he made it a point to turn ninety degrees and repeat the same sequence.

"Now you try," he said.

After several attempts to copy an elaborate series of hand movements with direct thrusts, and left jabs, he started to laugh. I finally got the joke. "You're making me do the hand movements to Coordination Set."

"You fell for it," he said, joining in my laughter. "But the angle of the thimble really does matter in terms of how wide or narrow the search is."

He grabbed my hand and bent it nearly all the way back to make the thimble do a search. Suddenly Albert Jackson Cage's complete legal history appeared on the wall.

"Now you've got it," he said. "Now point at the last paragraph."

I focused the thimble on a paragraph displayed on the wall. I spread my fingers as Cage had demonstrated. The display now posted Cage's indictment in this case. The display was brief—only one charge for this final trial, conspiracy to receive stolen property.

"I've never had a conspiracy to receive stolen property case before," I said. "You met with a guy who planned to give you stolen property? Tell me what happened."

Cage paused, and for a moment I though he wasn't going to say anything. Then he said, "Well, I got a text from someone-- someone from Dragon Moon because it came from a thimblewho told me to meet with a guy named Roman Ulibarri to pick up a new thimble prototype when I was doing a run down to the Playas site. Roman was going to sell me the magic thimble."

"What's the magic thimble?"

"It's something a scientist, a Dr. Yu at the labs had just come up with at the Los Alamos labs—it can be controlled with brain waves. It was way beyond the thimbles we already have at Dragon Moon, which are basically small smart phones. And, I was just supposed to pick one up."

For one moment, that almost seemed plausible, almost seemed innocent. A supervisor tells an employee to meet someone to check out a new tool for work, sort of like getting a new iPhone from your buddy who works at the Apple store before it comes out. I did that myself one time for my boss, and I didn't ask the buddy how he got the phone.

But then I realized he said the phrase "someone from Dragon Moon."

"Why didn't you know for sure who it was?"

"The text came from an unknown thimble. Kirlian used a lot of different thimbles, but because of the digits at the end, I figured it was one of ours. It's not like anyone else has one."

"Can we look up the text itself?"

"Just say, thimble display text on so and so date."

I used the thimble to find the texts in the vast trove of evidence. The text said MEET ROMAN ULIBARRI AT PLAYAS SITE, along with some follow-up confirmation texts.

"You don't know for sure that it was Kirlian?"

"I'm pretty sure it had to be him, or someone working for him. Kirlian would have access to my thimble via his."

The smell in the room suddenly grew worse, as if his thoughts were activating sweat glands. Was Cage lying?

"Did you know the magic thimble prototype was stolen before you tried to buy it?"

He waited a second, a guilty second. "If I didn't know for sure that it was stolen," he said, "they can't charge me with conspiracy, can they?"

"Let me check. Thimble, display New Mexico statute for conspiracy to receive stolen property." I used the thimble to scroll to the statute that Cage was being charged under. "The statute says you knew, or should have known, the thimble was stolen. Should you have known that this new magic thimble prototype was stolen?"

He didn't say anything.

"How did this other guy, Roman Ulibarri, get the magic thimble from a scientist at the lab?"

Cage maintained his silence.

I opened my fingers and asked the thimble to "display criminal complaint" to find the actual police report from the file. "It says here that this janitor, Roman Ulibarri, taped the conversation with you, described this advanced piece of technology, and said you definitely should have known that it was stolen when you agreed to pay for it."

"It's pronounced Ro-*man*," he said, putting the emphasis on the second syllable. "Isn't it illegal to tape me?"

"The state can get around it, if the other party had a thimble that could record and you had a thimble that could record, the state would argue that you had the assumption of risk that you were being recorded."

"Well, I thought I was doing a deal with Roman that was part of my job."

"Just following orders as part of your business."

"That's it exactly."

"Okay, once again, did you know that Ro-man had stolen the new, improved, magical thimble?"

Cage frowned. "I was set up."

"We have a trial in a week and I don't want to look like a complete asshole. Who is this Roman, this janitor who tried to sell you the magic thimble that you claim you didn't know was stolen from the most secure lab facility on earth?"

He thought for a moment. "Roman Ulibarri was a janitor at the lab who did handyman work for some of the scientists at their homes. These science guys aren't particularly handy. So, I figured he had permission."

"How do you know him?"

"He used to load and unload some of the trucks up there."

"Where did you meet, exactly?"

"We met in a café by the Playas site. He was visiting his sick mom over on the other side of the border in Palomas, or somewhere near there. Roman told me that he was doing some work for a scientist at his house, handyman stuff, for a Dr. Yu. He got something from Yu that I might find valuable. Like I said, he told me it was cool."

"It was cool?"

"It was cool. I didn't ask any questions."

"But you were doing this as part of your job, or at least you thought that, because someone from your employer texted you, right?"

"I guess so."

"That's called entrapment," I said. At least I thought it was called entrapment. I had lost confidence in my legal abilities after the conversation with Mary Alice.

Before we could go any further, the CO came in without knocking. Cage covered my thimble with his left hand, and everything on the wall vanished before the CO noticed anything amiss.

The CO frowned. "It's lockdown. This meeting is over."

I was left alone in the room after the guard took Cage back. But, I felt a glimmer of hope. At least I had a tool.

Yahima was waiting outside in the lobby as I left. "Please get my husband out."

"I'll do what I can, but I can't help him if he won't let me."

"I'll tell him that."

"Please do, because unless he tells me what's really going on, you're going to spend the rest of your life seeing him in places like this."

"I will visit my husband wherever, forever. Wouldn't your

wife do that for you?"

I didn't have an answer to that.

• • •

When I left the correctional facility, Mapquest directed me to head west over a ridge to meet up with the interstate through Las Cruces. Unfortunately, I was lost the minute I hit my first roundabout in the desert. Roundabouts belonged in quaint New England towns with white churches; not in census designated places like Chapparal with correctional facilities.

This census designated place wasn't quite desert, not quite rural, and barely a place. Mobile homes were spread randomly through the area, along with the occasional gas station and Family Dollar store. I lost my bearings by the second roundabout and third Family Dollar.

An hour and three more roundabouts later, I ended up over the border in a strange land where I realized I was no longer a licensed attorney. Yes, I was in Texas. Thankfully, it was not that hard to cross back into New Mexico, and I didn't need a passport. I found my way onto the interstate and was home a few hours later.

27. Honeymoon Suite

May 31, 2018

Luna ignored my texts the next day, and for some reason there were no visiting hours at the hospital. It was on lockdown, just like a jail. I didn't know if there was a quarantine or a shooting. In Albuquerque, it could be both.

I never heard when the hospital re-opened for visitors, but Luna worked her magic to get in to see Marley. I don't know whether she flashed her bar card or her mother card. When Luna finally called me from the Hotel Chaco the next night, she had already eaten at the hospital with Marley and didn't want to meet me for dinner. She waited a long, long moment, though, before she gave me her room number.

Luna wanted to see me again? I jumped into the shower and smothered myself with cologne. Then I changed into my nicest jeans and a polo shirt that she had bought for me at an outlet store on a road trip. She'd told me that it was the "ultimate shirt." This ultimate shirt was either blue or black depending on the light, and had an actual polo logo on it, not a dragon, thank god. I hoped she still liked it. I wanted to look good for Luna while she was still legally my wife.

I had trouble tucking in the ultimate shirt. It didn't want to stay put. "In, out, in out, pick one and go with it," was a saying in our family when it came to untucked shirts.

I went with "in," and eventually the shirt complied.

The Hotel Chaco was brand new and was now ranked number one with a bullet for Albuquerque hotels on TripAdvisor. I did love the mix of ancient and ultra-modern. When Luna opened the door to the room, she was dressed in a blue sweatshirt that had both Korean and English lettering on it. It showed a Laser Geisha holding a light blue light saber, and she was firing a beam over her left shoulder. The fiery caption on the shirt said LASER GEISHA BLUE, but the blue was crossed out and replaced with the scribbled letter spelling out TURQUOISE.

At first I thought the word had been scribbled by a child, but I realized that the anime female warrior in the middle—presumably Laser Geisha Blue--was indeed made of turquoise. This was some kind of ironic Asian anime shirt, popular with the smart young set in Seoul."Jen gave it to me," she said. "Apparently, her Asian adventure is nearing its end."

I didn't want to tell her what Denise had told me, that Jen might be adventuring in a mental hospital. Luna glanced at her phone. She had one of those screensavers that alternated backgrounds. The first scene showed her father the doctor, taking her temperature when she was seven. The second scene showed her holding up baby Marley. I waited for a third scene that showed me, but the picture reverted to the one of her father. I wasn't on her phone or in her life.

Before I could hug Luna, she put up a hand to stop me. "You don't want to catch my insomnia," she said. "Stay right there."

Luna opened the mini-bar and brought out an exotic brand of tequila, and after a few seconds of blending, created the world's ultimate margarita that put the authentic one from the Pink Store to shame. "It's my own invention, it's called a turquoise geisha of course. By the way, I love that shirt. It's very thoughtful of you."

I loved being called thoughtful for a change. I smiled. After pouring a turquoise geisha for herself, we clanged glasses.

"To Marley's good health," she said.

"To Marley!"

The drink was sweet and salty with a surprising kick at the end, kinda like Luna.

"So, Laser Geisha Turquoise, what's next?"

"I'm entering the case," she said.

"Which case?"

"State v. Albert Jackson Cage."

"Isn't there a conflict of interest with Laser Geisha Turquoise involved in litigation with Albert Jackson Cage's employer?"

She handed me an entry of appearance and a brief that waived defense co-counsel's appearance of impropriety. "I wrote this on the plane."

"I'm impressed."

"I reviewed what's happened so far on the nmcourts.com website. You need my help. You're lost. Admit it."

I was embarrassed, but she was right. I needed all the help I could get. I remembered what the attorney general had said about my needing Luna. She had been right. I looked around the honeymoon suite. It might have been a partner's office of a big Albuquerque firm—law books and documents mixed with Native American pottery. Luna was having a honeymoon with the law.

"I admit it," I said. "I am lost in so many ways. I do need your help."

"You might think that this simple conspiracy to receive stolen property case is nothing, but it's the way we take down Dragon Moon. This really is the most important case you've ever had."

"I've represented murderers."

"Dragon Moon has murdered people before, and they'll murder again if we don't stop them."

"Why do you hate Dragon Moon so much?"

"You know the story of my father." She pointed to the image of the man on her phone. "He was a small-town doctor in Crater, New Mexico, but he got involved with people who were then called the Mensa Mafia. Those people later became Dragon Moon. They got him involved in an illegal prescription drug ring while we were still in Crater. At first, he did it to help poor people who couldn't get the drugs they needed, but he got in so deep that he had to fake his own death to protect his family. He hid from us, moved to Mexico, and then re-married and raised Selena and Mia. I guess he had a taste of the good life and built an empire. When I found him again, his little empire came crashing down and he spent the rest of his life in prison. It was a wasted life."

To Luna, having a wasted life was worse than a venereal disease. I was wasting my life, Dew was about to waste hers, and she would be damned if she couldn't save Marley from wasting his in a hospital suite.

"I know all of that. So, you blame the Mensa Mafia—which ultimately became Dragon Moon—for taking your dad away from you, for him leaving your mom?"

"It's more than that. I don't want the same thing that happened to my dad to happen to me. I want to be there for my son for my entire life. I want to be someone he can be proud of. You have no idea how badly I want to take down these bastards."

"I don't necessarily want to take down Dragon Moon. I want to save my client, but Cage is being set up. What should we do to save him?"

"What's your theory of the case?"

"Entrapment. Dragon Moon set him up. He gets a text, presumably from someone working for his employer—either

Kirlian or someone working for Kirlian—and the text directs him to buy the new magic thimble prototype from Dr. Yu, and don't ask if its stolen."

She laughed at me. "You understand that you can't be entrapped by a private party, it has to be state action. You also have to file a motion in the first week if you intend to use entrapment, and you didn't do that."

"Oh yeah. I guess you're right." I felt the color drain out of the ultimate polo shirt.

"What about duress?" she asked.

"Doesn't duress mean that you commit a crime because you're afraid for your life?"

"You should know that cold. I don't know if I can love a man who doesn't know the difference between entrapment and duress."

I couldn't tell if she was being serious. "Then you're saying he was under threat of death by Dragon Moon?"

"Do you have any idea how vicious Dragon Moon is?"

"I guess not. How do we find that out?"

She pointed to the mass of documents that she had printed. "We need to interview Dr. Yu, the Los Alamos scientist who invented the thimble. We also need to talk to Roman Ulibarri, the witness who allegedly stole the property and conspired with Cage. Roman Ulibarri's charges were dropped and he got an immunity deal to testify against Albert Jackson Cage. Don't you research your cases?"

"I hadn't gotten around to it," I said. I really was a bad lawyer. "But I can do that now. Watch this!" I took out my thimble and put it on my finger. Using my newfound thimble skills, I managed to find the immunity agreement and project it onto the wall.

We read the agreement together. The attorney general of

New Mexico had given Roman Ulibarri total immunity, meaning all pending charges would be dropped if he testified against Cage and provided truthful testimony in all cases involving the Dragon Moon corporation.

Luna's eyes lit up. I could see her calculating stock values in her head.

"Show me more," she said, taking a gulp from her drink.

Over the next fifteen minutes, I proceeded to demonstrate how all her printed piles of paper could be shrunk to the size of the thimble.

"Why did I ever leave you?" she said, looking at more files that involved Dragon Moon.

"Do you love me or my thimble?"

"Both. That thing's incredible. You're pretty good with your fingers."

She smiled at me. Almost fifty, wearing an oversized anime sweatshirt with gray streaks in her hair and eyes that hadn't seen sleep in days, Luna was the sexiest thing I'd ever seen. She touched my shoulder.

"Maybe I can stay the night?" I asked. "This *is* the honeymoon suite."

"Let's see what happens tomorrow."

"Should I pick you up?"

"I'll drive," she said. "I'll pick you up at six in the morning. You've heard of honeymoon in Las Vegas? We can honeymoon in Los Alamos."

I couldn't wait.

28. Subpoena Envy

June 1, 2018

The next morning, Friday, Luna met me at the base of the building, right on Central Avenue. She even had a thermos of delicious coffee for me after I belted myself in.

"I got this from India," she said. "It's called Kama Sutra coffee."

She moved the car forward before I could come up with a witty reply, but damn this coffee tasted good. Best coffee ever!

"Dew and Denise don't have summer school today, so they're staying with Marley. Selena can take the late shift." I hadn't asked, but Luna wanted to make damn sure I knew that she would never leave our son alone.

She drove us in her Subaru to the Los Alamos National Laboratory (LANL) to meet Professor Yu and Roman Ulibarri. When we arrived at the main gate of LANL, Luna showed two witness subpoenas that had been signed by Judge Chairez. Luna must have magical powers if she got the subpoena papers signed so quickly. I had subpoena envy.

The guard printed up the LANL "short time" passes. "So here's a pass for Dan Shepard and Luna Cruz to visit two people on site. You have one hour, if you stay one minute longer these badges will self-destruct."

"Seriously?" I asked.

"I don't know," he said. "No one with a temp badge has ever stayed here more than an hour."

"Thanks," Luna said.

"Go see Dr. Yu first," the guard said and directed us to a big, open lot, which offered parking for technical areas 200-250. Some buildings had names, and some had numbers. My gut instinct was that the numbered buildings were where people did research they didn't want to put their names on.

This part of LANL was near the mountains, but felt more like a factory than an alpine college campus. After a few wrong turns and a polite, but firm, encounter with security, we arrived at the correct building. When we opened the door to a big warehouse. Inside, a surprisingly short but heavily armed guard in a tan uniform escorted us toward a small office at the end of the first-floor hallway. Strange sounds came from the other side of the wall. It sounded like they were testing smaller versions of the A-bomb inside the mop closet.

Along the way, Colonel Herring passed by with two military escorts. Her blue Air Force camouflage uniform made her ridiculously conspicuous against the plain walls of the building. She eyed me strangely, but otherwise ignored me. She hugged Luna.

"Hope to see you at the board meeting," she said to Luna.

"Hope so too," Luna replied.

"What was that about? I asked.

"She wants my votes."

After the Colonel had left the hallway, the short guard opened the door, as if onlhy one door could be open at a time. Inside, we encountered Professor Yu, wiping his eyes. In his thirties, he had a long black beard and looked as if he hadn't slept for days, just like a hardcore PlayStation gamer. I had thought my living space messy, but at least mine wasn't filled with hazardous waste containers right next to an unmade cot.

"I'm Luna Cruz," said. She had conspicuously cut off the third name on her badge, my name. "I have a subpoena to interview you, Dr. Yu."

"I'm Dan Shepard," I said when he looked at me as if I was Luna's driver. "I'm an attorney."

"Dr. Yu." He didn't bother to shake hands, but he commented on my thimble immediately. "I invented that," he said. He seemed reluctant to say anything more, but Laser Geisha Turquoise turned on the charm. She touched him on the shoulder, and it was as if her touch was a Vulcan nerve pinch designed to persuade instead of stun.

"May we see the latest version of the thimble, the so-called magic thimble?" she asked, her hand still on his shoulder. Her rendition of the Vulcan nerve pinch worked wonders on this lonely scientist.

He took us down the hallway to a windowless room the size of a squash court, half of which was occupied by a giant computer server. He then opened a receptacle on the mainframe and took out a metal skullcap, the size of a yarmulke, which was connected by wires to the mainframe.

"Do we need clearance to see this?" I asked.

He shrugged as if he didn't care whether he was supposed to show this to us or not. He closed his eyes. No sound came from the wires. In a few seconds a blank holographic sphere the size of a basketball appeared in the middle of the room.

"That's incredible," I said.

"Not really," He said his eyes still closed. "I can only do that in this room, with a direct connection to that massive server directly behind me. They lose electricity in Espanola, down the valley, whenever I turn it on."

"And Roman the janitor stole your technology from this building?" I asked. Security was tight at LANL. This wasn't an aisle at an Albuquerque Walmart. You couldn't shoplift the gigantic mainframe, or even the skullcap with all its wires by slipping it into your pocket.

"Not exactly," Dr. Yu said. "Roman stole a prototype from my house in White Rock, it's a suburb near here. Roman stole the magic thimble."

He said the words "magic thimble" as if they were in a foreign language.

"How did Dragon Moon get involved?" Luna asked.

"I made a deal with Dragon Moon regarding the first thimble prototype, and the first prototype only, which I was legally able to do under my contract with the lab. That thimble you are wearing is already obsolete. My recent improvements on these models were not covered by the original patent for the older models."

"I've reviewed your patent applications," Luna said. Was she bluffing? "So what is the magic thimble?"

On the mainframe, he pointed to an unframed picture of a young Asian boy with glasses beneath wild black hair. The kid just looked smart. "That's my son, Hikaru," he said. "A Japanese name, I know. We named him after Mr. Sulu on *Star Trek*. My Hikaru came up with the idea to calculate the various probable outcomes for all New Mexico court cases. With the new thimble, the magic thimble, we can revolutionize the practice of law."

"The shoftim system," I said, hoping I impressed Luna with my research. "With the magic thimble, attorneys can decide whether to plead or take a case to trial, right?"

"That's only the beginning. Someday we won't need attorneys at all. No offense."

"None taken," Luna said. "Can we see it in action?"

Yu closed his eyes and concentrated. First, a hologram cube appeared in the center of the room, about three feet off the ground. The cube was about the size of a banker's box. The box showed a still image of his house, a modest home in the Los Alamos suburb of White Rock, which was on the next mesa over.

His eyes still closed, his brow even more furrowed, he said. "Thimble show interior. The image of the outside of the house faded into an image of the inside of his garage workshop where he was working on something with a soldering iron. Nearby, a figure was moving some large boxes. Near the image of the man was a label that read ROMAN in funky letters. The computer-created images looked like clay figures in non-descript clothing, like that Taiwanese animation company that produced humorous YouTube videos. Still, seeing these three-dimensional figures projected holographically in thin air was impressive. Who knew what the possibilities would be a hundred years into the future?

Yu was excited by his own creation and talked rapidly. The thimble now displayed Kirlian's home in relation to Yu's. Did he direct it to do that with his brainwaves? The animation showed Roman talking, and Kirlian walking to Yu's garage. The small hologram of Yu demonstrated the thimble, and Kirlian shook his hand.

"Roman must have given him five sample thimble prototypes before Kirlian finally signed the deal," Dr. Yu said out loud.

A flat two-dimensional image showed a contract with the Dragon Moon Corporation signed by Yu and Kirlian.

Luna looked over the contract in the air. She tried to touch it, but her hand went right through it without disturbing the image.

"Dr. Yu," she said, her hand still in the middle of the document, as if trying to download it by osmosis. "We are only interested in a theft of the latest prototype, the so-called magic thimble allegedly taken from your house by Roman Ulibarri."

Yu now used the thimble to display another holographic video of the same garage. Startled, Luna removed her hand from the display. Had she received a small shock? She didn't say.

"I was having trouble with the magic thimble," Dr. Yu said, his eyes closed. The image of the thimble was now the size of a human head, but resembled a metallic black ski mask with several random eyeholes. A few small pieces of metal revolved around the thimble. I thought of one of those IKEA instruction guides, as Yu demonstrated how each part would fit onto the thimble.

"A few of the tiny pieces fell off and my solder stopped working," he said. "Roman volunteered to take the thimble and solder the pieces onto it, because he has very good hand-eye coordination. After he took my thimble, I never saw it again."

The hologram showed Roman taking the thimble away

"So, he had permission to take the magic thimble?"

"He did, but he was supposed to bring it back the next day with the parts soldered on."

The image now showed Roman driving away in an old car. A final close-up of his face showed him smile. Yu opened his eyes, and the image disappeared with one last, fleeting glimpse of Roman's Cheshire grin.

Luna looked at me. We weren't doing good cop bad cop; we were doing Coordination Set kata. She had done the inward and outward blocks and it was time for me to do the simultaneous kick and punch.

"Then it's possible that Roman thought he had authority to make another deal with Dragon Moon?" I asked. "Or with our client, Mr. Cage?"

"I suppose so," Yu said, "but I most certainly never gave him direct authority to sell it to a third party, even someone like Dragon Moon who I've dealt with before."

"Then it is possible that Cage did not know it was stolen when he met with Roman," I said.

Dr. Yu open his eyes and stared at the hologram in the middle. It had become a cloud. He looked winded. Maybe directing the image had expended considerable energy. He took three deep breaths before speaking. "I have no idea. I suppose so."

"Then there might not be a conspiracy to receive stolen property?" Luna asked, tagging in.

"I'm a scientist not a lawyer, but I suppose so."

Dr. Yu abruptly removed the skullcap. He placed it back in the receptacle on the mainframe, and touched the picture of his son, as if for luck. "That's it for the day."

"Where's Roman?" Luna asked. "We have a subpoena to talk to him as well."

"He's still working at the lab," he said. "It's a big lab, as you know. I make it a point to no longer have any contact with him. I must return to my work now. Good day, Mr. Shepard, Ms. Cruz."

I stared at the spot where the hologram had appeared. I could still see an afterimage of Roman's grin when I closed my eyes.

29. All Roads Leads to Roman

Our one hour had flown by and when we exited Yu's building the guard told us that our time had expired. After sending and receiving a few texts on his phone, the guard informed us that we could meet Roman outside the LANL gate at the end of his shift at five. Neither of use wanted to tempt LANL security, so we drove past the gate house and parked by the side of the road, near the bridge over the canyon. Whenever the ground shook from a test inside the lab, I worried that we'd fall into the canyon below.

While we waited, Luna and I talked about life, about dreams and her fears for both Dew and Marley. She worried that it was already too late for Dew, but didn't explain what she meant.

Selena sat with Marley at UNM hospital and Luna had been calling every half hour or so to check in. "He's fine!" Selena yelled through the phone. I could hear her clearly, even though Luna had the speaker function turned off. "He will heal better if the phone doesn't ring all the time."

Luna sighed and we waited some more. At precisely five o'clock on a Friday, the worker bees started heading home to Santa Fe and Espanola. LANL might be the home of the most brilliant scientists in the world, but it also had an army of janitors, carpenters, and security workers who were just regular Joes, or, since most came from northern New Mexico, regular Jose's. Most couldn't afford to live up here on the hill.

Luna texted Roman to meet us outside the main gate, and he texted back that he was driving a beat-up Chevy Malibu with a racing stripe. Luna stood on the side of the road and as soon as she saw him, flagged him down by waving at him. He pulled over to a shoulder on the edge of the cliff, and she walked to his vehicle. I strained my ears toward his car, couldn't hear their conversation.

Luna came back to the car, smiling. "He said to meet him at Buffalo Thunder."

. . .

Roman didn't wait for us to turn around. He took off like a LANL laser beam and crossed the bridge over the steep canyon. I did my best to keep up, but we were in Luna's Subaru. Traffic wasn't bad as we went through town, and as we passed the Hilton Garden Inn at the top of the mesa, I realized a motorcycle was following us. Not just *a* motorcycle, *the* motorcycle.

"It's Mia," I said. "That's the same helmet she wore before."

Luna glanced out her rearview mirror. "Are you sure?"

We sped up and passed a truck. The motorcycle sped up and passed a truck. "Yes. Why would she follow us?" I asked.

"She probably thinks we have the new, improved thimble and wants to see what we are doing with it. But here's the most important thing to remember about Mia, other than that she's my half-sister . . ."

"What's that?"

"She's crazy. She does not act logically."

"That runs in the family."

She didn't laugh. "Seriously. She changes her moods like the wind."

"Denise said that she's possessed."

"Denise said that?"

"We actually had a conversation. Denise is an expert on the paranormal and she thinks Mia is possessed by an evil geisha spirit."

"She's right. My half-sister probably suffers from

dissociative identity disorder. What you would call multiple personalities. One of those personalities is clearly evil."

As if on cue, we passed the *decanso* where Kent Dorfman, the original attorney on the case, had driven off the cliff to his death, presumably after being forced off the road by one of Mia's evil personalities. Roman's Malibu went even faster, weaving dangerously in and out of traffic. The motorcycle was now just two cars behind us.

The Subaru was excellent on the turns. We passed a few more dinosaur cars, but the motorcycle kept coming, passing other cars on the curves and crossing the double lines.

There were some mysterious flatbed vehicles with hazardous waste markings on their payload of large cylinders. These might be the Waste Isolation Pilot Project (WIPP) trucks that took nuclear waste from Los Alamos down to underground storage in Carlsbad. WIPP trucks were only supposed to drive at night, I thought. Then again, those cylinders could be either nuclear warheads or evil nanobots in this neck of the woods.

I did some quick passes on double lines myself, narrowly missing a WIPP truck heading uphill.

"You're good," she said.

"Thanks," I said as I negotiated another quick pass.

Maybe it was all the driving I had been doing lately, or perhaps my nerves had been steadied by martial arts. I stepped on the gas.

Luna grabbed my bicep, and I found I was shaking. After her touch, I stopped the shaking and tightened my grip on the wheel. After a quick pass of another WIPP truck, I slowed down at the closest thing to a straightaway. There were two WIPP trucks ahead, and I didn't want to pass them both. The motorcycle came closer. Finally, we came to the bridge over the Rio Grande. One of the trucks in front of us must have stalled, as the brake lights and hazard blinkers came on as it dramatically reduced speed.

I slammed on my brakes and managed to avoid the vehicle. Mia swerved to avoid us, but ended up plunging into the shallow, stony waters of this northern stretch of the Rio Grande. The motorcycle exploded, and an ash landed on a cylinder of the truck still in front of us and Luna and I both held our breath.

Thankfully, the ash went out.

We pulled to the shoulder and stopped. "Should we stay to talk to the cops?" I asked.

"What do you think?"

I drove over the bridge to the other side. The tangled wreckage of the bike was smoking in the cool waters of the Rio Grande. We didn't see Mia. She could be alive, but we really didn't want to stay and find out.

30. Thunder Down Under

The Buffalo Thunder casino, a few miles to the south, was in Pojoaque, but not really of Pojoaque. It was run by the Hilton Hotel chain. Presumably the casino got its name because a million buffalo made the sound of thunder as they stampeded across the open range. This massive resort was hardly the place for cowboys or buffalo boys; the only open range here was the resort's verdant golf course.

The Australian male revue, The Thunder Down Under, was playing the casino ballroom tonight so the parking lot was filled with giddy female patrons, killing time before the show started.

Thunder and lightning rumbled in my own gut as we pulled into the casino parking lot. The last time I had been here had been for a state bench and bar meeting. I was one of three lawyers who manned a booth sponsored by the state bar exhibiting our photography of New Mexico. I viewed it as a great honor by my peers. But Luna did not, and kept texting me that I shouldn't be there, screwing around with my hobby.

At the booth, I displayed some of the photos that I had taken in my travels on the breakdown docket. I was so proud when a justice of the New Mexico Supreme Court bought a photo I had taken of a sunset over Sierra Blanca reflected in the lake below. A district attorney of an outlying jurisdiction also liked my photo of a rainbow over a miniature golf course castle.

"That's amazing," the district attorney had said. "You could be a professional photographer. Can I buy it for my daughter?"

The magic of that special day faded on Luna's third phone call, the first one I had answered. "I need you here now!" she had said. "Right now!"

At first I thought she was being cruel, especially as another justice of the supreme court was looking at my photo of the turning leaves in the Sandia mountains.

"But this is my passion!"

"You don't have time for passion. You need to focus on law."

"I need to focus on something I'm good at."

"You don't have that option. I need you here, right now. I'm worried about something."

The senior partner at the largest civil rights firm in New Mexico, a firm that recently won a fifteen-million dollar police brutality verdict on a contingency fee, liked a photo of a sunrise over Exit 263 and wanted an autographed print. "You have an amazing eye," she said. "You really know the state."

I hung up on Luna.

When the phone rang for a fourth time, I deliberately turned it off and kept it off. I didn't call Luna until I was heading home. Luna, however, wasn't home when I arrived. A note read that she was at the hospital with Marley, and she wasn't sure that he was going to make it. That was the first of many hospital visits for my son.

Back in the present, we entered the resort and found Roman sitting by the pool. He had a shaved head and big muscles. We followed him to the wedding chapel, which looked like a white version of Georgia O'Keeffe's painting of the Ranchos Church, and sat at a bench facing the golf course.

Luna smiled at me. I smiled back. Even though this was an ersatz version of the Ranchos Church set on a golf course next to a casino/resort run by Hyatt, I felt the heartbeat of

New Mexico here. Well, I felt the heartbeat of Luna.

Luna did her Luna thing: a spoonful of sugar to make the interrogation go down. She had once joked that as a woman of a certain age, she was a "cougar" to young men like Roman. Roman was a handsome man who had charmed many female scientists, and when he smiled at Luna, we all knew he was looking for another conquest.

She had already done considerable research while we were waiting in the car in between her phone calls to the hospital. "Your charge was dropped so you could testify against Cage, right?" she asked Roman.

"That's correct," he said, "and the attorney general's office pulled some strings so I could keep my job at LANL until this blows over."

"I'd like to hear your side of the story," she touched his shoulder.

Roman gave a convoluted story that was identical to Yu's. He had frequently delivered thimble prototypes to Kirlian. But, he was vague on whether he had permission to take that final prototype—the magic thimble—from the garage and sell it to Cage.

Luna was ready. She produced a copy of the first contract between Yu and Dragon Moon. She was trying to convince Roman that he didn't legally embezzle the magic thimble prototype.

"You introduced Kirlian to Dr. Yu?"

"Yes, but—"

"That led to a binding contract regarding the original thimble."

"Yes, but—"

"You had permission to take the new, magic thimble?"

"Yes, but —"

"And you had done a prior deal with Kirlian?" she asked.

"Yes, but—"

"Kirlian, since he became chief counsel for Dragon Moon, is very hard to get a hold of."

"I guess so."

"But Albert Jackson Cage worked with Kirlian, correct?"

"Yes."

"Who set up the meeting?"

"I don't know. I got a text from an unknown number. It was from a thimble, so probably someone from Dragon Moon."

"Did Kirlian have access to a thimble?"

"He did."

"How would they know you had the thimble?"

"Word gets around. My wife says Los Alamos is like what do they call it-- a little sewing circle."

"So somehow the word got to Kirlian through the sewing circle that you had a stolen thimble?"

"It wasn't necessarily stolen at that time, but I'm sure he somehow found out that I had something he might find useful."

Damn, she was good. Time for Coordination Set again. I went in for the kill. "That means Kirlian probably texted Cage?"

"I have no way of knowing that, but sure, he could have done it."

"That means Cage might have thought this meeting was kosher."

"Kosher?" He didn't know the word.

"That the meeting was part of his job description," I said, "like you thought it was part of yours."

"Yeah, sure."

"That means Cage might not have known that the item was stolen when you guys had your meeting?"

Roman thought for a moment. He even stared at the chapel as if asking for divine intervention.

"I guess so," Roman said.

"Good question, Dan." Luna said. "Roman, let's talk about your immunity agreement. The attorney general's office wants you to make it look like this was some kind of illegal transaction, but it was perfectly legal, correct?"

"Yes."

"No conspiracy."

He shook his head. "No."

"No receiving?"

"No."

"No stolen property."

"I guess so."

I had to butt in. "Then why did you tape the conversation?"

He shrugged. "Just in case it wasn't, how you say, just in case it wasn't kosher."

One question too many. Luna frowned. She decided to take over.

"But, then again, the meeting could have been kosher."

"Yeah, sure. I wanted protection either way."

That was good enough for Luna. We shook hands with Roman and he excused himself and we sat on the bench next to the Buffalo Thunder wedding chapel. A Native American woman in a Buffalo Thunder uniform came over to us. "Are you the couple who wanted to renew their vows?"

· · ·

When we returned to the Subaru, Luna decided to drive. "We can win this one," she said. "They're trying to go forward on a conspiracy to receive stolen property on something that wasn't stolen and wasn't a conspiracy. We might not even have to do the duress defense. We can win on reasonable doubt."

"We're a great team," I said. "You've got that all on tape, right?"

She frowned. "I thought you were taping it," she said. "I can't think of everything."

I felt a herd of buffalo thunder through my veins. Maybe the thimble did effect my latent psychic abilities. I knew right then that something bad was going to go down. Luna dropped me off at the lofts. "Meet me at the hospital tomorrow."

31. *Family Affair*

June 2, 2018

I arrived at Marley's UNM hospital suite at nine the next morning, Saturday. Luna had already arrived but kept glancing at an iPad. Marley looked fantastic and seemed to be growing healthier before my eyes. Had there been a miracle in India? I didn't know that it was possible for him to grow so fast in just a few days, but it looked like he had sprouted at least an inch. His smile lit up the room, and when I walked in the door he did some karate chops in my direction. I hoped every chop took him one step closer to vanquishing his illness.

Dew and Denise had returned from their successful mock trial tour and practiced for the international competition in a corner. Denise was speaking, albeit softly. They nodded at me, but didn't get up.

There was a strange silence, and it took me a moment to realize why. There were no Beatles songs playing on the Muzak. That couldn't be a good thing.

"He's going to get out of the hospital next week, hopefully for good," Luna said to me, and then turned to Marley. "Are you ready for your life to finally begin?"

She went to our son and grasped his shoulder with her left hand. She then touched a finger to his finger, as if giving him the gift of life, just as God did to David in the Michelangelo painting.

"Marley, I'm doing all of this for you," she said. "I'm giving you a life."

I loved my son dearly, but I sensed that Luna loved him more. Luna loved him more than life itself and I had no doubt that she would give her life, her very soul, for this little boy.

I hoped it wouldn't come to that.

Marley looked like he was about to say something, but stopped himself. He then looked at me and did the inward and outward blocks of Coordination Set, which had become our private code. I wish I knew what he meant.

I did the inward block and then outward block right back at him. Was he going to talk?

No, not yet.

He was trying to communicate. I had an image in my mind of Marley saying his first words soon, real soon. And when he did, he was going to tell me the secrets of the universe and the meaning of life.

Then again, that could just be wishful thinking on my part.

· · ·

Luna was satisfied that Dew and Denise could keep Marley company, so we moved down to the UNM Children's Hospital lobby on the first floor. The lobby was modern, but cluttered with art designed to make children feel comfortable as possible. I wasn't sure how well it worked. Kids were crying all around us. I had always distrusted Muzak, but now there was no ambient noise whatsoever in the lobby. All the hospital noises, the tears, echoed through the lobby even more.

We wanted to sit, but every chair was occupied by nervous parents; most were checking their cell phones. This hospital served all comers, so it felt a little like the courthouse lobby where people continually checked on loved ones who had committed crimes.

A couple got up from the far side of the room and Luna and I dashed over. We spent the next few hours preparing for trial, interrupted only when Luna checked on Marley. She came back stronger after each break, as if she drew strength from him. We spent the first hour analyzing potential jurors, and the next writing questions for the two witnesses. Luna also had the entire corporate structure of Dragon Moon saved on her computer. Luna wanted to show that the alleged transaction was just business as usual and not a conspiracy. She first practiced her questions on me, and I tried to anticipate the witnesses' responses. Every moment I was with Luna, I realized that she was a far better lawyer than I would ever be.

After she had finished her questioning, she went through some mail that she had left in her briefcase. She opened one envelope to find the material witness warrant for her in a Federal case that involved Dragon Moon. It was signed by a Federal judge; a mandate that she show up for a deposition at the U.S. Federal Court Building in downtown Albuquerque. She got up and threw it in the trash.

"Shouldn't you deal with that?" I asked.

"What are they going to do, arrest me and throw me in jail?"

As someone who had spent a night in jail for contempt, I tried to convince her that as good a lawyer as she was, she was not above the law. The warrant was serious. But before I could complete my argument, Selena came in to the lobby with her new girlfriend, a friendly Navajo woman. Selena seemed excited. "Mia called again. About the proxy vote."

"Dan, we've got to deal with this," Luna said. "Kirlian is still trying to get Mia's proxy for the election." Luna touched her sister on the shoulder and the two of them walked to an elevator.

I knew Selena's new girlfriend, Heidietta Hawk, who sat down in the chair next to me. She was the sister of Heidi Hawk, the boxer.

"Selena was in love with my sister," Heidietta said, "and when my sister died, we found we had a lot in common, too."

"So, Selena went from one sister to the other? That's kind of odd."

"Your family is practically inbred compared to ours," Heidietta retorted.

After Luna and Selena went upstairs, Dew and Denise came down. "They kicked us out," Dew said. I wasn't sure whether it was Luna or hospital staff who had told them to come down.

"Since my mom won't help me, can you help us practice our direct examinations for mock trial?"

"Sure."

A Hispanic family had gathered round to hold a prayer circle next to us. Dew began cross-examining Denise using her courtroom voice. "Isn't it true?" she asked repeatedly.

The family asked us to keep it down. Like that was going to happen. We just moved to another corner. Dew was good, even though she tended to skip and go right for the juicy dramatic questions without laying a proper foundation. Denise's answers were still a little too short, but she was getting better.

"Use your mom as your model," I said to Dew. "She does her homework and lays the case out step by step."

"I prefer to be like my dad," she said. "People don't remember the little foundational things; they remember the big moments. I call them 'Marlow moments.'"

"What's a Marlow Moment?"

"It's when the truth is finally revealed."

"There are no Marlow moments in real life."

"Well, there should be," Dew said. "If you do your job right."

. . .

Luna and Selena joined us in the lobby hour later. "It's all going to work out!" Luna said.

"What's going to work out?"

"Everything. Marley's going to be fine, we're going to win the case, and we're going to take down Dragon Moon, In that order."

"Amen," I said. The prayer circle next to us contracted until it became a group hug. Our group looked at each other, well, why not?

"Prayer can't hurt," Luna said.

As we held hands, I looked around at the group and remembered what I said when I had taken my first road trip with Luna and Dew so many years ago, when we had camped out in a small hotel room near Carlsbad Caverns.

"Boy, are we a close family," I said.

"True enough," Selena said. "Luna, it's time for the family to step up. I think you need more time to prepare for trial. You might be better off going to Deming the night before the trial."

"I could, but I've got to be here with Marley as much as possible."

"Don't kill yourself if you don't have to. Heidietta and I will stay with Marley. Dew and Denise can practice here at nights. You need a break," Selena said.

"Are you sure?"

"You need to be relaxed for trial," Selena said. "You haven't slept in days. I know you can't sleep in a hospital room, and if you don't sleep, you're no good to anyone—not your son or your client."

Luna closed her eyes, as if she was psychically asking Marley or God for permission. She finally nodded at Selena before looking at me.

"Okay, then. Dan we're going to Deming tomorrow to get a good night's sleep before trial on Monday."

"One car or two?" I asked.

"One," she said.

· · ·

Sunday afternoon, as Luna and I drove south on I-25 toward Deming, she abruptly turned off on the Elephant Butte exit. Luna knew the perfect place to park where we could see the sunset light up the butte behind the reservoir. In that moment, the man-made lake nestled among mobile homes might have been Cabo San Lucas.

"We never had a honeymoon," she said.

"This is our rattlesnake honeymoon."

"Can you hear it?"

I heard the heartbeat of New Mexico. And then I realized that wasn't it. I had heard Luna's heartbeat all along. "I like our rattlesnake honeymoon. But are we going to go on to Deming?"

"Who said we're going to Deming tonight?"

We soon found ourselves at the Blackstone Inn in Truth or Consequences—in the Twilight Zone room.

Best night ever was in Room 7. We were in Room 7, of course.

32. Luna County

June 8, 2018

When I woke up the next morning, I found I'd had a good night's sleep for the first time since the shooting. I had once called Luna "asnoreable"—adorable while snoring. She certainly was asnoreable at this very moment. Everything was finally perfect. I didn't want to get out of bed to face any other truth or any other consequences.

Luna, however, woke up and smiled at me. "We've got to get to court. Let me use the bathroom first, I take longer."

"You're worth the wait."

The shower, I knew, had hot mineral waters coming out of one nozzle. Luna, of course, took longer than expected. After I showered, we changed into our power suits. I went with my rattlesnake boots and a power blue, excuse me, a power turquoise and black striped tie that Luna picked out for me. She went with the same combo, so we matched. Damn, we were cute.

"Laser Geisha Turquoise!" she shouted with pride at the mirror.

"And I'm the *Culebra Abogado*. Don't you mess with this crazy *vato*!"

• • •

Luna drove the Subaru across the last stretch of desert, and smiled when we crossed the Luna County line near the spinning turbines of the gigantic wind farm. The turbines were really spinning today.

"They named a whole county after you," I said.

"I would have picked another county," she said with a smile.

• • •

Twenty-six miles later, we arrived in downtown Deming and headed down a main drag of one story Victorian buildings. Luna parked by the old courthouse with its commanding tower, the one that had held the trial of Pancho Villa a hundred or so years earlier. It still said LUNA COUNTY COURTHOUSE on the side of the building, but it had been converted into a county governmental complex.

"You're a hundred years too late," I said as I directed her across the street to the new boring, modern brick building.

"I like the old courthouse better," she said. "It looks English, like a court of chancery or whatever they did in Queen Victoria's day. This new building looks like a bank designed by an out-of-state committee—columns in the front, adobe in the back. It has no soul."

"Hold on," I said. We had parked in the dirt parking lot. I listened again. It didn't matter. I could be anywhere and if I was with Luna, I could hear the heartbeat of New Mexico.

"What's wrong?" she asked.

"Absolutely nothing."

"By the way, did you bring your padfolio?"

"I didn't think I needed it."

"You always need it, but you can borrow mine."

She handed me a blue padfolio. The outside of the padfolio was engraved LUNA LAW and contained pens, a crisp legal pad and all the relevant case law in one of the pockets.

Inside the new Luna County courthouse, Judge Chairez was already in the courtroom, along with Shaharazad. The judge had gone back to her turquoise judicial robe. Shaharazad matched, which make them the turquoise twins. Well, since we were also wearing turquoise, it felt like a family reunion in Deming Rock City.

The attorney general herself, Mary Alice Forrest, would

handle this hearing personally. Since we were in blue, they must have subconsciously known to wear red. She had Raphael and the paralegal standing behind her. Together, they looked like a posse. The attorney general wore a power red pantsuit—the Hillary Clinton look on steroids look. The other two wore non-descript gray that, except for their red bow ties, almost made them disappear. Red versus blue, it was like a gang war. When Luna came to counsel table the paralegal vanished. I wasn't sure where she went.

"You're bringing in the cavalry," Mary Alice said to me. "Luna Law."

"I'm bringing in my wife," I replied.

The guards brought Cage out from the back. He wore a suit that he must have picked up from the reject bin at the Otero Correctional Center. That's where they kept the clothes the released inmates didn't want to take with them. He had lost weight, but that was not a good thing. He was wearing a size fifty suit.

Before we started, he wanted to talk with us in the jury room behind the courtroom.

"What's going on?" he asked. "Who's the woman?"

"This is my wife," I said. "Luna Cruz Shepard. She's the best lawyer in the state."

"I've heard of you," he said to Luna. "You've got a great reputation. Luna Law, right?"

"I might be changing the name if I merge with another firm," she said. "We'll see how the trial goes."

I gave him an update. "We're doing a duress defense, how Kirlian put you in a position of fear that reasonably forced you to conspire to receive stolen property."

He looked unusually nervous. "Do I have to say anything?"

"No," I said. "At least not yet."

"Promise?"

"I can't make that promise just yet."

We returned to the courtroom where Luna handled some pre-trial matters. She filed the waiver and had an emergency amended witness list. She smiled when the judge granted all her requests.

"Counsel, we will bring in the juror panel," the judge announced.

Because of Luna's extensive pre-trial research, we already knew which jurors to pick. Luna's theory was that we wanted people with military backgrounds, because they would be sympathetic to a guy like Cage, the war hero. Deming had a low cost of living, so it was a haven for retired military.

I wanted to show off for Luna with my *voir dire*, and used an old defense attorney chestnut about how proof beyond a reasonable doubt required you to not hesitate in the graver affairs of life.

"What are the graver affairs?" I asked the jury pool.

"Buying a house," said one potential juror.

"Getting married," said another.

I thought of asking about marital standards, but didn't. Instead, I went with an obvious one—making a left turn. People smiled, and I made eye-contact with Juror Number 12. "When you're driving, and have another person in the car with you, you signal and look both ways before making a left turn, even though your passenger tells you it's safe to turn. Why?"

Juror 12 nodded. "Because I have kids in the car."

"You make sure because you care, right?"

"I always look both ways when I have kids in the car,"

said Juror 12. "You have to be careful.

Juror Number 13 looked exactly like Gollum, the man from the previous trials. It took a few glances to make sure that it was not him, but someone else. "So, when you're out on Lomas Boulevard and you need to make the turn on Fourth Street, if you have any doubt at all, you hesitate, right?"

He stared at me. "Where's Lomas Boulevard?"

Ugh. I was in Deming, and not in Albuquerque. Luna shook her head. I then asked a few people if they could be fair and impartial. We kept the Gollum lookalike on the jury.

"He smiled at you," Luna said. "Even though you made a mistake he thinks you're human, and hopefully will give you, give us, the benefit of the doubt."

After a short break where we picked twelve jurors and two alternates, it was time for the trial to begin in earnest.

"Are we ready, counsel?" the judge asked.

"The attorney general of the great state of New Mexico, Mary Alice Forrest, is ready for the prosecution."

"Luna Cruz of Luna Law is ready."

"I'm ready too," I said.

Luna sat closest to the podium, making herself the *de facto* lead counsel. That was fine by me. Cage sat next to her and I sat at the far table, as far away from the jurors as possible.

Mary Alice Forrest walked to the podium with pomp and circumstance, as if addressing thousands instead of twelve plus two. "Your honor, ladies and gentlemen of the jury, this is a relatively simple case. A man named Roman Ulibarri stole a piece of technology from an esteemed scientist, Dr. Yu. Someone then set up a meeting between Mr. Ulibarri and the defendant, Albert Jackson Cage. We don't know who set up the meeting, but that's not at issue."

Luna scribbled notes on her opening statement outline. WHO SET UP MEETING?

The attorney general continued. "Mr. Ulibarri met with Mr. Cage, the defendant, and tape-recorded the conversation. It was clear that the defendant knew, or should have known that the item, a communication device known as a magic thimble, was stolen. The defendant then made a cash offer to Mr. Ulibarrri to purchase the magic thimble. That would be a conspiracy to commit receiving stolen property. We ask that you find the defendant guilty by the end of the day."

Luna already had her opening printed out, but had space for notes to respond to Mary Alice. When the attorney general sat down Luna picked up her ten-page outline and went to the podium. "Ladies and gentlemen of the jury, the wrong party is on trial here. The Dragon Moon Corporation should be on trial. Dragon Moon is evil."

She made a dramatic pause that got the rapt attention of the jurors, who probably wondered what Dragon Moon was. The attorney general could have objected, but at that instant she and Luna were united against a common enemy.

"Counsel says we do not know who sent the text to set up the meeting between Roman Ulibarri and our client, Albert Jackson Cage, but the evidence will show that the text originated from someone connected with Dragon Moon, and we will call a witness who can verify that."

Was she going to call Kirlian as a witness? I checked her perfectly organized trial notebook. He was on her amended witness list, and a subpoena had been issued. Why hadn't she told me?

Luna continued. "Our client acted out of fear. Fear for his

life, fear for his family. We will demonstrate that the Dragon Moon Corporation, an evil corporation, has a history of intimidating their employees to such an extent that Albert Jackson Cage felt he had no choice but to make a deal with Roman Ulibarri. Mr. Cage is a war hero, a man who put his life on the line for our country, and yet he was reasonably afraid of immediate body harm by Dragon Moon."

"Objection!" the attorney general said. "Prejudicial."

"Your honor," Luna said. "I am permitted to make reasonable extrapolations based on the evidence at hand."

"You may proceed."

"Albert Jackson Cage served our country overseas in the triangle of death, driving supplies to our fighting men and women. His motto was to do his duty, to not leave anyone behind. He felt that by making this deal, he was doing his duty to his employer. He acted under duress, and with a fear that would make a reasonable man take an action he knew was wrong."

Luna listed the elements of the duress defense, and added the fact that Cage felt he was compelled to perform the actions that he did due to an immediate threat by Dragon Moon.

The jurors looked at her and nodded in unison.

The state put Dr. Yu on the stand as their first witness. He wore a gray suit with no tie. With a stylish goatee and shaved head, he looked like a Silicon Valley hipster out for dinner at the newest Asian fusion joint. I couldn't help but feel a bit jealous of this brilliant man who was younger than I was.

On the attorney general's direct examination, Dr. Yu discussed his dealings with Dragon Moon. Dr. Yu had developed several prototypes of the thimble before the incident—prototypes X-1 through X-6. The attorney general showed the jury an illustration of how the thimbles had evolved over time. It was similar to the diagram showing man's evolution from the apes, except this time, each thimble grew smaller and thinner. X-1 went all the way down the index finger, while X-6 just reached the bottom of the fingernail. X-7, the stolen magic thimble, was small, but had several metal part the size of pimples grafted onto its sides

I probably had an X-5.

Mary Alice did a quick pivot. "Let's talk about the thimble on the far end of the chart, the X-7, the so-called magic thimble." She then showed a slide of the X-7 as "state's exhibit one." The jurors were not impressed.

"What's the difference between the X-1 through the X-7?" she asked.

"The X-7, the magic thimble, can be manipulated by brainwaves," Dr. Yu said. "It can create primitive holographic images. Author, inventor, scientist, futurist, and explorer Arthur C. Clarke once said that if technology becomes sufficiently advanced, it might as well be magic, so that's why I gave it that nickname."

"Like this?" Mary Alice played a video on the screen of Dr. Yu using his mind to create a computer animation.

"I want one!" this Gollum said.

Dr. Yu then testified about his eureka moment at his garage, and that Roman took the thimble ostensibly to solder something onto it and didn't return it.

"Roman stole it!" Dr. Yu shouted. Then he looked at my client. "Cage tried to buy what was rightfully mine!"

The jurors seemed unimpressed at the outburst, and the attorney general continued. "Even if Roman Ulibarri had authority on the X-1 through the X-6, did he have authority to keep the X-7?"

"No, he did not."

"Did he have authority to make a deal with Dragon Moon regarding the X-7?"

"No, he most certainly did not have authority to make a deal with anyone."

"Did he steal the X-7 when he took it ostensibly to repair it, but did not return it?"

"He did. He knew he should have brought it back!"

"And if someone agreed to buy an X-7 from a janitor without any paperwork?"

"That's conspiracy to receive stolen property."

"Objection, that's making a legal conclusion," Luna said. "He has not been qualified as an expert."

"Sustained," The judge said. "The jurors are to disregard that statement."

. . .

Luna walked to the podium as if Dr. Yu was the only person in the room. She did not look at anyone else. She asked Dr. Yu about his first transactions with Dragon Moon on the X-1 through the X-6, and how much money Dr. Yu had made. The attorney general objected on relevance and the judge limited how much Luna could ask about the earlier models.

Luna was incredibly prepared, but the judge ruled against her at every turn. When Luna tried to bring up our conversation with Dr. Yu at the lab, Mary Alice objected again, as Yu's statement was neither recorded nor sworn to. Luna gave me an angry look. Why hadn't I remembered to tape the conversation?

The judge called Luna and Mary Alice to the bench. I

stayed back at the table with my client, so didn't hear what happened. As they walked back, Mary Alice smiled, and Luna frowned. Without a recording, we couldn't impeach Dr. Yu with his prior statements.

Luna shook her head and sat down.

• • •

The state's next witness was Roman Ulibarri. I would be responsible for questioning him, as Luna felt that I had to do something to earn my fee. The direct examination by Raphael was solid, but not flashy. While he might have worked at a lab, Roman Ulibarri was an everyman, a jack of all trades. He cleaned things up at the lab, but also helped the scientists at home doing everything from yard work to washing their cars. He even emptied the cat litter for one elderly scientist.

Our blue-collar, retired military jury saw themselves in Roman, especially the retired enlisted men. Roman was a hardworking guy who just tried to get ahead.

Raphael then asked how he obtained the magic thimble.

"I stole it," Roman said plainly. "I wanted to make a quit buck."

"Objection!" I shouted. "You told us you had permission."

Raphael was prepared for my outburst and told the judge to admonish me for shouting. The objection was overruled.

Roman said he put the word out on the street that he had a magic thimble for sale. When he talked to us, he had said that the thimble wasn't necessarily stolen at the time he got the word out. He changed his story when he testified that he e-mailed some contacts and definitely said it was stolen.

"Who are these contacts?" Raphael asked.

"I don't know their real names. I provided the emails to the FBI, and it's my understanding that the investigation is still ongoing." Raphael didn't press. He asked about what happened next.

Roman then testified that once the "sewing circle of LANL" got word that he had a thimble, someone had texted him to set up the meeting with Cage to unload the thimble.

"How did this party know you had the thimble?"

"I told you. Word gets around. That's all I know."

"Who texted you about setting up a meeting?" Raphael asked.

"I don't know, but it came from someone with an early thimble. I can tell by the code at the end of the text. I figured it was Kirlian."

The state displayed the text on the wall. There were some strange symbols at the end of the message that must have indicated that the text indeed came from a thimble.

"This wasn't from one of your earlier contacts?"

"Not that I know of. None of them had thimbles, so their messages wouldn't have the same code at the end."

"Can you read the message for us?"

"Meet Cage in Deming."

"So, you met with Cage in Deming to unload the magic thimble?"

"I did."

"Why did you record the conversation with the defendant?"

"Just in case. In case it wasn't kosher." He smiled at using this new word for him. "For my own protection if there was a situation like this."

The state then introduced the recording of the conversation between Roman and Cage. Some of the parts that had been inaudible bad been cleaned up. Damn, the state had deliberately provided us a scratchy version. Here,

Cage clearly stated "I can probably get you a couple of grand up front for that little magic thimble thing," when before we had heard only static.

"Pass the witness," Raphael said.

I tried to discredit Roman using his prior statements to us when Luna and I were at LANL, but since we didn't have a recording, it was impossible. I repeatedly asked the question "You have no personal knowledge whether or not Cage knew it was stolen, do you?"

Roman answered the same way everytime. "He should have known I had stolen it."

After the fourth "asked and answered" objection, I finally sat down.

"If we lose, it's all your fault," Luna said when I sat down.

Mary Alice called a cop to do the obligatory prosecution things—establish chain of custody and venue—and then the state's case was complete in less than an hour.

"Your honor, the Great State of New Mexico rests its case."

"Does the defense have any motions?"

Luna made me do the motion for directed verdict, which was almost impossible to win. Luna had written some talking points for me on the pad in my padfolio. "Even in the light most favorable to the state, the state has failed to prove a *prima facie* case," I said at least three times. I pronounced it differently each time, just in case. A prima facie case meant there was enough evidence to submit the case to a jury. It didn't necessarily mean that the jury would find the person guilty.

Back at the defense table, Luna got busy scribbling new questions for our witnesses while the judge denied our motion. Luna put her pen down and stood up after the judge finished. "We're prepared to put on a case your honor."

"Let's come back after lunch," the judge said.

The jurors headed out to eat at the Mexican restaurant across the street, so we went to the Pic Quik to grab some sausage and green chile pizza slices that were sitting under a heat lamp. This was the same Pic Quik where I had lost my wallet. Today the cashier smiled. "Hope you can afford the pizza, *ese*."

I made it a point to pull out my wallet to pay. Luna practiced her questions and reviewed the notes on her lap top as we sat on a stoop. The pizza was terrible. Even though we were forty-six miles from Hatch and the best green chile in the world, this pizza was topped with some greenish rubber chili with an "i."

· · ·

Kirlian waited for us on the steps of the courthouse. He wore a gray polo shirt with the dragon logo—business casual boring. It was as if he didn't want to look too evil for the afternoon's testimony. Kirlian had shaved off his goatee, too, and I realized he was only about thirty years old. He looked quite innocent.

"Are you sure you want to do this?" Kirlian asked. "Put me on the stand?"

I looked at him. "You hired me to zealously represent Mr. Cage. This is zealous representation. The z word."

"I'll be the one asking the questions," Luna said. "I'm even more zealous than my husband."

He shrugged and stared at her, ignoring me. "I'm just going to take the fifth every time."

"I'm counting on it," she said.

· · ·

"Your honor, defense calls Karl Kirlian," Luna said when

were back in the courtroom.

After Kirlian was sworn in, Luna's first questions were about the founding of Dragon Moon by Kirlian's father, Luna's father, and another party named Dellagio, who was Denise's father.

"Ms. Cruz Shepard, is this relevant?" the judge said. "All three of those people are dead."

"Your honor, this case involves an alleged conspiracy by the employee of a corporation. I need to lay a foundation that explains the background of this conspiracy."

"Is your argument entrapment then?" the judge asked dubiously.

"No, it is duress. It is our contention that Dragon Moon left Mr. Cage with an immediate fear of bodily harm and it was reasonable for him to act the way he did. I want to address the reasons why Dragon Moon's action felt to Mr. Cage that he was genuinely, *reasonably*, afraid for his life, and that caused him to feel he had no choice but to take the meeting with Roman Ulibarri."

She then cited five minutes of statute and case law, and why a reasonable person would be so in fear of bodily harm from a corporate entity and thus commit an illegal act.

I expected the Mary Alice to object, but insead she said, "Your honor, I believe the corporate history of Dragon Moon is extremely relevant to this case." She wanted to know this story as well. When the cross-examination resumed, Luna did more talking than the witness. She asked a long question and then, as forewarned, Kirlian took the fifth.

In Luna's mind, her father was a saint who was tempted to go down a bad road because of the Kirlian family. Every time Kirlian asserted his fifth amendment right not to testify, he looked weaker and Luna looked stronger.

Luna then shifted to how Dragon Moon made its fortune. In the next ten questions, she emphasized how it was Kirlian's father, not her father, who made deals with the Mexican cartels to provide prescription drugs without prescriptions to drug addicts in America.

Still no objection by the attorney general, and again, Kirlian took the fifth, ten times in a row.

Luna then shifted to Dragon Moon's efforts to become a more legitimate business, but even that was troublesome to Luna. Kirlian's father had invested in gold and diamond mines where workers died from inhumane conditions.

"Diamond mining is a good metaphor for greed, isn't it?"

Kirlian looked to the attorney general for an objection, but none came. Luna then talked about miners who had been murdered when they protested inhumane work conditions.

"I take the fifth," Kirlian said five more times.

She then asked him about the Chinese company that had contracted with Dragon Moon to mass produce the thimble. The company had one of the worst records of human rights violations, and some of their workers had committed suicide.

"Your workers feared for their lives, didn't they?"

Finally, the judge had had enough. "Ms. Cruz, could you please get to the case at hand?"

"One more question in this area, your honor." She didn't wait for the judge to respond. "Mr. Kirlian, considering Dragon Moon's history of employee intimidation, don't employees have a reasonable fear for their jobs, and perhaps even their lives?"

"Objection!" Mary Alice shouted. She had allowed Luna to bash Dragon Moon, but now that Luna was returning to the case, she would fight back.

"He can answer," the judge ruled.

"I take the fifth."

"Now, that we've established Dragon Moon's sordid history," Luna said, "we'll start talking about the case at hand, your honor." Luna asked Kirlian about the thimble, but he took the fifth each time.

Luna now smiled at the twelve jurors and two alternates. She had all fourteen in the palm of her hand. I had counted. Kirlian had taken the fifth forty-nine times.

Luna didn't have a thimble, but she was a wizard with power point. She displayed the series of texts on a white screen so the jurors could see them.

"Did you send these texts to Roman Ulibarri and Albert Jackson Cage?"

We all expected Kirlian to take the fifth one more time, and when he did so, it would be damning. He would be the evil puppet-master pulling on poor Cage's strings, one who hid behind the constitution rather than admit his evil actions.

"No, I did not."

"What?"

"I did not send those texts," Kirlian said. "May I demonstrate with my thimble?"

Before Luna could respond Kirlian used his own thimble to highlight the series of digits and symbols after each text. "Those digits indicate that the texts were made by an earlier thimble prototype, an X-2. The X-2 was stolen during an earlier burglary."

"Do you have a copy of the police report?" Luna asked.

"As a matter of fact, I do."

He used his thimble to produce the police report --about five times normal size--on the white screen, replacing the earlier images.

"This report has nothing to do with the X-7, the magic thimble prototype that was stolen," she said.

He now manipulated the screen so it showed both the police report and the images from the texts. "No, as I said, this was from a primitive model, the X-2. I can tell from the digits at the end. Also, the second round of numbers indicate the text was sent from out of the country. By the look of the IP address, I would say the text to your client came from Mexico."

He now displayed a copy of his passport on the screen and the pages magically flipped to show his entry and exit stamps. "Here's my passport, which indicates that I did not leave the country during the time those texts were sent."

Luna looked down at her notes in her padfolio as if searching for the next question.

"And, as this X-2 thimble was stolen," Kirlian continued, "I have no way to contact whoever sent those texts. I can assure that given the date and the location of where and when it was sent, no one at Dragon Moon sent those texts. We no longer have any facilities in Mexico, nor do we conduct any business there."

So much for the duress defense.

Luna abruptly sat down. "Pass the witness."

Mary Alice cleaned things up during her cross-examination of Kirlian. She might not have liked the man, but she wanted to win this case. This early prototype of the thimble, the X-2, had been stolen. That theft had nothing to do with the theft of the X-7, the magic thimble. However, the X-7 was indeed stolen by Roman when he did not return it. Whoever set up the meeting between Roman and Cage regarding the X-7 had nothing to do with Dragon Moon.

There was no duress. There was no entrapment. Cage knew or should have known the X-7 was stolen. And, he conspired with Roman to make a deal to receive stolen property.

"Did you ever threaten Mr. Cage?" the attorney general asked.

"No, I did not. I even hired a lawyer for him, that man sitting next to the lead counsel, Ms. Cruz."

Luna tried one more time on re-direct. "But still, there's a chance that Mr. Cage did not know that the magic thimble was stole when he got the text from an unknown party."

Kirlian didn't hesitate. "Mr. Cage is smarter than you might think. He knew or should have known that the texts did not come from me, and he knew or should have known that the thimble was stolen."

"Objection," Luna said. "He's giving an expert opinion on an ultimate question that should be left to the jury."

"You're right, Ms. Cruz," the judge said. "The jurors should disregard the statement by the witness that the defendant knew or should have known that the thimble was stolen. They should not take the statement that the defendant knew or should have known that the thimble was stolen when they make their deliberations."

By repeating the admonition twice in her authoritative voice, the judge had further reinforced Kirlian's statement. The jurors smiled.

Luna frowned. "Your honor, can we take a break?"

"Do you have any more witnesses?" the judge asked.

"I don't know," Luna said.

33. Land of Entrapment

As the jury was in the jury room, Luna, Cage and I went to a cramped "conference room" by the front door. The ceiling was low enough for the meeting of the New Mexico chapter of the Lollipop Guild from *The Wizard of Oz*.

"So much for the duress defense," Luna said. "I thought he was going to keep taking the fifth."

"I was set up," Cage said apropos of nothing. We sat in silence for another moment. Was the ceiling getting even lower?

Suddenly I had a hunch about Kirlian's burglary. Using my own thimble, I said, "Thimble, produce police report of Kirlian burglary in Los Alamos, 2014."

The thimble produced a report, along with some eyewitness testimony regarding a suspect fleeing the scene. Once we saw *how* the suspect was fleeing, I gasped. It now made sense.

"You've got to testify as to who really sent you the text," I said.

He didn't make eye contact.

"This is our last chance. I'm trying to save you here."

"Pat Chino."

"Who is Pat Chino?"

"Look it up. Let's see if you can figure it out on your own." It was an implicit challenge. This was a legal arts kata. If I didn't show him my moves correctly, he wouldn't respect my abilities as an attorney, and wouldn't help me any further.

Pat Chino? I had never heard that name before. Using the thimble, I searched government records to locate the name, and then searched medical records with the thimble. Pat Chino had never seen a doctor in the United States, ever.

I felt a pinging in my head. I closed my eyes, and had a

vision of Marley trying to communicate me. No, I was thinking of hospitals, and Marley popped into my head as a logical progression. Marley had gone to a clinic in India. Perhaps this Pat Chino had gone out of the country as well. This was just a logical chain of thought, not anything psychic, right?

The next illogical inference that popped into my brain was that this Pat Chino person would know about the clinic in India. With some help from Luna, who had been to Bangalore, we accessed some patient records. India lacked the strong HIPAA privacy protections that we had in America.

With the thimble, we accessed Pat Chino's records at the Indian clinic and obtained several photographs. I displayed them on the wall, including before and after photos from the surgery.

"Oh, my god!" Luna said.

We could access the patient's prescriptions as well. Pat Chino had been prescribed Crotaladone by Dr. Gandi. It was starting to click. "So, in the first case you were charged with you were really getting the Crotaladone for Pat Chino?"

"Maybe," he said. "We had never met, but I finally met Pat in Playas, right before I met with Roman," Cage said. "And Pat had revealed to me about the Crotaladone."

"You didn't tell us that," I said.

"You didn't ask me if I ever met the person. I just told you that when I got the texts I thought they had come from Kirlian. I really thought that at the time. I thought I was getting the Crotaladone for Kirlian"

"And this person in this picture is the one who talked with you?" Luna asked. Luna walked up to the image displayed on the wall.

"Yes."

"Ladies and gentlemen, we have achieved entrapment," she said. "You were right, Dan."

I looked at Luna. "We can now show state action that we didn't know about before," I said. "You're the real lawyer here. What motions do we need to file to make this work, since we didn't raise the issue before trial?"

She opened her laptop and within seconds had templates available. "I can fill these out in a matter of seconds and have them ready. We can get all three cases dismissed, even the two where you, Cage, have already been convicted."

Cage still didn't look up. He wasn't happy. "So, I got to testify?" Would he wimp out as he had before?

Luna had previous success with that Vulcan nerve pinch. I now did one on Cage and grabbed his shoulder with my right hand. "You taught me about honor," I said. "Well, right now, I swear on my honor that I will do everything possible to protect you. I understand what's going on. And we can win this case."

He clasped his hands in prayer and closed his eyes for a moment. He then opened them and looked me in the eye as if he had just received divine guidance. "Okay. I'll testify."

• • •

We went back into the courtroom at one in the afternoon. "We call Albert Jackson Cage to the stand," I said. My career, my marriage, and perhaps my life were all at stake here. I thought about Dew's dad, Marlow. This would be my Marlow Moment.

Cage walked to the witness stand and took an oath to testify truthfully. He looked serious as he did it. I hoped my hunch, my "shine," whatever you wanted to call it, was on the money. If not, I could be disbarred.

Mary Alice, Raphael, and the paralegal sat at the state's table. Kirlian sat behind them. I noticed that Dick Sobchak with Dragon Moon Security sat in the same row. Several big men in black US Marshall windbreakers filled the last row of the courtroom. Why were they here?

I didn't want to get to the Marlow moment too quickly, as I wanted Cage to be comfortable answering questions. Luna had written the questions out on the padfolio pad, to make the questioning flow better. Thanks Luna!

I had Cage begin by recounting his war record, about saving Yahima.

"I love you baby," he said. She was sitting directly behind us.

"I love you too," she said, tearing up.

We briefly went through his background at Dragon Moon, then moved on to the case. When Cage got the text, he originally thought it came from Kirlian. After Kirlian's testimony regarding the IP address and the numbers at the end of the text, he stated that he agreed that the text did not come from Kirlian—or from anyone at Dragon Moon.

"You also know that Mr. Kirlian's thimble had been stolen?"

"Yes."

"Did you know the text came from a stolen thimble?"

"Yes, I did."

"Then why did you meet with Roman?"

"Because someone told me it was okay. That everything was cool. I thought I was the one doing the set up, but it turns out they were setting me up. They double-crossed me."

"And you met with this someone—the person who set you up—prior to meeting with Roman Ulibarri?"

"I met with the person in Playas about an hour before the

meeting with Roman Ulibarri."

"Did that person give you a name when you met?"

"Yes. Pat Chino. I figured it was an alias."

There was a gasp from somewhere in the courtroom. I couldn't tell who it was from.

"Is that person in this room?"

"Yes."

"Could you point that person out?"

He pointed to the paralegal.

34. Ms. Trial

The judge excused the jury, and the room became mobbed with a dozen Luna County Sheriff's Deputies. Mary Alice was in a fighting stance, as if she was ready to hit me with a left-right combo, and then do a spinning rear kick at Cage's midsection. "How dare you accuse my employee of a crime without any evidence? Your honor, I'm asking for sanctions against Mr. Shepard."

I looked at Luna. Tag, you're it! Luna stood. "Your honor, I've obtained police records and hospital records, all of which we accessed in the last few minutes. We are asking for sanctions against the Attorney General's Office of the Great State of New Mexico for extreme prosecutorial misconduct! They either knew or should have known that their employee had initiated contact with the defendant."

"Your honor," Mary Alice was practically screaming. "If they are claiming entrapment, they needed to file the proper paperwork before the deadline."

"There's an exception, of course," Luna said, "when there is deliberate state action that would constitute prosecutorial misconduct and the state has failed to provide exculpatory evidence." She had a stack of copies of case law and she started to walk toward the judge.

The judge banged his gavel, and silence fell on the room once the echoes faded. I could hear the breathing of the US Marshalls in the back row. They were clearly waiting for a cue, but it hadn't come yet.

"What are you proposing?" the judge asked.

Luna looked at me. Tag right back at you.

"Your honor, I'm proposing that we call the person in question to the stand," I said pointing to the paralegal. "I will only ask one question."

The judge looked at the police reports and medical records. "I think I know what question you will ask, and I am very curious as to the answer. Ma'am, will you please take the stand?"

The paralegal, who was apparently named Pat Chino, walked toward the podium. She debated her options, then walked to the stand and was sworn in. I had thought the paralegal was Native American, but after her injuries, her fall from the rooftop, this young woman had clearly had her entire face rebuilt in India. Looking at her eyes, I now recognized her.

"Ma'am, can you please state your name?" I asked.

She looked around. She looked at the marshalls and then back at me.

Luna decided to help me out. "Please answer the question, young lady." That sounded odd, the paralegal wasn't particularly young. "We are prepared to take a DNA swab from your mouth forcefully, if necessary," Luna said. "There is no fifth amendment right not to answer a simple question about your identity." Luna lifted a stack of cases. She was ready to go.

The judge looked at the paralegal. "Please answer the question."

"What is your name?" I asked.

The paralegal smiled. It was the first time I had ever seen her smile. Her teeth were a little too perfect, as if they'd been replaced by dentures after a fall "That's a little complicated." I recognized the voice instantly.

"Do your best, young lady," the judge ordered.

"My birth name is Anna Mondragon. I later changed it to Mia Luna Mondragon, after my half-sister, Luna Cruz, who is sitting at counsel table."

I was about to ask another question, but the paralegal stopped me. "Your honor, I am requesting a lawyer and do not wish to answer any further questions now. You can take me into custody and hold me in direct contempt if you wish."

All twelve Luna County deputies took Mia into custody. I went back to the defense table, and gave Luna a high-five.

"Your honor," Luna said. "I move to dismiss all of Mr. Cage's charges."

The judge stopped Luna. "I want briefs on this issue. I'm taking this under advisement."

"Your honor, I want the opportunity to investigate this matter," Mary Alice pleaded "I had no idea."

"We will have a hearing on this matter next Friday," the judge said. "When I am back in my home, I mean my home court up in Santa Fe."

Cage looked at me. "Your honor," I said. "Can Mr. Cage be released pending that hearing?"

"Yes. Mr. Cage, you are free to go pending final resolutions of all your cases next week."

Luna and I could not feel any better than when they released Cage right there in the courtroom. Yahima hugged him. She then hugged Luna and me in turn. "I love you guys!'

Luna looked at me. I looked back at her. Then we kissed right there in front of everyone. Happy ending!

"I love you, Dan."

"I love you, Luna."

"Maybe we have a future in this Luna Law thing."

"How about Rattlesnake Luna?"

Suddenly, there was more commotion in the courtroom. A few US Marshalls rushed to Kirlian, who directed them to come to us.

"Luna Cruz?" the biggest of the marshalls asked. He

flashed a badge, but there was no doubt that he had the authority of the entire Federal government behind him.

Luna smiled. "Luna Cruz Shepard."

The marshall did not smile back. "Luna Cruz Shepard, I have a material witness warrant for your arrest. Will you please come with me?"

Before she could say anything, another marshall grabbed her fists and attempted to cuff them. Luna was wearing some nice turquoise bracelets, but he pulled them off and threw them on the ground.

"Dan, do something!" Luna said. The marshalls now dragged her away. One of them stepped on one of her turquoise bracelets with his heavy black boot, crushing it.

I tried to pick up the pieces. Hopefully, I could put it together, put our lives together. But what could I do?

No, there wasn't going to be a happy ending today.

PART VI

CRASH OF THE EAGLES
SET TWO
FINAL OPTION

35. Prisoner of Azkaban

I hurried out to see three US Marshalls carry Luna to a black vehicle, an RV, and then set her down on a seat inside. They slammed the back door to reveal a Federal logo with the words PRISONER TRANSPORT. Another sign reminded everyone to stay at least ninety feet behind.

I had keys to Luna's Subaru and tried to follow the RV as it headed toward the interstate, and hopefully stay at least ninety-one feet behind.

One block later, an unmarked van behind me flashed some blinking lights. They weren't a police vehicle's regular rotation of red and blue, these were different, green and yellow. When I didn't immediately stop, the lights became more intense, as if firing green and yellow photon torpedoes. Genuinely afraid that my car would catch on fire, I pulled over.

Dick, Kirlian's bodyguard, approached. "Do you like interfering with the Feds?"

"You're not a Fed," I said.

"Well, they just radioed and asked me to talk to you nicely," he said. "If you keep following them, they will not talk to you as nicely. They're taking her to AZ-NM."

It sounded to me as if he said Azkaban. "Isn't that the mystical prison in the Harry Potter books?" I vaguely remembered a Potter film called *The Prisoner of Azkaban*.

"AZ-NM Correctional Facility," he corrected me. "It's in Crater, New Mexico."

"Crater, New Mexico? Does that town still exist?"

Dick didn't say another word, returned to his van, then deliberately revved the engine. He flashed the photon torpedo lights once more, then followed in the direction of the marshalls' van. I could see him head eastbound on the

Interstate 10 on-ramp before his vehicle vanished from sight.

Should I follow? This wasn't one of the Fast and the Furious movies where I could jump onto the van like Vin Diesel. This was my real life—the last and the litigious. Still, I wasn't going to let it go. I could follow them discretely to whatever facility and play lawyer. Hopefully, I could use the thimble to produce the appropriate paperwork to spring Luna.

Driving eastbound on the interstate, I drafted five different motions. I displayed the motions on the windshield as I kept the car in cruise control and steered with my elbows. On my third draft of a motion to review a condition of release, a state trooper pulled me over, presumably for weaving.

I had just won a jury trial and still looked somewhat respectable in my suit. I didn't have bloodshot, watery eyes or slurred speech. Still, I was apprehensive when I handed the officer my license and registration.

"I'm sorry I was drafting legal documents."

"You can go, but be careful," he said. "Don't draft and drive." I put the car in cruise control, one mile under the speed limit. The trooper followed me the next thirty miles to the Luna County line.

Once I was back on Interstate 25, I was on the famed stretch known as the *Jornada del Muerto*, or the Journey of the Dead Man. It dated as far back as conquistador days. A few hours of *jornada* later, I turned west on Highway 6 near Los Lunas, and crossed through even more *muerto* stretch of high desert. There weren't even any lights from oncoming traffic. If the road to Chapparal was like Mercury, I was now on the dark side of the Moon.

Eventually, red lights started bobbing in the distance. Was it a UFO? No, it was the lights of the RV, ten miles or so ahead of me. The high-altitude air was free from both air and light pollution out here, and visibility went on seemingly forever.

Highway 6 eventually intersected with Interstate 40. At least that brought the lights of traffic. I soon took the exit for Crater, New Mexico, the home of the AZ-NM facility. The census designated place of a few hundred souls was Luna's home town. She had been the district attorney here for a while, before she had been voted out. I could only imagine the utter humiliation, the utter devastation of being a prisoner in your home district.

Other than a truck stop, this was a ghost town, well a ghost census designated place. Some towns went through boom and bust cycles. Crater went through bust and buster cycles, and things were clearly in a buster form. The truck stop and the casino were already shuttered for the night. A casino that closed at eight in the evening? This town had gambled and lost. Hell, Luna had gambled and lost.

Every single storefront was empty, although one did have a sign proclaiming FEMALE VOCALIST WANTED. A piece of wood fell off the porch as I drove by. I sure hoped that poor Anna Maria, the former *American Idol* contestant, wouldn't leave her job as a night janitor only to end up singing in an abandoned building with a back-up band of ghosts.

A sign directed me to the AZ-NM prison facility. This place had been nicknamed the Discount Prison back in Luna's day. At first glance, new management had at least spent a few bucks on floodlights and barbed wire. When I arrived at the front entrance of the facility, the sign announced ARIZONA NEW MEXICO CORRECTIONAL FACILITY,

A SUBSIDIARY OF THE DRAGON MOON CORPORATION.

My heart sank even further.

Even worse, there was an annex labeled SUPERMAX at the far end of the parking lot past two more layers of barbed wire.

I pressed an intercom at the front of the outer fence. They had a video-monitor at least. The Native American woman on the screen had a badge that stated that she was the warden. This place was really cutting costs if the warden doubled as the receptionist. It might have changed owners, but this was still the discount prison.

"My name is Dan Shepard. Is Luna Cruz Shepard here? I'm her attorney."

"She's in Supermax and is not allowed any visitors at this time, legal or otherwise. You need to leave immediately."

Prison in your hometown was bad. Supermax in your hometown was super bad.

• • •

When I returned to Albuquerque, it was almost ten. I checked in on Marley at UNM Hospital. Selena and Heidietta were leaving for the night, and the nurse only gave me a second to give him a hug before visiting hours closed. The Muzak blackout continued.

I didn't get any psychic images. He was asleep. I sure didn't want to wake him and tell him the bad news about his mother.

In the lobby below, I told Selena and Heidietta what had happened, and we all started crying. Before we knew it, we found ourselves joining in another family's prayer circle. The family's preacher was there, and became confused when we told him we were praying for Luna. He assumed she was the child and not the mother."

"God bless, young Luna," he said.

"Amen," I replied.

. . .

My front door was open when I arrived at Greystoke, and I stepped in to find the place had been ransacked. Amid the mess, I saw a one-page search warrant on top of the dining table. It was signed by the same Federal judge who had signed the material witness warrant for Luna. Apparently, Luna had several boxes of documents relating to Dragon Moon that were crucial to ongoing litigation. These boxes could be "seized" by the Federal government and taken into evidence.

I vaguely remembered helping Luna carry three cardboard banker's boxes up after her step-mother's funeral. We had loaded them into the closet. Those boxes were gone, along with most of Luna's overcoats.

The authorities had also "seized" an old manuscript of mine that had been buried in another box in that closet. Would some poor agent at the FBI would have to read my unedited eighty-five thousand words in hopes of finding clues about Luna? Maybe they could get it to the right people to get it produced as a film. I almost smiled at the thought.

Our bed was unmade and the pillow cases ripped. The entire apartment looked terrible. I was going to file a complaint with the authorities until I realized that this was way I'd left it. The rips had come from Suri, when she had tried to wake me. If I ever wanted to get Luna back, I knew I'd have to clean the place up or she'd take one look at it and turn around.

It was close to midnight, but I still had two Red Bulls left in the fridge. After chugging them down, I windexed every inch of the apartment until it was immaculate. Luna would be proud.

. . .

The next morning, after perhaps two hours of sleep, I called a contact at the US Attorney's office, Joey Manzano. He agreed to look up Luna's situation and said he would meet me for lunch.

We met at a high-end lunch place called The Grove, which had been featured in a scene in the old TV show, *Breaking Bad*. In the show, Walter White poisoned the evil Lydia's stevia tea in the final season. The Grove was famous its healthy, but pricey fare. With its white walls and open patio, it could pass for a seaside bistro in Santa Monica or Malibu. Manzano wore a light blue suit and skinny tie, and fit right in with the other Hollywood types jetting in to check on local film productions. Did my crumpled suit mark me as a local hick?

"Your wife is still in the Supermax unit over in Crater," he said after we sat down. "She's in solitary, since normally it's a male facility."

"Why Supermax?"

"She's a material witness against Dragon Moon in like five different cases—the FBI is looking at them, the SEC, and the bankruptcy court."

"Why does the FBI want her?"

"I don't think you understand. The material witness warrant was issued by Dragon Moon. They want to question her as part of their defense against the various Federal lawsuits and criminal investigations."

"They can do that? And lock her up in their private facility?"

"Material witness warrants can be used for somebody *material*, someone absolutely crucial to their case. They can keep that person in custody indefinitely, if they fear she's a flight risk or dangerous. And the AZ-NM facility has a valid contract with the Federal government to house inmates."

"Luna's not a flight risk, and the only person she's dangerous to is me if I don't do the dishes. Don't you think that Supermax is overkill?"

"Well, the fact that in the past six months she went to India and to Juarez was a factor in the Federal judge thinking otherwise."

"Going to Mexico for your step-mom's funeral and flying to an India hospital for your kid's surgery doesn't seem like it should count against someone."

"That's not the real reason," Manzano said. "Not by a long shot. Did you know her dad went to prison for being part of a prescription drug cartel? That's a factor. Many of the people involved in that cartel were founders of Dragon Moon. That's another factor. She also has the documents about the founding of Dragon Moon. When she visited her father in prison, presumably she had conversations about where the bodies were buried, so to speak, and father-daughter conversations would not be privileged."

"Bodies were buried? Dragon Moon is dirty? But they're a Federal contractor. They had to pass some security check, right?"

"That's why all this is so serious, so 'material witness warrant' serious. Dragon Moon is trying to go straight, like the Corleone Olive Oil Company in *The Godfather*."

"Just when I thought I was out, they pull me back in," I said, doing a very bad imitation of Al Pacino in *Godfather III*.

He ignored me. "Billions are at stake. Your wife is just a pawn in the game between Dragon Moon and the Feds. Both sides need her right now."

"Can I talk to her? Are there visiting hours at Supermax, like on Thursday afternoons?"

"Did you really just ask that?" He laughed. "All access to her is limited by court order. You can only contact her through her lawyer."

"I thought I was her lawyer."

"She listed a different name."

"Who?"

"Selena Mondragon. I've never heard of her."

"She hired Selena?" I was disappointed that Luna had retained Selena, but it was probably for the best. I couldn't act rationally. Blood was thicker than marriage, and Selena was blood. I was just marriage. "Selena's her half-sister."

"You sure married into a crazy family."

After eating our artisan sandwiches at record pace, Manzano excused himself and I called Selena. "I'm at The Grove," I said.

"I used to waitress there," she said. I vaguely remembered that she had once served me here. I hope I had tipped her well.

"What's going on with Luna?" I asked.

"We're meeting with the FBI in a few minutes, the CIA after that, and with some US Attorneys later this afternoon," she said.

"Can I come?"

"No. This will be held in the US Courthouse, in a restricted room."

I didn't even know there *was* a restricted meeting room in the gigantic Federal courthouse. I wasn't admitted to the Federal bar and couldn't even handle a traffic ticket on the nearby Cibola National Forest, or speeding at the Los

Alamos lab. I could see why Luna had retained Selena. Selena had failed the New Mexico bar a few times, but when she finally passed she had retained the information, and later had also been admitted to the Federal bar. I had never bothered to fill out the application, much less find someone to be my reference. I couldn't even represent someone on a parking ticket on a Federal facility on base.

I gulped the last of my tea. I had added stevia of course, in honor of *Breaking Bad*. Hopefully no one had poisoned me. I sipped it anyway.

"Is she all right?" I asked.

"No. The stress is getting her. When she heard she could be locked up for up to six months on one of these warrants, she nearly had a nervous breakdown. They have her in solitary in the Supermax, although they will eventually move her to the women's prison max facility over in Fort Worth."

"That doesn't sound like much of an improvement."

"At least it's a female facility and they can put her in general population."

Luna mixing among maximum female criminals didn't sound like an ideal situation. "Tell her I love her."

"She knows," Selena said. I was expecting Selena to add that Luna loved me back. "Should I put money in her jail account so she can buy candy bars at commissary or make phone calls?"

"Money isn't an issue, yet. The main issue is that she's off her meds."

Ever since the shooting, Luna had survived through medication. Locked up in a cell coming down without Crotaladone might make her snap.

"I'll be at Marley's hospital room tonight around seven,"

I said. Come by if you can."

"We should be done late today. I'll do my best."

• • •

That evening I did the early martial arts class at the new program at the center downtown. I worked on my "cognition," visualizing my opponents as human instead of merely punching into the air at ghosts.

The instructor with the breathing tube then had a fantastic suggestion. "You're a lawyer. Just think of martial arts as litigation." He had to type those words into a tablet so they could then be said out loud by a computerized voice that emanated from the machine.

"You mean that a punch is like a law suit, and the defense is like an answer brief?"

He nodded.

So, when someone tried to grab my lapels, I thought of the appropriate response as if preparing a brief, step by step. In this case, it was a step back with my left foot to gain stability at the same time as giving a right punch. This was of course the Kimono Grab defense, which was now basically a counterclaim. I could call it a Kimono Counterclaim. I loved it. Thinking like a lawyer made me a better martial artist. Hopefully, thinking like a martial artist would make me a better lawyer.

• • •

After a quick shower, I visited Marley in his gigantic suite in the hospital. Thankfully, the Muzak was back on, but for some reason was now playing orchestral versions of Elton John. I hated Elton John.

Both Dew and Denise were there, along with Denise's grandmother, Nurse Song.

"Great to see you all," I said. "How's Marley?"

A doctor came in, beaming. "I knew you were coming, so I wanted to tell you in person. It's like a miracle. He can be released tomorrow."

I hugged the doctor, and he didn't push me away.

"He's not out of the woods, yet," the doctor said. "He will probably keep having to go to India every year for checkups. At least until we can offer the treatment or follow-up care here."

I felt tears of joy when I looked at my son. He still was getting bigger by the day. He did a friendly chop in my direction, and I hurried to his bedside to give him an awkward hug. He hugged me back. If you put a shell to your ear, you can hear the sea. In Marley's heartbeat, I could hear New Mexico, I could hear Luna.

Then he hiccupped and I had a full-on panic attack. Without Luna, I would have to care for him alone.

"I don't know if I can take care of him," I said, my knees weak, my eyes tearing up.

Nurse Song came over to give me a helping hand. "We can take care of him until Luna's situation clears up and you get back on your feet. I still live in the old group home and we have a room already set up for him."

"Am I off my feet?" I asked.

"We're all off our feet," Dew said. "My mom is gone and I miss her. I never thought she would go to jail just for being a witness, or not being a witness. Talk about a crime that doesn't give you street cred on the yard in Supermax."

"She's not going to last the next twenty-three-hours in lockdown in Supermax," I said, "much less the six months they can keep her there. We've got to figure a way to get her back."

"Knock, knock," called Selena. She wore an olive-green

business suit that made her look vaguely military, as if she'd just been injured in the desert. If memory served, she had been Laser Geisha Green, Laser Geisha *Verde* as she used to say. Selena's limp was worse today, and she walked as if she was tiptoeing through a minefield. She might have avoided stepping on a land-mine, but the stress had made her entire body tight.

She pushed her cane down hard on the ground with every step as she went to the bed and hugged her nephew. "That's from your mom. She misses you so much."

Marley grinned and reached out to touch her cheek.

Selena then told us to gather round. "We might as well have a family meeting," she said. "I've got a message to play. And let's do it here, because Marely needs to hear this."

"I didn't know we were still a family without Luna," Dew said. She was right. Luna was the glue that held this random group of laser geishas and rattlesnakes together.

We stole some chairs from an empty room and formed an impromptu circle in the middle of the hospital suite. Selena put her phone in the middle of the group and pressed play. I thought for a moment that with Dr. Yu's thimbles, that this would be a hologram, but even on the small screen it seemed as if Luna was right there in the room with us.

In the grainy video, Luna wore an orange jumpsuit and shackles. Laser Geisha Turquoise had rusted. I guess orange was the new turquoise. It had only been twenty-four hours, but she had aged a decade. She was shaking, and Selena's sloppy camera work made it worse.

"I love all of you," she said. "They won't break me!"

We muttered encouragement as if she could hear us.

"Dan, I love you," she said.

"I love you too," I said to the small phone.

"Nurse Song, please help Dan take care of Marley. He can't do it alone."

"No problem," Nurse Song said.

"Dew, please prepare for the mock trial competition. You can't glide on your ability alone. This is your last chance. Take it seriously. I don't want you to end up on the pole."

"Did she just say she didn't want me to end up on the pole?" Dew asked. "Like she's afraid I'm going to become a stripper if I lose?"

We re-wound a few seconds. Luna had actually said "I don't want you to end up *in a hole.*"

We felt some relief, but ending up in a hole for losing a youth-based mock trial competition, even a metaphorical hole, still sounded horrible. Dew was on the edge of tears.

"I'll do my best," Dew said to the phone. "I'll do my best, Mom." Dew said she only called Luna, "Mom" when Luna deserved it. Luna sure deserved to be called Mom right now.

Denise looked at the screen, but Luna did not mention her. Denise frowned. Her Aunt Luna was more of a mother to her than her own mother, so that hurt.

"And Marley, my son, I love you. I am doing this all for you!"

Selena re-wound the video and pointed it at Marley so he could hear. He pointed toward the phone and began to cry. Nurse Song comforted him. I did need help.

What was it that Luna doing for Marley? Before she could say anything else, a US Marshall yanked her away. "No filming allowed!" The video abruptly ended with the marshall's voice echoed through the room. Marley was still crying. In fact, we all had a tear. Luna wouldn't last more than a few days.

A doctor came in on his rounds, "Let's talk outside,"

Selena said.

Nurse Song stayed with Marley and the rest of us went to a balcony with a great view of downtown Albuquerque and the desert horizon beyond. The moon was setting right over the convention center.

"Luna fired me after that," Selena said. "She's totally paranoid without her meds so she actually kicked me out of the meeting room before the next deposition. She's now representing herself from her jail cell, and she's probably doing a better job of it then I was. She already had several motions drafted, as if she knew this was coming."

"How long will they hold her?" Dew asked.

"Indefinitely. There are several ongoing Federal cases against Dragon Moon. Dragon Moon might be able to hold her for the next six months, until those trials are over. Not only are they holding her in their own jail, they're getting reimbursed by the Federal government for housing a Federal prisoner. They have the motivation to keep her there. Hell, if she has a medical condition, they will get paid a premium to treat her with their company doctor they employ. It's called the prison industrial complex."

"Is it Kirlian doing this?" I asked.

"As an acting chief counsel, he filed the motions to hold as a material witness. He's putting pressure on her, keeping her in lockdown to force her to give up her proxy vote and gain control of the company at the shareholder vote."

"How can we save her?" Denise was the one who spoke up. "Is there something Dan or Selena can file, even if Aunt Luna is representing herself?"

Selena shook her head. "Not before the shareholders meeting. There's no CEO with authority over Kirlian right now. Kirlian is acting CEO until the meeting and the vote.

We checked the corporate by-laws. Luckily, there's a big group of shareholders who want him out of the picture entirely. Hopefully, if a new CEO is elected we can convince that person to file the appropriate paperwork with the judge to drop the hold."

They looked at me. I was supposed to come up with a plan. I took a deep breath and remembered the mock trial competition.

"You guys are doing mock trial that day in the same building, the convention center, right?" I asked.

"We're in the Kiva Auditorium in the West Hall of the convention center. Dragon Moon is meeting in the East Hall," Dew said. She pointed westward to the convention center, about a mile away. We could see the two separate halls connected by a skybridge.

"Well, after you do the mock trial—"

"After we *win* mock trial," Dew interrupted.

"After you win, Denise, you're the only one who has access to both events. You go in to the shareholders meeting and do some recon. Then we approach the new CEO and give him or her Luna's paperwork ready to sign. Maybe we do a "hold harmless" form saying that Luna won't sue them for false imprisonment if they let her go. We do it while the cameras are rolling to maximize the pressure."

Selena pulled out a few pieces of paper. "Luna already prepared a release order and a hold harmless form that says she agrees not to sue them. She dictated it to me during a bathroom break before she fired me. I can get everything in order with the electronic filing system in Federal court tomorrow, so all we have to do is serve them."

"Can you serve the new CEO sooner? Maybe we don't have to wait until the CEO appears at the mock trial award."

Selena frowned. "They won't accept service of process, as Kirlian told me they won't have a registered agent in New Mexico until after the board ratifies that corporate bylaws at the board meeting, something like that. It's all a sham, but they can file paperwork to tie the whole thing up in court until the new CEO is on board."

"Can't you do anything?" I asked.

"Not anymore," Selena said. "Luna made me sign a proxy of my shares over to her."

"Why did she do that?"

"She was hoping the increased number of shares would give her more clout at the shareholder's vote, but it backfired. Now, Dragon Moon wants her locked up even more."

"Who's going to be the new CEO?" I asked. "How does the vote work?"

Selena showed us a pie chart on her phone that showed the various shareholders of Dragon Moon as different colored slices. I recalled those election night maps, but here Selena showed the various scenarios for the shareholder votes on the pie.

"If Kirlian gets these blocks of shares he wins," she said. Fifty-one percent of the pie was now red. "But if Luna votes with Herring and Yu, someone else can win like that doctor from India who's on the board." Selena now made the fifty-one percent of the pie green.

"And if Luna votes with Mia and Denise," Selena now turned the most of the pie turquoise, Luna's turquoise, "they can elect whoever they want. Maybe Luna's friend, Diana Crater gets elected. Or maybe that emir from Dubai, Ahmad Assed, can be brought in. Like I said, I don't know the politics any more. I can't even get into the meeting now because I gave Luna my votes."

"Then it's up to me," Denise said. "After Mia, I probably have the biggest block of voting shares. I'm a big deal—to Dragon Moon at least. I just wish my mom was here to see me be a mock trial hero and help Aunt Luna get out."

"Denise, you can't serve him," Selena said, assuming the new CEO would be a man. "It would have to be someone who's not on the board."

"I wouldn't be able to serve them," I said, perhaps a little too eager. "I'm a party as wife to Luna."

"There is no conflict," Selena said. "Luna prepared the suit as Luna Law versus Dragon Moon. She must have anticipated the issue. You can do it, since you don't really work for Luna Law. You can serve the new guy."

To serve or no?

I now had the vision in my head. I would have to be the one to finish this, serve the papers and save Luna Law, save Luna. There was no question.

"I'll do it," I said. "I'll go right up to Kirlian or whoever it is, serve them and say 'Let my Laser Geisha Go!'"

Dew frowned. "You guys have to understand something. This is my big moment. This is the biggest moment of my entire life. Assuming we win, we're going to get a big trophy *and* scholarships. I don't want Luna spoiling *my* life."

I stared at her, not quite believing what I had just heard. "Well, let's play it by ear," I said cautiously, still looking at Dew. "Selena, I'll take a copy of the papers once you do whatever you need to do online. Let's just pray that Dew and Denise win and we'll see what happens then."

I thought back to my martial arts training. They had us in a stranglehold. What was the defense to such a hold— crash of the eagles, final option. I was going to have to strike them hard in the neck.

I snuck past the nurses to see Marley after everyone else had left. "I will save your mom," I told him. He was awake and smiled. He nodded. He opened his mouth, then closed it without uttering his first words.

Not yet. But soon . . .

. . .

I drove back home. There were some new documents on the printer with the file stamp of Federal court, indicating that they were good to go. Selena must have printed them remotely on my computer with codes supplied by Luna. My wife thought of everything. All I had to do is serve them on the new CEO. I put the documents in the blue Luna Law padfolio Luna had given me.

"Luna Law," I said. I was starting to like the sound of it.

36. Santa Fe Trial

June 15, 2018

After her trials with Cage around the state, Judge Chairez was finally back home in Santa Fe District Court for Friday's hearing. Checking the calendar online, I noticed that Pat Chino, AKA Mia Mondragon, would be arraigned on her charges immediately after Cage's hearing on our motion to dismiss all his cases. It was not only a matter of judicial expediency to have both matters held at the same time. I was legally entitled to notice of all of Mia's hearings under the New Mexico Victims of Crime Act. Luna was also entitled to notice, as she too was a victim. I had mixed emotions of being in the same courtroom as Mia, although I guess in her guise as a paralegal I had been there many times already.

I did a tally of Mia's crimes in my head. Mia had killed a waiter at the Parq Central Hotel and then killed Marlow. That was two counts of first degree murder. She had shot me, shot Selena, and shot at Luna. That was three counts of attempted murder, or at the very least aggravated battery with a deadly weapon. And that was just in one day.

After she became a fugitive, she had obtained fraudulent documents to change her identity and then committed passport fraud when she came back from her surgeries India. She lied on a government application to obtain the job at the attorney general's office. She had probably killed her lawyer, Kent Dorfman, as well as Axtell Pile. She had also pushed me down in the snow and taken my thimble, which would constitute a robbery. I even bet she didn't have a valid license, registration, and insurance for her stolen motorcycle, and had left the scene of several accidents.

Mia would die in state prison if she was convicted of even half of those crimes. Despite my defense attorney bias, I hoped Mia would receive the death penalty for what she had done to our family.

No more winging it in court. I woke up before dawn and prepared this time. I knew every variation of a 5-802 habeas petition (a type of motion to throw aside a verdict), a judgement notwithstanding the verdict, and a motion for a new trial based on newly discovered evidence. I put all of them in the blue Luna Law padfolio next to the other motions.

I wore a power blue suit and turquoise tie, of course. I also wore my rattlesnake boots. Time to be the Rattlesnake Lawyer one more time. Or maybe I was the Rattlesnake Geisha. I even remembered my black padfolio and stocked it with all my paperwork for the day. I was alone, but Luna was with me in spirit. Santa Fe meant Holy Faith, and I had holy faith that I would see her again soon.

I met Cage in Santa Fe at the First Judicial Courthouse. The three-story building felt like a palace after all the small courthouses I had visited over the past few weeks. A family of Long Island-accented tourists confused the courthouse with their four-star hotel and stood outside wondering why the crowd entering looked like criminals. Cage held hands with Yahima. They looked cute together, and matched in khakis and blazers.

We went to the third floor and had an amazing view of the adobe expanse of Santa Fe. The attorney general was standing in the hallway with her posse. She wore a dark green power suit that made her look diminished, like she was the attorney colonel, the attorney major, or God forbid, demoted all the way down to the attorney lieutenant.

Raphael was right behind her, looking like he wanted to be somewhere else. I always wondered what it would have been like to have the security of a state job, without having to eat what I kill as a private attorney. Still, government jobs could be just as fraught with peril if you hitched your wagon to the wrong horse. They could all sense that this hearing was not going to be much fun. I kept expecting to see their usual paralegal behind them, but she had been replaced by a new one, a short man in a plaid suit and bow tie.

Inside the cramped courtroom, Judge Chairez and the court reporter, Shaharazad, entered together. They also matched, again with the turquoise. Why did turquoise always make me think of Luna?

The judge called the court to order, and called our case.

"Attorney General Mary Alice Forrest for the State of New Mexico," said Mary Alice. She didn't say "great."

"Dan Shepard for the defendant, Albert Jackson Cage, who is present," I said.

"Where is Ms. Cruz Shepard?" the judge asked.

"She's with us in spirit." I presented the judge with my habeas petition and gave a copy to Mary Alice.

"Your honor, we can save everyone some time." Mary Alice said. "We are not opposed to Mr. Shepard's habeas petition and having the two prior judgments against Mr. Cage dismissed. And, in the interest of avoiding any appearance of impropriety, I am resigning my post immediately."

Mary Alice looked at me and nodded. She had just been doing her job, and presumably knew nothing about Mia.

"Your honor," I said. "We're not asking for any sanctions against Ms. Forrest."

"Then it's ordered," the judge said. "All of the cases

against Albert Jackson Cage have been dismissed. Sir, you are free of the jurisdiction of the court."

Cage hugged me. When I looked around, I saw Kirlian, Colonel Herring, Dr. Yu, and a few others I didn't recognize sitting behind us in the wooden benches of the gallery. They must have slipped in behind us. Colonel Herring now wore a red civilian suit and Dr. Yu had freshened up, his hair combed back while sporting a black suit and red bow tie. They followed us out as we left the courtroom.

"What are you doing here?" I asked Kirlian. Cage and Yahima stood behind me. They were my rattlesnake posse.

Kirlian wore a blacker than black suit with a tie that might have been made of pure gold. Dick, Kirlian's body guard, stood behind him, not in a uniform, but in a blazer and half-open shirt, like the bouncer from hell.

"I just wanted to see the end of the case," he said. "This is what we retained you for and your representation is now over. Here's a letter discharging you from your service. I also wanted to tell your client that he can have his job back."

"Thanks," Cage said. "But I'm hoping to get a job as a runner for my man the Rattlesnake Lawyer over here. You need a driver?"

"You got it, AJ," I said with a smile.

I wanted to test Selena's assertion that I couldn't serve Kirlian. I had the papers in my padfolio, I started to remove them when Dick grabbed my hand. Had they been expecting me to serve them?

Kirlian frowned. "As I told Ms. Mondragon, I am not a registered agent of the corporation," he said. "My status is uncertain, to say the least. I will not accept service and I can tie that up in court indefinitely. You can serve the new CEO after the board meeting."

"You can release Luna, can't you?"

Kirlian smiled. "That's above my paygrade. One of these nice people will probably be the one who has the authority to make that decision next week."

I put the papers back in my padfolio. "I'll see one of you next week then."

Kirlian tried to turn into the gracious hosts for his guest. "Mr. Shepard, I believe you know Dr. Yu and Colonel Herring. They're both interested in learning more about Dragon Moon's legal affairs, so I invited them to the hearing. Also, right behind me is Dr. Gandi, from India who's also on our board."

"You run the clinic that my son went to?"

Dr. Gandi shook my hand. "It was a pleasure to meet your son. He has incredible potential. We hope that we can stay involved in his treatment."

"Thank you." Then I frowned. It was time to stop being nice to these assholes. "Now, back to my wife. Where is she?" In my black rattlesnake boots, I towered over Kirlian.

"As I've said, I don't have the authority to release her, or to drop the material witness hold until after the shareholder meeting and the new board is in place."

"I'll keep that in mind," I said. "You're up for CEO as well, right?"

"I'll leave that to the shareholders," he said with a weak smile.

The Dragon Moon party turned away abruptly and headed down the hall. I hurried back inside. Judge Chairez was now arraigning Mia, who had a long-haired public defender standing beside her.

In addition to the contempt of court charges, the judge was also arraigning her on the murder of Sam Marlow, the waiter, and aggravated battery charges, including the one against me.

"Conditions of release? Mr. Shepard, you are one of the victims, do you wish to address the court?"

I didn't know whether I was supposed to be sworn in. Apparently not, since no one approached me. "Your honor, this young lady killed my best friend, the father of my wife's daughter. She shot at my wife and shot me. I believe that she assaulted me up in Taos, not to mention her new charges. I ask that she be held without bail pending the final resolution of all of her trials."

The long haired public defender with a bow-tie was a better advocate than I ever would be. He responded about Mia still having the presumption of innocence. He argued to lower the bond down to a million dollars, cash only.

A million dollars, cash only? She would have to lasso the moon down to bond out. I gave Mia a dirty look on the way out, and pointed my thimble at her. Judge Chairez gave me a dirty look, reminding me that she could hold me in contempt and lock me up in Supermax next to my wife.

I walked briskly out of the courthouse and was enveloped by a sunny Santa Fe day. Despite everything that had happened over the last few weeks, I loved this great state! I loved the adobe and the blue skies of the city of Holy Faith. I hoped I could get Luna out so we could share moments like this. I stood in the sun to take a deep breath.

A reporter stood next to the courthouse, talking about Mary Alice's resignation and how the state would be dropping its lawsuits against Dragon Moon. I didn't know whether to be happy or sad.

As I walked away from the courthouse, Dr. Dreadlocks approached me. At first I presumed he was another tourist who was confused about the location of his hotel. "The Inn at Lorretto is two blocks that way," I said.

"You look like you know this courthouse," he asked. That's when I recognized him from the medical clinic, and from his time serving papers on Luna.

"I know every courthouse," I replied. The man did not seem to recognize me.

He carried two very big briefcases. "Where would I go to bond out a woman who just had court?"

I looked at the two briefcases. How much cash was in there? "What's her name?"

"Mia Mondragon."

37. El Funko Segundo

I wanted to get out of Santa Fe, out of the First Judicial District, before Mia was released from the courthouse—just after I had spoken out against her. I didn't want to be her victim one more time. Would she follow me south? I wasn't thinking straight so I got lost in the crooked Santa Fe streets, then somehow reversed myself on Paseo de Peralta and found myself headed north.

By the time I passed the Santa Fe Veteran's Cemetery, I felt the urge to disappear for a bit. As Bruce Springsteen said in the song "Hungry Heart," "I took a wrong turn and I just kept going."

I headed north toward Taos. On the way, I stopped at the El Rancho Church and said a little prayer outside. Taos Pueblo was closed. The Taos hum, or heartbeat or whatever I had heard the first time, was silent. Still, something was drawing me up to Taos Ski Valley where this whole adventure had begun.

I drove past the massive Blake Hotel in the center of the village of Taos Ski Valley, then drove up a few of the switch backs, now that the road was dirt rather than snow-packed. When I pulled over it was at approximately the same place this had all started, but there was no A-frame here anymore, just a hole in the mud. Had the A-frame ever been here at all?

It was incredibly green here, but there was still some virgin snow on top of the jagged peaks surrounding us. While it might have been summer on the calendar, winter never really let go of this part of the world.

I took a few more breaths of the high-altitude air. Not everything had changed. The rope was still there and the sign that this was the area boundary, and not to cross. This time, I was on the outside, looking in. If I could do it all over again, would I still have crossed under the rope?

I wasn't sure.

I felt a burst of energy coming over me. To calm myself, I did my katas and ran through all the techniques. I only had fourteen minutes of material after all.

I looked around at this utterly perfect alpine valley. I was ready for anything. I would do whatever it took to save Luna.

38. Mock and Roll All Night

Loud music announced the arrival of Dew and Denise in the apartment next door at Greystoke. It might have been that horrid K-pop, J-pop or some other kind of Asian pop that I couldn't identify. It just sounded like rapid successions of noises to me. I had become my late father regarding the music of this younger generation.

I knocked and Dew opened the door. Since they had been splitting their time between Greystoke and Nurse Song's, their place was even messier than my apartment.

"You really should clean all this up," I said.

"You're not my father," Dew said. "I'm getting legally emancipated from my mother this summer, so I don't have to wait till my birthday."

"Then I'm your evil step-father, Dew. Right now, we're all under a lot of stress. I'm hoping that your mom gets out next week, and she's still your mom until you turn eighteen or get legally emancipated or whatever. And don't you think that when she comes home after being locked down in a prison cell, the last thing she wants to see is your mess?"

Dew said nothing. I had known Dew from even before I had dated, much less married, her mother. What had happened to that sweet girl who accompanied her mom on our trip to Valles Caldera so many years ago? She kept staring at me.

"If we all work together to clean this up," I said. "I'll tell you your father's secrets to winning trials."

That worked, and I helped Dew and Denise make the place almost fit for human habitation. The one thing about the k-pop music is that is sped up our heartbeats and we raced to keep up.

· · ·

"We're going to run through your entire mock trial right now." I said. I looked through the case file on Dew's freshly cleaned table and had to laugh. As this was an international tournament filled with all-stars, the theme was Star Wars, sort of. Copyright infringement was a scary thing, sop the names came from a galaxy *adjacent* to the one far, far away.

The competition's fact pattern concerned whether Hand Solitary should be charged with first degree murder for shooting someone or something named Greedy in the Most Icely Cantina. The facts were unclear whether Hand fired first. Teams had to be prepared to argue both sides of the case, meaning they had to play the roles of both the Imperial Prosecutor and the Rebel Alliance Public Defender.

My heart was with the rebels, the defense side. Dew would be lead counsel along with someone named Rayne Herring from Clovis High. I wondered if this Herring was related to Colonel Herring. Denise would play two witnesses—the defendant Hand Solitary, when the team did defense; and bounty hunter Bobby Faith when the team did prosecution. The final member of the team had not yet been named.

I watched Dew practice her opening statement and then stopped her. She still relied on Marlow moments and didn't always lay a proper foundation. I was much the same way. Luna had cured me of this, for the most part. I also used my newfound martial arts approach of thinking of every question as an attack and then formulating the appropriate response.

I hated giving a lecture to Dew, but I gave it anyway. "Lay a foundation, or the Marlow moments won't work."

"You sound just like my mother," she said.

"That's a good thing. Your mother is better lawyer than

I'll ever be." I gave her some more advice from my first mentor, Pete Baca. I was older now than Pete had been then.

Dew's next take flowed much better when she added a few lines. She then did the opening for the prosecution side and was just as good.

"Let's try your direct examinations," I asked.

She questioned Denise as Hand Solitary, the defendant. Denise wasn't bad, just a little quiet as she recited the facts that caused her reasonable fear to justify self-defense, even though Hand had fired first.

"Now practice cross-examination," I said to Dew. "Denise has got to get used to it from the other side."

Dew practiced cross-examination and Denise could parry every question with her light-saber quick wit, but Dew and I were surprised when Denise started to cry at the end.

"What's wrong?" I asked Denise.

"This will be the biggest moment of my life. I wish my mom could be there."

"I'm sure she's proud of you," I said. "Is that what's bothering you?"

"Not even. It's my birthday and none of you seem to care."

"We do care," I said. We had so much on our minds, that Denise was always getting lost in the shuffle. I looked at these two young women. This mock trial competition was the most important event in their entire lives. Their enthusiasm, their anxiety was contagious. It wasn't just the speedy K-pop music still playing in the background, but my heart was racing right along with theirs. These girls were the Rebel Alliance for reals and for the first time in my life I felt like their Yoda.

Dew practiced her closing argument again. She added a few extra sentences, cut out a few jokes, and she was already better than I had been after twenty years of practice.

"Your mother would be proud of you," I said. "You too, Denise."

"I know that if we win, we'll be able to get Auntie Luna back," Denise said.

And somehow, I don't know why, I just knew that these two teenagers were the key to bringing back Luna alive.

"I have one more thing to say to you girls," I said after another hour.

"What's that? Lay a proper foundation?" Dew asked.

"Don't talk too much and give narrative responses?" Denise added.

"No. May the force be with you!"

39. Kiva Fever

June 29, 2018

Nothing happened over the next few days. Nothing at all. I had no word from Luna. Selena did tell me that she was no longer at AZ-NM and had been moved to a hospital facility. She was unable to find out where. We tried to reach Kirlian, but he had left the country, had gone back to Armenia to handle family business. Even if we could serve Kirlian as acting CEO, he wasn't around to be served.

The wait made me even more frustrated.

• • •

On Friday, June 29, the mock trial event wasn't supposed to start until 9:30 in the morning, so I had time to run some errands. Unfortunately, Hollywood Joe's had closed. A sign read UNDER NEW MANAGEMENT, REOPENING SOON.

I saw Hollywood Joe getting into his car, lugging a bulky computer. "I had to do a re-write on *Heavy Starch*," he said. "But it's all good. They didn't get my character's motivation and want me to do a polish."

"Family's always a good motivation," I said.

'Family it is then," he said. "Good bye. Good luck with your story. Hope you get a happy ending."

I wanted to check my balance at the bank. I hadn't been serious about giving back the money. The bank was open, but Josephina, the hearing-impaired teller, was nowhere to be found. As the line was too long, I didn't bother to wait to find her. I would look it up online. Might as well catch up to the times.

When I drove down Broadway, I noticed that Culebra Kai was closed for the day. Odd, I thought, then forgot about it with the big day ahead.

I returned to Greystoke and met Dew and Denise in Dew's living room. They were dressed to kill. Dew looked like a miniature version of her mom in a blue suit, but wore a lavender bow, as opposed to a turquoise one.

"I'm Laser Geisha Lavender," she said. "The new one."

Denise was supposed to be a female Han Solo, but instead was dressed like Daisy Ridley's "Rey" from *Star Wars: The Force Awakens*. Denise looked delicate in off-white, but still radiated that she was ready to take on the Evil Empire with her toy light saber that was sheathed under her leather belt.

"People are coming from all over the world and we get to walk two blocks," said Dew. "We've got the hometown advantage."

"I hope so."

I went back into our loft and grabbed the Luna Law padfolio, with the paperwork inside to serve the new CEO. I felt like an assassin. I would serve him or her at the perfect moment, right as the cameras were rolling for the national news. The new CEO would have to act immediately, or watch a PR triumph turn into a PR debacle.

We walked the two blocks, but I made us stop in Civic Plaza before we entered the convention center. "Are you guys ready?"

Dew stopped. "I'm not religious, but I think we should say a prayer for our team, and most important for my mom."

Denise and I nodded. We prayed right there by the big concrete fountain before we crossed Third Street. I could picture Luna in my head, wearing her orange jumpsuit, hands cuffed behind her back. Lord, I would do whatever it took to save her.

I opened my eyes and we walked inside.

I had expected a lot of security, but all the big guys with

big guns were at the shareholders' meeting at the East Hall over the skybridge on the other side of Second Street. No one expected anything dangerous to go down at a mock trial competition in the West Hall. Their mistake.

Next to the escalator, everyone had to pass under four gigantic hanging promotional posters. The first read DRAGON MOON IS LOGISTICS with images of trucks with happy truck drivers, including Cage and Pile. The next poster read DRAGON MOON IS LEGAL TECHNOLOGY with a picture of Kirlian in the courtroom using his thimble to display a crime scene photograph with glowing yellow tape on a courtroom wall. A third one stated DRAGON MOON IS CORRECTIONS, and displayed AZ-NM. The final poster read DRAGON MOON IS ANYTHING YOU CAN DREAM, with Dr. Yu and his thimble pointing a laser beam toward a nearby galaxy. Right behind him, Dr. Gandi used his thimble as an x-ray machine to illuminate someone's intestines.

I discretely flipped off the banners. A banner should read DRAGON MOON IS KIDNAPPING! DRAGON MOON IS STOCK FRAUD! DRAGON MOON IS EVIL!

A small digital camera crew was on the left filming the banners. They weren't TV news, but film makers. I recognized, Allegra Kunis, who had been a witness in one of my cases. She was now a full-fledged documentarian, and even sported a raspberry beret.

"We're here at the International Mock Trial Championships," she said in front of the camera, "where Dragon Moon is showing the lawyers of tomorrow the technology of today! And cut!"

Selena, in her olive-green business suit, hurried over to us. Well, as much as she could hurry. "I worked the phones and got a rooting section for you all," she said.

We rode the escalators and entered the Kiva Auditorium on the second floor. It wasn't that crowded, since the international teams didn't bring their own fans. Some kiva. There were less than a hundred people in an auditorium that could seat over two thousand. This looked less like the world championships of mock trial, and more like a high school play dress rehearsal. That didn't mean this wasn't a matter of life and death for the girls. It was.

As she walked us down the aisle toward the stage, I saw our fans, and Denise whooped with joy. "Mom!"

"Denise! Happy birthday!" Denise's mother, Jen Song, the original Laser Geisha Pink hurried up the aisle to greet her daughter with a big hug. Jen also wore a business suit, as if she had indeed been fighting evil in the courtroom, rather than the asylum as her daughter had suggested. Laser Geisha Pink was now forty. My how time flew. Like her daughter, she had one pink streak in her hair.

She then gave me a polite handshake, as if to avoid the appearance of impropriety. I thought back to our big adventure back, when I had a conflict contract with the state, and her own adventures as Lawyer Geisha Pink when she saved Susie Song, the famous golfer. That was another lifetime ago.

"I'm so sorry about Luna," she said.

"We've got to get her back."

"Whatever it takes," Jen said. "We're here for her." Susie Song, the now retired golfer stood next to Jen. I didn't know she could now walk unaided. There was even a bounce in her long stride as she came over to shake my hand.

"Where were you guys all this time?"

Jen laughed. "You could write a book about what we did in Asia over the last year. "We cut our adventures short for

Denise."

With her cryptic smile, a Harry Potter-like scar on her forehead, and newfound wrinkles under her eyes, she clearly had a story to tell. I hoped that someday someone would write that book. Hell, I would write it myself if I had time, but I doubted that would ever happen.

Nurse Song and Selena then came over. Nurse Song wore surgical scrubs and was holding Marley. Marley did a chop in my direction, hitting my face. He giggled. I chopped back, but stopped my hand inches from him. He laughed again.

I thought he would say something out loud. I could see a mental image when I closed my eyes, as if he was trying to communicate with me. But then he stopped. He seemed exhausted by the effort.

Not quite yet. But I felt it would be today. Selena's attention was on her iPad. Was Luna contacting her? She didn't say.

"Dan!" I recognized that voice and found I had a surprise of my own. There was my own mother, standing next to Marlow's mother, Fanny. Both were dressed in sharp business suits, as if they could go on stage to argue the motions along with the kids.

"I'm here for my granddaughter," Fanny Marlow said.

"I'm here as moral support for you," said my mom.

"Don't you mean for her?" I asked.

"No, you're the one who looks like you need support."

My mom gave me a hug. I sure needed that today.

After a few minutes of catching up, Dew and Denise were rounded up by their coach, who was with the other members of the team: a visibly pregnant young woman in a loose-fitting business suit and an Asian boy who looked like he was in seventh grade. I picked up the glossy program off a seat. The pregnant teenager was Rayne Herring from Clovis High School, and the Asian boy was Hikaru Yu from Los Alamos Middle School, the teammate who was the last to make the team. He wore a furry outfit that made him resemble a teddy bear. With his odd mannerisms and head turned down, he had Asperger syndrome written all over him.

"Hey Dan!"

I recognized the girls' coach, the former APD officer, Bebe Tran, who per the program was now a third-year law student at UNM while simultaneously getting her medical degree. Tran's hair was now tinged with gray and she wore round, wire-rimmed glasses. The former prostitution decoy could now pass for a Vietnamese Yoko Ono in Yoko's later years.

That seemed odd, too. In a state with over ten thousand lawyers, why would our all-star team rely on a law student, albeit a brilliant one?

"Can you help me?" she asked. Bebe Tran was carrying a big cardboard box that she brought to our section. She opened it to reveal light blue t-shirts. The New Mexico Mock Trial All-stars were now "Team Turquoise."

"For my mom," Dew said. "For Luna."

"For Luna!" we all said as we put on our shirts. "Team Turquoise!"

Team Turquoise—a know-it-all who had failed her driver's test, a silent young psychic in a white toga, a pregnant seventeen-year-old about to drop an elephant, and a kid in a teddy bear outfit, all ccoached by a former Albuquerque decoy cop who was still in school.

I loved them already! Go Team Turquoise!

The team hurried backstage, but not before Dew said.

"Remember, don't disturb us, no matter what happens. My whole life depends on it!"

A few minutes later the lights went down. "Dragon Moon Corporation, the new leader in legal technology, presents the International High School Mock Trial Invitational." I recognized Kirlian's slight accent as the voice giving the announcement. "And now your host, the honorable New Mexico First Judicial District Court Judge, the honorable Veronica Chairez."

Judge Chairez came out in another turquoise robe. The eight teams marched onto the stage to the *Star Wars* theme, the happy one. I could visualize all the worlds of the Rebel Alliance sending their young legal warriors. On the other hand, this reminded me a bit of *The Hunger Games* as well, with these young people as the tributes of the conquered districts who were about to fight to the death.

Yes, this was an invitational of a handful of students, and not a true championship, but it was still a big deal to the teams involved. Dew and Denise waved at us before getting back into character. Our whole plan, Luna's life, depended on them winning.

"Since this is an international competition featuring eight counties, we have special guests here to sing the various national anthems," said Judge Chairez. "Here is my cousin, Anna Maria Villalobos from *American Idol*, and someone very special to her."

Anna Maria came out to the stage with her ten-year-old daughter, Jaylah. Anna Maria let Jaylah sing the high notes as they sang the national anthems together. This kid would someday surpass her mother. Anna Maria then hugged Judge Chairez.

We'd already had several family reunions today in the

Kiva. I felt hopeful that we would have one more tonight. "Luna, I'm going to save you," I said out loud. Everybody nodded.

"She's no longer in Supermax," Selena said, glancing up from her iPad.

"Where is she?"

"I don't know."

Luna could be anywhere in America. She might be on her way to the women's facility in Fort Worth or even Guantanamo, if it was still open. The stakes of serving the new Dragon Moon CEO were getting higher, and the paperwork in the Luna Law padfolio on my lap felt even heavier.

The theme from *Star Wars* began again and two teams marched out as the competition began. Team Turquoise went first. I recognized Colonel Herring, now in civilian clothes, sitting two rows back. She might as well be a drill sergent when she shouted, "Go Rayne!"

Rayne clutched her belly, nervously. I wondered if her child would be a lawyer someday with this early exposure to the law.

I thought of all the military movies, where Dad was a great hero and the son was a screw-up who had to live up to Dad's legacy. This was the first time I had seen this cliché with a military mom and her daughter.

I had never met Rayne, but I was already rooting for her. Make the Colonel proud Rayne!

Right behind the Colonel, Dr. Yu, dressed casually, was there with some colleagues. "Go Hikaru!" he shouted.

Our team faced a team from India, who all spoke with impeccable English accents and dressed in preppy blue blazers with green Slytherin ties like they had come straight out of Hogwarts. Our team played the defense side. Rayne became the weak link on the team when she did a poor direct examination of Hikaru, who was playing Chuy Baca, the defendant's best friend. Apparently Chuy Baca was a Wookie, which explained Hikaru's costume, although he looked more like an Ewok. He also had a high-pitched voice, which made his answers even less believable.

It would be up to Dew and Denise. I was more nervous for them than for my last trial. But, within seconds, I had nothing to fear. Dew was smooth as the lawyer, and Denise stood her ground as Hand Solitary. The force was with us.

Judge Chairez banged her gavels after Dew's closing argument and then conferred with two other robed judges. A minute later she announced a unanimous win for Team Turquoise.

In the next round, they faced a team from China, but played the part of the prosecution. Rayne stuttered through a weak opening, and that had me worried. Denise was a bounty hunter slash investigator named Bobby Faith. Rayne seemed confused when she did her questioning, but Denise carried the day with her answers. Denise as a witness called the shots for Rayne the lawyer, rather the other way around.

After she finished, her mother Jen yelled "You rock, Denise!"

"We love you Denise!" Susie added.

Denise blushed, and she seemed to grow a few inches taller. The judge banged her gavel and called everything to order.

Dew then had to question Hikaru Yu, who now was Dart Vedder, chief of the Imperial Police. Hikaru wore a black plastic uniform with the Darth Vader helmet, but without the facemask. The helmet was way too big for his head and wobbled every time he nodded.

Dew was undaunted. She was indeed channeling her late father, and got the poor kid to answer every question the way she wanted. She even used a few of my tips, but made them her own.

When I saw Dew, I saw Luna. Someday, Dew would surpass her mother. She could probably be the best lawyer on the planet someday. Dew's closing arguments made me want to lock up that evil Hand Solitary right away.

The Chinese team knew the "law," (the law is simplified in mock trial competition) but had some trouble with the language barriers. Unanimous again for the New Mexico All-Stars.

"Go Team Turquoise!" I found myself shouting. This wasn't just for Luna and Dew and Jen and Denise, this was for Hikaru and Rayne and their parents, their issues.

In the final round, Team Turquoise faced a team from Arizona with four Native American kids. This team had a greater claim to turquoise, but their team color was silver. Their captain was a young Navajo woman named Jane Dark, who was supposedly the best lawyer in the competition. The young woman had dyed her hair a fiery red.

"Jean Dark?" I asked. I thought of Jeanne D'Arc the French spelling for Joan of Ark.

"No, Jane Dark," Selena said. "Her mom is the warden at AZ-NM."

The Arizona team had a dozen fans on the other side of the auditorium, including the warden. She now dressed in a Crater High Lady Comet School sweat shirt. Luna had one just like it. The warden held up a little Lady Comet pennant and shouted "Go Jane Dark!"

"Jane Dark! Jane Dark!" Her other fans shouted.

When it was her turn, Jane gave an opening about how our legal system needed "predictability, accountability, and equality." She was the only competitor in Dew's league. She might even be better. I would hate to see them tangle for real someday.

In a vicious cross-examination, Jane tried to confuse poor Denise as Hand Solitary, but Denise must have channeled Harrison Ford himself in every bad ass role from *Star Wars* to Indiana Jones to the new *Blade Runner 2049*.

She was good, but I had no idea how the judges would score it.

Dew then gave the closing argument. She opened by asking "To be or no? That's what Hamlet would ask if he lived in New Mexico."

The audience laughed politely. She was originally going to use my "look both ways when crossing the street/reasonable doubt argument," but went off script. "I don't have a driver's license," she said. "I failed the exam, so I have to rely on my mother and father to drive me."

Dew called me her father. I was touched for a moment, even if it was just part of a closing argument in a mock trial invitational.

"My mother always told me that even when I told her it was safe to make a left turn, she still looked both ways, because if there was an oncoming car, I would be the one who got killed. There's reasonable doubt, a hesitation, because you care."

She looked directly at Kirlian who now sat in the front row. "I'm asking you to care about the defendant in this case, Luna Cruz Shepard!"

Dew was supposed to have said the "defendant in this case, Hand Solitary," of course. This was clearly intentional.

She then dropped the microphone and walked back to the defense table. Dew as the daughter of my third cousin, was my third cousin once removed, but at that instant she was my daughter.

Tran looked devastated. "Dew, how could you?" she whispered. "You just lost it for us."

"No, I didn't." Dew said.

But had she? Jane Dark did the rebuttal for Arizona, and mentioned that the defense team couldn't even remember the name of their client, and that alone should be grounds for a guilty verdict. Everyone else in the auditorium murmured agreement.

I expected Judge Chairez to announce the winner right there, but she told us we'd have to wait until seven that evening when "the new CEO of our sponsor, Dragon Moon Corporation, will come out to personally congratulate the winner and present the scholarships."

We had three hours to kill. "That's your cue, Denise," I said. She excused herself to go to the board meeting in the East Hall.

"I'll let you know what's going on," she said.

Dew told us again not to cause any trouble. "I only did that on close because I knew we had enough points to win. This is our moment."

I hoped that she was right.

"At least I hoped it was our moment," she said.

• • •

Over the next few hours, Denise regularly texted us updates about the Dragon Moon meeting and their various shareholder rule disputes. I DON'T REALLY UNDERSTAND WHAT'S GOING ON, BUT NOBODY SEEMS TO LIKE THE PEOPLE WHO ARE CURRENTLY RUNNING FOR CEO. THEY WANT TO OPEN

IT UP.

Selena suddenly looked up. "I'm not a persona non-grata anymore. Apparently, they need me to draw up a contract or something. I'm allowed to go to the shareholder's meeting for the big vote. Do you still have the paperwork?"

I pointed to the padfolio, "Can't you take it?"

"No, I'm now part of it again," she sounded like she had mixed emotions. "You have to do it. No matter what. Serve the new CEO," she said.

"I got this," I said. "This is all going to work out. Wherever she is, we'll go get Luna for a victory drink."

After Selena left, the rest of us took the Albuquerque Rapid Transit bus under the bridge and over to Farina, the famous artisanal pizzeria. Since it was early enough, our big group found a table outside. Dew sat at the head of the table, as if she was already the head of a big law firm. She was right. This was her moment. But moments never last, do they?

The cocky Dew who had dropped the mic was long gone. She kept muttering that she hoped she hadn't blown it, hoped she hadn't ruined her life. Her grandmother kept telling her that she had guts. Win or lose, everybody still loved her. Her real father, Marlow, would have been so proud of her

I sat between Dew and Nurse Song, who was holding Marley. He was extremely well behaved in her arms, but occasionally he looked off into the middle distance, as if searching for his mommy. I touched his cheek.

"You know he's still not out of the woods," Nurse Song said. "He'll need medical attention the rest of his life. And that's going to be expensive."

"I know," I said, "but he's worth it."

Marley chopped at my shoulder. I didn't want to think how we would afford his future care. We would work it out when Luna got back. I just wanted to enjoy the moment. If we had to take him back to India for another treatment, we would find a way—even if I had to drive him there myself, if that was possible.

Dew talked about the competition for a while and then looked down at her phone. "The guy from Stanford said that if I win today I can start there in January, with a full ride in their pre-law technology program. God, I hope I didn't blow it."

"And if you don't win?"

She shook her head. "CNM." She was referring to Central New Mexico Community College which was a great community college, but it wasn't Cornell, much less Stanford. "My mom keeps telling me that if I go to CNM I'll fail out. Maybe she was right when she said I would end up on the pole for reals."

"She said 'in the hole' not 'on the pole.'" I reminded Dew.

Dew shook her head. "I think she really meant pole." Luna and I had talked about Dew's lack of focus, and how that would affect her if she went to a community college.

"I don't do well on wait lists," Dew said. "If we lose and I don't get off the wait list, my mom will think I'm a total failure—and I will be."

"I'm sure she doesn't think that," I said. "I was waitlisted my first go-round to college—good test scores but low grades. I had to get my grades up at a local state school before I could transfer to an ivy league college. Then, when I applied to law school, I got waitlisted at three of the best schools in the country—Duke, Georgetown, and Northwestern."

"I don't remember where you went to law school," Dew

said, her mouth still filled with the meaty ingredients of the salsiccia pizza, a type pf Italian sausage.

"I did all right in the end," I said, "but it doesn't matter. Where you go to school, your grades, your scores, your extracurricular crap doesn't matter once you get to the real world."

"It matters to me," she said. "It matters to *her*." Her being Luna.

"I didn't get into Stanford for law school," I said. I didn't know why I was getting so angry as my past academic failures flashed before me, but my heart beat a little faster. "They wrote me a rejection letter that said 'We congratulate you on your outstanding academic achievement' before telling me the odds against me, and rejecting my ass even though I was on the 95th percentile on the LSAT. And I turned out all right. You'll be all right if you go to CNM for a semester or two to get your grades up."

Dew practically spit out her food with rage. "I don't want to just be *all right*. My mother won't be satisfied with me if I am just *all right*! I wasn't put on this earth to be just all right. And she is right. If I don't win this contest, I don't know what's going to happen. My life is over for reals! Why did I have to mention my stupid mother in my closing argument?"

A hush came over the room. Marley cried before the din of a nearby ART bus drowned out the silence. People started talking again. None of us had much more to say after that. We sat in silence and finished our meal.

After I took my last bite, I picked up Marley who had finally calmed down, even though he kept looking for Luna in the middle distance. Again, I felt one of those psychic flashes. I saw Dew taking over the world and then dying in an apocalypse in the distant future. I wasn't sure whether it was because she had won or lost the competition.

I stared at my son, but couldn't read Marley's dark eyes, Luna's eyes. He opened his mouth and then closed it.

"I know you're going to say something tonight," I said.

He looked at me solemnly and nodded.

. . .

We got back on the ART bus at six, just as I got a text from Denise. MIA IS HERE.

Dr. Dreadlocks had bonded her out, but who put up the money? One of the CEO candidates to sway her bloc of voting shares? Kirlian? He would certainly have the funds.

But then why would Mia agree to be here? That, too, soon became obvious. Dragon Moon was a logistics company. After Mia voted her shares, she could be in the back of a Dragon Moon truck headed over the border into Mexico by the end of the evening.

As we exited the bus at the convention center stop, I received another text. LUNA IS NEARBY. THEY SAID THEY'RE GOING TO—

The message stopped. Had someone taken Denise's phone? They're going to what? They're going to get Luna? They're going to throw her in the pit? They're going to kill her as part of their evil human sacrifice? Had they just taken her from Supermax to sway her vote as well?

I considered charging the room of the shareholders meeting in the East Hall, but the unarmed guards standing in front of the sky-bridge looked menacing. I needed to time to think, alone. Instead, I excused myself as our group entered the Kiva Auditorium. I snuck into the men's room closest to the sky bridge, because once I was inside the auditorium I knew it would be hard to leave with Dew sitting near me.

The men's room was empty when I went into the last stall over, but soon two other gentlemen came in. They didn't see me in my corner with the door closed. One was Dr. Yu, the other the South Asian. Indian, most likely. Through the crack, I saw they were both wearing Dragon Moon lanyards.

"Was your boy okay when he heard he wasn't going to win?" Dr. Yu asked.

"I'm surprised that they didn't let Rajiv win. They're trying to buy my clinic in India and we gave the free plastic surgery to that girl on the board. But a few third world clinics and a face reconstruction aren't worth as much as the thimble."

With a lean and another squint, I recognized Dr. Gandi. He ran the clinic in India that had treated Marley. His clinic had also done the plastic surgery on Mia.

Dr. Yu shrugged. "My son has never smiled in his life. When they told me he would win, I had no choice but to vote the way I did. And the Colonel, she's going to give us that exclusive deal with all the air force bases. It was a no-brainer."

"I'm amazed Kirlian lost in the shareholder vote," Dr. Gandi said. "He did take out the attorney general and get that litigation dismissed."

"It wasn't enough," Dr. Yu replied. "Too many loose ends."

I wondered what they meant by loose ends. They did their business, and left. So, this whole thing was fixed in exchange for voting shares of stock to vote out Kirlian? Why would anyone want to fix a mock trial contest? I thought again about Rayne Herring. She was hardly anyone's idea of an all-star. Was this about her winning to please the

Colonel? Yu's son might have been brilliant, but he was terrible as a mock-trial witness, and had nearly cost us the tournament in every round.

I thought about the other teams. Jane Dark was the real deal, but her mother wore a Crater High sweatshirt. Crater High was in New Mexico, so why was Jane on the Arizona All-Star team as opposed to New Mexico's?

While AZ-NM had a future as a lucrative private prison facility, it was nothing compared to the value of the contracts with military bases or equipping the courthouses with the shoftim system. I could see why they fixed the contest. Maybe it was more like the brutal dystopian world of *The Hunger Games* after all.

One thing was for sure, Dew and Denise thought this was real. This meant everything to Dew. I didn't want to see them get their hearts broken.

Still reeling, I walked to the entrance of the Kiva Auditorium. A thick velvet rope now blocked the double doors. Dick recognized me, and opened the rope. "Congratulations," he said. He even opened the door for me.

Why would he congratulate me? As I walked down the aisle I noticed several people in the far northern sections, in the back rows, sections XX through ZZ. We were in the front in row A. The auditorium seating was comparable to that of a medium-sized high school basketball court. I could still make out the faces in the back.

I recognized Hollywood Joe, Josephina from the bank, and Martiska and Spartan from Culebra Kai. All of them wore lanyards with the flaming red Dragon Moon logo. Cheyenne from Costco was chatting with all three Gollums who had served on the juries. Even my neighbor who had worked on Facebook now wore a Dragon Moon lanyard.

Hollywood Joe walked over to me. "Dragon Moon is going to put up the money to make my film. All I got to do is add one more action beat to the script."

Before I could ponder the meaning of the phrase "one more action beat," I saw Cage and Yahima. They didn't seem happy to see me and turned their backs. Before they turned, I read Cage's lanyard. It said CALL ME AJ!

I knew Cage had been an employee, but when had Yahima started work for Dragon Moon? Albert Jackson Cage had sworn that he would never work for them again, and now he wanted these assholes to call him by his nickname? I had been stabbed in the back.

"*Et tu,* AJ?" I asked, feeling like Julius Caesar must have when he got stabbed in the Senate during the Ides of March.

Suddenly it hit me. They all were employees—all employees of Dragon Moon, the real Evil Empire.

This was all a set-up! I already knew the mock-trial competition was a façade—a way to make Colonel Herring's pregnant daughter feel good about her future, or get Dr. Yu's kid to develop his social skills, or whatever.

Now I knew it was worse than that, far worse. Maybe the only reason Dew and Denise had even made this supposed all-star team was to persuade Luna to give up her proxy vote. I was part of it, too. Maybe the only reason I won the case was Kirlian's plot to take down the attorney general before she could file some securities fraud suit. I had my moment of clarity. Maybe it was a psychic vision from Marley, but I could now picture the entirety of this whole mess. Dragon Moon had been watching me, watching us, the last few months.

Cage and Yahima looked at me and shrugged. Had all his cases been a ruse too? Was the board playing some deeper game? Had Kirlian planted Mia in the attorney's general's office to get Mary Alice to resign in disgrace just before the stock went public? Hell, Mia'd had her plastic surgery at one of their clinics in India.

The last three months was all a big mock trial. Was the Rattlesnake Lawyer just doing a silly little game like Dew and Denise? The mock trial was a lie; was my whole existence on earth just a mock life, one big lie?

"This is all bullshit!" I said.

Everyone looked at me. "Don't steal my thunder!" Dew shouted from below. "Don't ruin the best moment of my entire life!"

"It's fixed!" I said to her.

That was the worst thing I could have said. As if on cue, Dick came through the open doorway, grabbed my shoulder and started to pull me up the aisle. "It's time for you to go," he said. The padfolio dropped to the floor.

I expected everyone to follow me out, but Dew lifted her hands.

Team Turquoise didn't budge. They wanted to see Dew win. Marley started to cry, but stopped when Nurse Song comforted him. He did a karate chop in my direction, as if telling me to fight my way through. Not a bad idea. Still, I let Dick haul me out by my shoulder without resistance. What was the defense to that? Was there was a purple belt move called Broken Wing? No, not yet.

I expected Dick to stop once he had hauled me all fifty-two rows up out to the exit of the Kiva Auditorium, but he stood with me as we rode the escalator down, and then he pushed me out the door of the convention center, onto Third Street, out to the vast expanse of Civic Plaza.

Dick then waited by the door. He would stand guard until

I slithered back home. I only had two blocks to walk back across Civic Plaza to the Greystoke or I could go back to the office and hide for the rest of my pitiful legal career, excuse me, my mock legal career.

I now heard the Muzak playing a sappy orchestral version of the Beatles "Revolution." The trumpets telling me that "It's gonna be all right."

I started to cross Third Street on the pedestrian crosswalk. I thought of my stupid *voir dire* argument in Deming: look both ways. Dew had said it even better, "look both ways, hesitate because you care." I looked both ways. But then I stopped, as if someone had thrown a brick at my head. I had a mental image of Luna in a suit, wearing handcuffs and walking within the gray walls of the convention center. Luna was inside the building in the East Hall by the shareholder's meeting. The image was blurry. Was Denise was sending me a mental image?

I formed another mental image. It felt like Dr. Yu's thimble was displaying a vivid hologram in the middle of my head. This must have come from Marley. He kept chopping his hand repeatedly. Save her, daddy! Save her!

Even the convention center bell tower that had looked like the ruined one at the San Geromino church was ringing loud and clear. Warning! Warning!

I was about to step off Third Street. There was a ninety-nine percent chance that I had just had a hallucination caused by stress and lack of sleep. There wasn't actually a bell in this tower at the convention center after all. Ninety-nine percent chance that this was just my sub-conscious doing some wishful thinking.

But what do you call that one percent? Reasonable freaking doubt? Something that causes you to hesitate in the graver affairs of life? This was as grave as it got. My wife was back there in the building behind me. I could now hear her tell-tale heartbeat pounding in my skull. It wasn't going to be all right. If I wanted to save my marriage, save my soul, save my family, I had to go back and rescue her.

I didn't step off Third Street. Instead, I turned around and took a few steps back to the convention center entrance. I remembered Oppenheimer's words—Time to become Death, to become Shiva, the destroyer of worlds.

Dick grabbed me by my lapels and pulled me into him for a head butt. It took a second, but I realized that even though I was wearing a suit, he was doing the attack for Kimono Grab. I stood back with my left foot, punched with my right, then raked down his arm, did a chop to the neck and gave a kick to the groin. Dick went down in agony.

I didn't have a plan, but I entered the convention center, ready for anything. Retreat was no longer an option. It never had been. I had fourteen minutes of material, but I only needed ninety seconds to go up the escalator to make it into the Kiva. Just then, somebody tried to punch me from three o'clock. Before the punch even came close to my face, I responded with Monkey Elbow. The guy went down. Now there were two guards between me and the escalator. The first did a left-right combo. He went down after Circle of Glass. The next did a right-left. Damn, I liked Whirling Mantis.

I stepped onto the up escalator. Was there a gunshot? I didn't care. At the top I made a turn toward the Kiva. I was going inside and they weren't going to stop me.

Somebody grabbed me by the neck and choked me.

No problem. Crash of the Eagles, Set Two, Final Option. When my half-fist was just a millimeter from his jugular I stopped.

"Sorry, I'm late," I said. "Traffic was a bitch."

• • •

It was Kirlian. I kept my half-fist near his jugular before finally pulling it back. He dusted himself, taking a minute to regain his composure. He was clearly rattled.

"Where's my wife?" I yelled.

"Your answers, whatever they may be, lie on the other side of that rope."

I looked over the rope just as someone opened the door from the inside. "Where is she? Is she still under arrest?"

"The answers to both your questions lie on the other side of that rope. I am no longer on the board. I don't really care anymore."

Do I cross over?

I had faced the same choice just a few months before. Do I cross, or stay here in ignorance? I felt another psychic pinging. I would not like what was on the other side.

40. . . . That is the Question

Spartan was now behind me. He wore a red Dragon Moon lanyard as well, which didn't surprise me at this stage of the game.

"What are you going to do?" he asked. "Make your move."

There was no retreat. I had come this far. I just had to know. Off on another side, I saw Diana Crater, the former New Mexico governor, and one of Luna's oldest friends.

"Go around the back to get backstage," one of the guards said. Was Diana the new CEO? If so, she could take me to Luna, but she vanished before I could ask her anything.

I nodded to Kirlian, lifted the rope and crossed into the Kiva. Spartan walked behind me.

I joined Team Turquoise and sat in the aisle seat. No one seemed that happy to see me return after my outburst. I picked up the padfolio which was on the ground. CNN was filming this. Perfect. I could still serve papers on the new CEO and it would make the news.

Dew looked at me. She wasn't going to drop the mic this time. She was going to pick up that award and hold it tighter than life itself.

"Don't steal my thunder," she said again.

"Don't worry, I've got this under control," I lied.

Perhaps after the new CEO came out, gave the award, and then mingled with the families. Then, after I asked politely, that person would take me backstage to meet Luna in whatever cell—or closet—these bastards were holding her in.

Colonel Herring was nowhere to be seen for her daughter's big moment. Was she the new CEO? Dr. Yu wasn't here either.

I looked at Marley. He nodded at me. If he could read my

mind, he liked my plan. He started moving his lips, as if practicing before he used them for the first time. He was going to say his first words in a moment. I just knew it. Then I picked up the papers and practiced saying "You got served," in English, Spanish, Chinese, and Hindi.

Allegra and her crew started filming, right next to CNN. Dragon Moon would have to let Luna go now, once this went out to the world. Allegra breathlessly recited narration in front of the camera. She was staring at cue cards indicating that she already knew the winner. "The new CEO will present the winning team with scholarships and . . ."

She misspoke a few times, but kept talking until the lights went down. "Don't worry," she told her crew. "We'll fix it in post-production."

Four other news crews all had their cameras focused on the front of the stage. It might not be live, but it was worldwide. This was my chance.

A spotlight now shown on the edge of the stage furthest from us. Judge Chairez returned to the stage. "Ladies and gentlemen, to announce the winners of the International Mock Trial Invitational, let me present the new 2018 board of the Dragon Moon Corporation and the new Chief Executive Officer."

Over-enthusiastic clapping came from the employee's section. Was this a corporate cult?

The judge smiled, her teeth glittering in the spotlight. "Hope it's not too much of a spoiler to say one of our board members was also on the winning team."

Dew shrieked with joy. If Denise was on the board and a member of the winning team, the New Mexico Mock Trial All-Stars were going to win. The fix was in? Was it because Herring's daughter was on the team?

I couldn't spoil Dew's moment, but I would face that CEO right after he or she gave the poor girl the trophy. I would let Dew have her thunder for a count of five and then I would tackle the CEO if I had to.

Since the theme was *Star Wars*, a DJ started playing the Imperial March, the theme for Darth Vader and the Evil Empire.

"How appropriate," I said.

Dew shushed me.

Diana Crater, the former governor, came out first. She had been a lousy governor, but was genuinely touched by the warm applause. Dr. Gandi looked very excited when his turn came. He now carried a banner that read ALPHA DRAGON IS MEDICAL! BANGALORE FACILITY.

Colonel Herring came out third and waved. No, she wasn't the CEO, just on the board. Even in her civilian clothes, she half-smiled like she had just been passed over for General. She then saw her daughter and mouthed some words at Rayne. The Colonel broke ranks and went to the edge of the stage and high-fived Rayne. "I love you Rayne," she said, loud enough for us to hear. "I'm so proud of you."

Rayne started crying. "I love you, Mom!"

Somehow that made it all worth it. The Colonel wiped away tears of her own.

Dr. Yu came out next. He pointed his thimble at his son, and a green spotlight shown on Hikaru. If this was his son's first smile, it had been worth the wait.

The music now grew louder. Did the empire bring their orchestra with them?

Selena walked out, holding her cane in her hand like a club, not touching it on the ground. Had Dr. Gandi had performed some surgery on her leg with his magic thimble?

Selena now had a lanyard and a badge. But, her walk indicated that if she hadn't joined Dragon Moon, they had joined her.

Selena had mentioned that their family went to extremes under pressure. It was in their genes. How extreme? What was going on?

"She's here!" she mouthed to me.

I opened the Luna Law padfolio and took the papers out. It was all good. This might be even easier than I thought. Luna could be free in a matter of moments.

Denise walked out next, looking scared. She was still in her "Rey" *Star Wars* costume and might as well have been ten years old, compared to everyone on the board. She waved at her mom and Susie, then looked in our direction and mouthed the words "I'm sorry."

Sorry? Sorry for what?

"We won!" Dew shouted at her. 'Be happy for me!"

Denise shook her head. "It's fixed," she said loud enough for us to hear.

And then Mia came out. I almost didn't recognize her. She was dressed in black, like a ninja in a business suit. She had an electronic monitor on her leg above her high heel. She, too, wore the lanyard and had a fresh badge.

She couldn't run in that outfit, or ride a motorcycle. Maybe she didn't have to. She probably would be whisked away to freedom right after this meeting. Mia pointed at me, made a pistol out of her hand, fired it.

I felt the sting of her imaginary bullet.

Whoever the new chairman of the board was had to have made a deal with the devil to get him or herself elected. Why? Why did anyone sell their soul to the devil for a few shares of stock? I thought of the usual answers—money, power, health, eternal life. Were they enough? Then I remembered something Hollywood Joe and I had discussed about screenplays. "Family is always motivation."

With fifty-one percent of the shares of Dragon Moon stock, this new CEO could save their family and themselves.

Was Kirlian the new CEO? No. He was still in the rear of the auditorium clapping politely, but he looked hurt that he hadn't made the final cut. It was getting harder for me to hold myself back. The padfolio felt like an anchor. Could this get any worse?

The music swelled as if Darth Vader himself was carrying the drum major of the Imperial Marching band. Dragon Moon was the Death Star to me, and this march was *Death Star uber alles*.

"And now, to present the trophy to the International Mock Trial Champions, to these future lawyers who will rule the world . . ."

Dew stood up, her whole body shaking with joy at those words. "Yes, yes!"

I now was on my feet, the padfolio on the ground, the papers in my hand. I was going to serve this person right now. A quick glance behind revealed that Spartan himself and half the Dojo were on their way to take me down. I didn't care. I would save my wife no matter what.

"Ladies and gentlemen, let me present the newly elected chief executive officer of Dragon Moon Corporation . . ."

I heard footsteps and saw a figure clad in black approach the stage from the wings.

I had always assumed that Luna, Selena, Denise, and Mia would use their combined fifty-one percent to vote Kirlian out and vote someone else in—someone like Diana Crater, someone like Colonel Herring.

What if I was wrong? What if they used their votes for something else?

Lighting from the rear shone on turquoise earrings, the five dollar earrings from Taos Pueblo. In the spotlight, I was even able to make out a clanging red Dragon Moon lanyard and badge.

I wouldn't need to serve the new CEO after all.

Marley pointed at the figure and said his first word. "Mommy!"

—the end—

About Jonathan Miller

Jonathan Miller has practiced criminal defense law all over New Mexico. He currently practices in Albuquerque where he writes and stays active in legal services that help the poor. Jon is a graduate of Albuquerque Academy, Cornell University, the University of Colorado School of Law, and the American Film Institute. He also wrote for the syndicated TV show Arrest and Trial and hopes to use his writing royalties to pay off his student loans before he dies.

Jon's books, *Crater County* and *Amarillo in August* both made the Tucson public library's master list of Southwestern books of the year, *Volcano Verdict* was a finalist for New Mexico mystery of the year, and his book *LaBajada Lawyer* is a finalist in the 2010 ForeWord book awards for Multi-Cultural Fiction.

49666938R00213

Made in the USA
San Bernardino, CA
01 June 2017